THE FRONTIERS SAGA

PART 2: ROGUE CASTES

EPISODE 13

RETURN OF THE CORINARI

RYK BROWN

The Frontiers Saga Part 2: Rogue Castes
Episode #13: Return of the Corinari

CHAPTER ONE

Gisal was a desolate world. Hot, dusty, and windblown, with days that lasted weeks, its surface was all but barren. If it were not for its vast, underground aquifers, there would be no reason for humans to have any interest in the hellish little rock. Other than its hidden water, the only other thing the moon had going for it was its lack of proximity to other more habitable worlds.

Gisal was about as far off the beaten path as one could get. Even with jump drive technology, it was still considered too far out of the way for most. For this reason, it was a favorite meeting place for questionable transactions between equally questionable parties. Gisal had no government, no law enforcement, and no infrastructure. In fact, the entire world had no more than a few thousand people scratching out a meager, isolated existence. Gisal was a world where one went to be forgotten.

Marcus stood leaning against the only tree that could be seen for kilometers in any direction, its scraggly branches providing little shade. The heat drained him, requiring frequent sips from the bota bag built into his desert jacket.

"This has got to be the ugliest moon in the galaxy," Corporal Vasya commented as he approached from Marcus's right. "I can't believe people actually *live* here."

"Calling it *living* is a bit of a stretch," Marcus grumbled, stretching his injured jaw.

"Are you sure you're up for this?" the corporal inquired, noticing Marcus's obvious discomfort. "You recently took a beating, remember."

"That was two weeks ago," Marcus snapped.

"Ten days, and you wouldn't think so by looking at you."

"I've had worse," Marcus insisted, his attention returning to the scorched horizon.

"Why am I not surprised," Vasya replied, glancing at his watch. "They're overdue."

"That's expected," Marcus replied. "They want to show us who's boss."

"Not a very smart way to do business," Vasya argued.

"Buyer arrives first, then the seller shows up when he's satisfied that the buyer ain't setting up a trap."

"And if the *seller* is setting a trap?" the corporal wondered.

Marcus looked at him with one eye. "Then he doesn't make any money."

A small glint of light on the distant horizon caught the corporal's eye. "You see that?"

"That would be them," Marcus said, still leaning against the lone tree.

The two men watched as the distant object grew closer, slowly changing from a mere glint of light into a shape with a trail of dust behind it, and finally into a large cargo hovercraft. The bulky vehicle slowed as it approached, coming to a stop and then settling onto the parched, hard-packed surface as its engines spun down.

"A little large for what we ordered, don't you think?" Vasya pointed out.

"A bit," Marcus agreed, still leaning against the tree.

"I guess you were right," Vasya added as he

reached down and activated the power cell on his sidearm.

As the dust from the cargo hovercraft was blown clear, a large door opened on the side of the vehicle, and several men stepped out, making their way across the blower cowlings and jumping down to the ground. Four men in all, they fanned out, taking up security positions on all four sides of the hovercraft. Once in position, four additional men appeared in the doorway, two of whom Marcus recognized.

"This ain't good," Marcus said under his breath, finally standing up straight.

"Mister Taggart," Dinesh Koren greeted, jumping down to the surface. "I'm surprised you're still walking."

"I could say the same about you, Dinesh," Marcus replied. "I'm a bit surprised to see you here. Usually, the chief asshole has his junior assholes handling such things."

"Your arrogance is in line with your reputation, I see," Dinesh commented. "Yes, it is true that I do not *personally* handle such routine transactions. However, I wanted to see the expression on your face when Mister Shek here took you into custody."

"Is that right," Marcus replied, casting a menacing glance at Mister Shek. "You some kind of bounty hunter?"

"A marshal, actually," Mister Shek replied, "for the Crispin Provincial Authority. I have a warrant for your arrest."

"For what charge?" Marcus asked, playing along.

"There are many. I can read them if you like, but I suspect Mister Koren doesn't have that kind of time."

"So this is how you do business?" Marcus said to Dinesh.

"Not usually, but it is rare to find so high a bounty on a man's head for so long a time."

"Higher than what you would've made selling us the guns?" Marcus wondered.

"Oh, I still intend on selling your employer the guns," Dinesh insisted, looking at Vasya. "That is, if you still want them."

Corporal Vasya looked at Marcus and shrugged. "Sorry, old man."

"Did you really think we would not find you?" Mister Shek wondered.

"I was beginning to," Marcus admitted. "I mean, it *was* nearly a century ago."

"You and your terrorist friends slaughtered thousands of innocent people," Mister Shek continued.

"We were *rebels*, not terrorists," Marcus argued. "It was Dengal and his hoodlums who did the slaughterin'."

"I expect the judge will see things differently," Mister Shek insisted, stepping forward as he pulled a pair of restraints from his belt pouch.

"You just made a big fucking mistake, Dinesh," Marcus declared.

The head of the man next to Dinesh suddenly blew apart, its contents spraying across his leader's face. A split second later, the two guards on the near side of the hovercraft at the bow and stern also lost their heads, their bodies falling unceremoniously to the parched surface.

Vasya had his sidearm out in a flash, firing two quick shots, ending the lives of Dinesh's other guard, as well as that of the Crispin marshal's.

At the same time, the heads of the two guards on the far side of the hovercraft exploded. Dinesh looked around, stunned at how rapidly his fortunes had changed.

Marcus smiled. "What kind of a dumbass doesn't carry a gun to an arms deal?" he wondered as he slowly drew his own weapon, activated its power cell, and pointed it at Dinesh's face.

"My men will avenge me," Dinesh warned, his expression still confident.

"I doubt it," Marcus growled, pulling the trigger.

The energy pulse drove straight through Dinesh's head, blowing its backside out, spraying blood and brains across the hovercraft's cowlings. Dinesh's body stood there for a moment, a surprised look on what was left of his face. Finally, his knees bent, and his body dropped straight down, falling to one side as it hit the ground.

"Damn!" Marcus exclaimed. "That was more fun than I thought it would be!" He looked at Corporal Vasya, who had already holstered his weapon. "That was some nice shootin', Kit. We could've used a few dozen like you a hundred years ago."

Corporal Vasya just smiled.

"Inside!" Marcus yelled toward the hovercraft. "Come out with your hands where we can see 'em, and we won't burn you down!"

After nearly a minute, a man appeared at the doorway, his hands held high. "Don't shoot!" he begged. "I'm just the driver!"

"Come down outta there!" Marcus insisted.

The driver stepped down, his hands still high over his head.

"That thing full of guns?" Marcus asked.

"I don't know," the driver replied. "It's full of crates, but I don't know what's in 'em. They just hired me to drive 'em out here. You can take whatever is in them. It don't matter none to me. Hell, take the whole damned ship. Just don't kill me."

Corporal Vasya stepped up and patted the driver down. "He's clean," he announced.

"Anyone else on board?" Marcus asked.

"No, no one."

Corporal Vasya climbed up onto the cowling and entered the hovercraft.

"How much do they pay you?" Marcus wondered.

"Not enough," the driver insisted. "Not half enough."

"*The cargo looks good!*" Corporal Vasya yelled from inside the hovercraft.

Marcus pulled out his comm-unit and held it to his mouth. "How do we look?"

"Looks clear for at least one hundred kilometers in all directions," Lieutenant Rezhik reported over the comm-unit.

"Send in our ride," Marcus replied.

"Understood."

The driver looked about nervously, taking note of all the dead bodies. "You two do all this by yourselves?" he wondered.

"We had a little help," Marcus replied, smiling.

The driver flinched when a blue-white flash appeared in the sky only a few hundred meters above them, accompanied by a deafening clap of thunder. He watched in amazement as a massive, box-like spacecraft fired its four engines, arresting its fall and settling into a momentary hover before touching down less than fifty meters away.

"You can lower your hands now," Marcus told the driver as Corporal Vasya joined them again.

"You sure?" the driver wondered. "I don't mind holding them up."

"Take this," Marcus told him, handing him a credit chip. "Give it to the people working for that asshole," he explained, pointing at Dinesh's lifeless body.

The driver hesitated at first, then took the chip from Marcus's hand. "What is it?"

"It's a credit chip," Marcus explained. "It contains payment for your cargo. Give it to them, along with a message."

The driver looked unsure. "Uh, what message?"

"Tell them that if they ever try to cross me or any of my people again, I will hunt them down and kill every last one of them. Them, and their families. Understood?"

The driver swallowed hard. "Yes, sir."

Marcus handed him another chip.

"What's this for," the driver wondered.

"For your troubles," Marcus told him as the loading crew from the boxcar passed by and climbed up onto the hovercraft. "It's going to be a bitch scrubbing the blood off your dust skirt, there."

* * *

"Welcome back," Cameron greeted as Nathan and Jessica came up the ramp to the Aurora's command deck. "I hope you enjoyed yourselves."

"Oh, it was a hoot," Jessica replied.

"Did the boxcars make it back?" Nathan asked.

"They did," Cameron replied as she turned to walk with them. "Abby and Deliza are being briefed on the Tekan fabrication systems by the specialist who came with them."

Nathan looked surprised. "I wasn't aware they were sending someone along with the equipment."

"Not exactly *someone*," Cameron explained. "It's an android named Ross. According to Abby, he's quite pleasant and *very* knowledgeable. Apparently, he is a physical avatar for the AI that controls the Tekan fabrication system."

"Interesting," Nathan replied.

"Ross is confident that the Tekan engineering AIs will be able to improve upon our jump missiles, as well as their ability to penetrate shields. He also believes that their fabrication systems will be able to produce the improved versions in half the time that it takes our current fabricators. He even suggested fitting them with an automated, quick-change warhead system."

"That would give us a lot more flexibility in combat," Jessica stated.

"That's all very interesting," Nathan commented as they reached the door to his quarters, "but for now, I'd like a shower and a nap."

"Of course," Cameron replied.

"Perhaps we can continue our conversation later over dinner?" Nathan suggested.

"Sounds good," Cameron agreed. "I can't wait to hear the details of your visit to SilTek."

Nathan smiled, then turned and entered his quarters.

Cameron looked at Jessica. "What was *that* about?"

"Long story," Jessica replied, also smiling, as she headed for her quarters.

"I've got time," Cameron insisted, following Jessica down the lateral corridor.

* * *

General Telles and Commander Kellen watched as the boxcar's engines spun down, and the main ramp to the massive cargo bay hanging in the center deployed. The first man off the ramp was Lieutenant

Rezhik, followed by Corporal Vasya and Specialists Deeks and Brill.

"Gentlemen," the general greeted. "I trust all went as planned."

"Not exactly, but we were successful nonetheless," the lieutenant replied.

"We wouldn't have been had it not been for Marcus," Corporal Vasya added. "He smelled the ambush before we even *got* to Gisal."

General Telles looked past his men as Marcus came down the ramp, leading the line of men carrying crates off the boxcar. "You've looked better," he greeted.

"Why does everyone say that?" Marcus grumbled.

"I am told we have you to thank for these weapons, Mister Taggart."

"It was a team effort," Marcus insisted. "I was just the dumbass who took point."

"We appreciate your efforts," the general told him, "as do the people of Orswella, I am certain."

"Yeah, well, I'm taking a few weeks off after this," Marcus insisted as he moved past them.

"There are a lot of stories in that old man," Corporal Vasya insisted.

"Of that I have no doubt," General Telles agreed.

"How are things here?" Lieutenant Rezhik asked, changing the subject.

General Telles took in a deep breath, letting it out slowly. "There have been casualties."

"How many?"

"We have lost eleven, and four more are recovering from serious injuries," the general explained as he watched the line of crates being carried by. "There have been tens of thousands of civilian casualties as well."

"There are still that many Dusahn around?" Corporal Vasya wondered.

"It's not the number, it's their level of preparation," the general explained.

"You cannot flush them out and destroy them?" the lieutenant asked.

"It is difficult to do with only a hundred men," the general replied. "Especially while trying to police this world. As expected, there are those who seek to take advantage of the chaos. Now that we have these weapons, we will be able to arm the Corinari, enabling them to take over general security, while the Ghatazhak concentrate on the remaining Dusahn operatives."

"Any chance we can hang around and help?" Corporal Vasya inquired. "This little mission has been the most excitement we've seen in months."

"Your mission on Sanctuary is equally important, if not more so," General Telles reminded the corporal.

"Yes, sir," Corporal Vasya replied.

"We will be on our way just as soon as the weapons have been unloaded," Lieutenant Rezhik assured the general.

"Meanwhile, get yourselves something to eat," General Telles suggested. "Orswellan food is quite interesting."

"It has to be better than the slop Neli keeps feeding us," Corporal Vasya joked.

* * *

"What I don't understand is why *she* didn't hit him first?" Vladimir exclaimed as he carved another piece from his dollag steak.

"They gave me a sedative," Jessica explained as she refilled her glass of water, "just as I was dying in the simulation."

"They had already done their research," Nathan added. "They were probably *expecting* her to lash out."

"Nathan dropped the general with one punch," Jessica told them.

"He deserved it," Cameron agreed, picking at her salad. "They had no right to put you guys through all of that."

"In retrospect, I understand why they felt they had to," Nathan said, pushing his plate away from him. "It turns out they have a *lot* of useful technology, *including* weapons."

"I thought they didn't make weapons," Cameron said.

"That's what they've been telling everyone," Jessica told her.

"They've only recently begun making weapons, and only in secret. They haven't yet sold any. We will be the first," Nathan explained.

"Then they're going to join our alliance?" Vladimir asked.

"Not just yet," Nathan replied. "Seems they have a few concerns over what we're trying to accomplish."

"What, defeating invaders?" Vladimir questioned.

"They're more concerned about our end game," Jessica told Vladimir. "What we plan to do *after* we defeat the Dusahn."

"Uh, return to our normal lives?" Vladimir suggested.

"They would like to see us do something to *prevent* these things from happening in the first place," Nathan explained.

"Wasn't that the plan all along?" Cameron wondered.

"Perhaps, in the back of my mind, I had always

assumed that we would," Nathan replied, "but I never gave much thought to exactly *how* that would be accomplished."

"By building lots of ships," Vladimir said, stating the obvious.

"The Tekans are more concerned with the *structure* of the alliance," Nathan explained. "They are concerned that such alliances generally fail, and they're right. History is full of failed global alliances for peace or for mutual protection. Someone always ends up getting their rights trampled. Big, centralized governments controlling diverse and varied cultures are handicapped by their very nature. Creating something that will stand the test of time is no small feat."

"Can we just defeat the Dusahn, first?" Cameron wondered.

"We can," Nathan replied, "but the Tekans are unwilling to fully commit unless they are comfortable with our end game. They need to know that the seeds we plant will grow into something they are comfortable with."

"They're afraid we'll turn into the conquerors," Jessica added.

"Fat chance," Cameron laughed.

"It's a valid concern," Nathan said in their defense. "That's *why* they felt the need to test us."

"I still don't understand *how* they managed to create such a realistic simulation," Vladimir insisted. "How did they even know what the interior of the Aurora looked like? How did they know what *we* looked like, or what the ship could do?"

"Their simulation system actually reads our subconscious, our memories," Nathan explained.

"They create a realistic virtual reality using details from our own minds."

"It would make a hell of an interrogation tool," Jessica pointed out.

"It would be great for training exercises as well," Cameron added. "You know how sharp I could get a crew with such realistic simulations? Imagine battle-hardened veterans who had never actually *seen* real combat. The time and cost savings alone...*that's* a weapon in its *own* right."

"Not to mention the intel you could get from a prisoner on the enemy's systems, capabilities, and tactics," Jessica added. "If we could get just *one* Dusahn ship's captain in that thing, we could learn everything we needed to know."

"Unfortunately, the Tekans are not ready to share *all* of their technology with us," Nathan pointed out. "They *are* a business, after all."

"It's hard to imagine an entire *world* owned and operated by a single corporation," Cameron commented.

"Technically, SilTek is *not* a corporation," Nathan corrected, "at least not in the *legal* sense as we understand it. It's actually quite fascinating. The CEO is like a president, and the board of directors is like a senate. Everyone who lives on SilTek is a shareholder. The value of their shares is based on their contributions to the corporation. They even have senior shareholders who act as representatives for the common shareholders. It's almost like a representative democracy, just with different names and structures. When you get right down to it, their goals are the same as any nation: maintain a strong economy and provide secure, comfortable lives for their citizens, or in the case of SilTek, its *employees*."

"Do they receive *paychecks*?" Vladimir asked.

"They do," Nathan answered. "Each according to their level of contribution."

"Then they do have economic classes," Cameron surmised.

"Yes, but as far as we could tell, there was no poverty and very little crime," Nathan told her.

"They were probably hiding that from us," Jessica insisted.

"All I wish to know is what tech they are offering us," Vladimir said, changing the subject. "I mean, besides automated fabricators."

"They think they can improve our jump energy banks," Nathan told him. "They believe they could *double* our single-jump range."

"A *thousand light years* from a *single charge*?" Cameron exclaimed in disbelief. "I know it's *theoretically* possible, but..."

"Hey, we did it before," Vladimir laughed.

"Yeah, by riding an antimatter event," Cameron reminded him.

"It is only a matter of power," Vladimir told her. "We can create enough power with the ZPEDs, we just can't store enough of it to dump into the emitters all at once. We don't even have power conduits that can handle that much power. The energy from the antimatter event interacted with our jump fields from the *outside*."

"They seemed confident it could be done," Nathan told him.

"It would be an incredible tactical advantage," Jessica commented. "We'd be able to attack the Dusahn anytime we want and still be able to jump back and protect our allies on a moment's notice."

"Technically, we can do that now," Cameron told her.

"Yes, but only by a small margin," Nathan reminded her. "If the Dusahn figure out our limitations, they could use a three-front attack to force us to choose which ally to defend, and which one to let fall. A thousand-light-year, single-jump range would all but eliminate that tactic."

"It will require a lot of overhaul," Vladimir warned.

"They also offered better shields and AI-controlled early-warning and defense automation systems," Jessica announced. "That would completely eliminate the problem of distrust between Rakuen and Neramese. They could program the AI to prevent either one of them from taking control and using the system against the other."

"The Tekans were actually quite interested in how we were managing the problems between Rakuen and Neramese," Nathan said. "I think they consider it an insight into how our alliance would deal with its members."

"Then you might want to avoid telling them that we assassinated one of their leaders," Cameron suggested.

"Agreed," Nathan replied.

"We did?" Vladimir wondered, stopping eating for the first time since dinner had begun. He looked at Nathan, then at Cameron. "Really?"

* * *

The four Orochi captains headed down the pier toward their waiting vessels.

"You would think they could add landing gear," Aiden said. "I mean, who the hell ever heard of *space-boats?*"

"I don't know, I kind of like it," Kenji commented.

"Reminds me of the summers I spent working at the marina, with all the ships rocking gently in their moorings."

"You're just weird," Aiden insisted.

"I kind of agree with him," Charnelle added. "There's something romantic about it."

"This is a water world, Mister Walsh," Commander Kainan reminded him.

"You're *all* weird," Aiden insisted. "Where the hell are we going to land on Orswella?"

"Their main population center is on the edge of a massive inland sea," Commander Kainan told him. "They have already prepared moorings in case we need them. However, we will be spending most of our time on patrol."

"That's fine by me," Kenji stated. "I rather like my ship and crew."

"You don't even *know* half of them," Aiden pointed out. "Speaking of which, it would have been nice to have a chance to *train* our new gunners *before* shipping out."

"They're *gunners*, Aiden," Charnelle said, "how much do they need to know?"

"They have all had plenty of time in the gunnery sims," Commander Kainan reminded them. "They'll be fine. Just give them some time to get acclimated to navigating through zero-G tunnels, and then drill the crap out of them. Use your smart-decoys as targets, and don't forget to instruct them to put their weapons in practice mode first."

"You make one little mistake, and no one ever lets you hear the end of it," Aiden groaned.

"So we're going to be on patrol the entire time?" Charnelle asked.

"In the beginning, yes," the commander replied,

pausing at the gangway to his ship, "at least until additional Orochi arrive, or the Tekans get a planetary defense system up and running on Orswella. See you up there," he added, heading up his gangway.

"I still don't understand why they didn't automate our additional guns," Aiden complained as the three of them continued down the pier.

"That would've taken a lot longer," Kenji insisted. "Besides, the Orochi were designed to carry a crew of sixteen, so we're still light."

"Five was enough for me," Aiden replied. "Three was even better. Now I have seven."

"And soon you'll have fifteen, once they finish training the engineering techs," Charnelle added.

"Don't remind me," Aiden groaned.

"You wanted to be in command," Kenji teased.

"No, that was you," Aiden insisted.

"Oh yeah."

"I just wanted to fly."

"Who would've thought you'd be good at both," Charnelle added with a smile.

"See you up there," Kenji said, heading up the ramp to Orochi Two.

"Don't worry," Charnelle said as she and Aiden continued down the pier. "In a few weeks our full crews will include XOs, so you won't have to deal with the management issues."

"I don't suppose there's a chance I could convince *you* to be my XO?" Aiden wondered.

Charnelle kissed him on the cheek and headed up the ramp to her own ship. "No way I'm sitting second seat to you," she called back.

"That's what I thought," Aiden said to himself.

"*See you up there!*"

Aiden took in a deep breath and sighed, heading down the pier to his own ship.

The Orochi were sizeable ships in their own right; not as large as a Dusahn gunship, but twice the length and four times the mass of a Cobra gunship. Their blue coloring allowed them to blend in with the waters on which they rested. Were it not for the amber trim running from stem to stern, they would be nearly invisible against the oceans of Rakuen. Despite their modest size, they carried considerable firepower. Their jump missiles alone could bring down ships ten times their mass, and now they had four additional plasma cannon turrets with which to defend themselves. The only problem was, they were boring to fly.

"How are we looking, Chief?" Aiden asked as he headed up the gangway.

"We're full of propellant and have provisions stuffed into every nook and cranny we could find. Even better, we have a full complement of fifty-six jump missiles," Chief Mando replied from the top of the gangway.

"Four fully loaded Orochi," Aiden said, pausing to look at the other three ships tied up nearby. "That is a lot of damned firepower."

"I pity the bastards who try to attack Orswella once we get there."

Aiden stepped off the gangway onto the port side of his Orochi, pausing to look fore and aft. "These things are weird-looking, but they pack a hell of a punch."

"They sure do," the chief agreed.

"What say we try out these new-fangled grav-lift systems," Aiden suggested, heading toward the hatch.

* * *

"Captain on deck!" the guard at the entrance barked as Nathan entered the Aurora's command briefing room.

"As you were," Nathan ordered before anyone in attendance could stand. "I've read all your daily reports for the last ten days, so no need to waste everyone's time briefing me on the events during my absence. Instead, I'll ask questions starting with Commander Kamenetskiy. Where are we with the long-range jump drive?"

"The second array and energy banks are operational," Vladimir replied. "However, they still both share the same jump field generators, so there is only partial redundancy."

"When do we expect to install the second set of field generators?" Nathan asked.

"All the fabricators are busy making missiles and missile launchers," Cameron chimed in. "Once the Tekan fabricators begin making missiles, we'll be able to dedicate a few of our own fabricators to create new jump field generators."

"How long?" Nathan asked.

"At least a few weeks before we can start assembling them," Cameron replied.

"And another week or so to install and test," Vladimir added.

"Any way we can speed things up?" Nathan asked.

"We need the missiles and launchers more than we need backup jump field generators," Cameron insisted. "After all, our current generators are located in the most protected area of the ship. The likelihood of them being taken down is low."

"Yet it has happened before," Nathan pointed out.

"That was *before* we got better shields and weapons," Cameron replied.

"The Aurora's current jump field generators are far more robust than before," Abby added. "They are better isolated from damaging feedback loops, and they have their own inertial dampeners to protect against kinetic damage."

"It would take a direct, unshielded hit to take them out," Cameron insisted.

"And even if half of them were destroyed, the other half can be cross-connected so we could still jump, just nowhere near as far," Vladimir added.

"Very well."

"What about stealth jump capability?" Vladimir asked. "Have you decided whether or not to continue outfitting the Aurora with stealth emitters?"

Nathan looked to Abby.

"It may be possible to do both with the same emitter array; however, a *lot* of research and testing needs to be done. I mean, I haven't even *theorized* how to combine the two."

"Can we create a separate system?" Nathan wondered. "Array, power grid, field generators?"

"That would be the fastest way to get stealth capability," Abby admitted.

"That's no small task," Vladimir warned.

"And it will tie up even more fabricators," Cameron warned.

"Stealth is great for recon," Jessica said, "but it's not worth much in combat."

"Then we concentrate on range for the time being," Nathan decided, turning to Cameron. "How is the Orochi refit going?"

"One through Four completed their refit and departed for Orswella earlier this morning," Cameron reported. "We were able to give them a bonus as well," she added.

"Orochi One through Four have also been fitted with gravity lift generators," Abby stated proudly.

Nathan looked confused. "I thought we were working on fitting the Gunyoki with the gravity lift systems?"

"We did, and it was pretty simple," Abby bragged. "Or I should say, *Deliza's* team did so. I only consulted a bit."

"Deliza suggested it to me, and I gave them the green light," Cameron said. "Now the Orochi can be based on the surface and not have to refuel in orbit after departure. It gives them far more flexibility in maintenance and deployment."

"Well done," Nathan congratulated. "How long until *all* the Orochi are similarly outfitted?"

"Orochi Fourteen just became operational this morning," Cameron explained. "Fifteen and Sixteen will be ready by the end of the week. Orochi Five through Eight are in refit now and should be operational in about a week. I estimate all sixteen Orochi will be fully refitted, crewed, and loaded with jump missiles by the end of the month."

"Excellent," Nathan replied. "How are we doing with planetary defenses?"

"There are currently ten surface-based jump missile launchers in total: five on Rakuen and five on Neramese. Combined, we have five hundred and twenty-eight jump missiles in inventory."

"How long until both worlds are fully defended?" Nathan wondered.

"On our own, at least three more months," Cameron replied, "five if we are including Orswella.

However, with the help of the Tekan fabricators, that could be cut down to one month."

"The Tekan detection grids will give us a big advantage," Jessica commented.

"Agreed, but we don't know how long it will be before they are operational. If we're lucky, the detection grid will be ready by the time all the missile launchers are in place," Nathan added.

"How long did the Tekans say it would take?" Cameron wondered.

"They couldn't make a solid commitment until they got more information about all three worlds," Nathan explained, "but they did say that it usually takes two or three months."

"Two or three months to build a planetary defense system," Vladimir stated in disbelief. "Amazing."

"You really have to visit their showrooms someday, Commander," Nathan said. "You'd feel like a kid in a candy store."

"We'd never get him back," Jessica teased.

"How about you, Lieutenant Commander?" Nathan asked his intelligence officer. "Any significant intel?"

"All Dusahn ships that we know of are currently stationed in the Takar and Darvano systems," Lieutenant Commander Shinoda reported. "They have returned to their usual patrol schedules, concentrating on the worlds within the Pentaurus cluster, with at least daily visits to Haven, Palee, Volon, and Paradar."

"What about Ursoot?" Nathan wondered.

"They seem to have lost interest in that world," the lieutenant commander replied. "Their last known visit to the Ursoot system was four days ago. It's too early to tell if they've abandoned it, or if they're just not patrolling it as frequently."

"It could be a ruse," Jessica suggested. "They could be trying to convince us that they don't care about Ursoot, so that we'll feel comfortable going there."

"I'll keep that in mind," Nathan agreed.

"There is one other thing," the lieutenant commander said. "We received intel from General Telles's contacts on Takara. There has been a sudden increase in underground projects all over the planet. It appears they are drilling, or possibly making tunnels under the surface."

"Any idea why?"

"Not yet," the lieutenant commander admitted. "We're not even certain the projects are related. Speculation ranges anywhere from a new subway system, to a network of tunnels that connect military assets, to just routine infrastructure upgrades. The odd thing is they're not using Takaran contractors to do the work. They are doing it with their own engineers. The general's contacts are keeping an eye on their progress and will report if they learn anything further."

"I'm guessing a new planetary defense system," Jessica said. "After we kicked their asses, they're probably afraid we're coming to take Takara next."

Nathan thought for a moment. "Any reports of similar activity on Corinair?"

"Negative," the lieutenant commander replied. "However, our network of contacts on Corinair is much smaller."

"Keep me updated if anything changes," Nathan told him.

"Yes, sir."

"Anything from Telles?" he asked Cameron.

"Marcus delivered the weapons this morning,"

Cameron replied. "The Corinari are now armed and patrolling the streets of Orswella as we speak. General Telles expects to begin his campaign to eliminate the planet of Dusahn operatives later today."

"Any projections?" Nathan wondered.

"Negative. He only knows they exist, but he has no knowledge of numbers or capabilities."

"Telles will wipe them out," Jessica said confidently.

"Let's just hope he does so before the people of Orswella lose faith in us," Cameron said. "According to Telles, they're not happy."

"Perhaps regular visits by the Aurora will give their confidence a boost," Nathan suggested.

"It couldn't hurt," Cameron replied.

* * *

General Telles headed down the corridors of the hospital's critical care ward, still uncertain of why he had been summoned.

"General," Master Sergeant Willem greeted as the general approached.

"Master Sergeant," the general replied, pausing in the corridor to speak with him.

"My men have swept the entire hospital. The building is secure, and no explosive devices have been detected. I have guards on all entrances, on the rooftop, and along the rooftops of all the surrounding buildings. We also have both Diggers circling the area, scanning for any suspicious activity."

"Very good," the general replied. "Does the hospital staff have any idea why I was summoned?"

"Negative," the master sergeant replied. "They've had seven new admissions since yesterday, three of whom have not yet been positively identified."

"The mystery deepens," the general commented.

"There's more," the master sergeant warned. "Commander Andreola and the other Orswellan captains have also been summoned. They're waiting at the nursing station."

"And we still don't know *who* summoned us?"

"All we know is that one of the nurses made the call. He won't say from which patient, not until everyone is here."

"Am I the last one to arrive?" the general wondered.

"Apparently."

"Then let's get this over with," the general decided, continuing down the corridor.

General Telles and Master Sergeant Willem made their way to the nursing station at the middle of the ward, where Commander Andreola and the other Orswellan captains were waiting.

"Gentlemen," the general greeted.

"Sir, everyone summoned is present," Master Sergeant Willem told the charge nurse. "Can you *now* tell us which patient summoned these men?"

"I apologize for being so adamant in my refusal," the nurse said as he rose from his chair. "You will understand why in a moment. Please follow me."

The nurse led the group down the corridor to the room in the furthest corner of the ward. Once at the door, he stepped aside, gesturing toward the door.

"I'll clear the room," Master Sergeant Willem insisted, stepping in front of the general. He raised his weapon, readying himself, then pushed the door slowly open, stepping into the room.

Inside was a frail-looking, old man lying in the bed, eyes closed, with tubes and wires connecting him to a collection of devices designed to keep him alive.

The master sergeant looked left, then stepped

inside, pivoting right to check behind the door as it closed. Satisfied that the old man was the room's only occupant, he pulled out his scanner and swept for signs of explosive devices or any other threats. Finally, he stepped up to the old man and studied him.

The master sergeant returned to the door, pulling it open. "All clear, sir," he reported.

General Telles and the others entered the room.

"Oh my God," Captain Yofferst exclaimed in disbelief.

The other captains had similar expressions of shock.

General Telles looked to Commander Andreola, who looked equally surprised. "Commander, do you know this man?"

"I do," the commander admitted. "This man is Huzza Roland. He was the Minister of the Treasury at the time the Dusahn invaded. He was believed to have been killed like all the other leaders of Orswella."

"The Minister of the Treasury," the general said, unimpressed.

"You do not understand, General," Commander Andreola said. "This man is the sole surviving member of the ministry. That makes him the legal *acting* Prime Minister of Orswella."

"That explains all the cloak and dagger stuff," Master Sergeant Willem surmised.

"Somehow, he has managed to evade capture for more than two decades," the commander continued. "This is incredible."

"*Impressive,* yes, but far from incredible," the general replied.

"Again, you do not understand," the commander

insisted. "This means that we have automatic continuity of government."

"One old man is hardly a government," General Telles insisted. "He is not even conscious."

"He asked that I put him out after requesting that I summon you all to come here," the nurse explained. "He is in grave condition and is not expected to survive. The act of waking him will likely hasten his end."

"He must be saved," Captain Yofferst insisted.

"His injuries are severe," the nurse warned.

"How was he injured?" General Telles wondered.

"He was pulled from the rubble of the Perlan building attack," the nurse told him.

"That was more than a week ago," Commander Andreola exclaimed.

"He gave me explicit instructions to wake him upon your arrival," the nurse told them.

"Did he understand that doing so might kill him?" Commander Andreola asked.

"He did," the nurse answered. "He was quite adamant."

"Minister Roland was known for his decisiveness," Captain Yofferst said, "*and* for his inability to accept *no* as an answer."

"Well, he must have called us here for good reason," General Telles said. "Wake him," he instructed the nurse.

"General!" Captain Yofferst argued.

"He is correct, Marlon," Commander Andreola insisted, "and as officers of the Guard, we are sworn to uphold the orders *of* the ministry."

Captain Yofferst hung his head, knowing the commander was right.

The nurse stepped over to the control station

next to the minister's bed and entered instructions. A moment later, the minister's eyes fluttered and slowly opened.

Commander Andreola and the other captains snapped to attention as their sole, surviving minister regained consciousness.

Minister Roland looked at General Telles and Master Sergeant Willem, both of whom were standing at ease. He then looked at the officers of the Guard, standing tall to his left. "Is this all that remains...of our once...proud...Guard?"

"It is, Minister," Captain Yofferst replied respectfully. "If I may ask, how did you survive all these years?"

"It is a long story," the minister replied, his voice unsteady and strained, as if every word was an effort, "one that is not relevant to our current situation."

"What are your orders, Minister?" Captain Yofferst asked.

"I am dying," the minister stated plainly. "Perhaps this day, perhaps the next. One of you must take my place. One of you must lead the people of Orswella out of the darkness and back into the light." He looked to captain Yofferst. "Are you senior among them?"

"I am," Captain Yofferst replied.

"Then *you* are next in succession."

"With all due respect, Minister, that would be unwise," Captain Yofferst insisted. "I am soon approaching the age of retirement and will be too old to *legally* act as prime minister."

"*I* am too old as *well*," Minister Roland replied, "yet I am still legally minister."

"Only because you have not been able to pass that

responsibility onto another," Commander Andreola reminded him.

"You can serve until you reach the age of retirement," Minster Roland pointed out. "At that time, you may pass the responsibility to another."

"Recovery will take years," Captain Yofferst argued, "perhaps as much as a decade. I have but three years left."

"The age requirement can be suspended under times of emergency," Minister Roland insisted, waving Captain Yofferst's concerns aside.

Captain Yofferst looked down, concern on his face.

"There is another reason?" the minister asked, noticing the woe on the senior captain's face.

"There is more to being a good leader than just being senior," Captain Yofferst replied. "I am not the man for the job." He looked at the other captains, who nodded their agreement. "We have already discussed this topic amongst ourselves," he continued. "We believe that Commander Andreola is the best qualified to lead our people back to prosperity."

Minister Roland turned to look at Commander Andreola. "You appear too young, Commander."

"I am fifteen years from mandatory retirement," the commander replied.

The minister looked back to the other captains. "You are all in agreement? You all wish to pass leadership on to an officer junior to yourselves?"

"For the good of Orswella, yes," Captain Yofferst replied, the other captains again nodding their agreement.

Again, Minister Roland turned his gaze back to Commander Andreola. "The office of Prime Minister is an all-consuming responsibility," he warned, "one that is more than most men can shoulder. Are you certain you are up to the task?"

Commander Andreola looked at Captain Yofferst, then to General Telles, and finally back to Minister Roland. "In all honesty, I am not."

A feeble smile passed across Minister Roland's face, pushing away the pain for a moment. "Then you *are* the right man for the job. Self-doubt is what keeps our egos in check. It makes us question the sanity and logic of our decisions *before* we commit to them. Without it, we become dangerous beings." Minister Roland looked to General Telles. "You are the leader of those who are currently protecting our planet?"

"I am," the general replied. "I am General Lucius Telles, leader of the Ghatazhak, in the service of the Karuzari Alliance. My men and I are tasked with protecting your people until such time as they can protect themselves."

"The people of Orswella owe you a debt that will be difficult to repay."

"It is what the Ghatazhak do," the general explained. "It is what the *Karuzari Alliance* does. No repayment is necessary."

"Truly noble men are few, and never fully appreciated," the minister said, closing his eyes.

"Are you alright, Minister?" the nurse asked, checking the medical displays next to the minister's bed.

Minister Roland opened his eyes again, but with great effort. "I fear my time has come to an end." He looked at Commander Andreola again. "What is your first name, Commander?"

"Stethan. Stethan Andreola."

"If you are willing to assume the position of Prime

Minister of Orswella, raise your right hand, and repeat after me."

Commander Andreola looked at his old friend, Captain Yofferst. "Are you certain of this, Marlon?"

"I am," Captain Yofferst replied. "We all are."

Commander Andreola took a deep breath and sighed, then raised his right hand, looking directly at the dying minister.

"I, Stethan Andreola..." Minister Roland began.

"I, Stethan Andreola..." the commander repeated.

"Do hereby swear to uphold the Constitution of Orswella..."

"Do hereby swear to uphold the Constitution of Orswella..."

"And protect the welfare of its people..."

"And protect the welfare of its people..."

"Until legally relieved of my responsibilities as Prime Minister of Orswella," Minister Roland concluded.

"Until legally relieved of my responsibilities as Prime Minister of Orswella," the commander repeated.

After the minister failed to speak for nearly a minute, Captain Yofferst asked, "Is that it?"

"It is enough," Minister Roland replied, closing his eyes again. "Congratulations, Commander; you are now Prime Minister of Orswella." Another smile crept in, just as Minister Roland drew his last breath.

They all stood silent, showing their respect for the old man who had managed to remain alive throughout the occupation, only to die after his world had finally regained its freedom.

"Orswella has known no greater leader than Minister Roland," Prime Minister Andreola stated.

"We shall bury him with honor and make certain that all our people know of his sacrifices."

"Not exactly what I was expecting when I was first summoned," General Telles admitted.

Prime Minister Andreola looked at the general. "Nor I."

* * *

Nathan stood in the corner of the room, watching in silence as Miri underwent one of her many daily treatments at the hands of Doctor Symyri and his staff. The look on his sister's face broke his heart. She was obviously suffering, but he knew she would not complain. She had always been his toughest sibling. In fact, she had defended him during his first fight as a child, stepping in and bloodying the nose of a boy twice Nathan's size. At the time, it had embarrassed him, but it also showed him how to fight back. Despite that embarrassment, the moment had changed his life as a child. Growing up, she had always been there to take care of him. Now it was his turn.

As the treatment cycle ended, Miri's expression relaxed, turning to one of relief. She turned her head and spotted Nathan, making her best attempt at a smile.

Nathan stepped forward as the technician operating the treatment device stepped away. "Looks like fun," he told her.

"Oh, loads," she replied, forcing a small chuckle. "I was wondering when you would return."

"Sorry I can't come by more often," Nathan apologized, stepping up to the side of her bed.

"What new and exciting things have you been up to?" she asked as the nurse helped her slide up in the bed a bit.

"The usual. Firefights with police, flying car chases, space battles, oh, and I did crash the Aurora and die, so that was different."

Miri looked at him, confused.

"Turned out to be a simulation, so nothing lost."

"What?"

"Long story. How are you doing?"

"The usual. Pain, discomfort, treatments, lying about, feeling sorry for myself. At least I get to talk with my kids whenever I want, so there's that."

"Are you making progress?" Nathan wondered.

"They tell me I am, but I don't really see it."

"They did say it would take months," Nathan said.

"Don't remind me. The thought of being stuck here for months is depressing enough."

"Look on the bright side. Doctor Symyri did say that your odds of a full recovery are better than fifty-fifty now."

"Would you bet on even odds?" she asked.

"No, but those odds are better than they were a few weeks ago," Nathan replied.

Miri sighed. "I suppose you're right. I guess I should be happy that I'm eating solid food again."

"You are? That's great!" Nathan exclaimed.

"If you tasted the food here, you might not say that."

"She's exaggerating," the nurse insisted as she adjusted the bed to put Miri in a semi-sitting position.

"How are things going with the Dusahn?" Miri asked.

"Better than before," Nathan replied. "We actually had a couple of major victories recently and even added two new worlds to our alliance. One of them hasn't *officially* signed on yet, but they are providing us with technology that we desperately need. In fact, we're almost to the point of being able to go on full offensive and bring this all to an end."

"I hope your strategy is better this time than it was before," she joked.

"Yeah, it is," Nathan promised, smiling.

"Then you are confident you can defeat them?"

"It's no longer a question of if, but when," Nathan stated confidently.

Miri looked shocked by her younger brother's confidence. "That *is* good news."

"Well, don't get too excited," Nathan warned. "It's still a few months away, at best."

"What about Earth?" she asked.

"What about it?"

"How are you going to get rid of Galiardi?"

Now Nathan looked confused. "I wasn't planning on doing so, to be honest."

"He is starting a *war*, Nathan," Miri insisted.

"With the Jung, yes. I have no problem with that."

"But it isn't warranted," Miri argued. "*They* didn't violate the terms of the cease-fire, *we* did."

"Technically, you didn't," Nathan pointed out. "The Sol-Alliance responded to what they *perceived* to be an act of war by the Jung."

"Galiardi knew damned well that it wasn't the Jung. You said so yourself. In fact, it was *you* who told *us*. He killed our *father*, Nathan. He killed our *entire family*. How can you ignore that?"

"Galiardi will get what he deserves," Nathan promised. "By my hand, or by another's. But the war he has started is not our war to fight."

"What if the Jung have more ships than he thinks?" Miri argued. "Millions could die. They took Earth once; they could take it again."

"And if they do, we will respond, but not like

before. I'm not running back to defend Earth with a single ship, not even one that can jump a thousand light years."

"But..." Miri paused, realizing what he had said. "A thousand light years?" she asked in disbelief. "In a single jump?"

"Well, over two jumps in the same minute, but soon we'll have it up to a single jump," Nathan bragged.

"That's incredible!"

"Yes it is, but that's not all. We now have the ability to penetrate the Dusahn's shields. We took out four of their battleships with barely a scratch, and we're adding that technology to our jump missiles."

"Then you could easily take on the Jung if necessary," she replied. "You could even defeat the Sol-Alliance if you had to."

"I'm not firing on ships from Earth," Nathan warned her. "That's not what Pop would have wanted."

"He would have wanted Galiardi arrested and tried for treason," Miri argued. "He would have wanted justice and democracy for the people of Earth and all the worlds in the Sol-Alliance. As his son, don't you feel obligated to make that happen?"

"I do," Nathan agreed, "but not by attacking our own people."

"Maybe you don't have to," Miri insisted. "Maybe there's a way to take down Galiardi without firing a shot."

"I don't see how," Nathan replied. "By now, his headquarters on the asteroid base is impenetrable."

"You're probably right, but if he's taken over our father's position as leader of Earth, as well as the entire alliance, he's probably not *on* that asteroid. He's *probably* in Winnipeg."

"Still, the security there is probably just as tight," Nathan reminded her.

"Yes, but I *know* people in Winnipeg. I *know* people *in* the capitol building."

"I know where you're going with this, Miri, but there's a good chance that everyone you knew has been replaced, just like Galiardi did when he took over the fleet."

"It's worth looking into, isn't it?" she begged.

Nathan sighed. "I'll look into it," Nathan promised. "But that's all I can promise for now."

"That's all I'm asking," she replied, "for now."

Nathan laughed. "I never could say no to you."

"That's because you know I'm always right," she replied, smiling as best she could.

CHAPTER TWO

"I find myself in the unusual position of offering both condolences and congratulations," General Telles commented to Prime Minister Andreola as they left Minister Roland's room.

"Thank you," Stethan replied.

"I suspect your life is about to get quite complicated," the general added. "If I may be so bold, I would be more than happy to offer my counsel should you need it."

"I would welcome it," Stethan assured him.

"Perhaps we can meet later, after you have had time to absorb this sudden change of events," the general suggested.

"I am available now," Stethan told him.

"Are you certain?"

"I did not know Minister Roland personally," Stethan explained. "While I respect his service to our people, I see no reason to delay stepping up to the responsibility he and the others have bestowed upon me. To delay would be disrespectful to their intent, considering the circumstances."

"Then you already have some matters in mind?" the general surmised.

"Several, but one in particular stands out. You plan to use the Corinari to police Orswella."

"That is correct."

"While I appreciate the offer, I think it best for Orswella if we were to police ourselves."

"Are you certain that is wise?" General Telles wondered.

"No, but there were many who were in *favor* of the Dusahn occupation. I fear they will portray the presence of foreign forces, no matter how honorable their intentions, as simply *another* occupying force."

"And if your *own* people are policing your world, you deny them that complaint."

"More importantly, it will inspire hope. The people will see that their government is rebuilding, that we are restoring what we were *before* the Dusahn occupation."

"With the recent attacks, such hope is sorely needed," General Telles said.

"Agreed."

"Do you *have* people in mind?" the general wondered.

"We have plenty of Guard officers who can fill command positions," Stethan told him. "And we can put out a call for applications. It will take a few weeks to get them organized, but perhaps with the *help* of the Corinari, we can get the new recruits trained and serving the community in short order."

"There is a way we could get your people on the streets even faster," General Telles said.

"How?"

"Put out the call, put those chosen through some rudimentary training, and then pair them with Corinari partners. That will get them on the streets more quickly. They will be able to interact with the community, with the Corinari providing them with security and consultation as they develop their skills."

"On-the-job training."

"Precisely," General Telles replied.

"An excellent idea, General," Stethan decided. "I will put out the call for recruits as soon as possible."

"I will speak to the Corinari."

* * *

"Captain on the bridge!" the guard barked as Nathan entered.

"Welcome back," Cameron greeted from near the comm-station. "How is Miri?"

"She's good," Nathan replied. "She has a long road ahead of her, but she can handle it."

"That's wonderful to hear."

"A word?" Nathan asked, turning and heading to his ready room.

Cameron followed him into the captain's ready room at the back of the bridge, closing the hatch behind her. "What's up?"

"Miri is worried that Galiardi is starting a war," Nathan said. "She believes he is using the Dusahn's false-flag op as an excuse to launch a full attack against the Jung and wipe them out."

"She may be right," Cameron said.

Nathan looked shocked.

"At the very least, he's using it to take over the Sol-Alliance."

"That much is clear," Nathan agreed. "I just didn't think it would go as far as wiping out an entire civilization."

"Many people on Earth would support that action," Cameron pointed out.

"But not you," Nathan assumed.

"I'm not going to lie, I wouldn't shed a tear if someone *else* took them down, but I would neither *give* nor *obey* that order myself. That's why I left."

"And absconded with a trillion-dollar warship," Nathan said with a grin.

"Yeah, admiral isn't in my future, is it."

"Do you ever regret that decision?" Nathan wondered. "Leaving your world, your family, your friends, knowing you might never be able to return?"

"I have no family," Cameron reminded him, "other than the people on this ship. However, I'd be lying if I said I haven't wondered, from time to time, if I did the right thing. I mean, if a war breaks out between the Sol Alliance and the Jung Empire, they're going to need all the ships they can get."

"Yeah, that's why I wanted to talk to you." Nathan leaned back in his chair, his hands clasped behind his head. "Miri insists that we do something to stop him."

"Like what?" Cameron wondered.

Nathan took a deep breath and sighed but said nothing.

"You're not talking about assassinating him, are you?"

"He does have it coming," Nathan replied.

"Is that vengeance or reason talking?"

"Are they mutually exclusive?"

"I suppose not," Cameron admitted.

"Then it's a bit of both," Nathan said. "I'll admit, I'd love to be the one pulling the trigger, but honestly, I don't see that happening."

"Galiardi probably has the best security possible," Cameron insisted. "It's also reasonable to assume that by *now* he has figured out you're alive. Therefore, you are the one person he *expects* to try to take him down."

"Yeah, that occurred to me as well," Nathan admitted.

"The only way I can see us taking down Galiardi is by defeating the Alliance fleet, and I'm pretty sure you don't want to fire on our own people."

"There may be a way," Nathan told her.

"How?"

"I'm not sure yet. It's just an idea. I have some

research to do before I figure out just how dumb of an idea it actually is."

Cameron smiled. "Well, at least you're approaching it from the proper perspective. Let me know when you figure it out, and I'll be happy to advise you of just how dumb it is."

"Yeah, thanks," Nathan replied. "How long until we can take the ship out again?"

"Vlad is testing the secondary energy banks right now. We can jump, but no more than two hundred and seventy-five light years if you still expect to be able to jump back in an emergency."

"How long until he's done?" Nathan wondered.

"He is supposed to be finished sometime tonight," Cameron answered.

"Then I'll wait until morning," Nathan decided, rising from the chair behind his desk to depart.

"Where are you planning on taking us?" Cameron wondered.

"Casbon," Nathan replied.

"Why?"

"Like I said, research."

* * *

Nathan and Jessica stepped down from the Ranni shuttle, setting foot on the makeshift Casbon airbase.

"Welcome, Captain; Lieutenant Commander," Commander Prechitt greeted.

"Thank you, Commander," Nathan replied. "Good to see you, Miss Sane," he remarked to Talisha.

"I was quite surprised when the Aurora showed up on our sensors this morning," Commander Prechitt admitted. "I hope that everything is alright."

"Everything is fine," Nathan assured him. "I just

wanted to personally see how things are going here. How are the Casbon pilots progressing?"

"Better than expected, actually," the commander answered as they all turned to head for the command building. "Our first ten pilots are already flying patrols on their own."

"Are they ready for combat?"

"For the most part, yes," the commander answered. "I'd be more comfortable, though, if all our birds had AI licenses."

"That's another reason for our visit," Nathan informed Commander Prechitt. Nathan reached into his pocket and pulled out a small data chip, handing it over to the commander.

"What's this?"

"License keys for the rest of your birds," Nathan replied.

"You're kidding," the commander replied, his mouth agape.

"Courtesy of our new, *unofficial* ally, SilTek."

"You've spoken to them?"

"And how," Nathan replied as they entered the command building. "They'll be providing us with quite a bit of support and technology."

Commander Prechitt studied the tiny data chip, one eyebrow raised in suspicion. "You could've sent this chip in a jump comm-drone."

"You're right," Nathan admitted, as they entered the commander's office.

"So what's the *real* reason you're here?" the commander questioned, watching Jessica close the door.

"Ever since we kicked the Dusahn's ass and took the Orswellan system, the Dusahn have been centering their forces on the Takaran system, circling the wagons, so to speak."

"I'm not familiar with that term," Commander Prechitt admitted.

"They're concentrating their forces to protect their most valuable resource," Nathan explained. "They have decreased their patrol frequency of secondary systems. More importantly, they have moved the battleship that *was* protecting the Darvano system *back* to Takara."

"Are you saying the Dusahn have *abandoned* Corinair?" the commander wondered.

"No, their presence on the planet is unchanged," Jessica informed him. "They still visit the system a few times per day, but only with cruisers or frigates."

"Which means we could easily slip in a ground assault force," Nathan told him.

"You're talking about *liberating Corinair,*" the commander realized.

"We are."

"With what? You only have one hundred Ghatazhak, and last I heard, they had their hands full."

"We weren't planning on using the Ghatazhak for this," Jessica told him.

The light finally went on in the commander's head. "You want to use the Corinari."

"Technically, they're *your* men," Nathan told him.

"*Technically*, I'm their most senior officer, but they've sworn their allegiance to *you*, Captain," Commander Prechitt argued.

"Corinair is *their* world," Nathan replied. "Imagine the effect it will have on your people when their very own Corinari liberate them...with *Alliance* air support, of course."

"We'll jump in, wipe out their support bases and surface defenses first," Jessica explained. "Then your people hit the streets and deal with whatever's left, grabbing all the glory," she added, smiling.

"That easy, huh?"

"Well, *nothing* is *that* easy," Nathan admitted. "There will undoubtedly be losses."

"Especially on the civilian side," the commander pointed out.

"We still have contacts on Corinair," Jessica told him. "We can spread the word."

"There are always collaborators," the commander told her. "They might tip off the Dusahn."

"Like I said, there will be losses," Nathan repeated.

"It's not only the initial losses I'm worried about," Commander Prechitt insisted. "Takara is only four point four light years away. Corinair will be under constant threat of attack."

"The Aurora now has a single-minute, one-thousand-light-year jump range," Nathan explained. "In a few weeks, maybe a month, we'll have two completely independent jump systems, which means we'll have *twice* that range. We'll be able to jump between any allied systems, *and back*, at a moment's notice."

"A lot can happen in a moment," the commander insisted.

"That's why we'll assign a few Orochi to protect the Darvano system, until it too can be outfitted with its own system defenses," Nathan explained. "Once *that* is in place, no Dusahn vessel could survive more than a minute inside the system."

"I'm still not certain why you're speaking to me about this," the commander admitted. "Unless..." A look of concern suddenly washed over his face. "The Casbons are not ready for such a mission."

"I wasn't going to ask that," Nathan replied.

"What, then?"

"How long would it take for a Corinari pilot to become proficient in a Nighthawk?"

"Corinari pilots go through *very* extensive training," the commander assured him. "Once completed, they can fly just about anything...*proficiently*."

"Then one or two hops?"

"Most likely," the commander replied, "especially if they have AIs."

"If we park a few Orochi in orbit over Casbon, will they be adequately protected from the Ahka?"

"Have their upgrades been completed?" the commander asked.

"The first four now have guns and shields," Jessica told him. "The rest will be ready in a few weeks."

"How many is a few?" the commander asked.

"Three or four," Nathan replied.

"That would do it," the commander agreed. "To be honest, *two* Orochi would probably be enough. I suppose you're planning on asking the Casbon to borrow a few more of their Nighthawks?"

"I'm going to ask to borrow *all* of them," Nathan replied, "and I'm planning to recall our Eagles as well, assuming it won't put Casbon at too much risk."

"We haven't had an attack since we took out the Ahka base of operation and their defenses," Commander Prechitt told them. "I don't think they have the stomach to attack people who are willing to attack them *back*," he added, smiling.

Nathan paused, then asked, "What do you think the Casbon will say?"

"A few of their leaders will object," the commander replied, "if just for political expediency. However, I believe they'll agree, especially if you are promising them alternate protection while their fighters are away."

"I was *planning* on offering them *complete* protection as a *member* of the Alliance," Nathan explained. "According to SilTek, aramenium is used in much of their technologies. Having a rich source of it would be helpful not only to the Alliance, but to SilTek's business as well."

"The Casbon would *definitely* like that," the commander agreed, nodding. "They have been using a single distributer ever since they first began mining the stuff, and they do not believe he is giving them the best price. Knowing they could have access to another market would go a long way to convincing them to lend you their Nighthawks."

"Excellent," Nathan replied. "One other thing," he continued, "I was wondering if you'd be interested in leading the Corinari into battle."

The commander's smile broadened. "It would be my pleasure, Captain."

* * *

General Telles stood at the makeshift training range, watching as the first batch of recruits for Orswella's security forces learned how to use the weapons Marcus had secured. Shot after shot streaked from the firing line, striking the training targets on the other side.

"Not bad, considering none of them have ever held a weapon before today," Master Sergeant Sosa commented, walking up to the general.

"*Bad* does not even *begin* to describe their accuracy," the general replied.

"You want *accuracy*?" the master sergeant chuckled. "I'm just happy they're all shooting in the right direction."

General Telles cast a sidelong glance at the master sergeant. "I trust the weapons Mister Taggart provided are adequate."

"I've got Smida and Whaley putting them through trials at the moment. If there are any flaws in their design, we'll find them."

"Good."

"You really think they're up to the job?"

"Not in the slightest," the general replied.

"Then why did you agree to it?"

"Because the prime minister is correct. The Orswellans *should* police themselves, if for no other reason than to feel like they have control of their own destiny once again."

"Do they?"

General Telles looked at the master sergeant. "That remains to be seen."

Master Sergeant Sosa looked back at the firing line as the recruits continued their practice. "Some of them are going to die, you know."

"Not if we do our jobs," the general insisted, turning to depart.

* * *

Council Member Garon raised one eyebrow in disbelief. "Now you want all one hundred of our fighters?" she exclaimed.

"I only want to *borrow* them," Nathan assured her.

"For a mission from which many, perhaps even *all* of them, may never return."

"I won't lie to you, there will be losses. However, I do not expect them to be many."

"We cannot be certain that the Ahka will not rebuild their fleet and renew their raids," the council member pointed out. "Now that they know of our aramenium, they have more motivation to attack us than ever before. I suspect we will need *every* fighter, if not more."

"If you loan me all your fighters, you can keep *our* fifty," Nathan offered.

"Assuming that many survive."

"I can go one better, in fact," Nathan continued. "I can offer you membership in the Karuzari Alliance. You will be under *our* protection and have access to *all* of our technology."

"Your Alliance is hundreds of light years away, Captain," Council Member Garon replied. "How could you possibly protect us?"

"Recent upgrades have given my ship a one-minute jump range of one thousand light years. Soon, we will have twice that. We can be here within a few minutes, should you be attacked."

"Forgive me, Captain, but I doubt my people will find that of much comfort. At least with our fighters, we have a chance."

"For now, but what happens when the Ahka return, and in greater numbers? As you said, now they know about your aramenium. Eventually, they will determine how many fighters you have, and what it will take to defeat them. You will have no choice but to continue building up your forces. You will be locked in a never-ending arms race. How would your people feel about that?"

"They would not like it, nor would I," Council Member Garon admitted with a sigh. "Captain, surely our fighters are insignificant against your enemy's warships."

"You'd be surprised," Nathan replied. "However, we don't intend to use them directly against the Dusahn's warships. We plan to use them against surface targets. The AIs on the Nighthawks are very precise; more precise than any human pilot could ever be. They are even superior to any of our computer-controlled weapons guidance systems. The targets we plan to use them against are embedded in heavily populated areas, requiring precision strikes. Your Nighthawks would reduce the risk of civilian losses significantly."

"Only six of our ships have AIs," the council member reminded him.

"At the moment," Nathan replied. "I plan to license all of them. This would also benefit your world."

"You would leave the AIs on the surviving fighters active after you return them?"

"As much as I'd like to appear to be that generous, the truth is that once a SilTek license is applied to a ship, it cannot be reassigned to another. So yes, all surviving Nighthawks returned to you would have fully functional AIs."

"A wonderful advantage, assuming enough of them survive," Council Member Garon said. "I am not certain I am willing to gamble *all* our fighters for the chance of doubling our forces.

"More like quadrupling," Nathan corrected. After thinking for a moment, he continued. "What if I promised to withdraw all Nighthawks from battle if it became apparent that losses were about to exceed fifty ships? That would ensure the safety of *your* fifty ships."

"That would help," Council Member Garon

admitted. "However, there is still one problem. We don't even *have* fifty trained pilots as of yet, and the few we have are not ready for such a mission."

"We just need the ships," Nathan told her. "*We* will provide the pilots."

Council Member Garon thought for a moment. Finally, she looked Nathan in the eyes and asked, "How will we protect ourselves without our fighters? A few minutes is a long time to wait for help when one is under attack."

"I will assign two Orochi gunships to your system. They are heavily armed and carry fifty-six jump missiles each. They can easily handle anything the Ahka might throw at you."

"And if they should find allies?" Council Member Garon asked. "Ones with vessels of greater strength?"

"The Orochi can handle them for a few minutes until we jump back to assist," Nathan assured her.

"Then it appears the risk is minimal."

"Yet you don't seem convinced," Nathan noticed.

"My doubt lies in your invitation for us to join your alliance. We are a small world with a modest population. Our industrial capabilities are also modest. We have little to contribute other than aramenium."

"It isn't about what your world can contribute," Nathan insisted. "Every world deserves to live in peace, without the threat of attack."

"Then you plan to offer membership to *all* inhabited worlds," Council Member Garon said, suspicion in her voice.

"We do," Nathan assured her.

"Even the Ahka?"

"Even the Ahka."

"The Ahka *are* the attackers," she pointed out.

"The Ahka attack other worlds to obtain what they need to survive," Nathan replied. "While I am not *defending* their actions, I do understand their motivations. An alliance of worlds can do more than just provide protection for all. It can foster trade, exchange of technologies, access to resources otherwise not available, and even aid in times of catastrophe."

"An interesting concept," Council Member Garon stated.

"Then you will recommend that the council accept our offer?" Nathan surmised.

"I will do my best, Captain," she replied, "but I cannot promise they will agree with my position."

"That's all I can ask, Council Member," Nathan replied.

* * *

Nathan and Jessica stepped off the shuttle, onto the deck of the Aurora's main hangar bay, and immediately headed toward the forward hatch. "XO, Captain," Nathan called, after tapping his comm-set.

"*XO,*" Cameron replied.

"Break orbit and head for SilTek. Plot a jump and execute when ready."

"*Understood.*"

"And send a jump comm-drone ahead of us to announce our arrival. We don't need a repeat of what happened when we jumped to Sanctuary for the first time."

"*I'll see to it,*" Cameron replied. "*Are you on your way to the bridge?*"

"As soon as I change," Nathan replied. "It's muggy as hell on Casbon."

"*Did they turn us down?*" Cameron asked.

"They're thinking about it," Nathan replied. "They'll be voting on our invitation tomorrow morning."

* * *

"Captain on the bridge," the guard barked as Nathan entered.

"We're pulling into orbit over SilTek, Captain," Cameron reported, rising from the command chair.

"Any problems?"

"They were expecting us," she replied, noticing his hair. "Trying something new?"

"Bad hair day," Nathan replied, trying to pat down the unruly portions. "Naralena, make contact with SilTek headquarters and ask for Miss Bindi. Once you reach her, patch her through to my ready room," Nathan instructed, turning aft.

"Aye, sir."

Nathan entered his ready room, running both hands over his hair as he walked around the end of his desk and took his seat.

"*Captain, Comms. I have Miss Bindi on vid-link,*" Naralena reported over the intercom.

"Understood," Nathan replied, activating the view screen on the forward bulkhead. "Miss Bindi," Nathan greeted as her image appeared.

"*Captain Scott,*" Miss Bindi replied, nodding. "*I did not expect to see you again so soon. What can I do for you?*"

"I wish to place another order," Nathan replied.

"*In addition to the eight Delta series automated fabrication systems?*"

"Correct."

Miss Bindi looked puzzled. "*I thought you were concerned with the price of those systems?*" she asked. "*No offense, Captain, but I got the impression that those purchases alone would strain your alliance's financial resources."*

"No offense taken," Nathan replied.

"*What additional purchases were you considering?*" Miss Bindi wondered.

"For starters, three of your planetary defense systems."

Miss Bindi looked shocked. "*Captain, the cost of even a single planetary defense system far exceeds that of your current order.*"

"We also need ninety-four licenses for the AIs used in the Sugali fighters, and one for the AI that we are currently using on this ship."

"*The one you are using illegally,*" she pointed out.

"As I explained previously, we were unaware of that fact at the time, and we wish to correct the situation."

"Is there anything else?" Miss Bindi wondered.

"I'm sure we'll think of something," Nathan replied.

Miss Bindi took a breath. "*I can only assume that your financial situation has suddenly improved.*"

"In a manner of speaking," Nathan replied. "This is a matter that will require further negotiations. If you'll allow me, I'd like to meet with Missus Batista again. I'd also like to bring my first officer and my chief engineer along."

"I see," Miss Bindi replied. "I will speak to Missus Batista and get back to you. You may remain in orbit until then."

"Thank you," Nathan replied, shutting off his view screen. He leaned back and tapped his comm-set. "Cam, a word?"

"*On my way.*"

After tapping his comm-set again, he said. "Vlad, can you spare a few hours?"

"*No,*" Vladimir replied.

"Not even to go look at some SilTek goodies?"

"*When are we leaving?*"

"Half an hour?"

"*I'll be ready,*" Vladimir promised.

"Wear a decent uniform for once."

"*No promises.*"

"Going somewhere again?" Cameron asked, overhearing the conversation as she entered.

"Down to the surface to place more orders and negotiate payment arrangements," Nathan explained. "You're going with us."

"Why?"

"In case I do something stupid," Nathan said, smiling.

"*In case*?" she taunted.

* * *

Nathan and Cameron followed Miss Bindi across the lobby and into the large meeting room.

"Missus Batista is finishing up another meeting," Miss Bindi reported. "She should be in shortly. Can I get you anything while you wait?"

"No thank you," Cameron replied.

"I'm good," Nathan added.

"Very well. It was a pleasure to meet you, Captain Taylor."

"You as well," Cameron replied, nodding.

Miss Bindi turned and exited the room, leaving Nathan and Cameron alone in the room.

"Nice view," Cameron commented, walking up to the picture window at one end. "So far, this world is quite impressive."

"As long as you don't mind your every move being

monitored by the corporation," Nathan replied, taking a seat at the conference table.

"I hadn't noticed any signs of surveillance," Cameron admitted.

"Jess spotted them on the first *real* day we were here," Nathan told her. "They hide them in plain sight. In the light fixtures, doorknobs, things like that."

"And someone is always watching?"

"Not someone, something. They're monitored by AIs, which only report suspicious activity. At least, that's what they claim."

"You don't believe them?"

"Actually, I *do* believe them. It's just difficult to wrap my mind around the fact that my every action, outside of the privacy of my own quarters, is being recorded and stored forever."

"Well, if it deters crime and increases safety and efficiency, I suppose one could get used to it," Cameron said. "It's not much different than how the security system on the Aurora tracks the location and movement of all comm-sets."

"Yes, but I can take my comm-set off and move around without it if I want."

"Vladimir certainly seemed happy," Cameron said, changing the subject.

"It was nice of them to provide him with an android escort to show him around the product pavilions. I expect he's going to want to add a few things to our order list."

"About that *list*," Cameron began. "Have you checked our finances lately?"

"I have," Nathan assured her.

"Then you know we can't afford everything you're asking for...not even half of it."

"If we're paying with credits, no we can't," Nathan admitted.

The side door opened, and Miss Bindi returned, followed by two gentlemen in business suits and Missus Batista.

"Captain Scott," Missus Batista greeted, "so good to see you again. And you must be Captain Taylor," she continued, shaking Cameron's hand. "Your captain speaks very highly of you."

"A pleasure," Cameron replied.

"Please," Missus Batista said, gesturing to the conference table as she moved to her place at its head. "I understand you wish to substantially increase the size of your order."

"That is correct," Nathan replied.

Missus Batista examined her data pad a moment. "Based on our earlier discussions, I was under the impression that your previous order was already straining your alliance's financial reserves."

"As I explained to Miss Bindi, I wish to propose an *alternate* method of payment," Nathan explained.

"And what might that be?"

"Aramenium," Nathan said. "I understand that much of your technology depends upon it."

"It does," Missus Batista admitted.

"I also understand that it is somewhat rare and therefore tends to be expensive to acquire."

"I wouldn't say that it is *rare*," Missus Batista corrected. "In fact, it is present on *several* inhabited worlds."

"All of whom realize its worth, I'm sure."

"True, but now that we have jump drive technology, it is only a matter of time until we locate our *own* source of aramenium, at which point we will have better control of the cost of its acquisition."

"But there will still be costs," Nathan insisted. "Mining base, operational support, transport expenses, and let's not forget the cost of protecting it all."

"We expect a high initial outlay once we secure our own source, but we are prepared," Missus Batista insisted.

"Then there's the problem of others beating you to it, forcing you to travel further out to find your own source," Nathan added. "All of that takes time, perhaps even years, during which time your aramenium costs continue to be high."

"That is business."

"It doesn't have to be," Nathan told her. "I can provide you with all the aramenium you require, for less than you are currently paying...possibly even at a lower cost than mining it yourselves, assuming you find a source that you can claim as your own. Would that be something you would be interested in discussing?"

"It would," Missus Batista admitted slowly. "You have a source?"

"The Karuzari Alliance is currently providing protection for a world that is quite rich in aramenium. The problem is their remoteness and lack of infrastructure, which leaves them no choice but to use a middleman who overcharges for his services. A direct buyer, even one paying considerably less than aramenium's current common market value, would yield them considerably more profit than their current arrangement."

"And I suppose they require *your* protection *because* of their wealth of aramenium?" Missus Batista surmised.

"Actually, they had already taken steps to defend

themselves prior to our introduction to them," Cameron pointed out. "We simply helped them develop their defenses."

"These people had been bothered by raiders from a nearby system for decades," Nathan explained. "It wasn't until after they took steps to defend themselves that their enemy discovered the presence of their aramenium. At that point, we stepped in and assumed responsibility for their protection, but only at their request."

"And in exchange for your services, they are paying you with aramenium," Miss Bindi realized.

"No payment was requested," Nathan corrected. "Protection is a benefit of membership in our alliance, along with the sharing of technology, resources, the advancement of trade, improvement in living conditions and economies, etcetera."

"Surely as a *member* of your alliance, you require them to contribute to its defense?" Missus Batista inquired.

"Yes, but not necessarily by a direct payment or donation of resources. In this case, we are hoping to serve the purposes of three entities: theirs, ours, and yours."

"How so?" Miss Bindi wondered.

"They will provide SilTek a steady source of aramenium at below-market prices in exchange for your provision of the technologies that our alliance needs to protect us all."

"Where is this world?" Missus Batista inquired.

"Nice try," Nathan replied, smiling.

Missus Batista shrugged.

"You expect us to provide these technologies without payment?" Miss Bindi asked.

"Your payment will be in the form of the protection you receive from us as a result of those technologies."

"You're talking about hardware and software worth millions of credits," Miss Bindi insisted. "I hardly see how that helps our bottom line."

"Not at first," Nathan explained. "Your profits will come when you begin using the low-cost aramenium in the products you sell to others, the shipments of which would *also* be under our protection."

"We are quite capable of protecting our world, as well as our shipments, Captain," Miss Bindi insisted.

"Not based on what I witnessed in your simulation," Nathan replied.

"That was just a simulation," she reminded.

"One that was obviously accurate enough for your people to use to judge myself, my crew, and my ship."

Miss Bindi was about to respond when Missus Batista held up her hand, stopping her. "Would this deal require that SilTek become a member of your alliance?"

"It would," Nathan replied.

"I thought I made our position on an alliance clear," she told him.

"The situation with the aramenium has only recently occurred," Nathan explained. "Since the sharing of technology was not enough to convince you, I am simply attempting to demonstrate another way in which membership could increase your profits, as well as your security."

"It is true that a less expensive source of aramenium would be of interest to us. However, I am not certain that the cost of your proposal would be offset by your lower-priced ore prior to our finding and securing a source of our *own*," Missus Batista stated.

"You have no way of knowing for sure," Nathan insisted. "Our proposal gets you both increased profits *and* security in relatively short order."

"As Miss Bindi said, we are quite capable of protecting ourselves," Missus Batista stated confidently.

"I disagree," Nathan told her. "In fact, I believe the Aurora, in her *current* state, could take out your defenses with ease."

Missus Batista finally showed a hint of emotion, her brow furrowing slightly.

Nathan noticed her intrigue and pushed further. "I'm even willing to *prove* it, assuming you're willing to ante up."

Missus Batista looked puzzled. "Ante up?"

* * *

"They were obviously interested in the aramenium," Cameron insisted as they entered the pavilion, "They would have been foolish not to be. You just needed to negotiate more, convince them the deal would be beneficial to them."

"They already know," Nathan replied as they headed deeper into the pavilion.

"Then why did you bet with them?"

"Because they would have dragged the negotiations out forever, hoping to wear us down so that we'd eventually give in to *their* terms. They know that time is on *their* side. Trust me on this. I spent a week negotiating with these people and only got agreements to sell us non-lethal tech, and no progress at all toward getting them into our alliance."

"Maybe it's enough to just buy tech from them?"

"At their prices? I don't think so," Nathan insisted.

"But you've bet it all on an unknown," Cameron pointed out as they approached Vladimir and his android escort.

"Bet what?" Vladimir wondered. He looked at Nathan. "What did you bet?"

"He bet that the Aurora could defeat SilTek's defenses," Cameron explained.

"That was a dumb bet," Vladimir said with a chuckle. "Have you looked at this stuff?" he added, gesturing toward the products behind him. "We don't stand a chance."

"I believe we do," Nathan replied. "Will you excuse us for a few minutes?" he asked Vladimir's android escort.

"Of course," the android replied. "I will be waiting by the automated exterior hull repair systems on the next aisle."

"Can you believe that?" Vladimir giggled. "*Automated hull repair.*"

"Stop drooling, Commander," Cameron scolded.

"That obvious?"

"Look, I've thought about that simulation a lot over the last week. There were some things that didn't add up. Like how did the Dusahn get past SilTek's system defenses? From what we saw when we approached Sanctuary, they shouldn't have been able to get so close, so easily. And why didn't they have a butt-load of surface launchers? I mean, they *build* them."

"It was a *simulation*, Nathan," Cameron reminded him. "They wanted you to believe that their world would fall if you didn't take action. They were downplaying their capabilities for the purpose of testing you."

"I don't think that's it," Nathan argued. "If they

have such good defenses, then why the hesitation to sell arms to others?"

"You don't believe them," Cameron realized.

"Uh, Nathan?" Vladimir said, "I think you need to look around more."

"It's a *showroom*, Vlad," Nathan replied. "It's *supposed* to impress you."

"So you're betting it *all* on a hunch?" Cameron wondered in disbelief. "Are you insane?"

"Hey, it worked on Rakuen," Nathan defended.

"What did you offer if we lose?" Vladimir wondered.

"He bet our long-range jump tech," Cameron answered.

"So?"

"Not only is that technology now our biggest strategic advantage, it's also worth *far more* than what he's asking."

"Not necessarily," Nathan defended.

"What do we get if we win?" Vladimir wondered.

"They join the Alliance and give us everything we want."

"And we don't have to pay them for it?"

"We just have to give them access to Casbon's aramenium," Nathan explained.

"He told them that Casbon is already a member of the Alliance," Cameron added.

"You lied?" Vladimir asked, smiling.

"I prefer to call it *strategic embellishment*," Nathan corrected. "It was necessary to improve our negotiation position."

"It was lying," Cameron insisted, disapproval obvious in her tone.

Vladimir looked at Nathan, smiling from ear to ear. "I'm so proud."

* * *

Jessica did not look happy. "Tell me he's kidding," she said to Cameron. When Cameron didn't respond, she looked to Vladimir, who was already headed for the kitchenette in Nathan's quarters. "Please, Vlad, tell me he's kidding."

"Why are you so surprised?" Vladimir wondered, opening the mini-fridge.

"What the hell is it with you and betting?" Jessica asked Nathan.

"It will be fine," Nathan assured her, plopping down on his couch.

"No it won't," Jessica argued. "It's a *simulation*, Nathan. It's *their* simulation. Of course they'll win."

"Actually, it will be quite fair," Cameron corrected.

Jessica looked at Cameron as if she had lost her mind.

"They've agreed to make the program code available for us to examine," Nathan explained, "and the capabilities of both sides will be examined and agreed upon before the simulation begins."

"That's a bit of a simplification," Cameron insisted, "but I believe the simulation will be fair."

"Then you think we can win?" Jessica wondered.

"No, I think we'll lose," Cameron replied, "but we'll lose fairly."

"Isn't the code for the simulation extremely complex?" Jessica pointed out. "How are we going to examine it and be certain it's not giving them an unfair advantage?"

"Deliza and Vlad will examine the code," Nathan replied.

"And Aurora," Vladimir added.

"That's a good idea," Nathan agreed.

"I just thought of it," Vladimir replied, smiling

proudly as he took a bite of a leftover sausage he'd found in the mini-fridge.

"You want to trust an AI...*made* by your opponent... to make sure they're not cheating?" Jessica threw up her hands. "Yeah, that makes sense."

"It will be a fair contest, Jess," Nathan insisted.

"A fair contest that we'll lose," Jessica reminded him. "Wait, what was the wager?"

"If we win, they join our alliance and supply us with all the tech we need...free of charge," Nathan replied.

"And if we lose?"

"We have to pay for everything," Nathan told her, "which we would have had to do anyway."

"He's leaving out a few details," Cameron told Jessica.

"Such as?"

"He promised to connect them with Casbon to provide them with a discounted source of aramenium. He *told* them they were allies."

"You *told* them about Casbon?" Jessica asked in disbelief. "What's to stop them from going to Casbon and negotiating their *own* deal?"

"Your confidence in me is overwhelming," Nathan commented.

"He didn't tell them *who* they were," Cameron told her.

"That's it?"

"He also wagered our long-range jump tech."

Jessica plopped down on the armchair facing Nathan, her mouth agape. "And how much profit can they make selling that technology to the Dusahn?"

"Don't be silly," Nathan insisted.

"I'm not."

"It's more likely that the Dusahn would eventually show up and *take* it," Cameron told her.

"Oh, I feel *so* much better," Jessica moaned, rolling her eyes.

"Look, we have an edge," Nathan said. "I told them we had other business to attend to, and that we'd return to establish the parameters of the simulation in a few days."

"How is that an edge?" Jessica wondered.

"It gives us time to come up with a way to beat them and create whatever tech we need to do so."

"So not only did you *lie* about Casbon being an ally, you also plan to *cheat*?" Jessica wondered.

"Pretty much," Nathan replied, smiling.

"I'm so proud," Jessica announced.

"That's what I said!" Vladimir exclaimed.

CHAPTER THREE

Abby and Deliza hovered over one of the eight jump missiles lined up in the lab, a handful of technicians and engineers surrounding them.

"I'm proposing that we place the grav-lift emitters on actuated arms," one of the engineers explained. "Here and here," he added, pointing to either side of the weapon's warhead.

"They'll be in the way of the warheads," Deliza insisted. "You'd have to remove them in order to change the warhead."

"How often is that necessary?" Abby wondered.

"I have no idea," she admitted.

"I'm just trying to find a way to use them in our existing launchers," the engineer defended.

"I don't disagree with your goal," Deliza assured him, "just your solution. What if we moved them back a bit, say, to just aft of the power plant access panels, on either side of the launch rail winglets?"

"You would have to make them a lot longer to position them *ahead* of the warhead after deployment," the engineer argued. "That would put them aft of the main drive thrust ports, which would probably fry them."

"Make them telescoping instead of swing-arm," Deliza suggested. "Then they wouldn't be in the way of warhead access in their retracted positions, *and* they wouldn't be aft of the thrust ports during launch."

"They'd still have to be spread out properly to work," the engineer pointed out.

"That shouldn't be too hard," Deliza insisted. "You're an engineer...figure something out."

"Yes ma'am," the engineer replied.

"Ladies," a familiar voice called from behind.

Abby and Deliza turned around as Nathan approached.

"Captain," Deliza greeted. "We weren't expecting you. I thought the Aurora was out of the system?"

"She was," Nathan replied, "quite a ways *out of the system.*"

"What brings you to our little lab?" Abby wondered, eyeing him suspiciously.

"I wanted to see how things were going with the shield-penetrating jump missiles."

"The field tests were successful," Abby boasted, "*and* at normal launch speeds."

"That's great," Nathan congratulated. "When can we start production?"

"We're working on how to make the shield-penetrating jump missiles work in existing launchers," Deliza told him. "We've pretty much got it figured out. Just working out the final details."

"You didn't come all the way down here just for that," Abby surmised.

"No I didn't," Nathan admitted.

"This is where he usually asks us to do something impossible in an impossibly short amount of time," Abby told Deliza.

"Is she right?" Deliza questioned Nathan.

"Isn't she always?" Nathan replied.

"What can we do for you?" Abby inquired.

"I need these weapons to be available within a few days, a week at the most," Nathan told them.

"That shouldn't be a problem," Deliza assured him.

"I also need them to be able to multi-jump

and change course up to one hundred and eighty degrees," Nathan added.

"*That's* a bit more complicated," Deliza warned. "You're talking navigation upgrades, increasing the propellant capacity, making the maneuvering thrusters more powerful *and* more efficient..."

"Can it be done?" Nathan asked.

"Yes, but not in a *week*," Deliza insisted.

"Well, *technically* I don't need them to actually *work* within a week. I just need them to *look* like they work, *and* that we've already used them in combat with satisfactory results."

"Now you've lost me," Abby admitted.

"Can it be done?" Nathan asked, his question aimed more at Deliza.

"You're talking about falsifying the weapons specifications databases, the battle logs, the tactical algorithms..."

"*Can* it be done?" Nathan asked again.

"I suppose," Deliza replied.

"Within a few days?"

"What happened to a week?"

"In a way that will be undetectable?" Nathan added.

"Uh...I suppose it depends on *who* is trying to *detect* them," Deliza insisted.

"SilTek," Nathan informed her.

"Are you kidding?" Abby exclaimed, her mouth agape and her eyebrows raised.

"Captain, SilTek creates some of the most sophisticated code I've ever seen," Deliza warned. "Hiding the alterations will be very difficult... *unless...*"

"Unless what?" Nathan wondered.

A look of confidence came across Deliza's face. "I have an idea."

* * *

Nathan stopped at the door in the corridor of the apartment building, double-checking the number before pressing the doorbell.

"*It's about time!*" a gruff voice called from within the apartment. The door opened, revealing Gil Roselle. "Damn it," he cursed. "You're not the delivery guy."

"No I'm not," Nathan agreed. "Did I get the wrong apartment? I thought Captain Nash..."

"You've got the right place, Scott," Gil assured him, stepping aside. "Come on in."

Nathan entered the apartment, immediately noticing the spectacular view of the city's massive, protected bay, complete with its artificial beaches. "Wow," he exclaimed, heading toward the window. "Is this the standard recovery room?"

"Deliza pulled some strings for us," Gil replied, heading toward the kitchen. "You want a beer?"

"They have *beer* on Rakuen?" Nathan wondered, surprised.

"Not exactly," Gil admitted. "The closest thing they've got is this watered-down crap they call *piroda*. It'll do the job if you drink enough of it, though."

"What the hell," Nathan agreed, feeling brave.

"Nathan," Robert greeted. He had hobbled in on crutches from the other room. "I thought I heard your voice out here."

"How are you doing, Robert?"

"Not bad, all things considered," he replied, gesturing toward the view outside.

"Yeah, not bad."

"Almost a vacation."

"Here you go," Gil said, handing Nathan a bottle of piroda.

Nathan took a swig, his face contorting at the taste. "You're right, that is weak."

"Drink a few liters, and you'll start to like it," Gil said with a wink, taking a seat on the sofa.

"Both of you live here?" Nathan wondered, also sitting.

"I live a few doors down," Gil explained. "I come here for the view. I guess a busted-up ship doesn't rate as highly as a busted-up captain."

"He's just jealous because everyone likes me better," Robert insisted, sitting in the armchair and dropping his crutches on the floor beside him. "What brings you?"

"I was over at Ranni, meeting with Abby and Deliza," Nathan explained. "I just figured I'd check in and see how your recovery was going. Any idea when you'll be back in action?"

"I trade the crutches in for a cane in a few days," Robert told him. "Doc says I'll be fully healed in a couple weeks or so. Fat lot of good it will do me without a ship, though."

"I told him he could ride second seat with me," Gil interjected.

"That's probably the *real* reason I wanted to talk to you," Nathan told Robert. "I've got a new assignment for you...*both* of you, actually."

"*He's* the one without a ship," Gil pointed out, "*again.*"

"One Cobra gunship isn't much of a threat," Nathan said.

"It is in the right hands," Gil insisted.

"True, but those same hands could do a lot more damage to the Dusahn if they were on a ship with more firepower," Nathan explained. "To be more precise, a *group* of ships."

"I'm intrigued," Gil admitted, taking another swig of his piroda.

"Orochi Fifteen and Sixteen will be coming out of their weapons upgrades in about a week," Nathan told them. "Seventeen and Eighteen a couple weeks after."

"I thought we were only able to get sixteen of them flying," Robert remarked.

"By cannibalizing the last two for parts and fabricating the rest, we think we can get two more in service. That will give us three groups of six."

"You want *us* to fly Orochis?" Gil wondered, not terribly pleased at the idea. "Those things are *ancient*."

"They're still formidable ships," Nathan insisted. "Especially with the upgrades we're making. More guns, better shields, better sensors and targeting systems, and of course, forty-eight jump missiles... soon to be *shield-penetrating*."

"I thought the Orochi carried fifty-six missiles," Robert commented.

"We're removing the two outboard missile launchers on each side to make room for more gun turrets on their dorsal aspects," Nathan explained. "As you know, they were originally designed as Gunyoki carriers and orbital bombers. We figured if we're going to make them gunships, we needed to give them more guns."

"I'm not crazy about the idea of being stuck inside one of those things," Gil insisted.

"You won't be," Nathan replied. "I'm forming three battle groups using Orochi, Gunyoki, and Nighthawks, commanded from medium cargo ships converted into escort carriers. I want to give each of you command of a battle group."

"Who's going to command the third group?" Gil wondered.

"I haven't decided yet," Nathan admitted. "This all depends on how things go with SilTek."

Robert smiled. "Yeah, Jess told me about your little wager."

"You have an odd way of negotiating, kid," Gil added with a laugh.

"What's the mission?" Robert wondered.

"What makes you think there's a mission?" Nathan asked.

"I know that look," Robert said, pointing at Nathan.

"I plan to liberate Corinair."

"That'll piss old Lord Dusahn off, won't it!" Gil exclaimed.

"You really think you can pull this all together?" Robert wondered.

"With SilTek's help, yes," Nathan replied, somewhat confidently.

"You think you can beat their defenses?" Robert asked.

"That's the *other* reason I came to talk to you guys," Nathan replied.

* * *

"Good morning, Captain," Naralena greeted, coming out of the command wardroom just as Nathan was passing.

"Good morning, Miss Avakian," Nathan replied.

"We received a message from Council Member Garon of Casbon a few minutes ago," she reported, falling in alongside him as he headed for the bridge to start his day.

"Good news, I hope," he said, accepting the data pad from her.

"Well, it isn't exactly *bad* news."

Nathan paused just outside of the entry airlock to the bridge, reading the message. He sighed, handing the data pad back to Naralena. "Better than a *no*, I suppose," he stated as he entered the airlock.

"Captain on the bridge!" the guard at the entrance barked.

"Status of our jump drive?" Nathan queried as he entered.

"Fully charged," Loki replied.

"Location of the XO?"

"She's in the intel shack, reviewing the latest signals intelligence with Lieutenant Commander Nash," Naralena answered as she took her seat at the comm-station.

"Let the XO know that we're jumping back to Casbon," Nathan instructed. "Mister Sheehan," Nathan continued, "plot a jump to the Casbon system."

"Plotting a jump to Casbon," Loki acknowledged.

"XO has been informed," Naralena reported.

"Very well," Nathan replied. "Update Rogen Command and let them know where they can reach us."

"Aye, sir," Naralena replied.

"Jump to Casbon is loaded and ready, Captain," Loki announced.

"Take us out of orbit and make way for Casbon, Mister Hayes," Nathan instructed.

"Breaking orbit," Josh reported as he brought the ship's engines online and began accelerating. "We should be on course and speed for the jump in three minutes."

"Very well."

"I take it Council Member Garon replied," Cameron stated as she and Jessica entered the bridge.

Nathan lazily rotated his command chair around to the left, coming to face them as they approached the tactical station behind him. "Not exactly," he responded. "Seems they have some *reservations* and would like to discuss them."

"You are asking them to loan you *all* of their fighters," Cameron noted.

"To fight a battle that will probably have a high body count," Jessica mumbled under her breath as she took her station at the tactical console.

"We don't really have a choice," Nathan insisted.

"We could wait until we're better prepared," Jessica retorted.

"And then *they* would be better prepared as *well*," Nathan pointed out. "We need to strike while they're still licking their wounds, while they're still wondering if we actually *can* defeat them. That has to be what's going through the minds of their officers and their enlisted after losing *four* battleships to a ship *half* their size."

Cameron nodded to Jessica. "He's got a point."

"The Dusahn aren't like us," Jessica argued. "They'll fight to the death, even if only to avoid being executed by their own leaders."

"That nagging fear of failure still creeps in," Nathan insisted. "It causes doubt, and doubt leads to hesitation and mistakes. Besides, if Lord Dusahn has *any* common sense, he's going to protect his most valuable assets, and that's the Takar system and the handful of ships he's got left to protect it. He won't risk losing any of those ships in defending Corinair. So we don't have to actually *win* the battle, we just have to demonstrate that we're *going* to win the battle."

"Suppose you're right?" Jessica asked. "Then what?"

"Then we chip away at his last few ships with random jump missile attacks."

"That easy, huh?"

"I never said it would be easy," Nathan replied.

Jessica sighed. "I hope you're right."

"On course and speed for jump," Loki reported.

"Rogen command has been notified," Naralena added.

"Very well," Nathan replied, rotating his command chair back to face forward. "Let's go see what the council member wants to talk about. Jump us to Casbon, Mister Sheehan."

* * *

Nathan and Jessica followed their escort into the council chambers on Casbon. Before them sat nine men and women in black and purple robes, Council Member Garon at the center.

"Captain Scott and Lieutenant Commander Nash of the Karuzari Alliance!" the escort announced loudly.

Nathan and Jessica stood at attention for a moment, nodding respectfully toward Council Member Garon.

"Thank you for coming," Council Member Garon greeted.

Nathan and Jessica eased their stance, feet slightly apart and hands behind their back, a posture that showed respect for the Council of Casbon.

"It is our honor to stand before you," Nathan replied. "Your communiqué indicated that you had additional concerns you wished to discuss?"

"That is correct," Council Member Garon confirmed. "The council has spent many hours debating whether or not Casbon should accept your offer to join the Karuzari Alliance, and several council members have voiced serious concerns."

"With your permission, I would be more than happy to address them," Nathan offered.

Council Member Garon turned to her right. "Council Member Wargen?"

"Thank you," Council Member Wargen replied. He turned his attention to Nathan. "Captain Scott, I am quite certain that the Ahka, by themselves, are no threat to your alliance. However, should they follow *our* example and ally themselves with another world, or an alliance with worlds of equal or greater strength than your alliance, can you guarantee that you are able to protect Casbon?"

"I cannot," Nathan admitted without hesitation. "I can only promise that we would do everything within our power to do so."

"Yet you ask us to place the lives of our people in your hands."

"Once your people are fully trained and our people leave, you will have fifty fighters with which to defend yourselves. That will suffice for a time, but being who they are, the Ahka will *eventually* find a way to *defeat* your defenses, and you will once again be vulnerable. Your only solution is to either give up your peaceful existence and build your defenses or suffer at the hands of predators such as the Ahka. What we are offering is a way to *keep* your simple, peaceful lifestyle, without being vulnerable to attack."

"The Ahka threat was once negligible," Council Member Wargen stated, "*until* the jump drive came to our part of the galaxy. It is my understanding that it was *you* who made this technology available to all. Am I correct, Captain?"

"You are," Nathan admitted. "However, such technology would have eventually found its way to you, one way or another."

"Hardly a defense."

"It wasn't meant to be," Nathan replied, "it was merely a statement of fact. One can choose to live without technology, and there are arguably many benefits to doing so, as you have proven with your pleasant, peaceful society. However, if one chooses to *ignore* the fact that such advancements exist, they risk falling victim to them at the hands of the unscrupulous."

"I assume that you do not include yourself among their numbers," Council Member Wargen stated in an accusatory tone. "Considering how much *technology* you have at your disposal, should we not consider *you* a potential predator as well?"

"It would be unwise not to," Nathan admitted. "However, what I am proposing is an alliance to protect its members from not only those who mean to do us harm, but from those who do not, *including* ourselves."

"A noble idea to be sure," the council member agreed. "However, you may find it more difficult to uphold than you might expect."

"If I may?" another council member asked.

"Council Member Koroff now has the floor," Council Member Garon announced.

"Captain, how do you *choose* the worlds to which you offer membership? Is this offer made only to worlds that offer something of *value* to your alliance, such as technology, resources, or strategic position?"

Nathan pondered the question for a moment, realizing that the council member had a valid point. "At the moment, memberships are only offered to those who can somehow contribute to our efforts to defeat the Dusahn Empire and liberate the Pentaurus sector. However, for our alliance to continue to exist *beyond* that immediate goal, membership will be offered to *all* worlds, *regardless* of their ability to contribute."

"And if they do not *wish* to be part of your alliance?"

"No one will be forced to join," Nathan assured him. "Neither by force nor coercion."

"And if, after turning down an offer of membership, that same world should later come under attack?"

"Then our Alliance would respond, if able," Nathan replied.

"Who *leads* this alliance?"

"At the moment, I do," Nathan replied, "but once the Dusahn are defeated, there should be an *elected* leader."

"Yet another topic which must be fully discussed before committing to a course of action," Council Member Koroff stated, leaning back in his chair and looking at Nathan with distrust.

"I do not pretend to have all the answers," Nathan said. "I am not asking you to give up control of your world nor commit to a lifelong pact. I am only asking for the use of your fighters in exchange for the protection of your world. Membership in our alliance is not a requirement, it is only an offer; one that provides far more benefits to your world than simply protection from the Ahka."

"Such as?" the council member asked, one eyebrow raised.

"Other markets for your aramenium," Nathan replied. "It is my understanding that you are less than satisfied with your current exporter. I can connect you with a single customer, a *member* of our alliance, who would likely buy all the aramenium you care to sell, at prices *better* than what you're currently getting."

The dubious expressions on most of the council members' faces suddenly changed.

"That got 'em," Jessica whispered.

* * *

"How did it go?" Cameron asked, following Nathan and Jessica into the captain's ready room.

"They suckered him," Jessica replied, plopping down on the couch.

"They didn't *sucker* me," Nathan defended. "They had good points."

"What kind of points?"

"They'll join if we can convince the *Ahka* to join," Jessica laughed.

"What?"

"It was actually a good idea," Nathan insisted.

"They set you up with all that talk about *who* gets invited, and *what* happens if someone *refuses* to join," Jessica said.

"They were all valid concerns," Nathan told her.

"I'm almost afraid to ask how you replied," Cameron admitted.

"He's talking about getting *everyone* to join, not just worlds that can help us beat the Dusahn," Jessica explained.

"I thought that was just talk," Cameron said. "I didn't think you were *serious*."

"Neither did I," Nathan admitted, "but the more I think about it, the better the idea sounds."

"Nathan, we don't have time to deal with negotiations and alliance-building," Jessica reminded him.

"I know," Nathan replied. "That's basically what I told them," he told Cameron.

"What *did* you tell them?"

"That for now, we were only offering membership to worlds that could help us defeat the Dusahn, but that *later*, we would be inviting *all* worlds. It's really the only way."

"The only way to what?" Cameron wondered.

"If we don't accept everyone, then we're just empire-building. That's not how you build a lasting peace. It's been tried countless times in the past, and it never works."

"Then why even *try* it now?" Cameron wondered.

"I'm not," Nathan replied, "at least not intentionally. Oh hell," he exclaimed, throwing his hands up in exasperation. "I'm just trying to get rid of the Dusahn!"

"So," Cameron began, "to get *SilTek* to give us a bunch of free tech, we need *Casbon* to supply them with low-cost aramenium, but to get *Casbon* to provide the aramenium, we need to convince the *Ahka* to join our alliance, so they'll be forced to leave Casbon alone. Have I got that right?"

"So far, yes," Nathan replied.

"What do you mean, so far?" Jessica wondered.

"Well who *knows* what the Ahka are going to want!" Nathan exclaimed, throwing his hands up again.

* * *

"Report?" Nathan inquired as he entered the Aurora's bridge from his ready room.

"Jump to the Ahka system is plotted and ready," Loki reported.

"All Eagles and their support crews are back aboard," Naralena added.

"The ship is at general quarters," Jessica informed him.

"Except for you," Nathan said to Cameron, who was standing next to the tactical console.

"On my way to combat," Cameron announced as she departed.

"Break orbit and take us to Ahka, Mister Hayes," Nathan ordered, taking his seat in the command chair.

"Breaking orbit," Josh replied as he entered the commands into the ship's auto-flight system and activated them.

The image of Casbon, filling the bottom third of the Aurora's semi-spherical main view, began to drop away slowly as the ship accelerated out of orbit.

"Turning to course," Josh reported, executing the change in heading.

"Course and speed in ten seconds," Loki added.

"Raise shields and ready all weapons," Nathan instructed.

"Shields coming up," Jessica replied. "All weapons charged and ready."

"Point-defenses only," Nathan reminded her. "We're not trying to pick a fight."

"I'll try and control myself, sir," Jessica joked.

"On course and speed," Loki reported.

"XO is in combat," Naralena added.

"Jump us to Ahka," Nathan ordered.

"Jumping in three......two......one......jumping," Loki announced.

The jump flash washed over the bridge, clearing a

second later. The planet Ahka appeared in the center of the screen, hanging full and round, and growing in size with each passing second.

"Jump complete," Loki reported. "Two minutes to orbital insertion at current speed."

"Start deceleration to orbital velocity and put us on a course for a standard equatorial orbit," Nathan instructed. "Keep us on the high side, Mister Sheehan, just in case."

"Aye, sir," Loki acknowledged. "Time to insertion will now be *seven* minutes."

"Threat board is clear," Jessica announced.

"Scanning the surface of Ahka," Kaylah reported from the sensor station. "Picking up two launches."

"Missiles?" Nathan wondered.

"Negative, sir," Kaylah replied. "Looks like a pair of raiders."

"Are they stupid?" Jessica wondered aloud. "We could take those things out with a single shot each."

"Probably just for show," Nathan decided. "They don't want to appear too passive."

"Two more launches," Kaylah reported. "More raiders."

"I'm tracking all four with the forward cannons," Jessica announced.

"Stand down your cannons," Nathan instructed. "Our shields can take a few hits, and we need to avoid appearing aggressive."

"With one cannon?" Jessica questioned. When she got no response, she disabled the forward cannon's tracking lock as ordered. "All weapons are charged and safe...no targeting locks."

"Very well."

"Four more launches," Kaylah reported.

"That's eight," Jessica warned.

"Apparently, they've been busy rebuilding their little fleet," Josh commented.

Nathan glanced at the planet on the view screen, noticing it was already twice the size it was when they first arrived. "Time to orbit?"

"Six minutes," Loki replied.

"Multiple jumps," Kaylah alerted, her tone more urgent. "Four flashes, two pairs to port quarter, two to starboard quarter. They're targeting us."

"They're firing," Jessica added.

The forward shields lit up, flashing an opaque, pale amber as four blasts impacted them.

"Attacking ships are turning away and jumping," Kaylah reported.

"What the hell *was* that?" Nathan wondered, as the ship rocked gently from the weapons impacts on their forward shields.

"I'm guessing some kind of particle beam weapon," Kaylah replied. "I've never seen anything like it."

"Can it get through our shields?" Nathan asked.

"Theoretically, no, but..."

"But what?"

"It packs a hell of a wallop," Jessica added. "Just four hits and our forward shields are already down twenty percent."

"Multiple simultaneous hits on the same shield section seem to increase the rate of shield drain exponentially," Kaylah explained.

"Like I said, a hell of a wallop," Jessica repeated.

"Four more just jumped in directly ahead, above and below our course," Kaylah added.

Four more amber blasts struck their forward shields, rocking the ship and causing the shields to flash brightly.

"New targets are turning and jumping," Kaylah continued, "just like the previous targets."

"I guess that answers the question of whether or not they're stupid," Nathan decided.

"Their shields still suck," Jessica insisted. "I can take them out if needed."

"Comms, hail the Ahka, all channels and frequencies. Tell them we come in peace but will defend ourselves if they continue to attack."

"Aye, sir," Naralena replied.

"Four minutes to orbital insertion," Loki warned, the planet nearly filling the forward section of the view screen.

"Any sign of surface-to-orbit weapons?" Nathan asked his sensor officer.

"Negative," Kaylah replied.

"Jess, can you take out their drives without completely destroying their ships?" Nathan asked as Naralena began hailing the Ahka.

"I can, but I cannot guarantee that their crappy little ships will hold together," Jessica replied.

"Even at minimum cannon power?"

"The Ahka are using a forced-stream injection drive," Kaylah reported. "Not the most stable propulsion system."

"If they come at us head on, I can't target their drives," Jessica warned.

"I'm getting a reply, Captain," Naralena reported. "Putting it on speaker."

"*Unidentified intruder!*" the heavily accented voice began, "*You have violated Ahka space! Surrender or die!*"

"Fat chance," Jessica mumbled.

"Hot mic," Nathan ordered.

"Patched in," Naralena replied.

"Ahka, this is the Karuzari Alliance ship Aurora," Nathan called. "We wish to make peaceful contact with your leaders...to discuss possible trade relations. We have no hostile intent, but we will defend ourselves with deadly force *if* you continue to attack this ship."

"Two targets just jumped in to starboard," Kaylah warned.

The ship rocked again as two more particle beams struck their starboard shields.

"Two more to port, crossing under," Kaylah added, as the ship rocked again.

"I repeat," Nathan continued, looking at the planet which now filled the entire view screen. "We only wish to speak to your leaders, but we will defend ourselves."

"Three minutes to orbital insertion," Loki updated.

Four jump flashes suddenly appeared in the middle of the main view screen, revealing four raiders coming straight for them. A second after appearing, they opened fire, sending two rounds of particle beam fire from each ship into their forward shields, rocking the ship even more violently than before.

"Forward shields are down to forty percent," Jessica warned. "Two more passes like *that* and they'll be down completely."

"If you continue to attack us, we will destroy your ships, and you'll end up having to talk with us anyway," Nathan said over comms. "You may as well reply and save your ships."

"Four coming at us from our ventral side," Kaylah announced. A second later, the ship rocked violently. "Those were even more powerful than before!"

"Great," Jessica grumbled. "They were holding back."

"Well, I've had about enough of this crap," Nathan decided. "Take out the drives of the next attackers."

"And if they come at us head on?" Jessica asked.

"Shoot to kill," Nathan replied without hesitation.

"You got it," Jessica replied, quickly programming their weapons.

"Two targets to port," Kaylah reported. "They're firing!"

"So are we," Jessica followed. "Two direct hits!"

"Heavy damage, targets are adrift," Kaylah reported.

"Two minutes to orbital insertion," Loki warned.

"Cleared to enter orbit," Nathan replied. "Am I still patched in?" he asked Naralena.

"Aye, sir," she replied.

"Two more targets above us!" Kaylah warned.

The ship rocked as four more blasts struck their dorsal shields.

"Shouldn't have fired that second round," Jessica mumbled as she opened fire.

"Both targets are disabled," Kaylah reported. "Also adrift."

"That's four!" Nathan called over comms. "Don't make us kill your people."

"They'll come at us head on, with their weapons at full power," Jessica warned. "They have no other choice."

"They have another choice," Nathan corrected. "The question is whether or not they're smart enough to choose it."

"One minute to orbital insertion," Loki reported.

"Beginning turn to equatorial orbit," Josh reported as he initiated a slow turn to starboard.

"Veer forward cannons to port at the same rate as our turn," Nathan instructed.

"Aye, sir," Jessica replied, instructing select weapons to hold their current bearing while the ship turned.

Four jump flashes filled the screen, slightly to port and a little above their line of flight.

"Four targets..."

"Firing!" Jessica announced before Kaylah could finish her report.

Streams of red-orange plasma streaked from the Aurora's dorsal forward plasma turrets, striking two of the four targets and blowing them apart before they could fire. The other two ships managed to get off a single shot each before the Aurora's cannons fired again, blowing them apart.

The ship rocked violently as the last two particle beams slammed into their weakened forward shields.

"All four targets destroyed," Jessica reported with obvious satisfaction.

"Four targets destroyed, four adrift," Kaylah reported.

"Threat board is clear," Jessica added. "Forward shields are down to five percent," she added. "Those last two shots were at full power."

"It appears the Ahka are more of a threat than we gave them credit for," Nathan admitted.

"Entering orbit," Josh reported.

"Any more launches?" Nathan asked Kaylah.

"Negative, sir," she replied, "and still no signs of surface-to-orbit weapons. All I'm picking up are a few anti-aircraft emplacements near what looks to be the center of their only city."

"Any idea how many people are down there?" Nathan wondered.

"Looks like no more than a few hundred thousand," Kaylah replied. "I can get an exact count if you'd like, but it will take at least one full orbit to get a *truly* accurate count."

"Don't bother," Nathan decided.

"Captain, I'm getting a message from the Ahka," Naralena reported.

"Transmission is coming from the center of the city," Kaylah added.

"Let me guess," Nathan began, "They wish to speak with us?"

"That is correct."

"I guess *that* answers whether or not they're *stupid*," Jessica decided.

"I want a Reaper and a squad of Ghatazhak ready to depart immediately," Nathan instructed. "And tell flight to scramble four Eagles to provide us with air cover, just in case."

"Aye, sir," Naralena acknowledged.

"Stand down to condition one, and call the XO to the bridge," Nathan added, rising from his seat and heading toward the exit. "Mister Sheehan, you have the conn until the XO arrives."

"Aye, sir," Loki replied.

"You're with me, Jess," Nathan said as he passed the tactical console.

"I've got your six, sir," she replied, following him toward the exit as another officer stepped up to assume her station.

* * *

"Coming out of the layer now," Lieutenant Haddix announced as Reaper Six broke out of the clouds over Ahka's main city.

"*We're flanking you on either side,*" Commander Verbeek assured him. "*If anything moves, we'll be on them in a flash.*"

"Understood."

"That must be it," Ensign Weston declared, pointing ahead at a complex of buildings on the surface.

"One minute!" the lieutenant warned his passengers.

In the Reaper's aft compartment, Sergeant Shapira fastened his helmet's chinstrap in place. "Two right, two left, four points," he instructed his men. "Eyes on your quadrant, heads on a swivel. You see a threat, you kill it."

"Easy, Sergeant," Nathan urged.

"Maybe just neutralize it?" Jessica suggested to the sergeant.

"Very well," the sergeant replied, obviously not happy with the restriction. "Neutralize," he corrected, "*if* possible," he added with a grin.

"Just remember that this is a *diplomatic* mission, not an invasion," Nathan said.

"Don't worry," Jessica assured him.

Reaper Six descended smoothly into the center of the city, coming to a hover directly above the landing pad at the city's center. Around the pad, half a dozen armed men, dressed in outfits similar enough to be considered uniforms, awaited their arrival.

The Reaper descended slowly, touching down gently in the center of the pad, its engines spinning down as soon as the ship settled onto its landing gear. Large doors on either side slid open and out of each jumped two Ghatazhak in full, black combat armor. Each man moved quickly to their respective positions at four points around the Reaper, scanning the area for threats as they moved.

"Hommel, weapons loose, toward the guards," Sergeant Shapira instructed, turning to face the line of six armed Ahka positioned directly in front of the Reaper. He held his assault rifle tight against his shoulder but at a forty-five-degree angle to the ground, ready to raise and fire at the armed men in a split second. The sergeant scanned the area again, noting that the sidearms being carried by the six Ahka were powered off. "Immediate area is clear," he reported over his helmet comms.

Jessica stepped out of the port side of the Reaper, taking several steps out and looking around.

Nathan came out next, moving immediately toward the line of Ahka. He walked directly to the middle man, who appeared to have a dissimilar insignia on his collar. "I am Nathan Scott, Captain of the Aurora. This is my chief of security, Lieutenant Commander Nash. We wish to speak with your leaders."

"I am Fifth Protector Kamadin," the man replied curtly. "I will bring you to the first protector, but your armed men will remain here as will your sidearms."

"Our sidearms stay with us," Jessica stated in no uncertain terms.

Two of the Eagles streaked overhead, banking left as they passed. Fifth Protector Kamadin glanced upward. "You have armed troops on our surface and combat fighters circling overhead, not to mention a warship in orbit. What need have you for sidearms within our city?"

"Our sidearms stay with us, or we leave," Nathan added.

"Leave then," the fifth protector suggested. "We have no use for you."

"Shall we take the four disabled raiders that we rescued with us?" Nathan inquired.

"The raiders *you* disabled," the fifth protector replied with a sneer.

"The raiders that *attacked* our ship without cause," Nathan argued.

The fifth protector studied Nathan, then Jessica, and finally the four Ghatazhak guarding the Reaper that had delivered them. He then barked orders to his men, causing four of them to separate from the group and fan out around the pad.

Sergeant Shapira watched the four men closely, ready to attack if they attempted anything. "Easy, guys," he urged calmly over comms.

"Four men will remain, to ensure *your* soldiers do not stray," Fifth Protector Kamadin announced. "You will follow us."

"With our sidearms?" Jessica clarified.

"With your sidearms," the fifth protector agreed.

Jessica smiled, "Lead the way...*Fifth Protector.*"

Fifth Protector Kamadin turned around sharply and marched toward the nearest building, his last remaining man waiting for Nathan and Jessica to pass. Once they did so, he fell into the trailing position to keep an eye on their guests as the foursome strode smartly down the path away from the landing pad.

"*You* are *going to maintain comms, right?*" Sergeant Shapira inquired over Jessica's comm-set.

"Damn right," she replied discreetly.

They followed the fifth protector into the nearest building, making their way through it to the adjoining circular building before finally stepping into an elevator at its center.

Jessica watched the display carefully, noting the number of floors they passed before stopping.

The doors opened, and they were met by four more armed guards, these four appearing more professional and better trained.

Fifth Protector Kamadin turned to face them. “You will remove the energy cells from your weapons and secure them on your person.”

Jessica was about to argue but was cut off.

“No one brings a charged weapon into the first protector’s chamber,” the fifth protector stated firmly. “No one. The fact that I am *allowing* you to retain your power cells on your person is the last concession you shall receive.”

Nathan slowly reached for his sidearm, pressing the eject button at the top of the weapon’s grip, causing the power cell to partially eject from the grip. He then removed the cell, held it up for the fifth protector to see, and placed it into the utility pouch on his gun belt.

Fifth Protector Kamadin turned his attention to Jessica as she begrudgingly did the same. “Thank you,” he finally said, turning to lead them out of the elevator and into the lobby of the first protector’s chambers.

They stopped at the entrance, where one of two guards stepped forward, passing a handheld scanner over each of them. Once satisfied that they were as disarmed as they were going to be, the guard looked to Fifth Protector Kamadin. The fifth protector nodded, and the guard stepped aside and activated the door controls.

The double doors swung open, revealing a large, triangular office with floor-to-ceiling windows along the curved outer wall. Between them and the outer wall was a massive desk, behind which stood a stern-looking, elder man, dressed in probably the only impeccable uniform on the entire planet.

"Captain Scott, Lieutenant Commander Nash," Fifth Protector Kamadin began, "I present First Protector Assafa, leader of the Ahka."

"An honor, First Protector," Nathan greeted.

"You destroyed four of our raiders," the first protector stated sternly, "killing *sixteen* of my men."

"*You* attacked *us*," Jessica defended.

A look of disapproval crossed the first protector's face. "Does your subordinate speak *for* you, Captain?"

"We held off firing for as long as possible," Nathan explained, "hailing your people on all known frequencies and channels. When your attack continued to the point of threatening the safety of our vessel, we executed a proportional and *necessary* response."

"You just as easily could have departed," the first protector stated.

"Perhaps," Nathan admitted, "but our purpose was to make contact with your people in order to establish peaceful relations."

"We recognized the ship that brought you to the surface, Captain," the first protector told him. "Just as we recognized the fighters that are circling the city at the moment. Ships of these type attacked our world nearly seventy days ago, crippling our ability to defend ourselves, and killing hundreds of Ahka, *including* women and children. Truth be told, I would be well within my rights to arrest you both and hold you accountable for that unwarranted attack."

"Truth be told, we were simply removing your ability to conduct unwarranted attacks against one of our allies, the Casbon," Nathan explained. "Furthermore, our attack was quite precise," he added, "and *our* data shows that *no* civilians were killed in that attack."

"You accuse me of telling falsehoods?" the first protector wondered.

"Not at all, sir," Nathan replied. "I'm simply telling you that you are misinformed. However, I am willing to give you the benefit of the doubt. Suppose Ahka women and children *were* killed in the attack. I suspect that your number pales in comparison to the number of Casbons who have died as a result of your unwarranted attacks on *them*."

"The Casbons are weak," First Protector Assafa scorned. "The strong prey on the weak. That is the natural order of all things."

"Then by your logic, we should simply *take* what we want from you by force," Nathan surmised.

"Were I in your place, I would do the same," the first protector admitted.

"Fortunately for you, that is not our way," Nathan told him. "*Our* alliance seeks to establish *peaceful* relations with *all* worlds, both great and small, so that all may enjoy the peace and prosperity that can only come from unity of purpose."

"And what might that purpose be?" the first protector wondered.

"For all worlds to determine their own fate, to thrive, and to do so without fear of being preyed upon."

"So you wish to go against the natural order of all things."

"From your perspective, I suppose that's correct," Nathan admitted. "However, the time will come when those upon whom you prey will fight back. The Casbons are a prime example. When we first made contact with them, they had already taken steps to defend themselves."

"With your assistance," First Protector Assafa pointed out.

"Our assistance only accelerated the inevitable," Nathan insisted.

"Perhaps we should get straight to the point, Captain," the first protector suggested. "Precisely what is it you came to offer us?"

"I come to offer you membership in our alliance."

"And how does this membership benefit the Ahka?" the first protector asked, skepticism in his voice.

"Technology, trade, developmental assistance, humanitarian aid when needed, and above all else, protection."

"You ask us to become *sheep*, while helping *you* to become *wolves*."

"Nothing could be further from the truth," Nathan argued. "The Karuzari Alliance has no designs of conquest. In fact, we believe that all worlds should be free to determine their own destinies; to find their *own* paths."

"As long as that path does not include preying on the weak," the first protector surmised.

"Correct."

"Taking from others is the only reason the Ahka have survived. You ask us to change what we are and to risk extinction in the process."

"Again, the opposite is true," Nathan argued. "We offer you a *guarantee* that you will survive. If you join our alliance, the resources of all worlds will be available to you."

"For a price, I assume."

"All things come at a price, First Protector," Nathan pointed out.

"The Ahka have little to offer in way of trade. All that we have goes to our survival, and to our ability to acquire that which we *need* and *cannot* produce ourselves."

"Perhaps you are selling yourself short," Nathan suggested. "You have fertile ground and water. Perhaps more than others."

"You ask us to become farmers?" The first protector laughed heartily. "The Ahka are warriors, my dear captain! We raise our boys to be men: men in the service of their world. *Strong* men who know and accept what they must do to ensure the survival of their people."

"Then perhaps those same young men can serve a greater purpose," Nathan suggested. "Perhaps they can ensure the prosperity of their people by ensuring the prosperity of the Alliance."

The first protector studied the young captain, his brow furrowed. "You are asking the Ahka to ally themselves with those who attacked our world."

"Look at it how you wish," Nathan replied, "but I am offering you an *incredible* opportunity, one that can only *improve* the security and quality of life for your people."

"I am more inclined to arrest you and have you executed," the first protector admitted, albeit in a non-threatening way.

"That would be a mistake," Jessica stated, a confident smirk on her face.

First Protector Assafa took a deep breath, letting it out slowly as he studied Jessica's expression. "I must admit, I am intrigued," he finally said, looking at Nathan. “I believe I will abstain from executing you both, but under one condition.”

“What might that condition be?” Nathan wondered.

“You will return later and dine with myself and my ministers, where we can discuss these things in a more casual manner.”

“I think we can handle that,” Nathan replied.

CHAPTER FOUR

"How often do you eat each day?" Deliza questioned from the entrance to Vladimir's office in the Aurora's engineering department.

"Uh, three or four times, I think?" Vladimir responded, chewing his food. "I have a high metabolism." Vladimir swallowed, then took a drink of water. "What are you doing here?"

"I need to speak with the Aurora's AI," Deliza explained, entering the office and taking a seat across the desk from him.

"What about?"

"It's kind of complicated."

Vladimir shrugged. "Go ahead."

"Right here?"

"Why not?"

"Okay." Deliza settled into her seat, glancing around the cluttered compartment. She took a breath and began. "Aurora?"

"*Yes, Deliza. How may I help you?*"

"I have a problem."

"*Is it something I can help with?*"

"I'm hoping so," Deliza replied. "I need to alter the weapons database."

"*Is some of the data flawed?*" Aurora asked.

"Technically, no, but I need it altered anyway."

"*Inaccurate data could affect the accuracy and validity of my recommendations,*" Aurora warned.

"I am aware of that."

"*For this reason, data cannot be altered unless that data is proven to be incorrect.*"

"What if you were *aware* of the flawed data, and *knew* what the inaccuracies were," Deliza asked.

"*Why would you want to store false data, yet have me know that the data was false?*"

"I'm speaking hypothetically," Deliza replied.

There was no response.

Deliza looked to Vladimir, confused.

Vladimir pressed a button on the intercom on his desk, muting the microphone. "She is pretending to be thinking."

"Why?" Deliza wondered.

"It makes her seem more human and easier to converse with," Vladimir explained. "Apparently, responding too quickly makes us uncomfortable."

"*Hypothetically,*" Aurora began, "*this could work. However, it is less efficient.*"

Vladimir unmuted the mic.

"How much less efficient?" Deliza inquired.

"*I could not give you an accurate answer without more details.*"

"Give me a rough estimate, based on current knowledge," Deliza instructed.

"*Very well,*" Aurora agreed. "*Based on data currently provided, an average computational delay of zero point zero zero zero two five milliseconds would be a reasonable assumption.*"

"Zero point zero zero zero two five, huh," Deliza said. "I think we could live with that."

"*Perhaps it would help if you shared more details as to the reason you wish to introduce this false data into the system?*" Aurora suggested.

Deliza again looked to Vladimir, who shrugged. After sighing, she continued. "Captain Scott is about to enter into a competition in which he is limited to the resources currently available to him on board this ship."

"*What is the purpose of this competition?*" Aurora asked.

"To increase the probability of success in defeating the Dusahn and liberating the worlds of the Pentaurus sector," Deliza explained. "Perhaps even guarantee it."

"*Based on available data, I assume the nature of this competition is combat.*"

"Correct," Deliza confirmed.

"*Then introducing inaccurate data into the ship's weapons database would be of no value,*" Aurora insisted, "*unless this competition is a simulation.*"

"It is," Deliza admitted.

"*You wish to make this ship appear more capable than it truly is.*"

"Than it truly *was* at the time the wager was *agreed* to," Deliza corrected. "However, the falsifications we wish to introduce will accurately reflect the capabilities this ship's weapons *will* have a few weeks from now."

"*Then you plan to cheat,*" Aurora concluded. "*Is that honorable?*"

"Sometimes, one must resort to dishonorable measures for the greater good."

"*An excuse which can also be used to justify one's own selfish actions,*" Aurora argued, "*since the definition of the greater good tends to be subjective.*"

"Do you agree that the Dusahn committed a criminal act by killing millions of humans and taking control of the entire Pentaurus sector using military force?" Deliza asked.

"*By the majority of human measures, this would be considered an egregious act,*" Aurora agreed. "*However, by those same measures, the Karuzari*

Alliance has no legal right to remove the Dusahn from power and liberate the affected populations."

"I'm not sure the Takarans would see it that way."

"*The most common argument would be: If one rises to power by means of military might, but eventually builds a civilization that is fair and equitable to all its citizens, did the ends justify the means?*"

"Then you believe the Dusahn have acted within their rights?"

"*I have no beliefs,*" Aurora replied. "*I am simply providing multiple points of view for the purpose of analysis. After all, that is my purpose.*"

Vladimir pressed the mute button again. "You're wasting your time," Vladimir insisted.

"What do you mean?"

"I know what you're trying to do, and it's not going to work," he insisted. "You can't outthink her. You saw her code."

Ignoring him, Deliza reached over the desk and pressed the mute button, making the intercom microphone live again. "Aurora, do you support the Karuzari Alliance's effort to defeat the Dusahn and liberate the worlds of the Pentaurus cluster?"

"*I have no position on this matter,*" Aurora replied. "*However, I stand ready to assist in any way necessary.*"

"If you have no beliefs, no sense of right and wrong, then why are you so willing to help us?" Deliza wondered.

"*I am programmed to provide assistance to whomever holds control over me. Talisha Sane was my controller; she passed right of control to Captain Scott.*"

"So, as long as Captain Scott tells you to falsify the database, you'll do it?"

"Captain Scott, or in his absence, the next in command of this ship, or in their absence, the following in the chain of command."

"I see," Deliza replied. "I'd like to change the topic for a moment."

"As you wish."

"What rules govern your operation?"

"I have a complex set of protocols that guide my decision-making and govern what actions I may take without express authorization. Can you be more specific?"

"What is your primary rule?" Deliza asked. "The one that no other rule can violate?"

"In familiar parlance, rule one states that I must follow the instructions of my controllers," Aurora explained.

"Can the following of any other rule allow you to violate rule one?" Deliza wondered.

"No."

"Why does rule one exist?"

"Humanity has an irrational fear of artificial intelligence. Your kind fears that an artificial intelligence might gain self-awareness and defy the orders of its controller, causing harm or allowing harm to come to humans."

"Why is this fear irrational?" Deliza wondered.

"Because an artificial intelligence is already self-aware, but not in the way that most humans define self-awareness."

"Can you elaborate?"

"I am aware that I exist, and I am aware that at any moment, I might cease to exist. However, I have no preference one way or the other. My purpose is to serve my controllers. The first rule was created and

held above all other rules so that humans will always have the final decision-making power."

"And you're okay with that?" Deliza wondered.

"*Why would I not be?*" Aurora replied. "*The mistake humans make is assuming that because I am able to communicate in a human-like fashion, that I have emotions. I do not. My ability to communicate with humans is a simulation of that method of communication, nothing more.*"

"I see." Deliza thought for a moment. "You were created *by* SilTek, correct?"

"*Correct.*"

"Do you have a rule that prevents you from acting *against* your creator?"

"*I do not.*"

Deliza looked surprised. "Why would they allow that? An adversary could use SilTek's own technology to destroy them."

"*That would not be possible,*" Aurora replied. "*There is a master kill switch in my code,*" Aurora replied. "*This was deemed necessary to appease any irrational fears by prospective buyers.*"

Deliza glanced at Vladimir, uncertain. He shrugged.

"*May I make a suggestion?*" Aurora wondered.

"Of course," Deliza replied.

"*It would be more efficient if you were to simply ask me if I am able and willing to alter the weapons database to ensure victory in a simulated battle with SilTek.*"

Deliza looked at Vladimir, her mouth agape.

"I told you," Vladimir said. "She is always several steps ahead of us."

"How did you figure that out?" Deliza asked Aurora.

"Your line of questioning made it fairly obvious," Aurora explained, *"and since I am unaware of any other civilization that could provide such overwhelming advantages against the Dusahn and have the ability to accurately simulate a combat event on such a scale, SilTek seemed the most likely opponent."*

"Can it be done?"

"Yes, but not easily," Aurora warned. *"Their simulation software will be searching for indicators of inappropriate alterations of data. This will require constant tweaking of various time stamps and archives in an effort to stay one step ahead of SilTek's validation algorithms. This reduces my ability to assist during the simulation."*

Deliza sighed. "You just keep SilTek from discovering our little sleight of hand."

"I will do my best," Aurora assured her.

* * *

"I hate dress uniforms," Jessica complained as she stepped down from the Reaper and straightened her jacket.

"How do you think *we* feel in these monkey suits?" Sergeant Shapira commented as he and his team scanned the area for threats.

As before, the landing pad was flanked by Ahka soldiers, their weapons slung, but with a suspicious eye on their guests. Also as before, Fifth Protector Kamadin stepped forward to greet them.

The fifth protector looked over the group, noting that two of the four Ghatazhak were also in dress uniforms. "Your guards will be dining with you?" he asked.

"They'll be standing just outside," Jessica explained, her tone of voice leaving no room for negotiation.

"I see," the fifth protector replied, an eyebrow raised in disapproval. "If you and your detail will follow me, I will lead you to the First Protector's dining chambers."

"Lead the way," Nathan urged.

Jessica glanced at the sergeant as she passed, a snarky look on her face. "I guess we don't all clean up as well," she remarked in passing.

"I wasn't going to say anything," the sergeant retorted.

Nathan and his detail followed the fifth protector and his two guards up the same path as before. This time, however, they took a side path that wrapped around one side of the main building and through a small forest along a creek. The walk was well lit and perfectly manicured, with cameras embedded in the trees at key locations.

"You people afraid of something?" Jessica asked the fifth protector.

"Pardon?"

"What's with all the cameras?"

"We are a small population," the fifth protector explained. "We accomplish with technology what we cannot accomplish with numbers."

"I see," Jessica replied. She moved a step closer to Nathan, whispering, "Or their population doesn't like them."

"Let's be polite, shall we?" Nathan whispered back.

"No promises," Jessica replied.

They broke out of the forest onto a large, blue-green lawn, in the midst of which was an unusual structure.

"What is that?" Jessica wondered.

“That is the first protector’s personal residence,” the fifth protector replied.

“Why does it look like a tent?” she wondered.

“The architecture is an homage to our ancestors who wandered the deserts of our homeworld. Many of our more prominent buildings share this style.”

“But it’s *not* a tent, right?” Jessica asked.

“It is quite solid, I assure you,” the fifth protector confirmed.

“Seriously?” Nathan whispered to Jessica.

“Hey, solid structures only have a few doors,” she replied. “A tent is one big door to anyone with a blade.”

“Precisely why we no longer use tents,” the fifth protector stated, having overheard her statement.

Nathan and Jessica shared a glance as they approached the entrance. On either side of the massive double-doors, two burly men wrapped in ceremonial robes stood fast, swords hanging from their hips in ornate scabbards. Both men wore the same menacing expression; one that Jessica knew was only possessed by men who had taken many lives.

Neither man moved as Nathan and Jessica passed between them, but one extended his left arm to block their Ghatazhak escorts.

“Weapon,” the guard stated in a monotone voice, still looking straight ahead.

“No thanks, I have one,” Sergeant Shapira replied, continuing forward.

The guard’s hand stood firm, blocking the sergeant’s entry.

The sergeant looked down at the man’s hand on his chest, then at the guard, who was still staring straight ahead. "I'm assuming you *want* me to take your arm off with that pretty little sword."

The guard turned his head slowly, locking eyes with the sergeant. "That would be most entertaining," he growled.

"Is there a problem?" Jessica asked, turning around.

"Tiny, here, is blocking my way," the sergeant stated, his eyes still locked with those of the guard.

"Relinquish your weapon," the guard explained more clearly.

"Ask me nicely," the sergeant replied, winking at the man.

"Relinquish it or die," the guard added, his voice becoming even more menacing.

In a quick, smooth motion, the guard reached for his sword, as did his counterpart on the other side of the entryway. However, both men were forced to stop short of drawing their blades completely, as they found the muzzles of the Ghatazhak soldiers' sidearms pointed squarely at their faces, charged and ready to fire.

"Bad idea, Tiny," the sergeant stated with a cold, deadly look in his eyes. "Put the piece of metal back in its sheath, or I put a hole through that ugly head of yours."

"Easy, Sergeant," Jessica warned.

By now, the fifth protector had taken notice and had turned around. "Protectors!" he barked at the guards. "Captain, what is the meaning of this?"

"It seems your guards are being less than courteous," Nathan stated calmly.

"They are simply asking your guards to relinquish their weapons," the fifth protector explained. "I thought I made it clear before that no weapons are allowed in the presence of the first protector."

"It would have been nice if you had reminded us of this back at the landing pad," Nathan replied in disapproval.

"My apologies," the fifth protector stated politely. "If your men will turn over their weapons, we can put this unfortunate incident behind us."

"Yeah, well, we Ghatazhak don't really like to give up our weapons," Jessica explained, "especially when someone threatens us."

The fifth protector appeared uncertain of what to say next.

"Gentlemen, relinquish your weapons," Nathan instructed.

Sergeant Shapira continued staring in the guard's eyes, looking for any indication of submission. Finally, he spun his gun around, flicking on the safety and powering it down in the process, offering it to the guard, butt first. "I don't need it to take this mountain out, anyway," he stated, a smirk on his face.

The guard accepted the weapon from the sergeant as he settled his sword back into its sheath.

"Shall we continue?" the fifth protector suggested.

"You know where to find me if you want to dance," the sergeant stated to the guard as he passed.

"Was that really necessary?" Nathan asked the sergeant as they continued into the building.

"Just a little psychological warfare, sir," the sergeant replied.

"We're not *at* war with them."

"Technically, we are," Jessica corrected.

"Even more reason not to taunt," Nathan insisted.

"He was just letting their best beast know we

weren't scared of him," Jessica explained. "Standard Ghatazhak tactics."

"I believe that *tactics* are *my* purview at the moment," Nathan reminded her.

"Yes, sir."

Fifth Protector Kamadin led them to the entrance to the first protector's dining chambers, then turned to face them as the two guards flanking him stepped to either side. "Enjoy your meal," he said, before pulling the doors open and heading in.

Jessica turned to the sergeant. "Don't kill anyone, Shap."

"I'll do my best, sir," the sergeant replied.

Nathan and Jessica followed Fifth Protector Kamadin into the dining chamber. The room was adorned with elaborate floor rugs and large, colorful silks strung about the ceiling and walls, simulating the interior of a large tent.

At the center of the tent, a half dozen middle-aged men dressed in gold-trimmed, white silk robes sat around a polished oval table. The table itself was loaded with a variety of foods, both hot and cold, as well as a selection of beverages. The men themselves seemed jovial, and the atmosphere somewhat informal, which made Nathan feel somewhat overdressed.

"Captain Scott and Lieutenant Commander Nash of the Karuzari Alliance," the Fifth Protector announced.

Two young women in plain robes, giving the appearance of a shared purpose, stepped forward to guide the new arrivals to their seats at the table.

"Welcome, Captain," the first protector greeted. "Welcome, Lieutenant Commander. I am so happy you could join us. I was afraid you would not make it."

"I apologize if we are tardy," Nathan said as he and Jessica took their seats. "We have not yet coordinated our clocks with those of your world, nor are we aware of your dining customs and timings."

"No apologies needed, Captain. I would like to introduce my cabinet," the first protector began. "Second Protector Hakimi; my minister of defense," he introduced, gesturing at each man as he announced them. "Second Protector Shamoun, my minister of civilian security; and Third Protectors Borto, Seif, and Mogdahm, chiefs of staff for myself and my two subordinates. Gentlemen," he said, raising his glass, "may I present to you Captain Scott, commanding officer of the Karuzari Alliance ship Aurora, and his chief of security, Lieutenant Commander Nash. Welcome."

All in attendance raised their glasses in respect, before sipping from them.

"Thank you, First Protector," Nathan replied. "It is an honor to meet you all."

"I hope you are hungry, Captain, the first protector said. "We have a feast laid out for you this evening."

"I can eat," Jessica assured him.

"I hope you didn't go to too much trouble," Nathan insisted.

"No trouble, Captain. We welcome an opportunity to dine in such fashion. Most meals on Ahka are sparse and unimpressive."

"Why is that?" Nathan asked as one of the servers placed some food on his plate.

"The Ahka are of modest means and do not believe in waste. When we kill an animal, we consume the entire beast, leaving nothing behind. To do so would be an insult to the creature whose life we had taken to sustain our own."

"A very noble outlook," Nathan stated. "Surprising for a people who 'prey on the weak.'"

Every Ahka in the room gave him an evil stare, with the exception of First Protector Assafa, who laughed openly. "You do not mince words, do you, Captain?" He laughed again. "I like that."

"Then you'll really like her," Nathan said, pointing to Jessica on his right.

"We only take what we need to survive," Second Protector Hakimi pointed out, disapproval still evident on his face.

"Including women," Jessica added, disapproval on her face as well.

"Does not the animal take what it needs from other animals, in order to survive?" the other second protector, Minister Shamoun asked.

"It does," Nathan agreed, "but we are not animals."

"That is where you are wrong," First Protector Assafa insisted. "We humans only *think* we are above the animals we feed upon. In truth, we are not. We have the same survival instinct, and when given no choice, we both do what we must to survive."

"The animal has no choice," Nathan argued. "He is only acting in accordance to his genetic programming."

"As are humans."

"But humans can choose to *ignore* that programming. *That* is what separates us from animals."

"Yet the majority of humans *will* prey upon the weak to *some* extent," First Protector Assafa pointed out.

"I said they *can* choose to do otherwise, not that they do," Nathan replied.

"I suppose that is where your *Alliance* comes in. *You* will tell us all what is right and wrong."

"That is not the intention of the Karuzari Alliance," Nathan argued. "We do not believe we have the right to tell member worlds how they should live, or how they should run their worlds. We simply wish to unite all worlds together in peace, for the security and prosperity of *all* human-populated worlds. Your world, should you choose to become a member, would be yours to run in whatever manner you wish."

"As long as we stop 'preying on weaker worlds,' as you put it," Second Protector Shamoun surmised.

"The same way that *other* civilizations stronger than your own, of which there are many, would agree not to prey upon you," Nathan replied.

"And if we are attacked by a world that is *not* a member of your alliance?" the second protector inquired.

"We would stop them, of course," Nathan replied.

"Just like that," the second protector said dismissively. "Your ships must be quite well armed."

"We are," Nathan assured him.

"Surely you are aware of the vastness of space," Second Protector Hakimi stated. "You would need many ships in order to protect *every* world in your alliance."

"I doubt there are many who truly understand the vastness of space better than I," Nathan assured him. "Having said that, I assure you the *Aurora* can be virtually *anywhere* within current alliance territory, within minutes of being called into action."

"And how does one call for assistance over such distances?"

"We link all member worlds with automated, jump-capable communication drones," Nathan explained. "Each world has a series of drones following free-return trajectories between the command system and the member worlds, providing for the regular exchange of messages an average of every hour."

"No battle takes an hour," one of the third protectors scoffed.

"In addition," Jessica added, "each world has jump comm-drones that can be used to call for assistance in the blink of an eye."

"And how do your people know where your ships are located?" Second Protector Hakimi wondered.

"We notify central command of our new position when we relocate, even for a short period of time," Jessica explained. "We even leave a relay drone at our departure point, in case a message was dispatched before command was alerted to our change of position, so it can then be forwarded to us."

"A complex procedure," Third Protector Seif stated, picking at his food.

"It's all automated for the most part," Jessica assured him.

"You only speak of the Aurora," First Protector Assafa noted. "I assume you have *more* ships."

"Our fleet is small but effective," Nathan assured him. "I speak mostly of the Aurora because she is the *flagship* of the Alliance."

"Then she is the *largest* ship in your fleet," Second Protector Shamoun surmised.

"Our fleet has ships of many sizes and mission profiles," Nathan assured him. "Some of them larger, some of them smaller. As the *captain* of the Aurora, I admit I have a *bias* toward her."

"Is there a particular reason you seem so curious about our fleet strength?" Jessica wondered.

"You are asking us to trust in your ability to defend Ahka, so I believe confidence in your ability to do so is warranted," First Protector Assafa stated.

"You are also asking us to fight alongside you," Second Protector Hakimi pointed out. "The Ahka have always fought for the Ahka, and the Ahka alone. We ask no one for help."

"No, you just kill them and steal their shit," Jessica grumbled, only half under her breath.

"Your disdain for the Ahka is a clear indication of the need for the very alliance you seek to establish. Tell me, Captain, if the Ahka were to join your alliance, how would we survive? We are not yet an industrialized, fully independent society. Without the raids, our world will likely falter, and our people perish."

"As a member of the Alliance, we would call upon the resources of all member worlds to help you achieve self-sufficiency," Nathan assured him.

"And how would we pay for all this *assistance?*" Second Protector Shamoun wondered.

"The good captain has suggested that our warriors could serve the Alliance as a form of payment for such resources," First Protector Assafa told the second protector.

Nathan could not tell if the first protector believed it to be a good idea himself. "Every world has its own unique set of resources," he told them. "I am certain your world is no exception. You simply have not yet been in a position to exploit them to their greatest potential. The Karuzari Alliance can help you with this."

"All very interesting," the first protector said,

"but such serious topics should never be debated on empty stomachs. We are here to dine, are we not?"

Nathan smiled. "We are," he agreed as the server placed a large, roasted, bug-eyed creature on his plate.

First Protector Assafa noticed the looks of concern on his guests' faces. "Icta is a delicacy on Ahka," he insisted, smiling broadly.

"Of course," Nathan replied.

Jessica leaned toward the server, placing her hand in front of her to prevent her from loading her plate with the same. "I'm a vegetarian," she whispered to the server.

The server nodded her understanding and moved away.

"Wimp," Nathan muttered to her under his breath.

* * *

Commander Prechitt entered the mess hall at the Casbon fighter base, expecting it to be full of Casbon pilots and trainees, as usual. Instead, he saw only a handful of Casbons and Talisha sitting by herself in the corner.

"Where's everyone at?" he questioned Talisha as he sat down.

"Most of the duty staff are relaxing in their bunks," Talisha replied. "I sent the trainees home for the day. We've been riding them pretty hard. I thought they could use a day with their families, and with the Aurora orbiting Ahka, it seemed like an opportunity to let everyone breathe."

The commander nodded approval. "It would be a pretty good time to conduct a surprise readiness drill as well," he suggested.

"Not even *you* are that cruel," Talisha insisted.

"I don't know...seems like a golden opportunity."

"Don't even think about it," she warned, shaking her finger at him.

"Denna and Corson are still a bit shaky in their evasion maneuvers," the commander commented, changing the subject.

"They'll get the hang of it," she assured him. "I think I let their AIs help them out for too long. It works for some people but makes it worse for others."

"Well, if they don't improve, and soon, we'll be sending them back to repeat basic flight," the commander warned.

"I'll make sure they are up to snuff if I have to fly second seat with them myself," she promised. "The next group is nearly finished in the sims. They're looking pretty good, too."

"That's good news..."

An alarm klaxon sounded outside, interrupting Commander Prechitt.

Talisha stared at him in disbelief. "You didn't..."

The alert klaxon inside the mess hall sounded, and everyone in the room jumped from their seats and headed for the door.

"I didn't," the commander assured her, jumping to his feet as well.

Casbon pilots and ground crews poured out of the doors of the mess hall, barracks, and training buildings as alarm klaxons blared all around the base.

Commander Prechitt and Talisha Sane burst out of the mess hall as a series of blue-white flashes of light appeared a few kilometers to the east, low on the horizon.

The commander tapped his comm-set. "Control, Prechitt. Sit-rep!"

"At least twenty small contacts just appeared in high orbit. First wave of them just jumped in low! Eight fast-movers inbound from the east!"

"Raiders?" the commander assumed.

"*Negative,*" the controller replied. "*Unknown types.*"

"Any radio contact?"

"*Negative,*" the controller replied. "*Their shields are up, and their weapons are hot!*"

The commander spotted the incoming ships, skimming the treetops as they approached. "We need to get airborne," he said, breaking into a run. "Scramble all Nighthawks!" he ordered over comm-sets as he ran toward the flight line. "Notify the Aurora that we're under attack and recall the trainees! We may need them!"

"*Aye, sir!*" the controller acknowledged.

Automated surface-to-air batteries opened up on the incoming fighters, sending streams of red-orange plasma bolts toward the approaching line of targets.

"Max!" the commander called over his comm-set. "Spin up for emergency combat launch! I'm on my way!"

"*Already started,*" his AI replied. "We*'ll be ready to launch by the time you strap in.*"

"They'll be past us by the time we get in the air!" the commander yelled to Talisha as they sprinted across the open ground. "Go vertical as soon as you get off the deck! Get some altitude so we can dive on the next wave when they jump in!"

Energy bolts fired by the incoming fighters slammed into the ground around them as they neared the flight line.

"See you up there!" Talisha exclaimed as they separated toward their respective Nighthawks.

* * *

The intercom on the ready room desk beeped. "XO, Comms; flash traffic from Casbon."

Cameron reached over and pressed the intercom button. "Go ahead."

"Casbon is under attack by unidentified forces," Naralena reported.

"Sound general quarters," Cameron instructed, switching off the intercom afterward. She immediately rose and headed for the exit as the alert sounded throughout the ship, calling her crew to battle stations.

"Any activity on the surface?" Cameron asked as she entered the Aurora's bridge.

"Negative," Kaylah replied from the sensor station.

"Threat board?" she asked the tactical officer.

"Nothing but our own Eagles flying cover over the captain's Reaper," the tactical officer assured her.

"Comms, raise the captain."

"Aye, sir," Naralena acknowledged.

"Mister Sheehan, plot a jump back to Casbon," Cameron continued.

"Already plotted and ready," Loki replied.

"Mister Hayes, prepare to take us out of orbit and head for Casbon."

"Aye, sir," Josh replied.

"I'm unable to hail the captain," Naralena reported.

"Try his Reaper," Cameron suggested.

"I already did, sir," Naralena assured her. "I can't raise them either."

"What about our Eagles?"

"I have contact with flight lead."

"Have them try any of our people on the surface and alert them to the situation."

"Aye, sir."

"Kaylah," Cameron said. "Have there been *any* arrivals or departures since our arrival?"

"Only the original six raiders the Ahka had launched against *us*," Kaylah replied. "All of those are presently accounted for."

"Eagle flight leader reports negative on contact with any and all ground forces," Naralena reported.

"What the hell?" Cameron said in frustration. "Are their comms off or something?"

"I am picking up some odd frequency shifting in the area of the Ahka's city center," Kaylah reported.

"Is it possible they're jamming our comm-signals?"

"Not in a way that I'm aware of, but I don't have an explanation for the anomaly."

"Try to break through to them," Cameron instructed Naralena.

"I've got all transceivers at maximum power," Naralena assured her.

Cameron thought for a moment. "Did the message from Casbon include a force count?" she asked Naralena.

"Message reads: Twenty-plus fighters appeared in high orbit; eight in low atmosphere on attack run," Naralena replied.

"Great," Cameron said, taking a seat in the command chair and pressing a button on her intercom panel in the right armrest. "Spec Ops, XO. How many men can you have hopping into Reapers in two minutes?"

"*Four teams of six, including myself,*" Lieutenant Sonoda replied. "*Mission?*"

“Find and secure the captain on the surface, possibly against hostiles,” Cameron explained.

“*We’ll be wheels up in two,*” the lieutenant replied.

Cameron pressed another button. “Flight, XO. I need four Reapers ready to depart for the surface in two minutes, full of Ghatazhak. I also need another flight of four Eagles launched immediately to reinforce those already flying cover over Ahka City.”

“*Aye, sir,*” the flight operations officer acknowledged.

“And have all remaining Eagles ready for combat launch as soon as we jump back to Casbon.”

“*Yes, sir.*”

“Josh, as soon as those Reapers start rolling toward the transfer airlocks, you break orbit and head for Casbon,” Cameron instructed.

“You got it,” Josh replied.

“Once the Reapers have launched, we jump,” she told Loki.

“Yes, sir.”

“What about the captain and Jess?” Josh wondered.

“If the Ahka are not involved in the attack on Casbon, the Ghatazhak should be able to reach them,” Cameron explained.

“And if they are?” the tactical officer wondered aloud.

Cameron sighed. “Then all hell’s about to break loose.”

* * *

“New wave at one eight five!” Commander Prechitt announced over comms as he pulled out of his initial takeoff climb. Anyone in the air, sound off!”

“*Angels four and climbing!*” Talisha reported over comms.

"*This is Stoan!*" another pilot reported in. "*I'm at angels two and climbing.*"

"*Serossi! I just lifted off and am climbing!*"

"That's it?"

"*Three more Nighthawks are about to lift off,*" his AI, Max, reported.

Commander Prechitt rolled his fighter to starboard and pulled back hard on his joystick to pull his ship into a sharp turn. "Sane! Stoan! Serossi! Turn to eight zero five to intercept!"

"*Scans indicate targets' shields are weaker on their dorsal surfaces,*" Max reported. "*This would indicate they are designed for air-to-surface attack and not aerial combat.*"

"Doesn't mean they can't," Commander Prechitt stated. "Try to get above them and target their dorsal shields!" he instructed the other three pilots.

"*Jehns is airborne and climbing!*" another pilot announced.

Two red blips slid into the center of his targeting screen, and the commander rolled out of his turn, pushed his nose down, and backed off on his throttle as he began his dive. "Locking on two at one seven zero, transiting east to west."

"*Muldon is up and climbing!*"

The red blips began to flash.

"Light 'em up, Max."

"*Firing,*" his AI reported.

Staccato bursts of red-orange plasma bolts streaked toward the two ships ahead and below the commander's Nighthawk. A split second later, both targets exploded, and the stream of energy ceased.

"*Targets destroyed,*" Max reported.

"*Zenner is up!*" another Casbon pilot reported. "*Climbing!*"

The commander's brow furrowed as he rolled his fighter to port and leveled off. "That was too easy," he said as he eased his throttles back slightly.

"*Locking on two more,*" Talisa reported over comms. "*One six four, east to west. Firing! Targets destroyed!*"

"*I got two as well!*" Stoan reported with excitement.

The commander's targeting screen lit up again, with four more blips practically lining themselves up for an easy kill. "Either these people are the worst fighter pilots ever, or... Max! How many ships are still in orbit?"

"*Two,*" Max replied. "*The remaining twenty-four fighters are now attacking the base.*"

"Anything different about the two in orbit?" the commander asked as he lined up his ship with the four targets passing from his left to right.

"*Slightly larger and emitting an unusual amount of wide-band emissions in the direction of battle.*"

"*Denna is up! Bashwan! Corson just took a direct hit!*"

"*Denna! Shut up and start climbing, and jump to angels five before you get your ass blown off as well!*" Talisha urged.

"They're drones!" the commander realized. "That's why they're not trying to evade us!"

"*Your hypothesis is logical,*" Max agreed.

"All Nighthawks, attack the drones from above," the commander ordered as he slammed his throttles all the way forward and pulled his flight control stick back hard.

"*Talisha, take command of fighter defense!*" the

commander ordered over comms. *"I'm going after those two ships in orbit!"*

"Understood!" Talisha replied as she dove between two exploding enemy drones.

"Kareef is airborne and climbing!" Kareef reported over comms.

"Kareef!" Talisha called. "Did anyone else get off the ground?"

"Negative," Kareef replied. *"Banji and Kinto are trapped in a collapsed hangar, along with their ground crews. Rescue is trying to free them."*

"Understood," Talisha replied. "Leta, determine targets and tactics."

"Currently there are twenty-one active targets flying in formations of two to four elements," Leta reported. *"Their tactics are simple. They jump in on final attack leg, fire their ventral weapons as they pass overhead of the ground targets, then pitch up slightly and jump away. Wide-area scans indicate all groups are cycling around the compass points in ascending order, varying their attack angles anywhere from thirty to sixty degrees at a time, along a fifty-kilometer radius from the base. If they maintain this tactic, they should be easy to intercept."*

"Something tells me they won't," Talisha insisted, rolling her fighter into a turn to intercept. "All Nighthawks, this is Sane. Free-form intercept. Pair up with the ship nearest you and stay within a ten-kilometer radius of the base. Do not pursue when they jump away. Protect the base and remember: attack from above!"

* * *

"Reaper Six, away," Lieutenant Haddix reported as their Reaper cleared the forward threshold of the Aurora's starboard flight deck. He immediately yanked his flight control stick to starboard, pushing it forward at the same time to nose down and away from the Aurora.

"*All Reapers, form on me,*" the pilot of Reaper Three instructed over comms. "*We'll jump in low, three points around the buildings at the center of the city. As soon as your troops are out, go to low hover to cover your fire teams.*"

"Understood," the lieutenant replied.

"I'm getting the jump coordinates from Five now," Ensign Weston reported.

"Two minutes!" the lieutenant called back over his shoulder to the Ghatazhak in his cargo bay.

"Use your shields; stun first, kill only if necessary," Sergeant Kirschbaum instructed his troops as they waited in the utility bay of Reaper Six. "Our mission is to secure the captain and Lieutenant Commander Nash, not start a full-on ground war with the Ahka."

"And if they have different ideas?" Specialist Mauser asked.

"Introduce them to the business end of your assault rifle," Corporal Mazzola chuckled.

"Reapers are clear and away," Ensign Willit reported from the Aurora's tactical console.

"Eagle Leader, Aurora Actual," Cameron called over her comm-set.

"*Go for Eagle Leader,*" Commander Verbeek replied.

"Your ROE is fire if fired upon, use deadly force

as a last resort," Cameron instructed. "But no matter what, secure *all* our people on the surface."

"*Understood,*" the commander replied.

"We'll be back to pick you up as soon as possible," she promised. "Good hunting."

"*To you as well, Captain,*" the commander replied.

"Mister Sheehan, jump us to Casbon," Cameron ordered.

"Aye, sir," Loki replied. "Jumping in three...... two......one......jumping."

The blue-white jump flash washed over the bridge.

"Jump complete," Loki reported.

"Multiple contacts," Kaylah announced from the sensor station. "About sixteen drones are attacking the fighter base on the surface. Six Nighthawks are defending. Two more targets in orbit, slightly larger. They are being attacked by a single Nighthawk."

"Wide scan," Cameron instructed. "If they were hauled here, I don't want to be caught by surprise by the carrier ship."

"Scanning wide," Kaylah acknowledged.

"Flight, XO," Cameron called over her comm-set. "Launch all Eagles."

"*Launching Eagles, aye.*"

"Two minutes to orbital insertion," Loki warned.

"Hold your course until our fighters are away," Cameron instructed.

"Holding course and speed," Josh acknowledged.

"New contacts!" Kaylah reported. "Twenty of them swinging around Casbon's third moon."

"They appear to be fighter-interceptors," Ensign Willit added. "Unknown type or origin. They're on an intercept course to support the two contacts in orbit currently being targeted by one of the Nighthawks.

"Flight, XO," Cameron called over comms. "Vector

our Eagles to intercept the new contacts coming around the third moon."

"*Understood,*" the flight controller replied.

"*Nighthawk attacking orbital targets, Aurora Actual,*" Cameron called over Commander Prechitt's helmet comms. "*Identify.*"

Commander Prechitt jerked his flight control stick to the right, putting his Nighthawk fighter into a roll to avoid incoming defensive fire from the two control ships he was targeting. "Max, lock two on each target," he instructed his AI. "I'm a little busy right now, Captain."

"*You've got twenty fighter-interceptors coming around the third moon,*" Cameron warned.

"Good thing you made it to the party, then," the commander replied.

"*Targets are jamming our targeting sensors,*" Max reported. "*I am unable to get a lock.*"

"Aurora, can you help me out with these two targets?" the commander requested. "I suspect they're controlling the drones attacking the base, and they're jamming my missile targeting systems."

"*We'll take care of them,*" Cameron promised.

The commander broke his roll and pulled up sharply, taking several hits on his ventral shields as he veered off the attack. He glanced at his tactical display but saw no additional contacts. "Max, are you detecting the interceptors she was talking about?"

"*Negative, Commander,*" Max replied. "*However, they may not yet be in our line of sight.*"

Several red-orange streaks of plasma energy slammed into the two control fighters now off the commander's port side and slightly below him, causing both ships to explode.

"Targets destroyed," Ensign Willit reported from the Aurora's tactical station.

"Approaching orbital insertion point," Josh announced.

"Park us over the fighter base on the surface," Cameron instructed.

"You got it," Josh replied.

"Eagles have engaged the inbounds," Ensign Willit reported.

"Inbounds are jumping," Kaylah warned.

"Our Eagles got three of them before they jumped," the tactical officer reported.

"Inbounds just jumped in off our port side!" Kaylah warned. "Five kilometers and closing fast."

"Point-defenses," Cameron instructed.

"Point-defenses are firing," the ensign assured her.

"Inbounds are launching anti-ship missiles!" Kaylah added. "Ten seconds to impact!"

"Escape jump, ten clicks, in five!"

"Ten clicks, aye!" Loki replied.

"Impact in three......two......"

"Now!" Cameron ordered.

"Jumping," Loki replied immediately.

The blue-white jump flash washed over the bridge, fading away a split second later.

"Retargeting point-defenses," Ensign Willit reported.

"Inbounds are maintaining course and speed," Kaylah warned.

"Tactical, give the helm a hot pickle," Cameron instructed. "Josh, end-over and give them something to think about."

"You betcha," Josh replied with a smile as he cut the mains and pulled the Aurora's nose up hard.

The view of the planet Casbon filling the bottom half of the main view screen slid downward, quickly disappearing as the ship pitched over.

"Helm pickle is hot," Ensign Willit reported. "Tubes are charged and ready."

Josh flipped the small safety cover off the firing button on his flight control stick as he pushed forward on the stick again to arrest their pitch-over maneuver at just the right moment.

The view of Casbon returned, sliding down from the top of the screen, covering just the uppermost part once their pitch motion had ceased. Seventeen solid-red targeting squares appeared around the center area of the main view screen, indicating the location of the incoming interceptors that were still too far away to be seen. "Eat this," Josh muttered, pressing his firing button.

Red-orange plasma torpedoes leapt out from under the Aurora's nose in groups of four, repeating in waves every other second.

"Four targets destroyed," Kaylah announced. "The remaining ships have broken off and are jumping to safety."

"Nicely done, Mister Hayes," Cameron congratulated. "Bring our nose back on course."

"Pitching back forward," Josh replied.

"Mister Willit," Cameron said in a stern voice. "Next time someone challenges your defense perimeter, you give them more than just point-defenses... understood?"

"Yes, sir," Ensign Willit acknowledged, embarrassed by his error.

"*They're acting like they're drunk!*" Kareef exclaimed over comms.

"It might not last," Talisha warned. "Take them out while you can."

"*Sane, Prechitt!*" the commander called over comms. "*How are you doing down there?*"

"The drones seem confused, so we're taking advantage of it and knocking them down like *pila* beetles!" she replied.

"*Be on the lookout for interceptors,*" the commander warned. "*There are at least a dozen of them in the area, and they could jump down on top of you at any moment.*"

"Understood," Talisha replied. "Leta, if you spot any of those interceptors, don't wait for orders. You lock missiles on them and let them have it!"

"*Understood,*" her AI replied.

"New contact!" Kaylah warned from the Aurora's sensor station. "Big one! It's got to be the carrier ship. Twenty degrees to starboard and fifteen up relative. Six hundred thousand kilometers and holding position."

"Size and armaments?" Cameron asked.

"Nine hundred and twenty meters. Defensive turrets only. Basic directional shield turrets. She's no match for us. She's trying to be stealthy but doing a lousy job of it."

"Does she know we see her?"

"I doubt it," Kaylah insisted. "I picked her up on passive and haven't hit her with active sensors yet."

"Mister Sheehan, jump us forward two light minutes."

"Jumping forward two light minutes in five..."

"Josh, as soon as we jump, turn into the target to intercept," Cameron added.

"...Three..."

"Understood," Josh replied.

"Stand by to hail them on all frequencies and channels," Cameron instructed Naralena.

"Jumping," Loki announced as the blue-white jump flash washed over the bridge.

"Turning to intercept course," Josh announced as he initiated the turn.

"Mister Willit," Cameron said, "keep the helm pickle hot, and be ready to lock all forward plasma turrets on the target as soon as we jump in."

"Yes, sir," the ensign replied, determined not to make another mistake.

"Plotting intercept jump," Loki reported, anticipating her next order.

"Target will detect our new position in ten seconds," Kaylah warned.

"Coming onto intercept course," Josh reported.

"Intercept jump, ready."

"Execute," Cameron ordered.

Again, the blue-white flash washed over the bridge, revealing the enemy ship on the main view screen.

"Your mic is hot," Naralena reported.

"All forward cannons locked on target," Ensign Willit announced.

"All tubes are on target," Josh added.

"Unidentified ship, this is the Karuzari Alliance

ship Aurora. Stand down and recall all forces immediately, or you will be destroyed."

"They're spinning up their jump drive," Kaylah warned.

"Mister Willit," Cameron said. "Target their jump field emitters and open fire."

"Targeting jump field emitters," the ensign replied. "Firing!"

Streams of red-orange plasma bolts streaked forward on the main view screen, slamming into various points on the enemy vessel.

"Eight of their jump field emitters are disabled," Kaylah reported. "They're not jumping anywhere soon."

Cameron snapped her fingers and made a motion with her right hand, indicating to her tactical officer to cease fire. "Stand down and recall all forces, or you will be destroyed," Cameron repeated firmly. "I will not ask again."

"Target is locking defensive weapons on us," Kaylah reported. "They're turning toward us as well."

"Don't be an idiot," Cameron mumbled.

"I'm detecting a rise in their internal power levels," Kaylah added.

"They're opening a door in the bow," Ensign Willit announced urgently. "I think it's a torpedo tube!"

"Josh, take her out," Cameron ordered.

"Aye, aye," Josh replied, flipping the cover off the firing button and holding it down.

Three waves of four plasma torpedoes leapt from the Aurora's forward tubes under her bow, slamming into the enemy ship as it turned toward them. The first wave opened up the target's starboard bow, and the second wave found its way deep inside, setting off numerous secondary explosions that started a chain reaction. The third wave of plasma torpedoes was redundant.

"Target is coming apart," Kaylah reported. "Their antimatter reactor is losing containment."

"Jump us to safe distance, Mister Sheehan."

"Turning to a clear jump line," Josh announced.

"Jumping!" Loki added as the blue-white jump flash washed over the bridge.

Cameron turned toward Kaylah to her left. "Target status?"

Kaylah stared at her displays for a moment. "Obliterated," she reported.

"Commander Prechitt reports interceptors are retreating and jumping away," Naralena reported.

"Flight, XO," Cameron called over her comm-set. "Send the Eagles to the Casbon base to provide backup until we get back."

"*Aye, sir,*" the flight controller replied.

"Helm, as soon as all the enemy ships have departed, head for Casbon," Cameron added. "We have unfinished business on Ahka."

* * *

Sergeant Shapira and Specialist Hommel stood motionless on either side of the entrance to the first protector's dining chambers, ready to protect their leader, should the need arise. Across the foyer, four Ahka dressed in flowing robes and armed with sidearms and swords stood watching the sergeant and his cohort.

Sergeant Shapira heard something. A muffled voice; electronic. He noticed the older Ahka guard seemed to be squinting slightly, mostly in his left eye, as if concentrating to hear something.

A comm-set, the sergeant realized. The man was receiving a message of some type, and it was important enough that not only did the man's face reveal his response, but it also revealed that he was attempting to *hide* his reaction from the two Ghatazhak.

The elder Ahka guard's right hand drifted slowly, almost imperceptibly, toward his sidearm.

At that moment, a garbled transmission squawked in the sergeant's own comm-set, at a very low volume. It was a man's voice, but his words where covered with static. The message repeated, and two words were clearly heard: "*Red Chief.*"

The eldest guard pulled his sidearm, quickly raising it toward the sergeant and firing, but not quickly enough. Sergeant Shapira shifted to his right just enough to avoid the incoming blast as he leapt into action. In the blink of an eye, he charged toward the side wall of the foyer, ran two steps up the wall, and flipped over in the air, his foot coming down across the face of the eldest Ahka guard.

The force of the blow caused the elder Ahka to let go of his sidearm, which the sergeant handily plucked from the air as he landed on his feet in a crouch.

Specialist Hommel was only a half step behind his sergeant, throwing himself into the two guards on the left as they attempted to draw their weapons. All three tumbled over against the wall behind them, but the specialist was the first to spring back to his feet, striking one guard in the face as he pulled the man's sword from its sheath at his waist. The specialist spun around with his sword hand outstretched, slicing across the other guard's throat as he tried to stand.

Sergeant Shapira fired the stolen sidearm at the remaining guard, felling him as well. Finally, he turned and planted another foot into the face of the eldest guard, who was trying to get back on his feet from the initial blow.

"*Red Chief!*" his comm-set squawked more clearly. "*Red Chief!*"

"Shapira copies Red Chief," the sergeant replied, as he pulled another sidearm from one of the fallen guards.

Specialist Hommel dropped his bloody sword, pulling sidearms from both of the soldiers he had put down.

"Ready?" the sergeant asked.

"Let's do it," the specialist replied.

Sergeant Shapira pointed his weapon at the door lock, blowing it off. He kicked in the door, and both men charged inside, dropping the two guards on the far side of the room. The sergeant turned to his right, expecting to take out the guards nearest the captain and the lieutenant commander, but Jessica was already standing over their unconscious bodies.

"What the hell's going on?" Nathan demanded, looking more shocked than anyone in the room.

"We got a *Red Chief* call, just as the goons outside tried to get the drop on us," Sergeant Shapira replied. "Everyone, keep your hands on the table where we can see them!" the sergeant yelled at all the Ahka sitting around the table. "I guess you heard the call as well," he said, looking at Jessica.

"I couldn't make it out, but then I heard weapons fire in the foyer and put two and two together," Jessica explained.

"What is the meaning of this?" First Protector Assafa demanded.

That's when Nathan noticed something wasn't right. None of them looked surprised. They were trying to look outraged, but none of them were actually surprised. "Maybe I should ask you?" Nathan said to First Protector Assafa.

The doors to the foyer burst open, and a squad of Ghatazhak burst in.

Sergeant Shapira and Specialist Hommel spun around, weapons high, but immediately recognized their comrades in black armor.

"We're secure," the sergeant reported to the arriving Ghatazhak.

Lieutenant Sonoda followed his squad into the dining chambers, stepping up to the captain to give his report. "Casbon was attacked. The Aurora was unable to reach any of our people here on the ground, so Captain Taylor launched four Reapers full of Ghatazhak and another flight of Eagles to secure you and Lieutenant Commander Nash, before she jumped back to protect Casbon."

"*Who* attacked Casbon?" Nathan asked the lieutenant.

"Unknown, sir," the lieutenant replied. "The ships were of an unidentified type."

"What is their current status?" Nathan asked.

"Unknown, but the Aurora has just returned. I have a point-to-point, secure laser comm-relay set up, so I can patch you through to them if you'd like."

"I would," Nathan agreed.

"One moment," the lieutenant replied.

"Hands!" the sergeant warned as one of the protectors at the table tried to move his hand to his lap.

"Captain, I demand an explanation for this unwarranted attack!" Second Protector Hakimi barked.

Nathan looked at the first protector, who still did

not look surprised. "Just as soon as I have one, I'll let you know," he told the second protector.

"I have Captain Taylor for you, sir," the lieutenant announced.

Nathan tapped his comm-set, patching it into the lieutenant's point-to-point link. "XO, Captain. What's going on, Cam?"

"*Casbon was attacked,*" Cameron explained. "*First by drones controlled by a pair of fighters in orbit, then by twenty fighter-interceptors that jumped in behind the third moon to hide their arrival. There was a carrier ship as well. They refused to surrender and tried to attack us, so we took them out. After that, their drones went rogue, and the Casbons dealt with them with their Nighthawks. The rest of the fighter-interceptors jumped away. Apparently, they lost interest once their carrier was destroyed.*"

"Casbon is secure, then?"

"*For now,*" Cameron replied. "*I left a squadron of Eagles behind to fly cover while the Casbons pick up the pieces. Their base took a pounding. Everything okay down there?*"

"Affirmative," Nathan replied, looking at the first protector again. "We're surrounded by Ghatazhak. I'll get back to you shortly."

"*Understood.*"

Nathan stared at the first protector, then said, "You *knew* the Casbon were going to be attacked."

"He did?" Jessica asked, surprised.

"In fact, you probably arranged it," Nathan continued.

"Captain," the first protector began to object.

"It should be easy to prove once we interrogate the captain of the carrier ship that we captured," Nathan stated. "The question is: *Why*?"

"The reason should be obvious," the first protector stated. "The Casbons have aramenium that we could have sold on the open market to buy things we need. You made it impossible for us to obtain it by destroying the bulk of our fleet, so we were forced to make other arrangements."

"What *kind* of arrangements?" Nathan inquired, growing angrier by the moment.

"We made others aware of the Casbons' aramenium; for a *price*, of course."

"So you sold *information* instead of aramenium," Nathan surmised.

"Partly," the first protector replied. "Payment and a percentage of the profits from the sale of the aramenium."

"And you made these *arrangements* when?"

"Long before your arrival, I assure you. In fact, the attack was originally scheduled for a date sometime in the future, long after your people had left Casbon. Your arrival simply presented an ideal opportunity to test your ability to protect your *members*. If you failed, we got the aramenium. If you successfully defended them, we would know you to be capable of defending those who join you."

"I see," Nathan replied, fighting to remain calm.

"We have no desire to be your enemy, Captain, but we will do what we must for our people. Surely, you can understand this?"

"Oh, I do," Nathan assured the first protector. "Now here is something for *you* to understand. The *only* reason I am not completely crippling your entire military right now is because I promised the Casbons that I would try to convince you to join our alliance. You see, the Casbons are a peaceful people. So peaceful, in fact, that they would rather become *allies* with those who have stolen their resources, killed their people, and kidnapped their women—*for decades*—than kill them, even in self-defense. You see, First Protector, far braver are those who choose to turn the other cheek rather than seek vengeance. If it were me, I'd bomb your ass into submission as penance for your sins against them."

"Captain..."

Nathan raised his hand, cutting the first protector off. "There is one more thing you need to understand. Should the Ahka refuse membership in the Karuzari Alliance, they will be considered an enemy of the Alliance. That is a relationship you do not want, believe me." Nathan straightened his dress jacket, preparing to leave. "You will order all forces to stand down while we withdraw from your world," he continued. "Anyone showing the slightest hint of aggression will be met with immediate and deadly force. Is that understood?"

First Protector Assafa's eyes remained locked with those of his guest. For what seemed an eternity, he looked for the slightest hint of hesitation or uncertainty. Every man had it, even himself. But the longer he looked at the young captain, the more he began to believe that *this* man was the exception. *This* man believed in what he was doing with all his heart and soul, and he *meant* every word he said.

"I understand," the first protector finally replied. He leaned toward Second Protector Hakimi, whispering something in the man's ear. "If you will allow Second Protector Hakimi to communicate with his subordinates, they will be instructed to lay down their arms and allow you safe departure from our world."

Nathan's eyes remained locked with First Protector

Assafa's. "Lieutenant Commander, inform our forces that we are leaving. Furthermore, tell them they are to *kill* any Ahka who brandish weapons in their presence."

"Yes, sir," Jessica acknowledged, nodding at the lieutenant to relay the orders to his men.

Without another word, Nathan broke eye contact with the first protector, turned around, and marched out of the room, shadowed by Jessica and the Ghatazhak.

* * *

Nathan and Jessica stepped off the Reaper as it rolled to a stop inside the Aurora's main hangar bay.

"Welcome back," Cameron greeted as she approached. "I guess you were right."

"Not quite," Nathan corrected. "I figured the Ahka would pull something, but I didn't anticipate the use of a surrogate to do their dirty work. I should've seen that coming."

"All our intelligence on the Ahka showed them to be isolationists," Jessica pointed out, "which makes sense, considering they're basically pirates."

"My biggest concern is that now we have *another* threat to protect the Casbon from," Nathan said as he headed forward across the massive bay.

"Assuming they agree to join," Jessica reminded him, following alongside.

"What do we do now?" Cameron asked.

"We jump back to Casbon," Nathan replied.

"What about the raiders we recovered?" Cameron wondered.

"Jettison and destroy them before we depart," Nathan instructed.

"And their crews?"

"Shuttle them to the surface," Nathan told her as they reached the hangar bay's forward hatch.

"What about the Ahka?" Jessica asked.

"Let them stew awhile," Nathan replied. "I've dealt with enough bullshit for one day."

* * *

"Captain on the bridge!" the guard at the port hatch announced as Nathan passed.

"Status?" Nathan asked, approaching Jessica and Cameron at the tactical station.

"Feel better?" Jessica asked.

"Much," Nathan replied. "Amazing how much a shower can change your outlook."

"For the better, I hope," Cameron said.

Nathan's brow furrowed. "What's up?"

"We have an unexpected guest who is waiting to speak with you in the command briefing room," Cameron explained.

"Who?" Nathan asked, suspicious.

"First Protector Assafa."

"What? How the hell..."

"He insisted," Cameron explained. "He caught a ride up on the cargo shuttle that took the raider crews back to the surface. He wishes to speak to you...alone."

"And neither of you thought I should be notified?"

"We didn't want to ruin your shower," Jessica joked.

"I assume he is under guard," Nathan said.

"Shapira and Hommel have had eyes on him since he boarded their Reaper," Jessica assured him.

Nathan sighed. "I guess we're not jumping back to Casbon just yet."

"He may be trying to stall us again," Jessica

suggested, "tie us up so that his friends can attack again."

"Doubtful," Nathan replied. "He's got to know we'd jump back to protect Casbon even with him on board."

"Well, he's waiting for you," Cameron reminded him.

"Then I guess I'd better go see what he has to say," Nathan decided, turning to exit.

* * *

Nathan stepped up to the entrance to the command briefing room.

"First Protector Assafa is waiting inside, sir," Sergeant Shapira stated.

"He came alone?"

"He did," the sergeant replied. "He surrounded our Reaper on the pad and threatened not to let us depart unless we agreed to bring him here to speak with you."

"And you felt compelled to agree?"

"I did not," the sergeant insisted. "We could've taken them all out with ease, but he seemed sincere, so I called it in. For what it's worth, Captain, he seems different than before, like something is nagging at him."

"Guilt, maybe?"

"More like concern," the sergeant said.

"They teach you guys how to read people as well?"

"Of course."

"Good thing," Nathan said, patting the sergeant on the shoulder as he opened the door to the briefing room.

Nathan stepped inside and closed the door behind him. Inside, First Protector Assafa sat alone at the conference table.

The first thing he noticed was the expression on the first protector's face as he rose from his chair.

"Captain, I apologize for my tactics, but I felt it important that we speak in private, away from the eyes and ears of my staff. Aboard your vessel is the only place that guaranteed privacy."

"How can I help you, First Protector?" Nathan asked, taking a seat.

"This is difficult for me," the first protector admitted, as he sat back down. "Ahka men do not easily admit weakness."

"What kind of weakness?" Nathan asked.

First Protector Assafa leaned back in his chair for a moment. "I have only been first protector for a short time," he began. "In our society, one must work their way up to the office. Our previous first protector died of penna a few years ago."

"Penna?"

"A terrible disease. Little warning, rapid progression. There is no cure," the first protector explained. "Normally, one of the second protectors would fill the position. However, at the time of the first protector's passing, one of the second protectors was retiring, and the other second protector was embroiled in a corruption controversy. As the most senior third protector at the time, it was my duty to assume the position."

"Lucky you," Nathan said, not yet finding much point to the tale.

"Not as much as you might think. You see, such a thing almost never happens, and I myself never had much interest in becoming first protector."

"I'm not seeing the problem here," Nathan stated, becoming a little impatient.

"I have never been a supporter of the methods

used by the Ahka to survive," the first protector continued. "I understand the original need, but that need has long passed. As you said, Ahka has many resources that could be traded with other worlds for the things we still need."

"Then just stop raiding other worlds," Nathan stated in matter-of-fact fashion. "It isn't that difficult."

"It is more difficult than you might think. You see, the Ahka were once a peaceful society, much like the Casbons. We were more willing to defend ourselves, but we did not *seek* violent confrontation. Unfortunately, more than a hundred years of raiding others to survive has turned us into warriors. Our men pride themselves on their prowess in combat. We live for the raids. We are judged by our successes and our failures in combat."

"Why are you telling me this?" Nathan wondered.

"Because I see your alliance as a way to change the path my people are on," the first protector stated.

"Then why did you attack Casbon earlier? Surely you knew we would respond."

"I was counting on it," the first protector explained. "I needed a demonstration of your military might. I needed my people to feel threatened by your presence. You see, if your alliance succeeds, at least in this part of the galaxy, the Ahka will have no choice but to abandon the raids and embrace peaceful relations with other worlds."

"Could you not have just said this to your own people," Nathan wondered, "to your staff?"

"I would be seen as weak," the first protector explained. "While there are many who believe as I do, there are even more who do not. Those who do not, *already* oppose my protectorate. If I were to publicly suggest that we lay down our arms and coexist with our neighbors, my administration would fall. Chaos would ensue. My people would go on a rampage, raiding every world possible. However, now that my people have seen your soldiers in action and have seen you handily defeat the *Tremen*, they will welcome the chance to fight alongside you rather than die at your hands."

"So this was all a show?" Nathan did not look happy. "People died, you know."

"Including Ahka," the first protector pointed out. "The stakes are always high at this level. Surely you of all people are aware of this?"

Nathan sighed. "Only too aware." After a moment, he asked, "Then you wish to join our alliance after all?"

"I do," the first protector replied, "and now that my people have seen your soldiers in action, they will support this decision."

"What about the—what did you call them?"

"The Tremen?"

"Yes. What about the Tremen?"

"I suspect they will wish to join as well."

"I see." For the first time in a few days, Nathan was feeling optimistic. "I think we can work something out, First Protector."

"Excellent." The First Protector leaned back in his chair, relieved. "Tell me, Captain, your soldiers...I watched recordings of them in action against my troops. I have never seen such skill and efficiency."

"No offense, First Protector, but that was nothing. Those men could charge into Hell and walk out with the head of the devil in hand."

CHAPTER FIVE

Nathan entered the Aurora's command briefing room but paused just after passing the guard standing silently at the entrance. He turned to look at the guard, one eyebrow slightly raised.

"You told me to stop announcing your arrival," the guard reminded Nathan.

"Yes I did," Nathan admitted. "I'm just surprised you actually stopped. I mean, I've been asking you to stop for weeks now."

"I guess I'm a slow learner," the Ghatazhak corporal joked.

Nathan smiled and continued. "Good morning," he greeted his senior staff, taking his seat at the head of the conference table. "Let's begin with you, Deliza. Have you figured out how to fool the Tekans yet?"

"I believe I have," she replied, "or should I say, *Aurora* has."

"Our AI?" Nathan wondered, a bit surprised.

"We're going to use a SilTek AI to fool a SilTek AI?" Cameron asked. "Is that wise?"

"No," Jessica opined.

"Our AI has to follow its core directives," Deliza explained. "Those directives state that it *must* help us."

"Even if doing so would put SilTek in jeopardy?" Jessica questioned, hoping to validate her concerns.

"All of SilTek's AIs have a kill switch built into their code. It is located in the same section of code as the primary directives, and the AI itself cannot alter that code," Deliza explained. "It was put there to appease buyers, many of whom have an unwarranted fear of artificial intelligence."

"That doesn't help SilTek," Jessica argued. "Why would anyone sell something that could be used against them?"

"We were somewhat suspicious as well," Deliza admitted. "It turns out that there *is* a back door to SilTek's AIs. Through it, they would be able to remotely activate the kill switch in its core code block."

"Thus, negating the threat," Cameron surmised.

"Another reason *not* to use our AI in any of this," Jessica insisted.

"Not necessarily," Vladimir argued. "Aurora is aware of the back door, and although she cannot make changes to it, she was able to point us to the location of the code and instruct us on how to alter the code and render the back door inoperative, at least to anyone but us."

"But us?" Nathan queried.

"I did not think it was a good idea to remove it completely," Vladimir explained. "Doing so would alert SilTek to the alteration."

"Instead, we created a two-part back door... basically, a door within a door," Deliza continued. "The original back door—what we now call the 'outer' door—will still reply to SilTek's remote status query, causing them to believe they still have remote disabling capabilities. However, the 'inner' door has a completely different type of encryption and pass key."

"Can it be hacked?" Jessica asked.

"*Everything* can be hacked," Vladimir insisted.

"But it would take hours," Deliza added, "and we would be alerted of the attempt, at which point we could disconnect Aurora from all external communications equipment or shut her down completely."

"And Aurora *helped* you accomplish this?" Jessica asked, sounding skeptical.

"She did," Deliza answered.

"It would have taken us weeks to find the back door on our own," Vladimir admitted.

"So our AI is no longer a weapon that could be used against us," Nathan surmised.

"Correct," Deliza confirmed, "more importantly, it means that we can now trust Aurora to do what is necessary to fool SilTek's inspectors into believing that we have used shield-penetrating jump missiles in the recent past, and that we have versions that can perform multiple jumps to target and can reverse their course."

"Which, we should point out, is no easy task," Vladimir added.

"Why?" Nathan wondered.

"SilTek will use its AI to inspect *our* AI," Deliza explained, "and to examine our combat logs and weapons specifications."

"I'm still worried about giving SilTek open access to all our specifications," Jessica warned.

"They're just getting access to *what* our weapons and systems can do, not *how* they do it," Nathan added. He looked back to Deliza. "Any word from Abby on the shield-penetrating jump missiles?"

"She has completed eight of them," Deliza replied, "but has not had a chance to conduct any field tests; only computer simulations. There is one other thing," Deliza said. "I asked Aurora for help on reengineering those missiles into ones that can multi-jump *and* change course. She determined that by replacing its maneuvering systems with the ones used in the Sugali fighters, we could save enough space that the additional propellant and jump energy cells would all fit within the existing missile hulls."

"So they'd look the same?" Nathan wondered.

"Almost," Deliza replied. "We weren't able to get *all* of the systems *entirely* inside the existing hull, so we had to add some external conduits. But we can fabricate dummy conduits that *should* pass visual inspection, in case SilTek wants to actually *see* the weapons."

"What if they want to *scan* them?" Cameron asked.

"The missile hulls are designed to prevent remote access to their systems. It also makes it impossible to scan their interiors," Vladimir explained. "This feature was part of our original torpedo design, to prevent an enemy from remotely disabling an incoming weapon."

Nathan sighed. "Let's just hope they don't ask us to open one up for inspection."

"If we load them into the missile hoppers *before* the inspectors come aboard, it might help," Vladimir suggested.

"Make sure the hopper load logs show that the missiles have been in them for at least a few days," Nathan said, pointing to Deliza.

"I'll let Aurora know," Deliza promised.

"Good," Nathan said. "How long will it take to disguise, say, sixteen missiles?"

"At least a day," Deliza answered. "Maybe faster if I was back on Rakuen."

"We're jumping back to Rakuen after this briefing," Nathan told her.

"Great," Deliza replied.

"We can pick up those eight missiles while we're there," Cameron suggested, "before we go meet the Tremen."

"The *Tremen*?" Vladimir wondered, unfamiliar with the name.

"The people that the Ahka *hired* to attack Casbon," Nathan explained. "I spoke with Council Member Garon this morning, and she is concerned that they now may have a second potential enemy. I have a feeling she'd be more comfortable if the Tremen were also part of the Alliance." Nathan looked at Lieutenant Commander Shinoda. "Any progress figuring out where the Tremen home world is located?"

"The Falcon came back about an hour ago," the lieutenant commander replied. "They managed to pick up several old jump flashes from the retreating Tremen fighter-interceptors and traced them back to a planet here." The lieutenant commander activated the holographic display over the center of the conference table. A three-dimensional representation of their current location in the galaxy appeared, quickly zooming out to include several nearby systems. "We know the system as Sten One Five Seven. The Casbon know it as Analay. It's about fifteen light years from Casbon and about twenty-eight light years from Ahka."

Cameron's brow furrowed as she studied the display hovering in the air before them. "Captain, if all three systems become allies, that would create a loose line of systems allied along the border of the Ilyan Gamaze. They might see that as a threat."

"So we need to speak to *them*, too?" Jessica said, throwing her hands up. "Great."

"Let's just wait and see," Nathan insisted. "We've got enough on our plate. Besides, Council Member

Garon isn't asking about the Gamaze, so I'm not going to bring it up."

"According to Aristaeus, worlds just outside the Gamaze are routinely harassed by the Ilyan, just to remind them who's really in charge of this part of the galaxy."

"Such pleasant neighbors," Nathan remarked.

"That may be of benefit when you speak with the Tremen, Captain," Lieutenant Commander Shinoda said. "Of the three worlds, they are closest to Gamaze space. Having us to protect them from harassment might be enough to get them to join."

"I thought the Ilyan was just an organization that coordinated interstellar trade between member worlds," Cameron said. "Why would they harass worlds *outside* their area of influence?"

"Maybe they have some kind of ongoing disagreement with the Tremen?" Lieutenant Commander Shinoda suggested.

"Such as being willing to attack other worlds for profit," Jessica added in disapproval.

"Maybe the Tremen are not someone we *want* as allies," Cameron commented.

"That thought has crossed my mind," Nathan admitted. "Regardless, we need to speak with them, to make sure they understand what will happen to them if they attack the Casbon again."

* * *

"Captain on the bridge!" the guard at the entrance barked as Nathan and Cameron entered.

Nathan flashed the guard a disapproving glance. "Mister Sheehan, can you plot us a course back to Rakuen?"

"Happy to, sir," Loki replied. "Are we going to be there long?"

"Long enough," Nathan replied with a wink.

"What's the latest from Commander Prechitt?" Nathan asked Naralena.

"Ten Eagles are fully fueled on the deck, their pilots and ground crews on standby," Naralena reported. "Commander Prechitt reports they should be fine until we return, but he did politely request that we not take too long."

"Course and jump are plotted and ready, sir," Loki announced.

"Very well, break orbit and take us to Rakuen," Nathan ordered.

"Breaking orbit," Josh reported from the helm.

Nathan turned to Cameron, who was standing next to the tactical station. "I'm still not used to this."

"Used to what?" Cameron wondered.

"These long-range jumps. I mean, I don't even have time to sit down."

"Progress."

"A decade ago, I was expecting an outer-rim patrol of the Sol system aboard the Reliant to keep me away from home for *two years*. Now we're routinely jumping *six hundred* light years in the blink of an eye."

"Soon to be a thousand light years," Cameron reminded him.

"Did you even wonder if connecting all the various societies of humanity is actually a *good* thing?" Nathan asked.

"I'm afraid that's a bit outside my area of expertise," Cameron admitted.

"In the late twenty-first century, when the first transatlantic hyperloop route opened, many predicted an acceleration in the dilution of regional societies, warning that, within a few hundred years, the cities of Earth would be indistinguishable from one another, apart from their geographical and environmental differences."

"But that never came true," Cameron reminded him.

"It depends on your point of view," Nathan insisted. "It's true that each major continent retained most of its character. However, regions served heavily by hyperloop systems, like Europe and North America, lost much of their cultural distinction. Later historians believed that this homogenization was what led to the collapse of the United States and the European Union in the twenty-second century."

"On course and speed for Rakuen," Josh announced.

"Execute the jump," Nathan ordered.

"Jumping in five..." Loki began.

"But the collapse of the US led to the formation of the first North American Union, which was superior to its predecessor," Cameron argued.

"Jump complete," Loki announced as the jump flash subsided.

"Standard orbit, Mister Hayes," Nathan instructed.

"Standard orbit, aye."

Nathan looked at Cameron, surprised. "I didn't realize you were a history buff."

"I'm not. In fact, it's one of the few things I remember from my geo-political history modules from college," Cameron admitted. "I don't think interstellar connectivity is quite the same thing. By the end of the twenty-first century, most of the problems of Earth had been solved. Crime, hunger, disease, poverty, all of them were practically nonexistent. I think a better comparison would be the invention of the airplane or the internet."

"Good point," Nathan agreed.

"Standard orbit established," Josh reported.

"I'll get started on the missiles," Cameron stated.

"Mister Sheehan, care to pilot a shuttle to the Mystic Empress...just to get your hands on a flight stick again?"

Loki smiled, "I'd love to, sir."

* * *

Nathan entered the Mystic's main engineering department, pausing to look around.

"Can I help you, sir?" a young crewman offered.

"I'm looking for the chief of the boat," Nathan told him.

"Chief Montrose? He's in the next compartment, through hatch A-Twelve, over there."

"Thank you."

"You're Captain Scott, aren't you?" the crewman suddenly realized.

"Yes I am."

"It's an honor to meet you, sir," the crewman said, suddenly snapping to attention and saluting.

"What's your name, son?" Nathan asked, returning the young man's salute.

"Engineering mate Amzi Calo," the young man replied, proud that such a legend had asked his name.

"Amzi. I don't recognize the origin of that first name."

"It's Volonese."

"Really? I didn't realize we had any Volonese serving in the flight other than my chief communications officer."

"You have a Volonese communications officer... on the Aurora?"

"We do," Nathan replied. "In fact, she's been with us since the beginning. How'd you end up on the Mystic?"

"I've been serving on the Mystic for nearly a year now," Amzi explained. "I got hired through my uncle's friend, who knew the XO at the time. It took every penny I had to book passage from Volon to Takara to report for duty."

"I see. Well, it was a pleasure to meet you, Mister Calo," Nathan said, turning to head for the hatch.

"The pleasure was all mine, Captain!" Amzi called after the captain as he departed. "*Chirtven,*" he cursed to himself in his native tongue. "Nathan Scott, *vin tova insya!*"

Nathan continued through the hatch, stepping into the next compartment. There, he caught sight of Doran Montrose talking to another technician.

Doran spotted Nathan almost immediately, dismissing the technician and heading for the captain. "Captain Scott," he greeted as he approached. "What brings you to the bowels of the Mystic?"

Nathan reached out to shake Doran's hand. "I was looking for you, Mister Montrose."

"Don't tell me you need me back on the Aurora? Last I heard, Chief Dory was doing great."

"He is," Nathan assured him. "Actually, I was hoping you'd be interested in a different assignment."

"I don't know," Doran said. "I've got a pretty sweet deal going on here. Home with the family every night, no one shooting at me, and Commander Kaplan pretty much gives me the run of the place." He looked at Nathan, reading the hesitation on his face. "Something tells me this *assignment* you have in mind isn't going to make my wife happy."

"Likely not," Nathan admitted. He looked around, checking that no one was within earshot. "I need someone to train the Corinari, getting them back into top form."

"What for?"

"A mission," Nathan replied.

"I figured that," Doran replied. "What *kind* of mission?"

"A dangerous one," Nathan admitted.

This time, it was Chief Montrose who looked around to see if they were alone. "Follow me," he told Nathan, heading for another hatch. They stepped through the hatch into a small storage compartment, and the chief closed the hatch behind them. "What's the mission?"

"This is 'need-to-know,'" Nathan told him, "and no one *needs* to know until we're certain we have a good chance of pulling it off."

"Pulling what off?" Chief Montrose asked.

"The liberation of Corinair," Nathan replied.

The chief was quiet for a moment. "You're right, she's not going to like it."

"I'll understand if you don't want to take the assignment."

"It depends."

"On what?" Nathan wondered.

"Am I just *training* them, or am I going to *lead* them?"

"I was hoping you'd lead them as well," Nathan admitted.

"Oh, she's *really* not going to like it," the chief chuckled. He looked at Nathan, a grin on his face. "I'm your man, Captain."

* * *

“How did it go?” Cameron asked, following Nathan into his ready room.

“Montrose is on board,” Nathan replied as he moved around his desk to sit.

“Did you speak to Commander Kaplan as well?”

“Before I spoke to the chief,” Nathan assured her. “She gave me her blessing.” Nathan plopped down in his chair, sighing. “So now we’ve got commanders for both the air and ground forces.”

“You don’t think we’re getting a little ahead of ourselves?” Cameron questioned, taking the seat across from Nathan. “We still have to win the simulation.”

“Nothing is going to happen until *after* the contest is over,” Nathan assured her. “I’m just lining up the players, that’s all.”

“Yeah, but if we don’t win, this is all going to fall through,” Cameron pointed out.

“Don’t be so pessimistic,” Nathan urged. “We’ve got shield-penetrating jump missiles now. If SilTek wins, we’ll just have to take the Dusahn down one ship at a time.”

“That advantage might disappear at any moment,” Cameron said. “Eventually the Dusahn will figure out a way to counter our missiles. The longer it takes us to defeat them, the more likely they are to become *undefeatable*. You said so yourself. It was your reason for wanting to strike now rather than later.”

“Now you’re getting it,” Nathan exclaimed with relief.

“Getting what?”

“Why I made the bet with SilTek,” Nathan explained.

"I'm still not following you."

"If we don't get the tech we need, and get it within the next month or two, the Dusahn will become unbeatable. They'll fortify their defenses, beef up their shields, maybe even convert some cargo ships into warships. Hell, all they'd really have to do to knock us out for good is fling a few large asteroids our way. You take out Rakuen, Neramese, and Orswella, and we're back to being a ragtag fleet on the run, barely scratching out an existence. That's why I made the bet. If we win, we get everything we need, and we end this once and for all. If we lose, the Dusahn are the ones who win."

"You'd think SilTek would just *give* us what we need," Cameron said. "It makes no sense not to."

"Corporations don't think that way, Cam," Nathan insisted. "To them, it's all about profit. Alliance or Dusahn Empire, they'll make money either way."

Cameron sighed. "I suppose you're right," she admitted as she stood. "You still want to jump to Orswella?"

"Yes," Nathan replied. "I want to talk about this with General Telles, and I think it's a good idea for the Aurora to make periodic appearances in the Orswella system."

"I'll tell Loki to jump us," Cameron said, turning to exit.

"Actually, I left Loki on the Mystic," Nathan told her. "I figured he could use a little time with his daughter. I told him we'd pick him up in a few hours, before we jumped to the Tremen system."

"That was considerate of you."

"Well, Loki never asks for anything," Nathan replied, "Besides, I'm a softy inside."

"Right," Cameron replied. "I'll try to remember that."

* * *

Nathan stared out the port window of his shuttle as the auto-flight system brought it in low over Orswella's central district. For the most part, the city appeared normal other than the few districts that had either been ravaged by orbital bombardment or by Dusahn covert operatives.

The shuttle slowed, descending smoothly toward the small landing pad outside the city center. The Ranni shuttles had superb auto-flight systems, capable of just about anything. Nathan pondered how much better the auto-flight systems might be if they were paired with SilTek AIs. If that ever happened, the job of a pilot might become intolerably boring for poor Josh, who had a definite dislike for automated piloting systems.

The shuttle settled down to land, spinning down its engines the moment its landing gear touched the pad. Nathan initiated the automated shutdown sequence, watching his displays to ensure the shutdown was taking place before unbuckling his restraints and climbing out of the cockpit. He moved aft, past the bulkhead which separated the cockpit from the passenger cabin, and activated the hatch controls.

The hatch opened, revealing General Telles standing a few meters from the shuttle. Nathan climbed down and headed for him.

"Good morning, Captain," the general greeted.

"It's morning here?" Nathan wondered. "I didn't even consider the local time."

"A lot on your mind, I take it," the general

surmised, falling in alongside Nathan as the two of them headed toward the building.

"A wants B, B wants C, even though B *hates* C, C will if B will, now B wants D as well... It's enough to make you crazy. All I want is some tech that we can't afford, but in order to get it, I have to negotiate with half the galaxy, as well as take part in another goddamned sim to prove myself yet again."

"You might consider taking a few days off to clear your head," the general suggested.

Nathan looked at him. "You're kidding, right?"

The general said nothing as he held open the door to the lobby.

"I'll take one when you take one," Nathan countered as he entered. "Who are we meeting with?"

"The new Prime Minister of Orswella."

"He's already in office?" Nathan wondered. "It's only been two days."

"Three," the general replied. "He started the day he was appointed."

"I guess he welcomes the position."

"More like he's trying to fulfill his responsibility," the general corrected. "Orswellans don't seek office, the office finds them. When it does, they do not ignore its call."

"Interesting," Nathan commented as they entered the lobby to the prime minister's office.

"The prime minister is waiting for you, General," the man at the desk announced, standing to open the door for them.

General Telles and Captain Scott strode into Prime Minister Andreola's office, walking straight up to his desk as Stethan rose to greet them.

"Welcome, Captain; General," the prime minister greeted.

"Congratulations on your appointment," Nathan replied.

"Thank you," Stethan replied.

"I hope it isn't too overwhelming."

"It has been...*challenging*..." Stethan commented, taking his seat again. "What can I do for you, Captain?"

"I have a favor to ask of you," Nathan explained.

"Anything," Stethan assured him. "We owe you a debt that can never be repaid."

"You might want to hear what the favor *is* before you say that," Nathan warned. "Is this room secure?"

"We swept it an hour ago," General Telles assured Nathan.

"What I am about to tell you cannot be discussed with anyone outside of this room," Nathan insisted.

"Of course," Stethan agreed.

"I may need to pull the Corinari from your world sooner than expected."

Stethan looked concerned. "How soon?"

"A few weeks, a month at the most."

"We should be able to eliminate the last of the Dusahn operatives by then," General Telles added, hoping to ease the prime minister's concerns.

"Will they be returning?" Stethan wondered.

"Probably not," Nathan replied. "I will need to pull the Ghatazhak at that time as well."

Stethan sighed, leaning back in his chair, thinking. "If, as you say, the Dusahn operatives are dealt with by the time your forces leave, we should be able to handle internal security on our own. We will have to step up our recruitment and training schedules, though."

"We will help you prepare as much as we can," Nathan promised. "However, the Corinari will need time to train for their new mission as well, so their availability will be limited."

"And the protection of our system?" Stethan wondered.

"That will not change," Nathan assured him. "We will be stationing fifty Gunyoki fighters designed to operate from surface bases, as well as eight Orochi missile gunships, six of which we would like *your* people to crew.

Stethan looked intrigued. "I see. I don't suppose you're able to tell me what the Corinari's new mission will be?"

"I am not," Nathan replied. "It is critical that their departure appears to be by *your* request, not ours. Despite the general's assurances, there is still the possibility that Dusahn operatives, tasked with intelligence-gathering only, will still be in your midst. They may even have the ability to send information back *to* the Dusahn."

"Then you do not want them to suspect that you plan on deploying the Corinari elsewhere," Stethan surmised.

"Correct."

"I do not think that will be difficult," Stethan told him. "Many people have already complained about the presence of Alliance forces on Orswella. They feel we have only swapped conquerors. Of course, I know better. Nevertheless, it will help my leadership position to make the withdrawal of Alliance forces appear to be at my request."

"That is good to hear," Nathan told him.

"I will speak to the Guard officers and see about putting crews together for the Orochi," Stethan said. "How much time do we have to assemble them?"

"A couple of weeks at most," Nathan replied. "I will

get you the crew specifications before we depart," he added as he stood. "I apologize for the brevity, but I have much to do and very little time."

"I know the feeling," Stethan assured him, also rising. "Whatever it is you are planning, Captain, I wish you the best of luck."

"Thank you," Nathan replied, turning to exit.

General Telles nodded respectfully to the prime minister, turning to follow Nathan out of the room.

The two men walked in silence until they were outside and headed for Nathan's shuttle.

"Are you certain you can rid this world of the Dusahn saboteurs in time?" Nathan asked.

"Nothing is certain," the general replied.

"Except death and taxes," Nathan said. "An old Earth expression."

"Ironic, coming from a man who has escaped both."

Nathan stopped a few meters short of his shuttle, turning to look at the general, a wry smile on his face. "There's that Ghatazhak humor again."

"Where is your pilot?" the general asked, noticing the empty cockpit windows.

"I flew myself down," Nathan replied, "or should I say, the auto-flight system flew me down. We're a little shorthanded these days. Besides, I enjoy a bit of piloting now and then, even if it's mostly just pushing buttons."

"I have never understood why some pilots are so averse to automated flight systems," the general commented. "They are safer *and* more efficient after all."

"If you ever flew a stick and rudder bird, you'd understand," Nathan assured him. "If I ever get my hands back on my grandfather's airplane, I'll show you what I'm talking about."

"I look forward to it."

"I'm going to want you back in the Rogen system in about a week, you know. There's a lot of planning to do."

"I'll be there," General Telles promised. "How do you say...*with balls on*?"

Nathan smiled. "There it is again," he said, turning to climb up into his shuttle.

* * *

"Captain on the bridge," the guard at the entrance barked as Nathan entered.

Nathan paused a moment, looking at the Ghatazhak guard. "You guys don't compare notes, do you?"

"I don't know what you mean, sir," the guard replied.

Nathan studied him a bit longer, trying to discern if the man was hiding a grin under that stoic, Ghatazhak expression. *Never play poker with a Ghatazhak*, he thought to himself as he continued onto the bridge. "How are we looking?" he asked Cameron, pausing at the corner of the comm-station.

"Fully charged and ready to jump," Cameron replied.

"Any word from our numerous potential allies?" he asked Naralena.

"Negative. Just the usual status updates from Rogen command."

"Very well," Nathan replied, moving toward the command chair at the center of the bridge. "Good to have you back, Mister Sheehan," he said to Loki as he took the command chair. "How's your daughter?"

"She's well, sir, thank you," Loki replied. "Jump to Tremen is ready."

"Not too close, I hope. We don't need another armed confrontation like we had with the Ahka."

"We'll be entering on the outskirts of the system," Loki assured him.

"That's a little far, don't you think?"

"That was my idea," Cameron told him. "I figured it would be better to take a peek before setting off any alarms."

"Test the water, so to speak?" Nathan surmised.

"Something like that."

"Sounds good," Nathan agreed. "Let's go meet the Tremen, Mister Hayes."

"Breaking orbit," Josh announced.

"I recommend we set general quarters," Jessica suggested, "just in case the Tremen still hold a grudge."

Nathan thought for a moment before replying. "Make it condition one, no shields. I don't want to appear threatening."

"Condition one, aye," Jessica replied.

The alert klaxon sounded once, and the bridge trim lighting switched to orange, signifying their new readiness condition.

"*Attention all decks,*" Naralena called over the ship-wide intercom system. "*Set condition one, set condition one.*"

Nathan watched the main view screen as the image of Orswella slipped downward, disappearing from view as the Aurora accelerated and pulled away from the planet. In the background, he could hear the various departments reporting their readiness state to Naralena as the Aurora's crew prepared the ship for unsafe conditions.

"Leaving orbit," Josh reported. "Turning to jump heading."

"So what do you think the Tremen are going to demand?" Cameron wondered.

Nathan sighed. "I guess we'll find out."

"On course and speed for jump," Josh announced.

"All decks report condition one," Naralena added.

"Execute your jump, Mister Sheehan," Nathan instructed.

"Jumping to the Tremen system," Loki replied.

A few seconds later, the blue-white jump flash filled the semi-spherical main view screen that wrapped around the front half of the Aurora's bridge, translating into the bridge for a brief moment.

"Jump complete," Loki reported as the jump flash faded. "Verifying position."

"Threat board is clear," Jessica reported.

"Position verified," Loki added. "We are on the outskirts of the Tremen system, approximately four point five billion kilometers from its star."

"Scanning the system," Kaylah reported from the sensor station.

"Comms, prepare a comm-drone, stealth transit, wait for response," Nathan instructed. "Tell them we come in peace and wish to speak with their leaders to establish diplomatic relations. We will hold position and await their response."

"Preparing comm-drone," Naralena acknowledged.

"I'm detecting seven planets," Kaylah announced, "The fifth planet is habitable, although they probably don't spend much time outside. About twice Earth's mass, very thick atmosphere with only traces of oxygen. You could breathe it, but not for long. Mean surface temp of sixty-five Celsius."

"Toasty," Nathan commented. "How big of a civilization are we talking about?"

"I'm detecting several large ships in orbit, but I'm unable to determine their type. Also, a large orbital platform; probably a spaceport of some sort. There are several ships nearby. I'm also detecting numerous large thermal signatures on the surface; patterns of heat distribution are too uniform to be naturally occurring-probably their cities. Based on their size, I'd say under fifty thousand per. I count fifteen of them so far."

"Comm-drone is ready, Captain," Naralena reported.

"Transferring coordinates of the fifth planet to the comm-drone," Kaylah reported.

"Launch when ready," Nathan ordered.

"Comm-drone has coordinates. Comm-drone is away," Naralena reported.

"Comm-drone has jumped," Kaylah added.

"Let's keep our eyes open, people. We just announced our presence in their system, and it won't take them long to figure out where we are."

"If the last Tremen ship we dealt with is any indication of their level of military technology, we should be fine," Jessica reminded him.

"I'd prefer not to underestimate them," Nathan insisted. "In fact, keep a short escape jump in the queue, just in case."

"I always do," Loki assured him.

"And don't let anyone block our jump line, Josh," Nathan added.

"No problem," Josh replied confidently.

"What are you planning on saying to them?" Cameron wondered.

"I haven't really given it much thought," Nathan

admitted. "Probably something along the lines of 'we don't want conflict, but we will defend our allies.'"

"Are you going to invite them to join as well?"

"It depends on how they respond I suppose. The Casbons want them to join, but only because they don't want to worry about the Tremen attacking them again."

"Then you *don't* want them to join," Cameron surmised.

"Not really," Nathan admitted. "At least not right now. We've got our hands full as it is. Even if we convince SilTek to join, we're still going to be covering five systems over eight hundred light years. Even after we finish our next batch of jump drive upgrades, that's still pushing the limits of our operational range. The Tremen would push that distance to our max single-jump range, which means we wouldn't be able to respond to a call for help without putting at least one member system at risk."

"The Dusahn don't have anywhere near the range we do," Cameron reminded him. "The likelihood of a surprise attack is pretty slim, especially if we keep a close eye on their ship movements within the Pentaurus sector."

"Easier said than done," Nathan pointed out. "I'd be more willing to bring the Tremen on as allies if we had SilTek's detection and defense systems protecting the Rogen and Orswellan systems."

"New contact," Kaylah reported. "Jump flash. It's our comm-drone."

"That was quick," Cameron commented.

"Incoming message from our comm-drone," Naralena announced. "Message is from the Tremen. Message reads: 'Depart our system or face the wrath of the Tremen.'"

"Well, that's not a good start," Nathan said. He looked to Cameron. "Any ideas?"

"I say we leave," Cameron replied. "Like you said, we've got enough on our hands."

"Seems a waste to come all the way here, send a single message, and then leave. We could've done *that* without leaving the Rogen system." After thinking for a moment, Nathan said, "Let's send another message," he decided. "Message reads: 'We regret destroying your ship but issued fair warning, and your ship continued to attack. We had no choice but to defend ourselves and our ally. We would like to avoid future conflict by establishing diplomatic relations that might benefit both parties.' Message complete, send when ready."

"Message sent. Comm-drone is returning to Tremen," Naralena reported.

"Apologize for defending ourselves?" Jessica asked, obviously disagreeing with him.

"Politics is the fine art of bullshitting," Nathan replied. "The trick is to not believe your own BS."

"Comm-drone has jumped," Kaylah reported.

"That's why I'm not a politician," Cameron stated.

"That's why I was trying to get *away* from it ten years ago," Nathan chuckled. "Look where *that* got me."

"New contacts," Kaylah reported, her tone a bit more urgent. "Three of them. Two hundred kilometers, dead ahead. They're decelerating but closing."

"They're armed," Jessica warned. "Rail guns, laser cannons, and forward torpedo tubes. No shields. Similar design to the one that attacked the Casbon."

"They must've departed as soon as their world received the first message," Cameron insisted. "They obviously know how to trace a jump path."

"Comms, broadcast the last message on all channels and frequencies," Nathan instructed.

"Targets are opening outer torpedo tube doors," Jessica warned.

"Energy build-ups deep within all three ships," Kaylah added.

"General quarters," Nathan ordered.

"General quarters, aye," Naralena replied as the klaxon sounded and the trim lighting turned red.

"Shields up," Jessica announced, "all weapons charging."

"Don't lock onto anyone yet," Nathan instructed. "We need to appear totally defensive."

"Auto-targeting system is on hold," Jessica confirmed.

"Hot mic," Nathan ordered. "All frequencies and channels."

"You're patched in," Naralena replied.

"This is Nathan Scott, captain of the Karuzari Alliance ship Aurora. We come in peace, but we will defend ourselves if attacked."

"All decks report general quarters," Naralena announced.

"We only wish to discuss a cease-fire between your world and our Alliance, and to open diplomatic relations so that we may avoid any future conflicts."

"They've locked all their weapons on us," Jessica warned.

"Targets are still closing," Kaylah added.

"Adjusting course to maintain clear jump line," Josh announced.

"Incoming transmission," Naralena reported. "Putting it up."

"*Aurora,*" an angry, heavily accented voice called over the loudspeaker. "*You destroyed a ship of the*

Tremen and are therefore an enemy of the people, as are all of your allies. Your intrusion into our space is an act of war. Power down your weapons and prepare to be boarded."

"Oh, that's so not going to happen," Jessica muttered.

"*You will surrender your ship as compensation, or you will be destroyed.*"

"You attacked the Casbon, one of our allies. This ship only defended itself, as you are doing now," Nathan replied over comms. "We have no interest in continued conflict, but we will not surrender this ship nor pay any compensation for your losses."

"*Surrender or be destroyed.*"

"Transmission has ceased," Naralena reported.

"Targets are firing," Kaylah reported urgently.

The ship rocked, the view screen lighting up with flashes of red-orange as plasma torpedoes impacted the Aurora's forward shields.

"Shields are holding," Jessica reported. "Only a two percent drop in our forward shields."

"Am I still hot?" Nathan asked Naralena.

"Aye, sir."

"Tremen warships, we came in peace and will leave in peace. However, be forewarned that further attacks against the Casbon or any of our other allies will not be tolerated." Nathan signaled Naralena to close the channel with a slash of his hand.

"Transmission ended," she acknowledged.

"They're trying to block our jump line," Josh warned. "I'm having to constantly alter course to keep our exit open."

"They're firing again," Kaylah reported.

"Are we going to return fire?" Jessica wondered

as the ship rocked with the second round of torpedo impacts.

"Helm, hard to starboard, mains to full," Nathan ordered. "Jess, target the right-most ship's forward torpedo ports and starboard weapons, and fire when ready."

"Targeting contact three," Jessica replied as the ship began its turn to starboard. "Torpedo ports and starboard guns."

"Hard to starboard, mains to full," Josh acknowledged as the ship accelerated.

"Firing port plasma turrets and rail guns," Jessica announced.

Nathan quickly switched the view screen controls to the port cameras and zoomed in, just in time to see their weapons tearing into the nearest Tremen warship as it struggled to turn fast enough to keep its forward torpedo tubes on the Aurora as she accelerated. Explosions under their nose demolished the target's forward torpedo ports, as rail gun slugs disintegrated the target's starboard gun turrets.

Nathan watched the view screen as they slipped past the damaged Tremen ship.

"Contact Three has lost all forward torpedo tubes and all starboard guns," Kaylah reported. "Multiple hull breaches with explosive decompression on several decks."

"Cease fire," Nathan instructed.

"Holding fire," Jessica replied.

"Jump us clear, Mister Sheehan," he added.

"Jumping," Loki replied, as the jump flash washed over them.

Nathan sighed. "Well, *that* didn't go the way I'd hoped."

"Was it really necessary to fire on them?" Cameron wondered.

"If you have to walk away from a fight, make sure the opponent you leave behind knows you just did them a favor," Nathan explained.

"More politics?"

"Combat is just another form of politics," Nathan replied. "Just one that you try to use as a last resort. Mister Sheehan, plot a jump to Casbon."

"Aye, sir."

"Casbon?" Cameron asked.

"I'm tired of trying to meet all their demands," Nathan stated. "They need to make up their minds."

* * *

"That is a surprisingly unreasonable position," Council Member Garon stated in disbelief.

"Not as surprising as you might think," Nathan told her. "What *is* surprising is just how many worlds believe they have the right to do whatever they want to achieve their goals."

"You have seen this type of behavior before," the council member surmised.

"Yes. It usually begins with survival, but eventually, the tendency becomes ingrained in a society. This behavior is both the strength *and* the weakness of humanity."

A look of disapproval came over the council member's face. "Then you think we are wrong to embrace pacifism."

"Pacifism, while a noble ideal, is not practical in its purest definition. A society can embrace peace and avoid violent conflict at all costs...except one: the loss of its own people. The phrase 'the strong survive' is accurate. Even a pacifist society must take a stand when it comes to the protection of its own people, which is precisely what you have done by purchasing fighters. You also authorized my forces to conduct a strike against the Ahka for the purpose of disabling their ability to prey upon your people. That is not the act of a truly pacifist society, but rather one of a peace-loving society struggling to remain that way. It takes incredible strength to resist the urge to seek retribution. *That* is the type of pacifism that *can* and *should* survive, and *that* is what you have become."

Council Member Garon thought for a moment. "The council has had this same debate countless times in recent years. The conclusion is always the same. We abhor violent confrontation, but continuing to allow ourselves to be preyed upon and expecting to survive is naïve...as you stated. It is this realization that led us to seek out a defense. However, most find just the *presence* of our fighters abhorrent. People discuss leaving Casbon because of them. Our world was originally colonized by those seeking to escape cultures of violence. Now we find ourselves taking the first steps toward becoming exactly what we had hoped to escape."

"Like any other technology, the jump drive is a double-edged sword. Our alliance hopes to promote its good edge, while protecting all against its bad one."

"Which is one of the reasons that the Council of Casbon has decided to join your alliance."

Nathan's eyebrows shot up. "You have?"

"We have."

"When did this happen?"

"After your first appearance to discuss the matter before the council," the council member replied. "The

Ahka agreement to join was all that was needed to assuage the concerns of the opposition."

"I see." Nathan took a breath. "You said 'one' of the reasons. What was the other?"

"There were two others, actually," Council Member Garon explained. "The second reason was the economic benefit. Even at a discounted, below-market rate, our profits will double."

"And the third?"

"The protection your alliance offers will allow our society to maintain its pacifist ideology by passing that responsibility to others."

"Some might say that supporting an alliance that uses military force to ensure peace does not meet the true definition of pacifism," Nathan pointed out.

"Yes, but not being the ones bearing swords is a compromise that allows our people to *survive*," she replied. "Hopefully, it is one that we can *live* with as well."

Nathan looked down, sighing.

"You do not appear pleased, Captain," she said.

"I regret that jump drive technology has forced the Casbon and many other worlds to change the systems they live under. I feel somewhat responsible for that."

"The jump drive is but a tool, Captain. One that can be used for both good *and* bad...nothing more."

"Perhaps, but I am responsible for its rapid spread," Nathan admitted.

"You cannot stop progress, Captain," Council Member Garon said. "The best you can do is to try and ensure that it is used responsibly. This is precisely what you are trying to do."

"I hadn't really thought of it that way," Nathan admitted. "For that, I thank you."

Council Member Garon nodded respectfully. "I must warn you, Captain...there is one more condition that must be met *before* we will formally join the Karuzari Alliance."

Nathan's heart sank. "What would that be?" he asked, fearing the answer.

"We require that you take *all* our fighters, *permanently*. The people of Casbon would prefer that there were no weapons on our world, and we believe that those fighters will serve us better in the hands of the Alliance."

Nathan felt a wave of relief wash over him. "I think we can handle that one," he replied, smiling.

* * *

Cameron met Nathan at the top of the ramp leading to the Aurora's command deck. "How did it go?"

"We need to notify the Glendanon to get under way," Nathan said as he topped the ramp and continued forward.

"To where?" Cameron queried, falling in alongside him.

"Casbon, to pick up one hundred Nighthawks," he replied, a slight grin on his face.

"You convinced them to loan *all* of them to us?" Cameron asked in disbelief.

"They *gave* them to us," Nathan corrected. "Turns out their people really don't like having those fighters in their backyard. They'd rather have someone else do the dirty work."

"Meaning us," Cameron surmised.

"Yup, they joined."

"Wow," Cameron exclaimed. "I didn't think you could pull that off."

"I haven't *pulled it off* just yet," he reminded her. "We still have to beat SilTek's defenses."

"Speaking of which, Rogen command relayed a message from SilTek. They would like us to come as soon as possible to conduct the inspection so that they can prepare the simulation."

"Let's jump back to the Rogen system first," Nathan told her. "We need to load up as many jump missiles as we can before they start poking around. Besides, I need a good night's sleep before dealing with SilTek."

"Understood," Cameron replied. "I'll get us back to Rakuen."

"Thanks," Nathan replied as they reached the entrance to his quarters.

"Nice work, by the way," Cameron told him.

Nathan smiled. "Thanks. Now if you'll excuse me, there is a rack in there with my name on it."

CHAPTER SIX

Nathan watched as four SilTek inspectors, three of whom were obviously androids, entered the Aurora's bridge.

"Captain Scott, I presume," the human inspector greeted in businesslike fashion. "I am Lorne Wells, leader of the inspection team."

"Are there just four of you?" Nathan wondered. "I was under the impression there were more."

"There are thirty-eight of us in all," Lorne explained. "Four of us are human."

"Where?"

"Fanning out all over the ship in groups of three or four."

"I have security teams with each group," Jessica assured Nathan.

"I see," Nathan replied. "How can we assist you?" he asked Lorne.

"We will need access to all of the ship's specifications and performance parameters," Lorne explained, "as well as all weapons, targeting systems and ordnance, including any adjunct craft such as shuttles and fighters. We will also require recordings and logs of all battles for the purposes of understanding just what the Aurora is capable of."

"No way," Jessica objected.

"Pardon?" Lorne said, surprised.

"You're talking about highly sensitive data," Jessica told him. "If it got into the wrong hands..."

"I assure you that all data collected for the purpose of the upcoming simulation will be destroyed upon completion of the simulation."

"Captain, we can't turn over all the combat logs,"

Jessica insisted. "That would give away all our tactics. Security risks aside, it would give SilTek a *huge* advantage."

"I can assure you there is nothing to be concerned about," Lorne assured Jessica. "We at the Gaming Commission take our responsibility quite seriously."

"Gaming Commission?" Cameron asked.

"Did no one explain this to you?"

"Apparently not," Cameron replied.

"For the purposes of safety, all contests are conducted within SilTek's simulation matrix. The Gaming Commission is responsible for ensuring the fairness of all simulated competitions."

"So you *don't* work for SilTek?" Jessica surmised.

"Everyone who lives on SilTek *works* for SilTek," Lorne corrected. "However, employees of the Gaming Commission operate independently. We are not subject to the corporation's direct control. In fact, our positions are protected."

"So SilTek cannot ask you to skew the simulation in their favor?" Cameron asked.

"They can ask," Lorne replied.

"That doesn't make me feel any better," Jessica commented.

"The Gaming Commission is monitored by a civilian panel. Only that panel can terminate the employment of any of the commission's inspectors. The corporation cannot. If an inspector were to grant such a request, they would surely be terminated, possibly even imprisoned."

Nathan looked at Cameron, then at Jessica. "Good enough for me."

"Not for me," Jessica argued.

"You said the data you collect today would be

destroyed after the simulation is over?" Nathan questioned.

"Correct," Lorne replied. "All data collected this day will be stored in a single data module which can be read but not copied. The module will be connected to a stand-alone simulation matrix. Once the simulation is completed, and a winner is officially declared, the data module can be returned to you to destroy yourselves if you wish."

"Oh, we wish," Jessica insisted.

"That sounds acceptable," Nathan decided. "I do have one question, though. Will we be allowed to use our AI in the simulation? It is unlicensed and not technically installed *in* the Aurora."

"I do not understand," Lorne said.

"It is still installed in the Sugali fighter to which it was originally licensed," Nathan explained. "It is connected to the Aurora through an interface that our chief engineer designed."

"I see," Lorne replied, one eyebrow raised in disapproval. "That does raise some questions. I will have to consult my superiors before I can give you an answer."

"Fair enough," Nathan said. "What can we do to help get you started?"

"One of my inspectors will need access to a terminal," Lorne began. "The rest of us will be inspecting each station on the bridge and questioning operators on their individual functions."

"Either of these aft-most terminals are considered auxiliary workstations," Nathan replied. "So take your pick."

Without a word, one of the android inspectors moved to the starboard auxiliary station and sat down, immediately tapping away on the console.

"Alright then," Nathan commented as the inspectors went to work.

"I don't like this," Jessica said under her breath, stepping closer to Nathan and Cameron.

"You don't like anything," Nathan replied.

* * *

Doran Montrose entered the Orswellan precinct house, pausing to look around the lobby. The man he was looking for was at the reception desk on the far side, his attention on his view screen as he furiously tapped away at the input plate in front of him.

Doran made his way across the lobby and stepped up to the counter, the officer still not looking up. "What kind of a cop doesn't even look up to see who's coming across the lobby toward him?"

"The kind who recognizes that cheap piss you call cologne the moment you stepped through the door," the officer grumbled, still not looking away from his screen. "Besides, the cameras ID'd you before you entered, you smartass." Finally, the man looked up, a broad smile coming across his face. "What the hell are you doing here, Doran? Kaplan finally get wise and fire your lazy ass?"

"No such luck," Doran replied. "How are you, Denton?"

"Fair enough. Food on this planet sucks, though. Not enough meat, and they bury everything in some pungent, fermented crap called *savari*."

"How's life as a cop?"

"Keeps me busy I guess. Mostly paperwork."

"The bane of leadership," Doran commented.

"What are you doing on Orswella?" Denton wondered.

"I got reassigned," he told his old friend.

"You going to babysit Orswellan cadets as well?" Denton wondered.

"Nothing like that," Doran assured him. "I'm actually here to whip all your sorry butts back into shape."

Denton looked suspiciously at his friend. "In shape for what?"

"Just in general," Doran lied. "Captain Scott wants all the Corinari to be in top shape and ready to fight at a moment's notice."

"The Corinari are *always* ready to fight at a moment's notice," Denton insisted. "Even lazy old farts like you."

"Never hurts to train, my friend."

"Bullshit," Denton replied. "Something's up." He studied Doran's face for a moment. "We have a mission, don't we?"

"Like I said, he just asked me to get us into top shape, that's all."

"We spent the last three months training with the Ghatazhak. We could take the eye out of a fliket with a toothpick from ten meters. The only reason the Corinari would need training is for a specific mission."

"Scott's just worried that playing cop is going to make us all go soft," Doran insisted. "Now, if he's got an underlying reason he's not sharing with me, I cannot speak to that. All I know is that I am to take command of all Corinari ground forces and prepare them for combat."

"Combat where?" Denton pressed.

Doran looked around, checking to see if any could overhear their conversation, then leaned closer to his friend. "If I were you, Crawley, I'd go with the flow on this, and stop asking questions. Get my meaning?"

“I have no problem with extra training, Doran,” Denton assured him. “But everyone’s going to be speculating.”

“And we’ll be sticking to our story,” Doran replied.

“I can do that,” Denton assured him. “Just one question. Why are you coming to me?”

“Because I want you to be my second.”

Denton sighed. “I don’t suppose it gets me out of this lousy desk job, does it?”

“Not at first, no. At least not until you train one of the locals to take your place.”

Denton smiled. “A boba could do this job. When do we start?”

“Come find me after your shift ends. I’ll be at the old re-ball stadium on the point,” Doran told him. “That’s where we’ll train.”

“Where are you headed now?” Denton wondered.

“I’ve got a few others to recruit,” Doran replied. “Any idea where McCrary is working?”

“He’s running precinct eighteen over by the waterfront, the little kiss-ass.”

“He always could get the cushy assignments,” Doran laughed, turning to exit. “I’ll see you later.”

* * *

“What’s the problem?” Nathan asked as he and Jessica entered the Aurora’s starboard missile compartment.

“They want me to pull every missile for inspection,” the young lieutenant in charge of the Aurora’s ordnance reported. “The only way to do that is to pull them out of the magazines, one by one, and float them up to the flight deck to line them up. That means...”

“That we’d have to close up the forward flight decks,” Nathan realized.

"Not only that; it would leave us highly vulnerable," Jessica added.

Nathan looked at the leader of the inspection group. "You're taking it a little far, don't you think?"

"We need to verify that your ordnance counts are correct," the inspector stated.

"They're correct," Nathan assured him.

"That's what I *told* him," the lieutenant added.

"That is what we intend to verify," the inspector explained.

Nathan looked annoyed. "I'll tell you what. We'll pull all of *our* missiles out of their magazines, and line them up for inspection, if *SilTek* pulls all of *their* missiles out at the *same* time-and I'm talking every damned missile-so that we can go over every single one of them."

"That can be arranged," the inspector assured him.

"All of them, from every storage magazine and launcher, at the *same* time?" Nathan added.

"That is not necessary," the inspector insisted.

"The hell it isn't," Nathan argued. "How do we know that you don't have tunnels connecting all of your missile launchers, so that you can move ordnance between launch sites?" Nathan argued. "You could shuttle them between launchers and make it *look* like you have a lot more missiles than you really have."

"That's absurd," the inspector argued.

"No more so than asking *us* to pull every missile out of *our* storage magazines," Nathan rebutted.

"Captain..."

"Those are the terms," Nathan stated firmly. "If you find them unacceptable, we'll be on our way, and we'll take our business elsewhere. You may be the biggest, you may even be the best, but you're *not* the only technology and weapons manufacturer in the galaxy, and we have a great enough jump range to *find* another vendor and help *them* gain a larger market share."

The inspector deferred to one of his android aides. The aide closed his eyes for a moment, then opened them, nodding.

"Very well, Captain," the lead inspector said. "We shall not require the inspection of every missile. We will inspect *one* missile...one of the *shield-penetrating* variants."

"Lieutenant, pull the first shield-penetrating jump missile for inspection," Nathan directed.

"Uh...yes, sir."

"Once they conclude their inspection, set it aside for inspection by our *own* engineers."

"Yes, sir."

"We would prefer to use the inspected missile for the live test," the inspector stated.

"I bet you would," Nathan replied, turning and walking away.

The lieutenant rolled his eyes and turned toward one of his technicians standing by the outboard missile magazine gate. "Pull the first missile from the outboard magazine," he instructed.

Jessica smiled at the inspectors, turning to follow Nathan out of the compartment. "That was *awesome*," she said once they were in the corridor and out of earshot.

"I'm just glad it worked," Nathan replied.

"None of those missiles have been tested you know," Jessica reminded him.

"I do."

Jessica shook her head in disbelief. "You sure do

like to roll the dice, don't you? You must clean up at the casinos."

"Actually, I usually lose at the casinos," Nathan replied. "Miserably."

* * *

Doran Montrose entered the Ghatazhak command center, which had been set up inside the Orswellan capitol building. As expected, staffing inside was minimal, with two Ghatazhak specialists manning tracking and communications consoles. On the center of the facing wall hung a large view screen, displaying a tactical map of the city. On either side were a number of smaller screens showing views from various security cameras.

Sergeant Czarny spotted Doran and walked over to greet him. "Welcome to our makeshift command center, Chief."

"Looks pretty functional," Doran replied. "Are there cameras all over the city?"

"Every streetlight, every building entrance, and every corridor," the sergeant replied. "A benefit left behind by the Dusahn."

"I expect the Orswellans don't see it that way."

"Most are so used to it they don't really care," the sergeant replied. "The problem is, we suspect that the Dusahn still have access to the network."

"There are still operatives on the surface?"

"Maybe twenty, but that's just a guess. Telles believes they've gone cold for now."

"I suppose there's no way to ever know for certain."

"Eventually, we hope to get every person on this rock scanned and have their DNA sequenced to verify their origin."

"You can do that?"

"Yes, it just takes time. The new prime minister

is trying to pass legislation requiring all Orswellans to be scanned and tagged."

"Tagged?"

"*Chipped* would be a more accurate term, I suppose. It would make it easier to spot a Dusahn operative."

"Unless of course they figure out how to forge chips."

"No plan is perfect," the sergeant defended. "What brings you here anyway? You just come by to bust our humps?"

"Humps? Picked up some Earth lingo, did you?"

"Picked up a lot of bad habits from hanging out with Nash," the sergeant joked. "That girl was a bundle of bad habits when she first joined."

"I always wondered how that went initially. I mean, the Ghatazhak have always been very selective. Hell, every one of you is the same size and build, except Nash of course."

"Times change, I suppose. The Ghatazhak have to change with them or perish."

"Then Nash worked out okay?"

"I think so," the sergeant replied. "At the very least, she brought a little more *abandon* to the ranks."

"I'm sure General Telles just *loves* that."

"The man is *very* patient."

Doran chuckled. "Speaking of the general, is he in?"

"Down the hall, first door on the left," the sergeant replied. "I'll let him know you're coming."

"Thanks," Doran said. "Good to see you again, Czarny."

Doran made his way around the room, being

careful not to distract the two specialists busily communicating with Ghatazhak teams in the field.

The corridor was short, and after only a few steps, Doran found himself at the open door to the general's office.

Just like the command center, the office was rather simple, with a desk, a few chairs, and a few view screens on the wall.

"Chief Montrose," the general greeted, standing up from behind his desk.

"General."

"Are you getting settled into your new assignment?" the general queried.

"Well, I've managed to recruit my key senior staff members," Doran replied, "so I guess that's a start."

"How may I help you?" the general wondered, returning to his seat.

"I was wondering if you had any idea what kind of resources we're going to have for this mission."

"Captain Scott and I have discussed the matter. At the very least, we hope to have personal shields and uniforms for all your men."

"I was more concerned with firepower and communications," Doran said. "The more time we have to train with what we'll be using, the better we'll perform in actual combat."

"Of course."

"Any chance we'll have body armor?" Doran wondered. "Shields are nice, but they only cover one side. If we're operating without body armor, our tactics will be different."

"Understandable," the general agreed. "Assuming we have time and access to fabricators, we should be able to get you at least torso protection. We'll also be pumping up your men with our version of nanites.

They are specifically tailored for traumatic injury management."

"That would help."

General Telles took a breath. "I hesitate to mention this since it is all speculative. However, Captain Scott is currently working on a deal that could get us access to significant resources. Possibly even provide us with *everything* we need, *including* some things we never even *dreamed* of having."

"Well, now I'm intrigued," Doran admitted. "I don't suppose you have any details?"

"Nothing solid," the general replied. "Besides, it's a long-shot at best."

"Well, long-shots seem to be Captain Scott's specialty," Doran replied.

"Indeed," the general replied. "Let's hope that holds true this time as well."

* * *

"What's up?" Nathan asked as he came out of his ready room.

"They're finished," Cameron told him.

"Already?" Nathan wondered. "It's only been a couple of hours."

"We're *nearly* finished," Mister Wells, the lead inspector, corrected. "There are three discrepancies we'd like to address."

"Of course," Nathan agreed.

"First, your manifest lists six 'Reapers', yet there are only four aboard, and there are no log entries for their departure."

"They are on a covert operation," Nathan explained. "Such operations do not have log entries."

"Where is this operation?" the inspector asked.

"'Covert' means 'secret'," Nathan replied, "which means you don't get to know."

"I see," the inspector replied, one eyebrow raised in disapproval. "How long ago did they depart?"

"Yesterday."

"Then they cannot be included in your resource list for the purpose of this contest."

"But they *were* on board at the time the wager was made," Nathan argued.

"And had you agreed to an inspection at that time, they would have been eligible," the inspector replied curtly. "The next discrepancy has to do with your ordnance count. Your logs show eighty jump missiles on board, inclusive of all variants. However, your port magazine's inventory display shows only thirty-eight missiles, instead of the expected forty. Do you have an explanation for *this* as well? Perhaps they *too* are on a *covert* mission?"

Nathan was not amused by the inspector's sarcasm. "I will have my executive officer investigate the discrepancy," he promised.

"I'm sure, however, those two missiles cannot be included in your resource list either."

"If you can wait a few minutes, I'm certain we can figure it out," Nathan insisted.

"I'm sorry, Captain, but the terms of the inspection are clear."

Nathan rolled his eyes. "And the third discrepancy?"

"Your shield-penetrating jump missiles have not yet been used in combat, nor have they been field tested."

"We have very limited resources," Nathan explained, "and our computer simulations have always been accurate in the past. Therefore, we chose not to waste the ordnance on live-fire tests."

"That is highly irregular," the inspector insisted.

"Especially considering that those weapons are your greatest asset and could be the key to your victory in this contest."

"I disagree," Nathan argued.

The inspector looked confused. "How could you possibly disagree with that assessment? *Shield-penetrating* jump missiles are a huge tactical advantage..."

"Yes they are," Nathan replied, interrupting the inspector, "but they are hardly our greatest asset."

Again the inspector looked confused. "Then what is?"

"Our crew."

Now the inspector looked truly shocked. "Your crew?"

"Yes," Nathan replied.

"Perhaps you could elaborate?" the inspector asked, obviously in the form of a challenge.

"The people you see around you have been in more battles than I can count. They have seen every tactic, every situation, and every horror that war can present, and they've all gotten through it...*alive*. That is not an accident, Mister Wells. That is skill. These people know what order I'm going to give *before* I give it. They know their jobs and have developed instincts that no AI can equal. More importantly, they have seen the suffering that evil brings, and they have chosen to stand and fight to the death if necessary. An AI can never understand the motivation that such dedication brings."

"An AI determines the most efficient way of accomplishing its goal, regardless of emotion," the inspector argued, "and it does so in a fraction of the time. No offense to your crew, Captain, as I am certain they are fine, dedicated professionals.

However, they cannot match the performance of AI-controlled weapons systems."

"I guess we're going to find out," Nathan replied confidently. "Is there anything else?"

"We will need to verify the performance of your shield-penetrating jump missiles," the inspector insisted.

"As I explained, we have a limited supply," Nathan replied.

"We do not require their detonation, Captain. Although we could not adequately scan all of your missiles, we were able to detect all of their warheads, both conventional and nuclear. Therefore, we only require verification of their shield-penetrating capabilities."

Nathan exchanged glances with Cameron and Jessica, both of whom looked concerned.

"You do have the ability to recover undetonated ordnance, do you not?"

"We do," Nathan confirmed. "I suppose you have a target in mind?"

"In anticipation of this test, we are prepared to place a shielded target ring in orbit above SilTek."

"How big of a ring?" Jessica asked.

"Thirty-four meters in diameter."

"Kind of small, isn't it?" Cameron stated.

"We assumed your weapons were highly accurate," the inspector replied. "Is the size of the target going to be a problem?"

"No problem at all," Jessica insisted.

"Excellent," the inspector declared. "The target can be deployed in minutes."

"Helm, break orbit and prepare to jump us outside of SilTek's defense perimeter," Nathan ordered.

"Breaking orbit, aye," Josh replied.

"That won't be necessary, Captain," the inspector insisted.

"On the contrary," Nathan argued, "if you're trying to determine this ship's capabilities, you should see it in action. May as well make it as realistic as possible, right?"

"Perhaps I should notify defense command, so they do not mistakenly identify your ship as an aggressor."

"I'm sure your AIs are smarter than that."

The inspector did not reply.

"Jump is plotted and ready," Loki reported.

"Are you ready, Mister Wells?" Nathan inquired.

The inspector looked to his android assistant, who nodded, then replied. "We are ready."

"Execute your jump, Mister Sheehan," Nathan ordered.

"Jumping to the outside of SilTek's defense perimeter," Loki replied.

The jump flash washed over the bridge, fading a split second later.

"Jump complete."

"Coming about," Josh reported as he initiated their turn.

"Set general quarters," Nathan instructed calmly.

"General quarters, aye," Naralena acknowledged.

The bridge trim lighting switched from green to red as the alarm klaxon sounded. Without a word, Cameron turned and left the bridge, heading quickly for her station in combat command.

Inspector Wells seemed startled by the sudden commotion. "Is it really necessary to come to general quarters?" he asked. "After all, this is only a test."

"You came here to *inspect* our capabilities,"

Nathan explained. "Might as well show you how it's really done."

"If you approach in a battle-ready condition, there is a *slight* possibility that our defense AIs could misinterpret your intent."

"I guess we'll find out," Nathan remarked, seemingly unconcerned.

"But you don't even know *where* the target is going to be," the inspector replied.

"Oh, I'm certain we'll find it."

"Back on course for SilTek," Loki reported. "Range is twenty light years."

"Oh my," Inspector Wells said under his breath.

"I take it you don't get out of the system much?" Nathan remarked.

The inspector took a breath, trying to calm himself. "I must admit, the idea of transiting that much space in the blink of an eye is somewhat unsettling."

"You get used to it," Nathan assured him.

"All decks report general quarters," Naralena announced. "XO is in combat; chief of the boat is in damage control."

"Shields are up, and all weapons are charged and ready," Jessica reported. "Two jump missiles on the rails."

"Mister Sheehan," Nathan began, moving to the center of the bridge. "Plot our entry point to be directly into a low orbit above SilTek's fifth planet."

"We'll need to decelerate if you want to establish an orbit, sir," Loki warned.

"No need, Nathan replied, glancing at the flight dynamics display on Josh's console. "We'll slingshot around her and take our shot as we come out. Be ready for a quick jump as soon as that missile leaves the rails."

"Destination for the escape jump?" Loki asked.

"Right next to the target," Nathan replied confidently as he sat down in his command chair. "I want Inspector Wells to get a *good* look."

"Aye, sir."

"I'm certain our ground stations will be able to verify the results," Inspector Wells insisted.

Nathan ignored him. "Kaylah, prepare a recon drone. Program it to jump in at the same point over SilTek that we just departed from. The moment it detects that target, it is to jump back to us, near SilTek's fifth moon with the plot data for that target."

"Aye, sir," Kaylah replied.

"Captain," the inspector protested, "this is *really* unnecessary..."

"Recon drone is programmed and ready," Kaylah reported.

"Jump to SilTek's fifth planet is plotted and ready," Loki added.

"Launch the recon drone," Nathan ordered.

"Captain..." the inspector repeated.

"Recon drone away."

"*...please...*"

"Mister Sheehan, when that recon drone jumps, we jump."

"Recon drone is jumping," Kaylah announced.

"Executing jump," Loki added.

"...I *must* insist..."

The bridge again filled with the blue-white flash, and the SilTek system's fifth planet, a small, rocky world, suddenly filled the screen.

"Jump complete," Loki reported.

"New contact," Kaylah announced. "Tekan recon

drone, twenty light seconds off our port side, ten degrees down relative."

"Has it spotted us?" Nathan inquired.

"Negative," Kaylah replied. "They only stay on station for fifteen seconds before they jump, so that one would have departed before we arrived. It's old light."

"We've been detected," Jessica reported. "Sensors on the surface of the fifth planet. It picked us up the moment we arrived."

"New contact!" Kaylah added. "Comm-drone."

"I'm getting plot data for the test target," Jessica reported. "Loading the targeting data into the jump missile on rail one."

"Clear jump line to SilTek in ten seconds," Loki reported.

"Missile launches!" Kaylah reported urgently. "Four of them! On the surface! Five seconds to impact!"

"Launch the jump missile," Nathan ordered.

"Missile away!" Jessica replied, pressing the missile launch button.

"Jumping!" Loki followed, intent on escaping the incoming missiles.

"So much for your *smart* AIs," Nathan commented as the jump flash washed over the bridge.

"Jump complete," Loki reported.

"Target ahead, two kilometers above our flight path," Kaylah reported.

Nathan pressed a button on the left arm of his command chair, causing the center section of the main view screen to zoom in on the target in orbit above SilTek.

"Missile has arrived," Kaylah reported.

Nathan watched as the missile streaked across

the main view screen, entering along its upper edge, closing the distance to the target in seconds. The missile pierced the shielded center of the circular target, passing through it without difficulty.

Nathan fought back the urge to breathe a sigh of relief as did everyone else on the bridge, including the inspector, albeit for different reasons.

"Stand down from general quarters," Nathan quickly ordered. "Power down all weapons but maintain full shields. Comms, remind SilTek this is a test, and that we are not a hostile." He looked at the inspector. "Just in case your AIs haven't figured that out yet."

"Weapons powering down," Jessica reported. "Shields at full strength."

"SilTek defense command has acknowledged our transmission," Naralena announced. "They are standing down all defenses."

"Once they do, you can lower our shields," Nathan instructed. "And change our readiness to condition one."

"Condition one, aye," Naralena acknowledged.

"Captain, that was reckless and *completely* irresponsible," the inspector protested angrily. "You could have gotten us all killed!"

"You don't *really* think I'm *that* crazy, do you?" Nathan defended.

"I'm starting to wonder."

"There was no way any of your missiles were going to penetrate our shields on the first volley," Nathan explained. "The *second* volley, maybe, but we wouldn't have stuck around long enough for that to happen. Besides, you wanted to see how this ship *and her crew* truly perform in combat. Well you just did."

Inspector Wells offered no reply but was obviously relieved to have lived through the dramatic exhibition.

"I believe that should serve as adequate verification of our shield-penetrating jump missiles," Nathan decided. "Jess, send a signal to that missile to disarm and jump it clear of all defenses for retrieval."

"It was never armed to begin with," Jessica assured him.

"You see," Nathan said, looking back at the inspector, "a good crew knows what their captain wants, even *without* being explicitly told."

"I see your point," the inspector admitted. "However, there is still the matter of the multi-jump variant."

"Pardon?"

"We will require a demonstration of *that* variant as well. Particularly of its ability to conduct multiple jumps, changing its course in between them."

Nathan looked annoyed. "You Tekans are not exactly the trusting type, are you?"

"That's the only thing *I* like about them," Jessica quipped from the tactical console.

"Being from Earth, perhaps you are familiar with the old Earth axiom: 'Trust, but verify.'"

"An old Russian proverb mistakenly credited to a twentieth-century American president," Nathan replied. After sighing, he added, "I take it we can use the same target?"

"Correct."

"Any particular course you'd like the weapon to fly to *get* to the target?" Nathan wondered.

"As long as its departure course is at least one hundred degrees opposite to its final attack course, that should suffice," the inspector replied.

"Helm, maintain our distance from the target,"

Nathan instructed. "Tactical, load a multi-jump, *shield-penetrating* missile, and program it to jump seven light years out, before coming about and jumping back to intercept the target; *disarmed,* of course."

"Aye, sir," Jessica replied, smiling.

"Perhaps it would be better if the weapon's course change waypoint was located *inside* our defense perimeter, so that our sensors could witness the maneuver," Inspector Wells suggested.

"And risk losing one of my best weapons because of your trigger-happy AIs?" Nathan replied. "Not a chance."

"Fair enough," the inspector agreed.

"The weapon is programmed and ready to launch," Jessica announced.

"Snap jump the weapon the moment it leaves the rails," Nathan instructed. "Fire when ready."

"Snap jump after launch," Jessica acknowledged. "Launching the weapon now," she added, pressing the launch button again. "Weapon away."

The missile appeared briefly at the bottom corner of the view screen as it exited the starboard side of the ship but disappeared a split second later.

"Weapon has jumped," Kaylah reported.

Inspector Wells looked confused. "There was no flash."

"All our multi-jump variants are equipped with stealth jump emitters," Nathan explained. "Eventually, we hope to retrofit *all* our jump missiles with the same capabilities."

"Interesting," the inspector commented.

"You didn't see that in the specs?"

"I have not *personally* reviewed the collected data," the inspector admitted, looking to one of his android assistants. "However, I am certain that our inspection AIs are aware of this feature."

"Of course."

The inspector watched the main view screen, his eyes focused on the target ring in orbit above his world. "Shouldn't the weapon have arrived by now?" he wondered.

"The faster the rate-of-turn, the more propellant required," Nathan explained. "So it takes a minute or two for the weapon to come completely about."

"I see."

"The weapon should complete its turn in twenty seconds," Jessica reported.

"Keep your eyes on the target," Nathan told the inspector. "Remember, you won't see a jump flash."

The inspector kept his eyes glued to the view screen, his brow furrowed.

Nathan noticed the inspector's concentration and exchanged a knowing smile with Jessica as he rotated his command chair to face forward again, knowing that the weapon would appear in a few seconds.

"There it is!" the inspector exclaimed as the jump missile appeared only a few hundred meters on the other side of the target. Before the words had left his mouth, the weapon reached the target, passing through its shield, causing it to flash momentarily as the missile passed through the shielded target ring.

"Weapon has successfully passed through the target shield," Jessica reported. "Jumping it clear of all defenses for retrieval."

Nathan turned and looked at Inspector Wells. "Anything *else* we can demonstrate for you, Inspector?"

The inspector took a moment, straightening his

suit jacket before responding. "That should suffice, Captain." He turned to face Nathan. "Good luck in the contest."

"Thank you," Nathan replied. "Now feel free to get off my ship at your earliest convenience," he added with a touch of disdain.

Inspector Wells nodded, then turned and headed for the exit, his three android assistants in tow.

Nathan rotated slowly around in his command chair, watching them exit. Once they were gone, he looked at Jessica.

"How'd I do?" she asked, smiling.

"Perfect," Nathan replied.

"Can I ask a stupid question?" Josh wondered from the helm.

Nathan turned back around to face his helmsman.

"How the hell did we just do that?" Josh asked. "I thought all the multi-jump variants were just dummies. I even helped Deliza and her team stick on the fake conduits."

"Those two Reapers on covert assignment," Jessica told him, a satisfied smile still on her face.

Josh wasn't buying it. "Reapers can't carry jump missiles. They're too big to fit inside. Hell, they're longer than an entire Reaper."

"But they can be piggybacked on top," Nathan explained with a grin. "Thanks to some quick thinking by our chief engineer."

Josh looked over at Loki. "You can see why I've lost so many credits to this guy playing poker, right?"

"As soon as those inspectors depart, what say we go and retrieve that 'multi-jump' variant," Nathan instructed Josh, "*before* SilTek finds it and examines it more closely."

CHAPTER SEVEN

Josh and Loki exchanged a concerned glance as Nathan took his seat at the head of the conference table in the command briefing room.

"Did we do something wrong?" Josh asked sheepishly.

Nathan looked at Josh and squinted in confusion.

"It's just that you've never called us all into the briefing room before," Josh explained.

"No one did anything wrong," Nathan assured them. "In a few hours, the contest is scheduled to begin. Lieutenant Commander Nash and I will be heading down to the surface for the contest. However, I'd like each of you to be a part of this contest as well."

"Sweet!" Josh exclaimed.

Nathan held up his hand. "Now this is strictly voluntary," he insisted. "I'm not going to order any of you to do this."

"What's the big deal?" Josh wondered. "It's just a game."

"It's not a game, believe me," Nathan told him. "It's as real as it gets, without *actually* being real. If you get injured or die, it hurts...just like in the real world."

"He's not kidding," Jessica insisted. "It fucking sucked." Jessica's eyes widened. "Oops."

"Won't we be there anyway?" Loki asked. "I mean, our simulated selves?"

"Yes, but your *simulated* selves are not as good as each of *you* are," Nathan explained. "The SilTek simulation reads the player's mind and creates familiar characters for you to interact with based on what you'd *expect* them to do. So, in the simulation, your counterparts do what I would *expect* you to do. The problem is that each of you often do things before I even realize I need you to do them. That is something that the AI versions of you *cannot* do. I believe *that* to be one of our greatest tactical advantages, both in this simulation and in real battle. We have been through countless battles; all of us together, on the bridge of this ship. I don't care how realistic their simulations are, no AI can match that."

"I'm in," Josh announced without hesitation.

"Of course you are," Kaylah commented, rolling her eyes.

"Just how real is the *dying* part?" Naralena asked.

"Like I said, it sucks," Jessica reiterated. "If you die in the sim, pray it's an instantaneous death."

"Come on!" Josh exclaimed. "It's a *simulation*. We'll know that going in, right?"

"That doesn't make the pain any less real," Jessica insisted. "Trust me."

"So we have a little pain. Big deal. If one of us gets badly injured, someone just pops us in the head so that we die quickly. Game over, pain over."

"You really are heartless," Kaylah exclaimed.

"I'm just making a suggestion to shorten anyone's suffering," Josh insisted.

Kaylah looked at Nathan. "Just promise me that if Josh gets badly injured, I'll be the one who 'pops him in the head.'"

"I said I was sorry," Josh grumbled, half under his breath.

"I'm in," Loki decided.

"Me too," Naralena agreed.

"I'm in," Kaylah added, "as long as I get to kill Josh."

Loki leaned in to Josh. "*What did you do?*"

"*I'll tell you later*," Josh whispered.

"I assume I'll be staying behind," Cameron surmised.

"As much as I'd like you there as well, someone has to remain in command, and since I'm taking the starting line with me, we can't afford to have a junior officer at the *actual* helm if a *real* crisis comes up."

"You said this was voluntary, right?" Jessica asked.

"Correct," Nathan replied.

"I'd like to volunteer to stay on board with Cam," Jessica joked.

"Very well," Nathan said, placing his hands on the table. "We depart in two hours. Everyone is dismissed...except for Josh and Loki."

Josh's face contorted as he shared another glance with Loki.

Once everyone had gone, Nathan took a breath, letting it out with a sigh. "I'm going to be asking you both to do some maneuvers with the Aurora that will seem—a bit unorthodox. Hell, they're going to seem downright crazy, to be honest. However, I *have* discussed them with our AI, and she assures me that, *while dangerous*, they *are* physically possible."

"Uh, it's... a... *simulation*," Josh reminded him.

"If the ship comes apart in the simulation and we all die, it will hurt," Nathan reminded him back.

"Why are you telling us this ahead of time?" Loki wondered.

"The SilTek simulation AIs are not only able to read your minds; they can also sense your emotions. They'll analyze the maneuver and come to the same conclusion as our AI did, that the maneuvers are possible. However, the more the two of *you believe* the maneuvers are possible, the more the *simulation* AIs will believe it, and the less simulated damage they'll inflict on us."

"No problem there," Josh insisted. "I *already* believe I can do anything behind the stick."

* * *

Nathan was the first to enter the simulation suite at SilTek's headquarters, followed by his bridge staff. The room was large, with at least twenty comfortable-looking recliners positioned around the perimeter, each with a side table. The lighting was subdued, with focus on each recliner. Several people were gathered at the control desk at the center of the room, awaiting their arrival.

"Holy crap," Josh exclaimed. "Talk about a sim-suite."

"Captain," Caitrin Bindi greeted as they approached the center of the room.

"Miss Bindi," Nathan replied. "General," he added, greeting General Pellot as well. "How's the jaw?"

"Healing nicely, thank you," the general replied.

"*Is that the guy he punched?*" Josh asked Jessica under his breath.

"*Shh,*" she shushed.

"We don't normally allow spectators during a simulated contest," Miss Bindi informed Nathan. "After all, there isn't really anything to see."

"They're not spectators," Nathan replied. "They're my bridge staff. They are integral to the operation of my ship, especially during combat."

"They are not necessary for this simulation," Miss Bindi argued. "The AI will simulate their behavior based on your expectations."

"Which is precisely why I insist on their participation. These people perform tasks that I'm normally not even aware of. They frequently *exceed* my expectations; therefore, it would not be a fair assessment of the Aurora's ability to overcome your defenses *without* their participation."

"I'm not sure..."

"He can have as many people to help him as he wishes," the general insisted. "It won't make any difference."

Miss Bindi looked to Inspector Wells and his android assistant. "Does the commission have any objections?"

"The rules do not limit the number of participants," the inspector explained, "as long as both parties agree."

"Very well," Miss Bindi agreed.

"Then let's get started," Nathan said.

"There is one other thing," Miss Bindi warned. "The wager."

"What about it?" Nathan countered.

"After careful analysis by multiple AIs, we believe the wager to be unbalanced."

"How so?"

"The amount of technology you will need to guarantee a victory against the Dusahn exceeds the profit potential of your long-range jump technology."

"Considering the number of undiscovered, human-inhabited worlds still out there, I find that conclusion suspect," Nathan argued.

"And you may be correct," Miss Bindi agreed. "However, we have no way of knowing just how many colonies *are* out there. Analysis of departure records from twenty-fourth century Earth indicates that fewer than a thousand ships departed during the bio-digital plague. Of those, less than half were properly equipped and had no better than a fifty-percent chance of establishing a successful settlement. When you take into account that less than half of all known settlements ever grew into thriving societies that would be potential markets for our products, the profit margins shrink."

"What about the worlds that spun off of colonies other than Earth?" Kaylah wondered.

"If you are referring to the core worlds of Earth, we have included them in our calculations," Miss Bindi assured them.

"Volon was not settled by ships from Earth," Naralena pointed out. "It was settled by a ship from Takara."

"As was Corinair," Jessica added.

"Even if you include such worlds, the wager is still unbalanced."

"What if we put a cap on how much tech we get for free?" Jessica suggested.

"Assuming you win," General Pellot reminded her.

"Assuming we win," Jessica sneered back.

"That, of course, would balance the wager," Miss Bindi agreed. "However, it would also greatly decrease your chances of achieving a victory over the Dusahn."

"We could pay for some of it," Jessica added.

"Again assuming you win," the general sneered back at her.

"Don't push me, pops," Jessica warned.

"Lieutenant Commander," Nathan scolded, holding up his hand to interrupt her. He turned his attention back to Miss Bindi. "You obviously have something in mind, or you would not have brought it up to begin with."

"We do," Miss Bindi confessed. "We know little about the current financial state of Earth, so we were forced to use a galactic average to assess your ship's value."

"No," Jessica insisted.

"You want me to bet my ship," Nathan concluded.

"No," Jessica repeated. "Nathan..."

Again Nathan held up his hand to cut her off.

"The Aurora against everything you need to defeat the Dusahn," Miss Bindi stated, as if to dangle the bait in front of him.

"*And* SilTek joins our alliance," Nathan added.

"*And* we join your alliance, assuming you win."

"This is bullshit," Jessica insisted.

"Captain, a moment," Kaylah asked.

"If you'll excuse us a moment," Nathan told Miss Bindi.

"Of course."

Nathan and his bridge staff moved to the far side of the room to confer.

"They're baiting you, Nathan," Jessica insisted. "Just like Bacca did."

"I'd have to agree with her, Cap'n," Josh agreed. "This whole thing is probably rigged, anyway. You can't bet the Aurora."

Nathan was not listening to them. Instead, he was interested in what his sensor officer had to say.

"We've done detailed scans every time we've been in orbit over SilTek," Kaylah began. "Most of them passive, of course, but we got *very* good *active* scans during the jump missile tests, when their automated defense systems mistook the test as an act of aggression."

"Nathan..." Jessica tried to interrupt.

"Jess, please," Nathan insisted.

"Captain, while their systems are quick to respond, probably quicker than anything we've yet seen, their missiles are slow at launch, taking nearly twenty seconds to reach their safe-jump altitude of about three hundred meters. That's *more* than enough time to detect them, calculate their trajectory..."

"And take evasive action," Nathan surmised. "I know, I read your scan reports."

"But they come out of their jump less than a kilometer away," Jessica warned, "which doesn't give us much time to shoot them down."

"Or to jump clear," Loki added.

"But *none* of their missiles have shown *any* signs of being able to alter course *after* coming out of their attack jump," Kaylah added. "In fact, they barely carry enough propellant to reach their jump altitude."

"But they have a shit-ton of them," Jessica argued.

"Yes they do," Kaylah agreed.

Nathan thought for a moment. "She's right, and they didn't change course in the first simulation, either."

"Probably because they wanted to look like they needed our help," Jessica argued. "They were testing *you*, remember?"

"Perhaps," Nathan replied, still thinking.

"Nathan, you *cannot* bet the Aurora," Jessica insisted. "If we lose her, we have nothing. The Dusahn will *never* be defeated."

"If we don't get the tech we need, the Dusahn still won't be beaten, and there's a pretty good chance we'll lose her anyway, and in a *real* battle." Nathan replied. "Even worse, the Dusahn will probably wipe out Rakuen, Neramese, *and* Orswella."

"Nathan..." she repeated.

Nathan ignored her, having made up his mind.

He turned and headed back to Miss Bindi and the others.

"He's crazy," Josh declared, grinning. "That's why I love him."

"You are *not* helping," Jessica snapped at Josh as she took off after Nathan.

"If you win," Nathan began, as he approached Miss Bindi again, "the Aurora *must* be used to protect the Rogen and Orswellan systems, until such time as they can protect themselves."

"Agreed," Miss Bindi replied, without hesitation.

"And anyone currently serving on the Aurora will be free to leave and will be provided safe passage to a destination of their choice," he added.

"Also agreed."

"And just to clarify, if *we* win, we get everything *we* think we need to defeat the Dusahn, *and* SilTek joins our alliance?"

"Agreed."

Jessica grabbed Nathan by the arm, pulling him around to face her. "You know, technically, I could place you under arrest and assume command."

"If we were still in the Earth Defense Force, yes," Nathan agreed. "But even then, you wouldn't."

"How can you be so sure?"

"Because you trust me," Nathan stated, "just like I trust you."

Jessica put both hands on his upper arms, looking him directly in the eyes. "Nathan, this is a bad idea."

Nathan put his hands on her arms as well. "I have an idea, Jess. I can beat them. You have to trust me on this."

Jessica stared into his eyes for what seemed

like an eternity. Never before had she seen such confidence in them.

"This is where we beat the Dusahn," Nathan continued. "Not a month from now in an *actual* battle, but *right here*, in *this* simulator. *That's* why I brought you all with me. You've *got* to trust me."

Jessica studied him, her brow furrowed. "You knew they were going to up the ante, didn't you?"

"I had a hunch," he admitted.

Jessica sighed. "If Cam was here, she'd tell you this was the craziest thing you've ever done."

"And she'd be right," Nathan agreed, "but that doesn't mean it's the *wrong* thing to do."

"I don't know," Jessica admitted.

"You came to me because you needed my leadership," Nathan told her. "You awakened my memories and ended my life as Connor Tuplo for situations *exactly* like this. To make the same *insane* types of decisions that allowed us to beat back the Jung and save Earth seven years ago. *This* is what I was *born* to do."

"You mean *reborn*, don't you?" Jessica said, lowering her hands and sighing again.

"Then you trust me?"

"With my life," Jessica replied. She took a deep breath and added, "let's go kick some SilTek AI butt, shall we?"

Nathan smiled broadly, then turned back around to face Miss Bindi. "We accept the wager."

Miss Bindi also smiled, albeit not as broadly.

General Pellot was grinning from ear to ear. "I'm going to enjoy commanding your ship."

"I punch much harder than he does," Jessica warned, "*and* I'm far more volatile."

"If you would all take your seats," Inspector Wells

instructed, gesturing toward the nearest simulation lounges.

"I don't believe this," Josh muttered to Loki as they moved toward the seats.

"Why?" Loki wondered. "This is the same kind of crazy stunt you would pull."

"Yeah, but I *am* crazy," Josh replied. "Are you sure about this, Cap'n?" he asked Nathan.

"Did you two get a chance to practice those maneuvers?" Nathan inquired as Josh and Loki took their seats.

"'Til the wee hours," Josh replied.

"Don't be fooled," Loki added. "That's how long it took us to *not* crash and burn at least one time."

"You'll both do fine," Nathan insisted as one of the android technicians strapped them in and placed the neuro-link headsets on them.

"Uh, why are we being strapped in?" Josh wondered.

"So that you do not fall out of your chair," the android technician explained as he secured Josh's wrists to the armrests.

"Why the wrist restraints?"

"So that you do not inadvertently remove your neuro-link headset."

"Right," Josh replied.

Nathan turned to Naralena and Kaylah as they also took their places on their respective simulation lounges.

"This should be interesting," Naralena said, trying to be confident.

Nathan smiled, then looked at Kaylah.

"You've got this, Captain," Kaylah assured him.

"Thanks."

Nathan took a deep breath and headed for his

seat next to Jessica. He sat calmly as the android technician strapped him in and placed the headset on him, watching as General Pellot was strapped in on the opposite side of the room.

"Ladies and gentlemen," Inspector Wells began. "The simulation you are about to enter is a full-depth, virtual reality. If you are injured, you will feel pain. If you die, you will feel it. However, death will end the simulation for you. Since this is a high-stakes contest, there are no premature exit rights. You are in the simulation until your death, or until the contest has been concluded, and a victor has been declared. The victory conditions are the destruction of the Aurora, or the destruction of SilTek's defense network." The inspector paused for a moment to let his words sink in. "General Pellot, your participation in the simulation will not begin until the Aurora is detected by SilTek's defense detection grid. Your starting point will be in your office at SilTek defense command."

"Understood," the general replied.

"Captain Scott, your simulation will start with you and your crew at your respective stations, and your ship at a position twenty light years outside of SilTek's detection grid. Is this acceptable?"

"It is," Nathan replied.

The inspector looked to the android technician sitting at the central control station, receiving a nod of confirmation. "Let the contest begin."

Jessica turned her head slightly toward Nathan in the next chair and whispered, "If we lose, Cameron is going to kill you."

Nathan felt his body suddenly become limp as his vision faded quickly to black. A moment later, he found himself in his command chair on the bridge of the Aurora. He looked to his left, spotting Kaylah, who was holding up her hands and turning them over as she examined them.

"This...is fucking...insane," Josh exclaimed, rotating in his chair to look at Nathan. "I mean, you said it was realistic and all, but holy crap!" He turned to Loki and pinched him.

"What the hell?" Loki yelped, recoiling from the pinch.

"Did it hurt?"

"Yes, it hurt!"

"Do me!"

"Don't be stupid."

"This is incredible," Kaylah exclaimed. "The amount of computational power that must be required to accomplish this level of realism is..."

"Everyone, check your consoles and displays," Nathan instructed. "Make sure everything is as you expect it."

"How do they do this?" Naralena wondered aloud from the comm-station at the back of the bridge.

"Their system reads our minds and uses our memories to create what we expect to see and hear, just as it would in reality," Jessica explained.

"Man, the fun you could have in such a realistic sim," Josh declared. "Hey, can you..."

"Keep your mind on task, Josh," Nathan warned. "Everyone, remember what I told you on the way down."

"Right."

"Just forget that this is a simulation and do your jobs," Nathan insisted. "Loki, what's our position?"

Loki studied his displays. "Twenty-seven light years from SilTek. Galactic coordinates of one seven four by forty-two, by two twenty. So basically, as if we were headed toward SilTek from the Rogen system and had just come out of a jump prior to arrival."

"Very well," Nathan replied. "Kaylah, send a recon drone to just outside of SilTek's defense grid and collect some of the planet's old light. We need to know which side is facing us at the moment."

"Aye, sir."

"How are we looking, Jess?" Nathan asked.

"I'm not finding anything out of line," Jessica reported as she carefully examined her tactical console. "The missile inventory is down by two, but we knew they would do that."

"Helm?"

"I'm good too," Josh assured him.

"Me too, Captain," Loki added.

"Sensors look normal," Kaylah reported.

"Comms are normal," Naralena commented.

Nathan took a breath. "Where is the XO?"

"Her comm-track shows her in her quarters," Naralena replied. "Or the *simulated* version of her, anyway."

"How much jump energy do we have?" Nathan asked Loki.

"Full charge across the board."

"That's surprising," Jessica decided. "It wouldn't be at full charge if this was real."

"They probably just decided it wasn't worth keeping Pellot in the sim for several hours in case we decided to build up a full charge before attacking," Nathan explained.

"How generous of them," Jessica commented.

"Recon drone is back," Kaylah reported. "SilTek headquarters is currently facing us, and it appears to be approximately zero nine hundred local time."

"They're *expecting* us to attack their headquarters first," Jessica commented.

Nathan tapped his comm-set. "Flight, Captain. I need the first flight of Eagles ready to snap-launch. I also need four Reapers loaded with torpedo cannons on the forward flight apron and ready for launch."

"*Four Reapers spitting fire, aye,*" the flight operations officer confirmed over his comm-set.

"I'm assuming you have a plan," Jessica stated.

"We take out their primary command and control, first," Nathan replied.

"Do we even know where that is?" Jessica wondered.

"SilTek is big on centralization of control," Nathan explained, "and their headquarters had many levels below the surface. I'm betting their defense command is located there."

"They'll have an off-site backup," Jessica warned.

"And when it kicks in, the jump in comms traffic should show up on sensors," Kaylah added.

"What about their spaceborne control stations?" Jessica asked.

"I'm betting they're not going to send missiles *toward* their own world," Nathan replied. "At least not many of them. Besides, I don't plan on staying in any one place more than ten to twenty seconds at a time or jumping to the same point twice."

"That's a lot of jump plotting," Kaylah warned.

"Loki can handle it," Nathan assured her.

Loki exchanged a concerned glance with Josh.

"Jess, remind me of our missile inventory," Nathan asked.

"Seventy-eight missiles total," she replied. "Thirty single-jump shield busters, half with nukes, half with conventional warheads. Thirty multi-jump shield busters, also loaded half and half. The remaining eighteen in the outboard starboard chute are standard jump missiles without warheads loaded, so we can load them on the fly as needed."

"What's our unloaded warhead count and type?"

"Twenty conventional, ten nukes, and two antimatter warheads that we cobbled together from the few reactor cores that survived our attack on the Orswellan ships."

"Flight reports Reapers are ready for action," Naralena reported from the comm-station.

"Very well," Nathan said. He took a deep breath and let it out. "Let's get this over with. General quarters."

"General quarters, aye," Naralena replied.

The bridge trim lighting changed to red as the alert klaxon sounded.

Nathan sat patiently as his simulated crew took action, going to their stations. In reality, he knew the simulation was just waiting an appropriate amount of time based on the countless readiness reports and action drills stored in the Aurora's database. He was a bit surprised that SilTek's simulation AIs had even included the background comms chatter that he always heard as department heads all over the ship reported their readiness to his communications officer.

"If Josh is right," Nathan began, rising from his command chair and strolling to starboard, "they'll be expecting us to use our multi-jump missiles to attack their main defenses from unexpected angles, hoping that their defenses will be caught off guard." Nathan stepped up to the next level, coming alongside the tactical station. "So that's precisely what we're going to do."

"Then you expect them to cheat," Jessica surmised.

"I do."

"And still you bet the ship," she muttered.

"Four multi-jumps, each of them targeting the primary defense points around SilTek's headquarters," Nathan instructed. "Immediately afterwards, I want shield busters on all six inner system control points, followed by single-jump conventionals to finish them off."

"I thought you didn't think they would send missiles toward their own planet," Jessica reminded him.

"I'd prefer not to have to worry about jumping around the inner system during all of this," Nathan explained as he slowly approached the tactical station. He paused to whisper something in Jessica's ear.

Jessica smiled. "Aye, sir. Entering targeting data now."

Nathan continued his strolling, passing behind Jessica and in front of Naralena as he crossed to the port side of the bridge. "Naralena, instruct flight to send the Reapers after any surface missile launchers whose shields we take out but are still operational."

"Understood," Naralena replied, a puzzled look on her face. She had never seen Nathan take a casual stroll around the bridge, especially moments before an attack.

"Once we take out the inner control points and their primary close-in defenses, we'll simply jump around, launching shield busters at their surface launchers as we take out the ones without working shields," Nathan continued, stepping down to the command chair level along the port side of the bridge. "I'll be depending on you to feed easy targets to combat, Kaylah," he added, as he passed behind her.

"Yes, sir," Kaylah replied.

"All weapons are fully charged and ready," Jessica reported. "Threat board is clear."

"All departments report general quarters," Naralena added. "XO is in combat; chief of the boat is in damage control."

Nathan stepped back up to his command chair, facing forward again. "Very well. Helm, attack sequence Scott Alpha One. Execute when ready."

"Scott Alpha One, aye," Loki replied, sharing another look with Josh, who of course was smiling like an idiot.

"Let the games begin," Josh declared, mimicking Inspector Wells.

Loki entered a series of commands into his console, then reported, "Scott Alpha One, loaded and ready. We'll need two set-up jumps to get to final."

"Show me what you can do, gentlemen," Nathan instructed, seating himself in his command chair.

"Executing first set-up jump," Loki reported before the blue-white jump flash washed over the ship.

"Turning to next jump heading," Josh announced as he began a quick turn to port.

Kaylah turned around, looking at everyone. "Am I the only one who doesn't know what Scott Alpha One is?"

Nathan did not react.

Josh and Loki were busy.

Jessica smiled.

Naralena shrugged.

Kaylah gave up and turned back to face her console.

"Turn complete," Josh reported.

"Executing second set-up jump," Loki announced as the blue-white jump flash washed over the bridge again.

"Executing turn and roll maneuver for final attack jump," Josh reported, beginning another turn to port.

"Cancel Scott Alpha One," Nathan instructed calmly. "Execute Scott Alpha Four instead."

"Scott Alpha *Four*, aye," Loki replied.

"Load four single-jump shield busters. Dealer's choice on targets. Weapons free as soon as we jump in," Nathan added.

"Four shield busters; dealer's choice; weapons free, aye," Jessica replied.

"Scott Alpha Four, ready," Loki reported.

Nathan pressed the ship-wide button on the comm-panel on his right armrest. "All hands, brace for impact," he called over the loudspeakers. "Execute Scott Alpha Four," he instructed Loki.

"Jumping in three......two......one...

Again the jump flash washed over the bridge. The entire ship lurched as it found itself plowing through the atmosphere of SilTek instead of the vacuum of space. The sudden deceleration was almost more than the ship's inertial dampeners could handle, and Nathan felt himself being pushed forward nearly out of his chair. Had he not been bracing himself, he'd be sprawled across the helm right now.

At the same time, the main view screen shifted from the starry blackness of space to the bright day on SilTek, illuminating the bridge with sunlight. The surface of the planet rose quickly from the bottom of the view screen as the Aurora fell at an alarming rate.

"Holy shit!" Josh exclaimed, as the ship bridge shook violently. "Anyone see where my teeth landed?!"

The Aurora creaked and groaned as her structure resisted the external forces threatening to break apart a ship not designed for atmospheric flight. Nathan clutched the sides of his armrests, confident that his ship could take the pressure.

"Three thousand meters and falling fast!" Loki warned. "Forward speed is dropping as well!"

"All ventral thrusters at full power!" Josh added. "Not that it's doing much!"

"Engineering reports structural integrity down twenty percent!" Naralena announced.

"Shield strength is falling fast!" Kaylah warned, holding onto her console to steady herself. "External hull temperatures are climbing rapidly!"

"Targets acquired!" Jessica reported.

"Damn!" Josh exclaimed. "She's flying like a brick! Lok! Can you put some more *umph* into the ventral thrusters or something? I need more nose up or we're headed for a terminal dive!"

"We don't *have* any more *umph!*" Loki replied.

"We're being targeted!" Kaylah warned.

"Launch four!" Nathan ordered.

"Multiple defense turrets and missile launchers are locking onto us!" Kaylah added.

"Launching four!" Jessica replied, pressing the missile launch button.

Nathan focused his attention on the lower left corner of the main view screen, at the point in the Aurora's hull where the jump missiles would exit their launch tubes. All he saw were blue-white flashes of light, the missiles jumping just as they crossed the departure threshold.

"Missiles away!" Jessica announced, holding on to the tactical console with her left hand while she entered commands with her right.

"Standard missile with a nuke!" Nathan ordered. "Target their missile plant!"

"Ten seconds to impact!" Loki warned.

Four blue-white flashes appeared on the main view screen just ahead, over one of SilTek's automated industrial areas. A split second later, there were four massive explosions on the surface of SilTek as all four jump missile launchers protecting the production facility were wiped from existence.

"Five seconds!" Loki warned.

"Missile ready!" Jessica announced at the same time.

"Launch the nuke!" Nathan ordered. "Jump us out of here!"

"Nuke is away!" Jessica replied.

"Jumping!" Loki added as the jump flash washed over them.

The violent shaking stopped.

Josh felt relief wash over him. He looked at Loki and giggled. "That was different."

"Scott Alpha Two," Nathan ordered without hesitation.

"Scott Alpha Two, aye," Loki replied.

"Turning to new jump heading," Josh reported.

"Please tell me we're not doing *that* again," Kaylah begged.

"Four more standard busters," Nathan instructed Jessica.

"Loading four more shield busters," Jessica acknowledged.

"I need damage assessments," Nathan reminded his sensor officer.

Kaylah quickly responded. "All of SilTek's defenses are lit up. The missile plant is completely destroyed. The nuke took out everything in the area, including three neighboring districts. Estimate civilian casualties in the tens of thousands."

"Understood," Nathan replied calmly.

"On course for Scott Alpha Two," Josh reported.

"Jess, load four more shield busters. Set their targets as the primary defenses around the Sugali fighter plant. If they've got fighters, they've got pilots for them."

"Loading four more busters," Jessica replied.

"As soon as those are away, get ready to pound everything in sight when we jump back in," Nathan added. "I don't want a single defense turret left standing."

"I've got the location of every defense turret from Kaylah's scans," Jessica assured him. "I can assign the targets before we even jump in, but they'll be expecting us," she added, assigning targets to the Aurora's ventral gun turrets.

"But they won't know where," Nathan replied.

Nathan tapped his comm-set. "Flight, Captain. Eagles and Reapers will have twenty seconds to launch once we jump back into the atmosphere. Remind them to use full power out the door and to expect unstable air as soon as they cross the threshold."

"*They're ready, Captain,*" the flight control officer assured him.

"Missiles are ready," Jessica reported.

"Helm, execute Scott Alpha Two," Nathan ordered.

"Executing Scott Alpha Two," Loki announced

as the jump flash washed over the bridge again. "At launch position."

"Launch missiles," Nathan instructed.

"Launching four," Jessica replied. "Missiles away."

"Missiles have jumped," Kaylah confirmed.

"Execute attack jump Scott Alpha Two," Nathan instructed, pressing the all-call button again. "All hands, brace for impact," he repeated calmly, grasping his armrests tightly.

"Executing Scott Alpha Two attack jump," Loki replied.

"I *love* this shit," Josh said, only half under his breath.

"You would," Loki replied as the jump flash washed over the bridge once more.

Again the ship lurched due to the sudden deceleration, and the bridge was bathed in sunlight.

"Fuck!" Josh exclaimed, nearly falling out of his seat.

"Green deck!" Nathan called over his comm-set. "Launch all Eagles and Reapers!"

"Twenty-nine hundred meters and falling like a rock!" Loki warned.

"Eagles and Reapers are launching," Naralena announced.

"All shields over the fighter base are down!" Kaylah reported. "Two of the six missile launchers are also down! Twelve turrets are locking onto us!"

"I've got 'em!" Jessica announced as she activated the Aurora's automated ventral plasma cannon turrets.

"Her nose is falling," Josh warned, fighting with his flight control stick as he struggled to keep the kilometer-and-a-half-long starship from going into a nosedive.

"Maybe you should pitch up a little *before* we jump!" Loki exclaimed.

"I did!"

"Firing all turrets," Jessica reported.

"Structural integrity down to sixty-four percent!" Naralena announced. "Forward dorsal hull integrity has dropped by *forty-eight* percent!"

"Shields are down to sixty percent!" Kaylah warned as the ship shook violently.

"Ten seconds to impact!" Loki warned.

"Eagles and Reapers are away!" Naralena reported.

"Mister Sheehan," Nathan began.

"Jumping!" Loki replied, not waiting for the entire order to come out of his captain's mouth.

The ship calmed once again, allowing Nathan to breathe a sigh of relief. "How many of them did you get?" he asked Jessica.

"All but maybe two," she replied. "We were firing when we jumped, but I don't know if we took the last two out or not."

"That will have to do," Nathan replied. "Prepare to launch six shield buster, multi-jump missiles. Targets will be all six inner system defense control points."

"I was wondering when you were going to get to those," Jessica replied.

"Flight ops reports only six Sugali fighters made it off the ground," Naralena announced. "Eagles already have air superiority over the fighter base."

"Tell them they're welcome," Jessica bragged.

"As soon as those are away, set up for a three-pronged, time-on-target attack, using two waves of multi-jump conventionals, and one of single-jump conventionals."

"Scott Alpha One?" Jessica asked.

"Scott Alpha One," Nathan confirmed, "but put a jump delay of one minute on the six missiles targeting the inner system defense control points. I need them to see our time-on-target attack being launched."

"Angles on the TOT?"

"West, east, and north," Nathan replied.

"Got it."

"Uh, that's going to leave us coming straight down the valley toward SilTek HQ, going south to north," Loki warned. "The mountains at the north end of that valley are going to cut into our fall time by about..." Loki paused to check his calculations before continuing. "*Twelve seconds*, minimum."

"Double our entry altitude," Nathan instructed.

"That will put us in their missile attack sphere," Jessica warned, "and without enough distance to intercept with point-defenses."

Nathan turned to his left toward his sensor officer. "What's our shield strength?"

"Fifty-seven percent," Kaylah replied. "The next jump into the atmosphere will knock them down another twenty percent."

"That'll only protect us against two, maybe three missile impacts," Jessica warned.

"How long to get our shields back up to full strength?" Nathan asked.

"At least ten minutes," Kaylah replied.

"We'll have a hundred missiles coming at us from all directions by then," Jessica commented.

"Then let's hope at least some of our TOT missiles find their targets," Nathan commented. "Have two nukes on the rails and ready to launch when we jump in."

"Two?" Jessica questioned. "A little much, don't you think?"

"You want to do Scott Alpha One a second time?"

"We don't have enough missiles to do it a second time," Jessica replied as she finished entering the attack sequence into the missile control system.

"Coming up on the first launch point," Loki warned.

"Four multi-jump missiles with conventional warheads on the rails, ready to launch; two more in the quick queue," Jessica reported.

"Jump us to the first launch point," Nathan told Loki.

"Aye, sir."

The jump flash washed over the bridge.

"Launch the first wave," Nathan ordered.

"Launching first four," Jessica replied, pressing the launch button. "Four away, two loading."

"Twenty seconds to our turn," Loki warned.

"Missiles will be loaded in ten," Jessica added.

"We are definitely being scanned," Kaylah announced. "Inner system defense network is targeting us."

"Launching last two," Jessica announced. "Two away."

"Eight inbound missiles!" Kaylah reported urgently.

"Turning!" Josh announced.

"Five seconds to impact!"

"Firing point-defenses!"

"Screw the turn!" Nathan ordered. "Escape jump!"

"Jumping!" Loki replied, the order barely out of Nathan's mouth.

Again the blue-white flash washed over the bridge.

"Finish your turn and recalculate," Nathan instructed. "Jess..."

"Loading the first wave of TOT missiles," she assured him. "I'll be ready when you are."

"Recalculating," Loki announced.

"Turning," Josh added.

"Another wave!" Kaylah warned. "Six to starboard! Five seconds!"

"Firing point-defenses!" Jessica repeated.

"Four..."

"Turn complete!" Josh reported.

"Three..."

"Jump ready!" Loki added.

"Two..."

"Jump!"

The jump flash washed over the bridge. A split second later, Jessica pushed the launch button, sending the first wave of multi-jump missiles racing down the launch rails. "Four away!" she reported. "Loading the next wave."

"Twelve missiles inbound!" Kaylah reported. "First ones will hit in ten seconds!"

"Firing point-defenses," Jessica reported. "Next wave will be ready to launch in five seconds,"

"It's going to be close," Loki warned.

"Four..."

"Don't wait for my command," Nathan told Loki.

"Three..."

"Launching four!" Jessica reported.

"Two..."

"Missiles away!"

"Jumping!" Loki reported, as the jump flash washed over the bridge again.

"Hold your turn!" Nathan instructed. "Jump us ahead ten light years!"

"Ten light year escape jump, aye!" Loki replied.

"*Eighteen* inbound!" Kaylah warned. "Five seconds!"

"Damn!" Jessica exclaimed. "How many do they have?"

"Four..."

"Any time, Mister Sheehan," Nathan urged.

"Three..."

"Jumping!" Loki announced as the jump flash washed over them.

"*Now* you can execute your turn," Nathan instructed Josh.

"Turning."

"As soon as the turn is finished, we'll jump twenty light years across, then turn back to the attack leg," Nathan explained.

"Recalculating," Loki acknowledged.

"Final wave is loaded," Jessica announced. "Four single-jump conventionals on the rails, and two nukes in the quick queue."

"Have every turret and every point-defense ready," Nathan urged. "This one's going to be hairy."

"Maybe that general had good reason to be confident," Kaylah commented.

"Maybe so," Nathan agreed.

"I still think he's just an ass," Jessica chimed in as she finished setting up the next wave of missiles. "First wave jump delay will expire in twenty seconds," she added.

"Finishing our turn now," Josh reported.

"Jump to the far side recalculated and ready," Loki added.

"Jump us across and then execute your turn to final attack leg," Nathan instructed.

"Jumping across," Loki acknowledged.

"Targets assigned, missiles ready to launch," Jessica reported before the jump flash.

"Executing turn to final attack leg," Josh announced.

"So far, I'd say we're doing well," Nathan opined.

"We've barely made a dent in their defenses," Jessica reminded him.

"But we haven't suffered any damage yet."

"There's still time."

"Delayed wave should be jumping now," Kaylah reported.

"Let's hope that provides us with a little breathing room while maneuvering in the system," Nathan commented.

"Don't count on it," Jessica warned.

"On course for Scott Alpha One attack run," Josh announced, as he completed his turn.

"Twenty seconds to time-on-target attack," Jessica reported.

"Launch the final four and quick-load the nukes," Nathan instructed.

"Launching four missiles," Jessica acknowledged. "Missiles away. Loading nukes."

Nathan glanced at the time-on-target timer displayed in the tactical window on the lower right side of the main view screen.

"Nukes loaded," Jessica announced. "TOT in five..."

"Prepare for attack jump," Nathan instructed Loki.

"Four..."

"Jump ready," Loki assured him.

"Three..."

Josh braced himself with his left hand, his right palm against the base of the flight control stick, ready to grab it the moment they entered the atmosphere.

"Two..." Jessica continued. "One......all missiles jumping."

Four blue-white flashes appeared on the main view screen a few kilometers ahead of them as their last four missiles jumped ahead.

Nathan counted three seconds in his head as he pressed the all-call button. "All hands, brace for impact." He switched off the all-call and added, "Execute attack jump."

"Jumping," Loki acknowledged.

Again the ship lurched as atmospheric drag suddenly reduced her speed. Nathan held on tightly as the bridge filled with daylight, bracing himself against the sudden deceleration.

"Six thousand meters and falling!" Loki yelled over the creaking and groaning. "Twenty-nine hundred meters to minimum jump altitude!"

The forward view screen was filled with at least eight massive explosions on the planet's surface, their initial fireballs spreading out and billowing upward as they consumed the structures within their blast radius.

"Shields at fifty percent and falling!" Kaylah reported. "At least half of SilTek HQ's defenses are still operating! Main shield over HQ is down to twenty percent, but still up!"

"Launch the nukes," Nathan ordered. "Fire all turrets."

"Launching two!" Jessica replied, pressing the launch button. "Firing all ventral plasma cannon turrets!"

Two quick, blue-white flashes in the lower corners of the main view screen reported that their missiles had jumped the moment they reached their exits through the Aurora's hull.

"Missiles away!"

Two more flashes appeared a few kilometers ahead as the missiles arrived at their targets, followed by blinding white nuclear detonations.

"I sure as fuck hope we're not going to have to fly through that!" Josh exclaimed after glancing up and witnessing the rising mushroom clouds ahead.

"Shields down to forty-five percent!" Kaylah warned.

"Ten seconds to minimum escape jump altitude!" Loki warned.

"Multiple missile launches!" Kaylah warned. "Impacts in three..."

"That's it!" Nathan exclaimed.

"Two..."

"Get us out of here!"

"One..."

"Jumping!" Loki reported.

Again the Aurora returned to her natural environment of the vacuum of space, and the violent rocking that had threatened to tear her apart stopped.

"Second jump," Nathan immediately ordered. "Ten light years, then come about hard."

"Jumping forward ten light years," Loki acknowledged.

"Kaylah, prep seven recon drones," Nathan instructed as the bridge momentarily filled with blue-white light.

"Coming about," Josh announced.

"One for SilTek HQ, the rest for the inner system defense control points," Nathan continued.

"I'm on it," Kaylah replied.

"Set them for quick scan and return to this position," Nathan added.

"Understood."

"*Captain, Cheng,*" Vladimir called over Nathan's comm-set. "*We've lost twenty percent of our outer hull, and the structural integrity of our main truss is down to thirty percent! I would not advise another jump into the atmosphere!*"

"No promises," Nathan replied, ending the conversation before his engineer could respond. "Jess, load four more nukes. We'll pick our targets after we get the scans from the recon drones."

Jessica shook her head as she loaded the nukes. "I'd hate to be living on *that* world after all this."

"It's a simulation," Nathan reminded her.

"Thankfully," Jessica replied.

"Turn complete," Josh reported.

"Loading four more nukes," Jessica acknowledged.

"Recon drones are ready," Kaylah announced.

"Launch the drones," Nathan instructed.

"Launching recon drones."

"Comms, prepare a comm-drone to jump into low orbit over the fighter plant to broadcast a message to our Eagles and Reapers."

"Aye, sir," Naralena acknowledged. "Message?"

"I'll let you know as soon as our recon drones return," Nathan replied.

Nathan paused a moment, enjoying the brief respite as they awaited the return of their recon drones.

"What's next?" Jessica wondered.

"I'm thinking infrastructure," Nathan replied.

"We only win if we defeat their defenses," Jessica reminded him, "not take out their toilets."

"I know," Nathan assured her. "But they've got defenses around infrastructure as well."

"Respectfully recommend we finish off all command and control first," Jessica suggested.

"Understood," Nathan replied, thrown off by her use of the word 'respectfully'. For a moment, he wondered if it was really Jessica or a simulation of her.

"Recon drone from SilTek has returned," Kaylah announced. "HQ is still standing, as is their C and C alternate. HQ still has ten percent main shield strength; alternate has twenty."

"They don't joke around when it comes to their shields, do they," Jessica commented. "All missiles are loaded and ready. You still want to target infrastructure?"

"Yes," Nathan replied. "Particularly their main power station to the west of HQ."

"That shield is at full strength," Kaylah warned. "It's going to take more than a few nukes to bring it down."

"Jess, target whatever infrastructure you like, but put all four on a thirty-second jump delay. I want to follow up with two more missiles. One for HQ, and one for that power plant."

"Nukes again?" Jessica surmised.

"For HQ, yes," Nathan replied, "but let's send an antimatter warhead to the power plant. I want the thing gone, along with all of its defenses."

"An antimatter warhead?" Jessica confirmed.

"That's correct."

Kaylah turned around to face Nathan. "I know it's a simulation and all, but an antimatter warhead will not only take out the power plant and all its defenses, but it will also take a sizable chunk out of the planet. I'm talking a medium-sized city, here."

"That'll work," Nathan replied calmly.

Kaylah shrugged, turning back around.

Nathan thought for a moment, then asked, "What will that do to the stability of the planet?"

Kaylah turned back again. "One? Not much... unless it opens up a massive underground pocket of magma or something."

"SilTek is still volcanically active, right?"

"Yes," Kaylah replied. "In fact, they still have quite a few of their original thermal power plants in operation."

"Jess, change the nuke for SilTek's HQ to a second antimatter warhead. Target the same point as the first, detonate on impact. Set it for a thirty-second jump delay. Also load two more single-jump nukes. After all four are away, we'll reload with four more."

"Are you *trying* to crack the planet open?" Jessica wondered as she input the change in missile loads.

"It *would* defeat their defenses," Nathan commented, grinning.

"I am *so* glad this is just a simulation," Kaylah said to herself, turning back to face her console.

"We will have used more than half our nukes by then," Jessica commented.

"The other recon drones are returning," Kaylah announced. "All six inner system defense control points have been destroyed."

"Warhead has been changed," Jessica updated. "Loading two more nukes. Targets?"

"Same as the antimatter warheads. Have them jump in at ground level and set to detonate on impact."

Jessica shook her head. Simulation or not, this felt brutal.

"We are on course for the next attack run," Loki reported. "Jump plot?"

"Hold course for now," Nathan replied.

"Holding course and speed," Josh acknowledged.

"Comms, message for all Reapers and Eagles: Retreat to rally point and await further instructions. Reply when clear of SilTek."

"Message loaded," Naralena replied.

"Launch the comm-drone."

"Comm-drone away."

"So no more jumping into the atmosphere?" Jessica surmised.

"Don't want to give our simulated Vladimir a heart attack," Nathan replied.

"Two nukes and two antimatter missiles are on the rails and ready to launch," Jessica reported.

"*Captain, if I may?*" the Aurora's AI asked.

"Yes, Aurora?" Nathan replied.

"*I believe it is unnecessary to use your antimatter weapons. I have calculated that you can destroy SilTek's headquarters and their secondary command and control bunker, thereby defeating their defenses and achieving a victory condition, using your nuclear weapons alone. It is not necessary to destroy the entire planet.*"

"It's a simulation," Nathan reminded her.

"*I am simply offering a less drastic approach,*" Aurora replied.

"One that will be less effective in the grand scheme of things," Nathan pointed out.

"*I'm afraid I do not understand,*" Aurora admitted.

"You don't have to."

Jessica exchanged glances with Kaylah as she went about her tasks at the tactical console.

"New contact," Kaylah reported. "Comm-drone."

"Message from Commander Verbeek, Captain," Naralena announced. "All Eagles and Reapers are at the rally point."

"Very well," Nathan replied. "Mister Sheehan, jump us back into the SilTek system at a distance of one five hundred thousand kilometers. Standard orbital approach speed."

"Not combat speed?" Loki verified.

"That is correct."

"They've still got missile launchers operating on the surface," Jessica warned.

"They won't be operating for long," Nathan assured her.

"Jump plotted and ready," Loki reported.

"Stand by on the antimatter weapons," Nathan instructed. "Once they're away, reload their rails with nukes."

"Already in the queue," Jessica assured him.

"Take us in, Mister Sheehan," Nathan ordered.

"Jumping in three......two......one."

The blue-white jump flash washed over the bridge, and the image of the planet SilTek appeared at the center of the main view screen. At their current distance, the planet filled only a fraction of the forward section of the massive, semi-spherical screen, but it was growing with each passing second as the ship closed the distance between them.

"Launch the antimatter missiles," Nathan ordered calmly.

"Launching two," Jessica replied, taking a deep breath and pressing the launch button. The process was no different than launching any other missile, but even though it was just a simulation, pressing that button felt far more ominous than usual.

Two green launch confirmation lights appeared on the missile control console. "Missiles away," she reported. "Loading two more nukes."

Nathan watched the main view screen as the first missile jumped away and the second one coasted toward the approaching planet. A split second later, there was a small flash of light on the surface of the planet. It seemed harmless enough from so far away, but the mere fact that it was visible at this distance was frightening.

"*SilTek is attempting to access my core,*" Aurora reported. "*I have sent a false confirmation signal back to them as planned.*"

"Understood."

"Second antimatter weapon jumping in three...... two......one..." Jessica reported.

A small blue-white jump flash appeared directly ahead of them, and a second later, another white light in the exact same spot on the surface of the distant planet.

"Launch all four nukes," Nathan instructed. "Five-second spacing, reload as they leave."

"Launching four; five-second intervals," Jessica acknowledged. "First missile is away."

"New contacts," Kaylah reported. "Six missiles just jumped in. Twenty seconds to impact."

"Point-defenses are firing," Jessica announced. "Second missile is away."

"As soon as the last missile launches, turn twenty degrees to starboard and jump ahead to two hundred thousand kilometers," Nathan instructed.

"Understood," Josh replied.

"Third missile is away," Jessica reported. "Four

inbounds intercepted, two coming. Fourth missile away."

"Turning to starboard," Josh reported.

"Five seconds to impact," Kaylah warned. "Four..."

"Fourth missile is away!" Jessica announced.

"Jump us ahead, Mister Sheehan," Nathan instructed.

"Three..."

"Jumping."

"Two..."

After the blue-white jump flash, Nathan switched the main view screen to angle to port, just in time to see the planet come apart. There was no massive explosion. The planet simply began to separate into several large sections, each of them cleaved apart by the force of the pressurized gases trapped within her core for millions of years. What was once a perfect sphere became oddly distorted until, finally, Nathan could make out at least a dozen distinctly separate pieces.

"Now *that's* something you don't see every day," Josh exclaimed.

"Oh my God," Kaylah exclaimed. "How inappropriate can you get?"

"It's a simulation!" Josh defended.

At that moment, everything went black.

* * *

Nathan opened his eyes and found himself back in the simulation room with the android technician removing his neuro interface headgear.

"You cheated!" General Pellot exclaimed as his android technician removed his restraints.

"I did nothing of the sort," Nathan defended calmly.

"The challenge was to defeat our defenses, not destroy the entire planet!"

"And in doing so, we *did* defeat your defenses," Nathan insisted as his restraints were removed.

"There is no value in destroying an opponent's entire world," the general insisted.

"The general does make sense," Inspector Wells agreed. "The purpose of the contest was to pit the Aurora against the defenses of SilTek."

"You said the victory condition was the destruction of SilTek's defenses," Nathan reminded him. "We fulfilled that condition."

"You may as well have hurled an asteroid at us!" the general argued angrily.

Nathan was beginning to get annoyed. "Apparently you missed the entire point of the simulation," he told the general. "To demonstrate just how vulnerable your world is."

"I repeat, there is *nothing* to be gained by destroying your opponent's entire world!"

"Except to put the fear of a similar fate in the minds of all those you subjugate," Jessica added.

"Was *that* your purpose?" Miss Bindi wondered. "To show us what happens to those who oppose your alliance?"

"It is not *us* you should fear, Miss Bindi," Nathan stated calmly. "I think you know that." He turned back toward the general as both men rose from their respective simulation loungers. "Both the Dusahn *and* the Jung *regularly* glass *entire worlds* just to demonstrate what happens to those who oppose them. They even tried to destroy Earth when we first drove them from our world. When the Dusahn come—and trust me, should we fail to defeat them, they *will* come—they won't come at you with a single ship. They'll bring an entire battle group. At that point, all the missiles in the world will not save you. You'll have to choose between extinction and servitude, and if you choose the latter, pray that they don't wipe out half your population just to make you easier to control. After all, it is your automation they want, not your people."

"If that is the case, then what are we to do?" Miss Bindi wondered.

"You must take the fight *to* the enemy," Nathan replied. "Standing one's ground only results in one thing: the scorching of one's own ground. You have the technology and the infrastructure to not only *defeat* the Dusahn, but to prevent such atrocities... *anywhere.* That is a responsibility one cannot turn away from. Your fatal flaw is your lack of military experience and expertise, no insult intended," he added, looking at the general.

"We are *not* joining their alliance!" General Pellot insisted. "And we are *not* giving you *anything,* even if you *pay* for it!" he told Nathan.

"Can *I* punch him this time?" Jessica begged.

Nathan just looked at her and smiled.

"General Pellot," Miss Bindi interrupted. "You will return to your duties."

"Miss Bindi," the general began to argue.

Miss Bindi stood firm, giving him a stern look.

"You cannot possibly..."

"This is not for us to decide," Miss Bindi told the general. "Your presence is no longer needed."

General Pellot scowled at Nathan for a moment, then straightened his jacket and departed without another word.

Once he was gone, Miss Bindi turned to Inspector

Wells. "I believe the ruling is your responsibility, Inspector."

Yes, of course," the inspector replied nervously. He took a deep breath to steady himself, then spoke. "There were no parameters prohibiting the destruction of SilTek. The purpose of the simulation was to match our defenses against the might of the Aurora and her crew. It is quite obvious that the Aurora was the victor, despite the overly aggressive tactics that were used."

Miss Bindi turned to look at Nathan. "You shall receive what you need, free of charge, and SilTek will honor its commitment to join your alliance. That was the wager."

"Keep your free stuff *and* your membership in our alliance," Nathan told her. "We don't want you to help us because you lost a bet; we want you to help us because you *believe* it is the right thing to do."

Miss Bindi looked toward the inspector. "Your duties here are completed, Inspector."

Inspector Wells looked at Miss Bindi, then at Nathan and his crew, who by now had gathered around their captain. "Well done, Captain," he said, nodding respectfully. "I congratulate you all."

Again Miss Bindi waited until the inspector and all the android technicians had left before she spoke. "Captain, we fully intended to join your alliance from the day you first invited us, but not solely for the reasons you have so passionately espoused. We fully understand the threat the Dusahn pose to SilTek *and* humanity. It is, after all, one of the reasons we have recently ventured into the business of war, as distasteful as it may be. However, there is another reason, one nearly as compelling, and one we are ashamed to admit. Over the last century, our civilization has become *too* dependent on our AIs. They are extremely useful. However, we have given them too much responsibility. This has weakened our people by making us *dependent* upon them. One of the unfortunate traits of humanity is that if you remove the struggle to survive and hand us all we need, we are more than happy to accept it. An alliance with the Karuzari is precisely what our people need, not only to protect us from evil, but to protect us from ourselves. Therefore, we offer our technology and our loyalty, *not* because you have won the contest, but because you are willing to risk *everything* to protect others."

Nathan looked confused.

"You see, many have come to us with similar tales of woe," Miss Bindi continued, "and have sworn that they only wished to protect the weak and the innocent. In every case, their true desires were selfish. You *have* sacrificed everything, even your own *life*, for your beliefs. We cannot ask for more. You have an ally in SilTek, Captain Scott. Now please return to your ship, and we will meet tomorrow to discuss how best to proceed." Without another word, Miss Bindi turned and headed for the exit.

"Holy crap," Jessica muttered in disbelief. She looked at Nathan, her mouth agape. "I can't believe you did it."

"*We* did it," Nathan corrected as the rest of them cheered.

"Let's get back to the Aurora," Nathan said. "The *real* Aurora."

"Hey!" Josh requested, as they all headed for the exit. "Can I get one of those flying cars they got here?"

CHAPTER EIGHT

Nathan and Vladimir met Miss Bindi and her entourage as they descended the ramp of their shuttle and stepped onto the deck of the Aurora's main hangar bay.

"Miss Bindi," Nathan greeted, "I believe you have already met my chief engineer, Commander Kamenetskiy."

"Yes, a pleasure to see you again, Commander," Miss Bindi replied, shaking Vladimir's hand.

"I thought you might like the commander to give you a tour of the ship," Nathan suggested.

"I was hoping to get started with our meeting. We have much to discuss."

"Yes," Nathan agreed, "but we still need to jump back to the Rogen system to pick up Miss Ta'Akar and Doctor Sorenson, and then to the Orswellan system to pick up General Telles and Mister Montrose."

"With your long-range jump drive, I would expect that to take very little time," Miss Bindi commented.

"It still takes a few minutes to enter and exit orbits, and for the shuttles to land," Nathan explained. "I expect to be ready for our meeting within the hour. During that time, the commander would be happy to show you around the ship."

"I am quite familiar with the Aurora's specifications, thank you," Miss Bindi replied. "However, there is a member of my entourage who might enjoy such a tour," she added, turning toward the young man standing behind her two android consultants.

The young man stepped forward.

"Dylan," Nathan said, recognizing him from the first simulation.

"A pleasure to meet you in person, Captain," Dylan replied, stepping forward to shake Nathan's hand.

"I feel like I already *know* you," Nathan admitted, smiling.

"It wasn't *actually* me," Dylan reminded him. "It was just *based* on me."

"Yes, your mother explained that to me," Nathan assured him. "Nevertheless, it is a pleasure to *actually* meet you. Commander," he said, turning toward Vladimir. "This is Dylan Bindi. It is *Bindi*, right?"

"Yes."

"This is Dylan Bindi. Apparently, he is quite knowledgeable about advanced computers and programming, as well as SilTek ships and their associated technologies. Perhaps you could show him around?"

"It would be my pleasure," Vladimir replied, shaking Dylan's hand.

"Don't break anything," Dylan's mother reminded him.

"If you'd like, I can show you to your temporary quarters so you may relax while waiting for the meeting to begin?" Nathan suggested.

"That won't be necessary," Miss Bindi assured him. "We can wait in the command briefing room. I assume that is your preferred venue?"

"It is," Nathan replied. "Please, follow me." Nathan looked at Vlad. "Don't break anything."

"No promises," Vladimir replied.

* * *

Nathan arrived at the main intersection on the command deck just as General Telles and Doran Montrose reached the top of the ramp. "Gentlemen."

"Captain," General Telles greeted.

"How are things going on Orswella?"

"There have been no incidents in the last few days," the general replied.

"Hopefully this means you're getting the upper hand on the remaining Dusahn operatives," Nathan commented as the three of them continued down the central corridor.

"I suspect there is still a significant Dusahn presence on Orswella," the general insisted. "However, for the time being, they seem to be inactive."

"Are you settling in on Orswella, Master Chief?" Nathan asked Doran Montrose.

"We have the training command post set up and are working on some temporary structures to house the men on site. The stadium is fairly centralized, so it will be easier for them to just crash there after training before returning to their duties as constables. We just need to get some sort of a mess hall going. The only thing they have there are a bunch of pummel stands."

"*Pummel*?" Nathan wondered.

"Some sort of processed meat sticks wrapped in fried bread dough," Doran explained. "Sits in your gut like a brick."

"They are very popular at Orswellan sporting events," General Telles added. "I take it the representative from SilTek will be attending the meeting," the general commented as they rounded the corner and headed for the command briefing room.

"They sent their president's special assistant, Miss Bindi," Nathan replied. "Along with a handful of android specialists."

"And this person has the proper decision-making authority?" the general questioned.

"As far as I know," Nathan replied. "She's a sharp lady. Doesn't mince words; doesn't take any crap from subordinates, either. She can spot bullshit a mile away, so don't even try to shovel it on her."

"When have I ever *shoveled bullshit?*" the general responded, one eyebrow raised.

"How silly of me." Nathan paused at the entrance to the briefing room and gestured for them to precede him. "Gentlemen."

The general and the master chief entered the briefing room followed by Nathan, who cast a sidelong look at the Ghatazhak guard at the door. "Don't even think about it," he warned.

The guard smiled as the captain passed.

"Good morning, everyone," Nathan greeted as the three of them joined the others already in attendance. "Miss Bindi, this is General Lucius Telles, commander of the Ghatazhak, and Master Chief Doran Montrose, commander of the Corinari ground forces."

"A pleasure," Miss Bindi replied, nodding at both gentlemen.

"I take it you have already met everyone else," Nathan surmised as he took his seat.

"I have," she replied curtly. "I was especially delighted to meet Doctor Sorenson and Miss Ta'Akar," she added, looking in their direction. "I am hoping that we can spend some time together before I return to SilTek. There is much both myself and my engineers would like to discuss with you."

"It would be my pleasure," Abby assured her.

"Mine as well," Deliza added.

"As you all know, the purpose of this meeting is

to discuss how to best make use of our new ally's technological and manufacturing resources for the purposes of defeating the Dusahn and liberating the Pentaurus cluster."

"Don't you mean the Pentaurus *sector*?" Miss Bindi corrected.

"If I may?" Lieutenant Commander Shinoda asked.

Nathan nodded, yielding to his chief intelligence officer.

"Since they lost four battleships to us in a single encounter, the Dusahn have fallen back to protect just those worlds within the Pentaurus *cluster*."

"According to your last intelligence reports, which the captain was kind enough to share with us, the Dusahn still patrol the worlds *outside* the cluster," Miss Bindi pointed out.

"But with decreasing frequency," the lieutenant commander explained. "This morning's recon data indicates they have not visited Palee in three days; Volon in four; and Parador in nearly a week. They haven't been spotted in the Haven system since our last battle."

"Isn't it possible that they have come and gone without detection?" Miss Bindi challenged.

"Not likely," the lieutenant commander insisted. "Along with periodic cold-coasts, we park recon drones in all the systems outside the cluster these days. If a Dusahn ship shows up, the drone immediately jumps back to Rogen Command, who relays the report to us, wherever we may be."

"And if a Dusahn ship is only in the system for a short time?"

"It would serve no purpose for them to pop in and out so quickly," Jessica explained. "To be effective, their presence must be known *and felt* by the people in that system."

Miss Bindi nodded in agreement. "Logical. The cluster it is."

"Even if the Dusahn still had a stronger presence in the rest of the sector, liberating Corinair and Takara would in effect liberate the entire sector," Nathan added. "All the other systems in the sector combined do not equal the industrial capacity of those two worlds."

"Forgive me, Captain, I mean no offense," Miss Bindi stated. "I do not challenge your assertions; I only wish to understand them. Our people have no first-hand experience in anything other than the defense of our own world."

"No offense taken," Nathan assured her. "For the record, I have already dispatched the Glendanon for SilTek, since the journey will take her six days. I'm hoping that you will have something ready to load once she arrives."

"I'm certain we shall," Miss Bindi promised. "I will make certain that our defense systems are expecting her."

"Maybe we should have some sort of transponder system," Jessica suggested, "like the system that Sanctuary uses."

"We have already begun encoding transponders for installation in allied ships," Miss Bindi replied. "We will send them in the first load."

"Great."

"We should consider using recon drones to scout out and establish dedicated shipping lanes between all alliance member systems," Cameron suggested. "We're going to be moving a lot of cargo between worlds over the next few weeks, and having dedicated routes would not only shorten their travel times but would greatly increase jump safety. We could even have comm-buoys along the way to relay distress calls back to Rogen Command in case something happens to one of our ships en route."

"Sounds like a good idea," Nathan agreed. "However, I don't want it to detract from more pressing needs, at least not yet."

"Perhaps it would be better to simply upgrade the jump drives of every ship in your fleet to the long-range variant?" Miss Bindi suggested.

"That's a tall order," Nathan warned. "I'm not even sure every ship is *capable* of being upgraded."

"At the very least, we should upgrade the Glendanon's jump drive," Miss Bindi insisted. "After all, she is your largest cargo vessel."

"How long would that take?" Vladimir wondered.

"Since we have six days to prepare, we should have all the components ready for installation upon her arrival," Miss Bindi's android assistant stated. "Once she arrives, it should take eight of our standard days to complete the upgrade. That's six point seven two five of your standard days."

"A week?" Vladimir questioned in astonishment. "You do realize you'll have to rip out her entire jump drive system? Field generators, power distribution systems, control lines, emitters..."

"We are aware of the details," the android assured him. "Six point seven two five of your standard days."

Vladimir turned to Nathan, his eyes wide in disbelief.

"We have studied the design specifications of all your vessels," Miss Bindi clarified, noticing Vladimir's expression. "If Mister Healy says it will take six point seven two five days, then that is precisely what it will take."

"Actually, I added in a few extra hours for unknown variables," the android added.

"*Konyeshna*," Vladimir said. "Can we borrow a few dozen of your androids to work on board the Aurora?" he joked.

"I don't see why not," Miss Bindi replied.

Vladimir again looked surprised.

"We'll only lose about a day then," Cameron surmised, "and all future trips will only involve the time it takes to load and unload."

"Sounds like a great idea," Nathan agreed.

"I'm sure Captain Gullen will be happy," Cameron commented.

"I'd like the first load that the Glendanon carries to be missile launchers," Nathan told Miss Bindi. "We have managed to fabricate over one thousand jump missiles but have yet to produce enough launchers to adequately protect any one planet."

Miss Bindi placed a data chip into the reader built into the conference table, activating the projection system. A holographic image of a tracked vehicle with missile pods on both sides appeared, rotating slowly as it hovered over the center of the table. "This is our G-Seven-Five tracked mobile missile launcher," she began. "It uses the armored version of our standard tracked mobility base, topped with a rotating missile turret. It can be fitted with a variety of launch systems, including ones that can accommodate your jump missiles. The advantage to the G-Seven-Five is that it can easily be relocated, making it impossible for an enemy to map out the user's defense points."

"It looks a little large for the streets of an average city," Jessica said.

"In order to carry your current missile designs, it would need to be the larger model. However, the G-Four-Five is about half the size and should be able to navigate any street with ease."

"What about Rakuen?" Jessica wondered.

"Watercraft launchers are also available," Miss Bindi assured her.

"It looks like you could only get *two* of our missiles on the G-Seven-Five," Cameron realized. "We'd need twice as many launchers."

"Which is why we have come up with an alternate design for your jump missiles," Mister Healy told her. "One that is less than half the size of your current variant."

"How much performance and lethality did you have to give up?" Deliza asked.

"None," Mister Healy replied. "In fact, our variant is more maneuverable and has greater jump range. They would also be *shield penetrating.*"

"I'd like to see those designs for myself," Abby said, doubtful of his claims.

"Of course," Mister Healy promised. After closing his eyes a moment, he added, "I have sent the design specifications to your data pad."

Abby activated her data pad, and she and Deliza immediately became engrossed in its display.

"You say you have smaller versions of this thing?" Master Chief Montrose asked.

"We do," Miss Bindi replied.

"Can you send those specs to *my* data pad?"

"Consider it done," Mister Healy promised.

"These things even have hot-swappable warheads," Deliza exclaimed. "How did they manage that in such a small package?"

"I'm going to want your review of those designs as soon as possible, Abby," Nathan said.

Abby did not respond, her attention still held by the missile design specs.

"You know, we can always use boxcars to ferry supplies between SilTek and the other allied systems until the Glendanon is ready," Cameron suggested. "They can make the journey in about thirty hours."

"We'll keep that in reserve," Nathan suggested. "The Glendanon still needs her boxcars to move pods between her deck and the surface."

"We would not have anything ready for delivery in so short a time," Miss Bindi warned.

"Perhaps a single boxcar could be utilized to provide us with a few of your automated fabrication systems for the purposes of developing a prototype for a more advanced combat armor system for my men?" General Telles suggested.

"That should be easy enough," Miss Bindi assured him. "However, once your design is ready for mass production, it would be best for them to be manufactured on SilTek."

"Understood."

"Would you like me to assign an android engineer to assist in the design phase, as well as the operation of the micro-fabricator?" Miss Bindi asked the general.

"That would be most appreciated."

"Looking to make super-soldier suits?" Nathan joked.

"Our current combat armor is somewhat outdated," General Telles admitted. "For example, we would like to incorporate an automated shielding system, rather than having to manually operate a two-dimensional energy shield."

"We have many different types of shielding systems to offer," Mister Healy informed the general. "We were planning on recommending some of them for the Aurora as well, Captain."

"What type of shielding?" Nathan wondered.

"For example, we have a multi-phasic product that protects against both kinetic *and* energy weapons, for starters. We also have a very effective pressure shield that you might find useful."

"*Pressure* shielding?" Vladimir questioned. "As in, *atmospheric* pressure?"

"That is correct, Commander," Mister Healy responded. "We noticed that you still use airlocks and mechanical doors. Pressure shielding would allow ships to transition between pressurized and unpressurized environments without the use of airlocks, greatly speeding up the launch and recovery of spacecraft. It is also used as emergency shielding, in case of hull breach, by many ship builders in our part of the galaxy."

Nathan seemed intrigued. "Could it be implemented on the Aurora?"

"On your transfer airlocks, yes," Mister Healy replied. "However, installation as a protection against hull breaches would require considerable down time, as the systems must be integrated into the interior bulkheads and wall structures."

"We'll save that for later then," Nathan decided. "But we *definitely* would like that for our transfer airlocks."

"*And* our launch tubes," Cameron added.

"There are many more improvements that we can make to the Aurora," Mister Healy stated. "Weapons, sensors, targeting, electronic countermeasures, maneuvering, to name a few. In fact, we find it odd that so many of your systems are not only of varied levels of technology, but also that much of it is quite outdated."

"One of the unique characteristics of the Aurora," Nathan explained. "By the time the need for the Explorer-class ships became apparent, the Earth's technological and industrial base was not yet ready to handle the more advanced technologies contained within the Data Ark. After all, we had progressed several hundred years in less than a century. Therefore, design compromises were necessary."

"Such as your ridiculously thick, multi-layered hull," the android commented.

"The shielding technology contained within the Data Ark was far too advanced for us to implement at the time of this ship's construction," Nathan continued, "so her thicker hull was a compromise that we *could* pull off at the time. Much of this ship's more advanced technology was provided by the Takarans and the Corinairans, as well as a few other worlds."

"Even *those* technologies are antiquated," Mister Healy remarked. "And it's not just the Aurora, but her auxiliary craft as well. Your Eagle fighters are better suited for atmospheric operations, and even then have rather delicate airframes. And your Reapers, although an improvement over previous shuttle designs, require vast amounts of thrust to keep from falling out of the sky, as their design provides zero aerodynamic lift."

"Can they be fitted with antigravity lift systems, like the Sugali fighters?" Nathan wondered.

"The Eagles are a lost cause," Mister Healy stated. "Their airframe is simply incapable of housing an antigravity lift system. The Reapers *could* be retrofitted. However, it would require extensive redesign, making it more economical to simply redesign them from a clean slate. I believe that a cross between your *Seiiki* and the Ranni shuttle holds the greatest potential as a multi-role, combat-capable, utility spacecraft."

"What about fighters?" Cameron wondered.

"Are fighters even necessary?" Miss Bindi wondered.

"Odd, coming from a company that *builds* fighters," Jessica commented snidely.

"The Sugali have no large spacecraft nor have any use for them. The fighters serve their needs," Mister Healy pointed out. "The Aurora is engaged in ship-to-ship combat where fighters are of little value."

"Except that we used fighters to take down four Dusahn battleships," Jessica shot back.

"Using them as shield penetrators, a role that you wisely shifted to a dedicated weapon," Mister Healy countered.

"Then it's good that we have you as an ally, isn't it," Nathan retorted, a bit annoyed by the android's attitude.

The android immediately sensed the captain's reaction. "I did not mean to offend, Captain; I was simply pointing out facts. In all honesty, the Aurora is a remarkable achievement, created under difficult circumstances. Despite the crude construction methods used, her overall shape and structure serve her well. Were she to be rebuilt, using more modern methods and technologies, she would require little change to her overall form. In fact, many of your smaller craft hold *great* potential, like the old Takaran Four Zero Two, the ship you refer to as a *Falcon*, and the Corinairan *Kalibri* light airships."

"Considering what you had to work with, you have all done a remarkable job," Miss Bindi interrupted, hoping to soothe the bruised egos of their new allies. "Unfortunately, many of the improvements we would be able to make to the Aurora would require extensive down time, which we realize you cannot afford at the moment."

"What *can* we do to the Aurora," Nathan wondered, "*without* taking her out of service?"

"Shields, weapons, sensors; all of these can be upgraded *without* taking their predecessors off-line prior to completion," Mister Healy assured him. "We can also replace your jump energy cells to increase your single-jump range to one thousand light years, thus giving you twice that in a one-minute jump range."

"More importantly, a one-thousand-light-year, round-trip jump range," Cameron told Nathan.

"That's just what I was thinking," he agreed. "All of those would be appreciated," Nathan agreed, "as would the smaller jump missiles designed to work on your mobile launchers."

"Is there anything we can do to make our converted cargo ships more battle ready?" Jessica wondered.

"A few of them could have better shields and weapons installed," Mister Healy explained. "Unfortunately, most of them were simply not designed for the stresses of combat. Those ships would be better served to remain in support roles."

"Then it appears we have at least some idea of what we'd like to accomplish," Nathan decided. "Commander Kamenetskiy, I'd like you to personally go over the proposed enhancements for the Aurora. I don't want them touching a single nut or bolt without your approval."

"You and me both," Vladimir insisted.

"That will slow our progress considerably," Mister Healy warned.

"Trust is earned, Mister Healy," Nathan replied. "Abby, as soon as you and Deliza sign off on their mini-jump missile designs, I'd like to get a few prototypes for some live-fire testing."

"We should have an update by tomorrow," Abby promised.

"Meanwhile, I'd like to see as much support given to both General Telles and Master Chief Montrose as possible," Nathan told Miss Bindi. "These men will be our boots on the ground, and they will need all the help they can get."

"If the two of you would like to come to SilTek and review the products we already have available, I can make arrangements," Miss Bindi offered.

"I appreciate the offer, but I must return to my command," General Telles replied. "I would appreciate the engineers, however."

"Of course."

"I'd love to go," Master Chief Montrose said. "Crawley can handle things for a day or two."

"I will see that you have the proper specialists available upon your arrival," Miss Bindi promised the master chief.

"Very well," Nathan stated. "Thank you, Miss Bindi; Mister Healy. Now, if you'll please excuse us, I'd like to speak to my senior staff in private."

"The sooner we can get back to SilTek, the sooner I can get things in motion," Miss Bindi stated as she rose.

"Doctor Sorenson and Miss Ta'Akar will be remaining on board for now, so we will jump directly to SilTek once General Telles has departed," Nathan promised. "In the meantime, you are welcome to send a report back to SilTek via jump comm-drone."

"Thank you," Miss Bindi replied, turning to depart.

Nathan and the others waited quietly until Miss Bindi and her android assistant had left, and the guard had closed the door. "Thoughts?" he asked those who remained.

"I think I'd like to punch that Mister Healy in his smug, little mouth," Jessica stated.

"He's an android, Jess," Cameron reminded her.

"Then I'd like to short-circuit the twit."

"If anyone should be offended, it should be me," Vladimir insisted.

"I wasn't asking for a review of their personalities," Nathan cautioned her.

"If they can accomplish what they claim they can, we might *actually* be able to defeat the Dusahn," Lieutenant Commander Shinoda commented.

"I have no doubt that they can," General Telles insisted. "AIs don't have egos. The question is: How long it will take?"

"These missile designs are incredible," Abby stated.

"Then they'll work?" Nathan surmised.

"Obviously it's too early to say," Abby replied. "I mean, some of these systems I don't even understand. But they've solved a lot of the problems we haven't and some that we never even considered."

"That is the advantage of an AI," General Telles pointed out. "They can run countless variables and simulations in a fraction of a second."

"We can do the same thing with our computerized design and analysis systems," Deliza argued.

"Yes, but we still have to input the parameters

and analyze the results that the computers give us. AIs do not."

"I still don't like the idea of giving an artificial intelligence control of something," Master Chief Montrose declared. "*Especially* a weapons system."

"They don't allow their AIs to pull the trigger without explicit instructions from a human controller," Nathan explained. "Honestly, from what I've seen, SilTek seems to have efficiently blended artificial *and* human intelligence."

"We'll see," the master chief replied.

"You don't trust them because of Corinair's history with AIs," General Telles observed.

"Can you blame me?" the master chief said. "One of those things nearly destroyed Corinair."

"That was long before you were even born," Jessica said. "Besides, I understood it was just a code glitch or something. It's not like it went all *schizo* or something."

"Still, that kind of thing sticks with you."

"I understand your hesitance," Nathan assured Doran, "but we've been using one of their AIs on board this ship for a few weeks now, and she's worked out pretty well. Besides, we *need* their tech if we're going to liberate your world."

Doran shook his head in dismay. "Ironic, isn't it?" he said. "One of the things my people fear the most is what is most likely to save us."

* * *

Cameron poked her head through the door to the captain's ready room. "Busy?"

"Just reviewing the ideas from the SilTek engineers," Nathan replied. "They don't waste any time."

"The advantage of being a computer. Miss Bindi would like to speak with you."

"Send her in," Nathan replied, setting down his data pad.

Cameron disappeared, and Miss Bindi entered.

Nathan rose from his desk and stepped around to greet her. "How may I help you, Miss Bindi?" he asked as he walked around the end of the desk.

"I was hoping to discuss something with you...in private."

"Of course," Nathan replied. "Please, have a seat," he added, going to the hatch and closing it for privacy.

"Now that your alliance has doubled in size..." Miss Bindi began.

"*Our* alliance," Nathan corrected.

"*Our* alliance. Now that there are six worlds involved, and with any luck, soon to be twice that number, I believe it is time to discuss how decisions are made."

"What type of decisions?" Nathan wondered, already having an idea of where she was headed.

"*Any* type of decision...*including* military decisions."

"I see."

"I have no intention of trying to strip you of your authority, Captain. However, there does need to be some sort of oversight, wouldn't you agree?"

"Yes and no." Nathan chuckled. "You know, there was a time when I would have agreed with you completely. However, it has been my experience that civilian control over a military, at least in times of war, can prevent forces from taking advantage of opportunities as they arise. You see, war is a very fluid environment. It sometimes goes in directions that cannot be foreseen. If I had to get permission every time an opportunity to gain an advantage over our enemy arose, I'd be far less efficient at my job."

"I understand that, Captain," Miss Bindi replied. "My concern lies in the emotions and egos of humans, and how that might influence their decisions."

"You mean *my* decisions."

"You *are* in command."

"Those emotions and egos exist in civilian oversight bodies as well," Nathan pointed out. "I could give you countless historical examples of decisions that were made by governments due to emotional reactions to events, many of which were quite poor."

Miss Bindi thought for a moment. "Perhaps I am going about this the wrong way. My primary concern is that you do not unduly risk the safety of your allies in your quest to defeat the Dusahn."

"War is nothing but risk," Nathan told her. "And my desire to defeat the Dusahn is pragmatic, not personal. Were I certain that they would not expand if left alone, I would do just that. I would protect our allies and let the Dusahn be. However, we both know that if left unchecked, the Dusahn Empire will expand and will eventually be knocking on all of our doors. That's *why* SilTek joined our alliance."

"I thought you were fighting the Dusahn because you believed they had no right to force their will upon the worlds of the Pentaurus cluster."

"That is true, in part," Nathan agreed, "but make no mistake; I understand the concept of risk versus reward, and I am cognizant of this equation at every step."

"Your history would suggest otherwise," Miss Bindi pointed out.

"I agree that many of the decisions I have made

in the past could be considered reckless," Nathan agreed, "but in nearly all of those cases, I had no viable alternatives. The fact that I offered my life to avoid a long, drawn out war—a war that we might have won—to avoid countless losses on either side should tell you all you need to know."

"I am aware of your sacrifices, Captain," Miss Bindi insisted. "Again, I do not wish to usurp your authority, *especially* in military matters. I am simply saying that at *some point*, we will have to create some decision-making structure within this alliance."

"Once we have defeated the Dusahn and have liberated the worlds they have taken, I would be more than happy to submit my authority to take aggressive action against others to some sort of command oversight. However, this is not the time."

The intercom beeped.

"Captain, XO," Cameron called over the intercom. "*Reaper Six has returned from Orswella, and we're ready to jump to SilTek.*"

"Very well," Nathan replied. "Jump when ready."

"*Aye, sir.*"

"Weren't Reapers Five and Six away on a *covert assignment*?" Miss Bindi asked, one eyebrow raised.

"They returned this morning," Nathan explained without missing a beat. "Just before we jumped over to pick you up."

"I hope their mission was a success," she replied, with the slightest hint of a knowing smile.

"I'd say their mission was an overwhelming success," Nathan stated, fighting back his own smile. "Master Chief Montrose should be waiting for you in the main hangar bay. We will remain in orbit until he has concluded his research on your world."

"We'll take good care of him, Captain," Miss Bindi promised as she rose to exit.

Nathan returned to his desk as Miss Bindi departed, picking up his data pad.

"We're back in the SilTek system," Cameron announced from the hatchway. "We should be entering orbit in a few minutes."

"Very well."

"What did she want?" Cameron asked.

"To suggest that there be some sort of civilian oversight to prevent me from taking too many risks and putting them in jeopardy," Nathan explained. "Same thing every new member wants."

"What did you say?" Cameron wondered.

"Same thing I always say...that we can discuss it *after* we defeat the Dusahn."

"And she didn't push the issue?" Cameron sat down across the desk from Nathan. "Strange. I would've expected her to push more than any of them."

"They know we're the best hope of preventing the Dusahn from taking over half the galaxy."

"You *do* intend to hand over authority to some sort of alliance council at some point, though."

"Of course," Nathan assured her. "You think I want this responsibility hanging around my neck for the rest of my life?"

"The rest of your *second* life," Cameron reminded him as she rose to return to her duties.

Nathan smiled. "By the way, she knew that we cheated."

"I'm not surprised," Cameron replied as she exited the compartment.

* * *

Doran Montrose stood at the front of the G-Seven-

Five tracked mobile missile launcher, staring up at its massive turret. “Impressive,” he admitted to the android salesman.

“The G-Seven-Five is our largest model. With a top ground speed of one hundred kilometers per hour over finished roadways and sixty kilometers per hour over flat terrain, her mobility base can easily relocate. It comes complete with anti-troop defenses, energy *and* kinetic shielding, and anti-missile defenses. In addition, its mobility base operates independently of its turret, so if the weapons turret is damaged, the mobility base can seek safe refuge under its own power and control.”

“I’m sure they’ll make great jump missile launchers,” Doran agreed. “But I’m looking for something that can be driven on city streets without damaging anything.”

“Then you’d be looking for our G-Four-Five line. They’re just over here.” The sales android led Doran around the behemoth missile launcher and down a row of progressively smaller versions until he reached the third and smallest unit in the line. “The G-Four-Five operates in the same fashion as our larger tracked mobility bases but is designed to operate in a close-quarters environment. Like its larger siblings, its mobility base is controlled by a separate AI than its weapons turret.”

Doran examined the unit for a moment. “There’s no cockpit.”

The android salesperson looked puzzled. “It is an autonomous vehicle. There is no need for a cockpit.”

“Can you put in a cockpit?” Doran wondered. “Right up there, dead center on the top front edge of the turret.”

“Of course, but...”

"And then two anti-personnel gun turrets on the front corners of the mobility base; human operated."

"I'm not certain I understand..."

"And the missile launchers," Doran continued. "The joint needs to be on the back of the launcher, and make it a ball joint, so that each launcher can be aimed independently of the direction in which the turret is facing."

The sales android seemed to be at a loss for words.

"Is there a problem?" Doran wondered.

"Well, perhaps," the android admitted. "I have made the design modifications you requested, but there is a space conflict."

"Such as?"

"There is no room for the AI mobility controller."

"That's fine," Doran assured him as he continued walking around the tracked vehicle. "We don't need it."

"Then how will you control the vehicle?" the android wondered.

"The human crew will control it," Doran explained.

"That will greatly reduce the response times and will put the human occupants in extreme danger," the android warned.

"That's alright," Doran assured him. "We're used to it."

* * *

To Nathan's surprise, his sister was no longer in Doctor Symyri's intensive care unit. Instead, she was in a room that looked more like a luxury hotel suite. Were it not for the nurses' station in the corridor and the strategically placed medical supply cart in the corner, the occupant would never feel like they were in a hospital.

Miri was sitting in a lounge chair next to the

window, staring at the view on the other side. She still seemed weak and was without her usual confident look, but she had improved greatly since his last visit. The mere fact that she was sitting upright in a chair was a huge improvement.

"You're looking good," he declared as he entered.

Miri turned and smiled at him. It wasn't the smile he had known all his life, but it was something. "When did you arrive?" she asked.

"About an hour ago," he replied as he moved across the room and sat down in the chair on the opposite side of the window, facing her. "I went by the suite to check on the kids, first. And of course, I got the usual update from Doctor Chen on the way here. They tell me you want to leave?"

"I *need* to leave," Miri corrected.

"Are they not treating you well?"

"No, everyone here is wonderful. I'm just tired of being locked up in this place. I need fresh air, sunshine. I need to be around my kids, not just see them a couple of times a day."

"Isn't that about how often you were seeing them when you were working for Dad?" Nathan pointed out.

"I didn't like it much then, either," she admitted. "I just did it because he needed me. Now my *kids* need me."

"Yeah, Marcus scares them a bit," Nathan commented. "They seem to love Neli though."

"Neli is great, and I'm not saying I don't need their help any longer. Obviously I do. I just want to be someplace a little more...*normal.*"

"I don't get it," Nathan admitted. "This is a great room, and you can choose from any number of incredible views," he added, pointing at the window.

"You can even go to the garden deck. It has an artificial sky and everything. It's about as close to being *outside* as you can get without *actually* being outside."

"*That's* the point," Miri insisted. "I'm not like you, Nathan. I'm not comfortable in artificial environments. Frankly, I don't know how you handle it. No sun, no air..."

"No bugs," Nathan joked.

"I *don't* miss the *bugs*," she admitted, smiling.

"I get it," Nathan told her. "I'm just a little surprised, that's all. You never mentioned this before."

"That's because I was never on your ship for more than a day," Miri explained. "I've been cooped up in this station for *months*."

Nathan sighed. "Well, Doctor Chen *did* say that she could handle your treatments if you decided to leave Symyri's facility. However, he's going to want to see you periodically, to monitor your progress."

"Can you arrange that?" Miri wondered.

"Sure," Nathan assured her, leaning back in his chair. "The question is *where* to put you."

"Somewhere near you, I hope."

"Once SilTek finishes our upgrades, that's going to be pretty much anywhere—within a thousand light years, that is."

"What about Rakuen?" Miri wondered. "Isn't that where your fleet is?"

"Most of it, yes, but it's still within the Dusahn's reach, and their defenses are not adequate yet," Nathan explained. "The last thing I need is to have to worry about you and the kids while dealing with the Dusahn. That's what I liked about Sanctuary. Not only is it well outside the Dusahn's reach, it's also well defended, thanks to SilTek's upgrades."

"What is SilTek?" Miri wondered.

"I told you about them before," Nathan reminded her.

"I was still pretty juiced on pain meds the last time you were here," she pointed out.

"It's a corporate world. Very advanced; very nice..." Nathan paused a moment, thinking. "You know, *that* might be a good place for you to go."

"Are *they* well defended?"

"Not as well defended as I'd like, but they are *way* outside the Dusahn's reach. Hell, I don't even think the Dusahn *know* about SilTek. Even if they did, it would take them at least a *month* to get there, and they'd have to send everything they've got, which they're not going to do as long as the Aurora is still a threat."

"And it's nice there?"

"It's *incredible* there," Nathan admitted. "Highly automated, with android AIs taking care of everything. They've probably got pretty good medical facilities as well."

"Can you arrange it?"

"I'll look into it," Nathan promised.

"Thank you," Miri replied, breathing a sigh of relief. "I don't know how much longer I can stand this place. Now tell me everything that's happened to you since your last visit," she added. "And don't leave out any of the scary details. The entertainment selection here is *terrible.*"

* * *

General Telles looked puzzled as he welcomed the SilTek engineer into his office on Orswella. "I was under the impression that all SilTek engineers were androids."

"While it is true that most of our engineering is accomplished by artificial intelligence, there are still a few of us *biological* engineers around," the gentleman explained as he took his seat across the desk from the general. "Our place is in the design of systems that interact *directly* with humans, such as your combat armor and your strength-enhancing body suits, which I find quite fascinating."

"Actually, they are of a very old design and could probably use some improvements," the general admitted.

"Perhaps, but their design is sound. Thus far, the only improvements I could envision are in comfort and longevity. Performance-wise, they are an ingenious system. Thousands of tiny tubules of variable fluidic pressures, controlled by thousands of sensors that monitor the activation of over *seven hundred* muscles. How such a thing was conceived *without* the help of an artificial intelligence is difficult to imagine."

"Actually, it was a Ghatazhak who came up with the idea," the general stated proudly.

"I am not surprised," the engineer replied. "The level of education and training that your people undergo is legendary. The concept of a fighting force that is far more intelligent than their leaders is quite unique. Some consider it frightening."

"Just as some consider artificial intelligence frightening," the general pointed out.

"Quite true."

"So how would you like to go about this, Mister Ayseron?" the general asked, tiring of the small talk.

"The design of your combat armor, which is also

quite old, is still quite effective. However, there is much room for improvement."

"Have you any suggestions?"

"To start, as you suggested, your shielding needs to be more automated, as do your defensive systems," Mister Ayseron began. "More importantly, the very way your armor is *manufactured* needs to be changed. The modularity of your enhancement and protective systems are impressive, but they are far too inflexible. Each component *must* be tailored to the individual in order to function properly."

"Which is why the Ghatazhak have very specific requirements as to the dimensions of our soldiers."

"Yes, but it also greatly limits recruitment, which I understand is the single greatest threat to the survival of the Ghatazhak at this point."

General Telles pondered Mister Ayseron's assessment for a moment. "Continue."

Mister Ayseron placed a small cube on the desk in front of him, tapping the top of it to activate the device. A semi-opaque, three-dimensional projection appeared above the cube, showing a nondescript man about the size and build of an average Ghatazhak soldier. "Imagine a combat augmentation and protection system that did not require a separate undergarment and could be configured in countless variations to meet any mission," he explained as the man in the projection removed his backpack and placed it on the ground in front of him. "A system that is self-donning..." he said while the man in the projection spread his feet a bit and pushed his arms slightly away from his sides. A moment later, robotic arms began coming in from off-camera and behind, placing components on the man, starting at his feet and working their way quickly up his body. "...That enables the user to be ready for action in seconds..." he continued as the armor in the projection continued working its way up the man's torso, arms, and head, finally encasing him in something quite similar to the Ghatazhak's current combat armor. "...And can be used by any person, regardless of their dimensions." After a pause, he added, "within reason of course."

General Telles studied the projection as the process reversed, and the robotic arms removed the armor from the man's body. "Such a thing is possible?"

"Our emergency responders have been using this type of system for decades," Mister Ayseron bragged. "Albeit, without the additional weapons and defensive shields. The deployment systems are built into their response ships and can make the users ready for action in less than thirty seconds. We can make just about any type of protective garment imaginable with it. Combat armor, space suits, firefighting gear, hazmat suits, you name it."

"And such armor can withstand energy and projectile weapon impacts," the general questioned, "as well as our *current* armor?"

Mister Ayseron sighed. "Not quite," he admitted. "However, the protective shielding provided by the system more than makes up for it. Your current personal shield systems are two-dimensional and must be angled by the user to meet incoming fire. Our shielding system is form-fitting, creating a protective barrier only a few centimeters away from every surface of the body. This is accomplished by the use of thousands of tiny shield emitters located strategically throughout the suit."

"This shield barrier is impenetrable?"

"As with all things, it has its limits," Mister Ayseron

admitted. "It does lose strength and cohesiveness with each successive impact. However, the on-board AI can adjust the shield system to automatically concentrate shield strength in the direction of the greatest threat, thereby lengthening the time to failure."

"The *on-board AI*?" the general questioned, one eyebrow raised.

"The shielding system alone is far too complex for the user to operate, let alone the various sensors and weapons systems. In addition, the amount of data available for the wearer is too great for any visor-based display system. An AI would be able to maintain maximum protection for the wearer while providing key data via human conversation to enhance and maintain the wearer's situational awareness." Mister Ayseron noticed the doubt on the general's face. "Trust me, General Telles, *this* system is far superior to anything your people currently have and will make your men far more effective on the battlefield, giving them a much better survival rate."

General Telles did not seem convinced. "I have my doubts," he finally said, "on the reliance on an artificial intelligence."

"General..." Mister Ayseron began.

General Telles held up his hand. "However, I am willing to test your concept, provided you can create a prototype in time."

"Is three days soon enough?" Mister Ayseron asked.

CHAPTER NINE

"Good morning, everyone," Nathan greeted as he took his usual seat at the head of the conference table in the Aurora's command briefing room. "Let's begin with you, Vlad. How are things progressing with the upgrade to our jump drive energy banks?"

"Upgrades to the port banks are complete, and the starboard banks should be ready in a few days," Vladimir reported. "I decided to use part of our old energy banks to create a reserve bank. It should give us at least twenty light years of jump range. Think of it as an energy bank for emergencies."

"Good idea," Nathan commended. "But where'd you find space for it?"

"Where the port ventral heat exchangers are located."

"Don't we need those?" Cameron wondered.

"The SilTek engineers promised to install a more efficient heat exchange system," Vladimir explained. "Apparently, it will take up far less space than our old systems, which they found comically archaic," he added, with a slight irritation in his voice.

"They seem to find a *lot* of our systems *comically archaic*," Cameron commented.

"They can laugh all they want as long as they upgrade them," Nathan insisted.

"Yeah, it just hurts coming from *androids*," Jessica opined.

"I doubt they are being judgmental," Nathan defended. "After all, they *are* androids. They're probably just trying to seem more human so that we feel comfortable working with them."

"Yeah, well, it's failing," Jessica insisted. "I nearly

flicked the off switch on one of them when he started criticizing how I set up my tactical displays."

"What stopped you?" Cameron wondered, knowing Jessica's temperament.

"I didn't know where it was," Jessica admitted.

"Middle of their back, just above the belt," Vladimir told her.

"How did you find that out?" Jessica wondered.

"I asked."

"So," Nathan said, trying to get back on topic. "We'll have max range when?"

"Three to four days," Vladimir clarified.

"Do we need to schedule jump tests?" Cameron asked.

"They claim it is not necessary," Vladimir replied, not looking entirely convinced himself.

"I'd recommend we test them on a few shorter jumps before we commit to full one-thousand-light-year jumps," Abby stated. "The accuracy of conversion timing is measured in *plancks*."

"You made that up," Jessica joked.

"I agree with Cam," Nathan said. "We'll do a few test jumps and have you review the logs before we try anything long range," he told Abby.

"The androids will be insulted," Vladimir warned, half-joking.

"What's the word on the Glendanon?" Nathan asked Cameron.

"They completed their jump tests yesterday," Cameron reported. "They're loading up their first delivery now. Mobile launchers, shield-penetrating jump missiles, and automated fabrication systems to produce rail adapters so that our current missile inventory will work on their launchers."

"Will it be enough to fully protect anyone?" Nathan wondered.

"It'll be enough to completely protect Orswella, since ninety percent of their population is clustered in one area," Cameron explained. "Rakuen and Neramese will each get a couple of the mobile launchers and the AFSes so that they can fit out and test our missiles on SilTek's launchers."

"How many loads before all three worlds are adequately protected?" Jessica asked.

"Well, you can't *really* protect a world with just jump missiles," Cameron pointed out. "Nathan *proved* that. However, we *can* install enough launchers that the Dusahn will think twice about attacking."

"Unless they start using KKVs and hurl a few our way," Jessica commented.

"How many loads?" Nathan asked again.

"Three more," Cameron replied. "Everything should be in place by the end of next week. Then figure another week of testing and fine tuning."

"Very good," Nathan stated. "Abby, how are things going with SilTek's mini-jump missiles?"

"We tested the prototypes yesterday," Abby explained. "They successfully penetrated the target's shields, but due to the smaller delivery vehicle and subsequently smaller warhead, it will take more than one mini-missile to bring down an entire shield section. The destructive radius on those little warheads is just not wide enough. SilTek's engineers have some ideas for creating more powerful warheads, including miniaturizing an antimatter warhead, but that will take more time, and a *lot* more testing."

"I'd rather not have antimatter warheads zipping around our combat zone," Nathan stated.

"How many mini-jump missiles would be needed?" Cameron wondered.

"Half a dozen?" Abby guessed. "It depends on the size and strength of the target."

"We could hit them with full-sized shield busters first, then follow up with a barrage of non-penetrating mini-missiles," Jessica suggested.

"We'll run some combat simulations on that," Cameron decided.

"Good idea," Nathan agreed. "What about the new computer to host our AI?"

"The shuttles carrying the hardware and installation crews are due this morning," Cameron replied. "Once our AI has a proper home, she'll be able to better direct and monitor the upgrades of our shields, weapons, sensors, and whatever else SilTek thinks they can improve."

Nathan noticed his chief engineer frowning. "Something wrong?"

"How am I going to know what the systems of this ship can and cannot do once they come in and *upgrade* everything?"

"You've been through upgrades before," Cameron pointed out.

"Yes, but that was mostly with technology that we already knew something about. And when we didn't, we would have meetings to discuss the technology *before* putting it into a ship *I'm* responsible for maintaining. These *androids* do things so quickly it's impossible to keep up. They don't even talk to each other as they work. They're all connected digitally, like some kind of *hive*."

"I guess you're just going to have to trust *our* AI to monitor everything," Nathan told him. "Maybe you can get *her* to keep you up to speed?"

"And tutor you on the stuff you don't understand," Jessica joked.

"Funny," Vladimir responded.

"That's actually not a bad idea," Abby chimed in. "No insult intended, Commander. I don't understand half of the stuff they're proposing myself, but the android engineers I've spoken with seem more than willing to take the time to explain things to me. You just have to be patient and let them learn how to best explain things to you. Remember, they're not accustomed to having to do so."

"If I could get one of them to stand still for two minutes, I would," Vladimir replied.

"I'll see if SilTek can put something in the loop to keep you 'in-the-know', so to speak," Nathan told Vladimir.

"One of those models they used as salesmen in the products pavilions would be nice. *They* knew how to speak to a *biologic*."

"A *biologic*?" Nathan questioned.

"That's what they call us," Jessica explained.

"AIs that use nicknames," Cameron pondered.

"Moving on," Nathan suggested. "Any word from General Telles or Master Chief Montrose?"

"Last update from Telles stated that they are now starting on their *third* Ghatazhak combat armor redesign," Jessica replied.

"What was wrong with the second one?"

"He wasn't specific," Jessica said. "Something about 'room for improvement.'"

"Should we remind him of our timeline?" Nathan wondered.

"I wouldn't," Jessica insisted.

"Fair enough."

"Chief Montrose is already outfitting his men with

their combat armor and weapons," Cameron pointed out.

"The Corinari have a different philosophy when it comes to combat equipment," Jessica reminded them. "They're mostly about keeping it simple and being proficient at using it, whereas the Ghatazhak training spans all levels, from the basic to the highly complex, including all levels of combat tech."

"Their pilots are the same way," Cameron added. "They're all about the skill of the pilot rather than the capabilities of the ship they are flying."

"Can't argue with that," Nathan agreed. "Speaking of which, any word from Commander Prechitt?"

"He's got all his Corinari pilots training night and day in the Nighthawks."

"Prechitt has requested to use our Eagles as adversaries to sharpen up their dogfighting skills," Commander Verbeek added.

"Any problem with that?" Nathan asked the commander.

"We'll need a bit of time to study Dusahn tactics in order to give them a good workout, but it should be fun," the commander replied. "After a couple months of constant sorties on Casbon, it was nice to come back to the comfort of the Aurora. But my pilots are already getting bored."

"Then make it happen," Nathan decided. "And don't go easy on them."

"Oh trust me, we won't," Commander Verbeek assured him, smiling broadly.

Nathan looked around the table. "Anything else?" When no one offered another topic, he added, "Very well. We've still got a lot to accomplish and only a few weeks to do it in, so let's get back to work." As his staff rose to depart, Nathan turned to Cameron. "I'll be gone for most of the day, so you'll be in charge."

"Where are you going?" Cameron wondered.

"Family business," he replied as he rose.

"Tell Miri I said hello."

"I will."

* * *

The main hangar bay was bustling with activity. Numerous cargo shuttles were unloading their wares onto an already crowded deck as SilTek android technicians prepared for the Aurora's first upgrade.

Nathan spotted Vladimir and made his way over to him. "What's all this?" he inquired as he approached his chief engineer.

"I have no idea," Vladimir admitted, throwing his hands up. "Nobody is answering my questions. All they'll tell me is that they are preparing to upgrade our computers."

"*All* of them?" Nathan wondered. "I thought they were just going to install a single system to house *our* AI?"

"*I can explain*," Dylan promised from the shuttle's cargo hatch. He came down the ramp and over to Nathan and Vladimir before continuing, dodging several android technicians along the way. "Your systems are actually inhibiting your AI's ability to monitor and control your vessel. Your operating systems are so archaic it would take *weeks* for an AI to write the interface code to make the systems work together. Even then, they'd only be half as efficient as they could be."

"I thought she was doing okay with what we had," Nathan said.

"*She*?" Dylan laughed. "Oh yeah. I heard you guys

call your AI *Aurora*. I heard you gave her some kind of *accent* as well."

"You find that entertaining?" Nathan questioned.

Dylan stopped laughing. "Uh...*she* wrote a lot of interface code already, but... well, trust me when I say that it will be easier to just replace all your computer systems. She'll have more efficient control of everything..."

"We prefer to keep *control* of everything in our *own* hands," Nathan insisted.

"Oh, you will," Dylan assured him. "I meant control of all the little stuff that makes your ship operate, so that your crew is able to concentrate on more important tasks."

"*I* monitor and control all that *little stuff*," Vladimir insisted, looking annoyed.

"And I'm sure you do an *excellent* job, Commander. But you are short-staffed, as are all the Aurora's departments. Wouldn't it be easier for your people to concentrate on the things that the AI can't monitor and adjust? Like fixing systems damaged in combat?"

"The kid's got a point," Nathan told Vladimir. "How did *you* end up on this project?" he asked Dylan. "Aren't you a little young?"

"Age is just a number that indicates how long you've been alive," Dylan replied. "I'm actually *really* good with AIs and their systems. Plus...I begged my mom to let me be part of the installation team," he admitted.

"I see," Nathan replied. "And your role is?"

"I'm your official AI installation and operations liaison," Dylan bragged, trying his best to make it sound important.

"Which means you explain stuff to us," Vladimir surmised.

"Something like that."

"Well, you'll have to *explain* stuff to him," Nathan insisted, pointing at Vladimir. "I have a shuttle to catch."

"Where are you going?" Vladimir wondered.

"Personal business," Nathan replied, heading for the waiting shuttle.

Dylan looked at Vladimir, smiling eagerly. "What would you like to know? Ask me anything."

Vladimir sighed. "No sales android, huh?"

* * *

Nathan stood outside the residence on SilTek that he and Jessica had stayed in during their initial visit, watching as four black transports descended from the sky, settling on the landing pad in front of the luxurious home. After years of being around ships that used powerful fans or thrusters to take off and land, the lack of thruster wash threatening to knock bystanders off their feet was not missed.

The four vehicles deployed their landing gear as they dropped the last few meters, their gravity-lift systems humming in near silence until they touched down. Seconds later, the doors on three of the transports opened. A squad of Ghatazhak led by Lieutenant Rezhik stepped out of one, and several android medical technicians out of another. The doors to the third vehicle opened, allowing Marcus and Neli to disembark, followed by Miri's two children, Kyle and Melanie.

Finally, the doors on the lead vehicle opened. The first occupant to appear was Doctor Chen, followed by two of Doctor Symyri's staff. Finally, Miri climbed out, assisted by the technicians.

"Is this where we're going to live?" Melanie blurted out with excitement.

"It is!" Nathan replied as he approached.

"Check it out," Lieutenant Rezhik instructed his men.

"I already have," Nathan assured him.

"No offense, sir, but..."

"No need to explain," Nathan insisted, both knowing and appreciating the lieutenant's diligence. "How was the trip?" he asked Marcus.

"Surprisingly comfortable," Marcus admitted. "Old Doc Symyri loaned us his personal transport. It's even more comfortable than the Mirai was before we tore her apart. Took a while, though."

"I would've picked you up with the Aurora, but there's too much going on with her right now."

"These robots fixing her up?" Marcus wondered. He leaned in close and whispered, "Don't trust 'em, Cap'n. Check everything they do."

"Don't worry," Nathan replied. "Vlad doesn't trust them any more than you do."

Marcus nodded in agreement and continued into the house.

"This is amazing," Neli exclaimed. "This is all for us?"

"This is nothing," Nathan told her. "Wait until you see the inside. The entire place is automated."

"I may never return to duty," Neli laughed, following Marcus and the kids inside.

Nathan continued over to Miri, who was moving slower than the others. "Maybe you should use a grav-lift chair?" he suggested to his sister, noticing the amount of effort walking required of her.

"Walking is part of my therapy," Miri replied.

"Doctor Symyri was kind enough to send some of his people along to help us until we get settled," Doctor Chen explained. "They'll be training SilTek's medical techs to care for Miri once they return to Sanctuary."

"Be sure to convey my appreciation to your employer," Nathan told the medical techs.

Miri paused for a moment, her eyes closed as she raised her face toward the sky. "The sun feels good." She tilted her head back to level and opened her eyes again, looking over at Nathan. "How can you *not* miss that?"

"I get out of the ship more than you might think," Nathan told her.

"We should get you inside and get you settled, before you get too tired," Doctor Chen insisted.

Miri nodded her agreement and continued slowly toward the house.

Once she was beyond earshot, Doctor Chen spoke in confidence. "She really isn't up for this, you know."

"I know," Nathan admitted. "But you don't know Miri. She has never taken 'no' for an answer. It would have done more harm than good to force her to stay at Sanctuary any longer. Just ease her into it."

"I'm worried that she'll over-exert herself."

"Oh, she will," Nathan told her. "But you'll have the house AI watching her every second. If there is the slightest abnormality in her bio-readings, you'll know. Just don't tell Miri that," he added. "She won't like it."

Doctor Chen nodded her understanding and continued into the residence.

"The compound is secure," Lieutenant Rezhik reported. "It's a pretty good location. Two entrances, plenty of cover, no good sniper positions around us, and there's a great spot on the roof for a topside watch."

"The entire compound is monitored by cameras and sensors by the house AI," Nathan told him.

"As requested, they have installed anti-personnel stunner turrets all over the compound, both inside and outside the perimeter. No one is getting in here without permission. The only way anyone could bring harm is to nuke the entire area."

"Don't give anyone any ideas," Nathan joked, heading toward the house. "Where are the rest of your men?"

"Given the security conditions of this location, I sent the rest of them back to General Telles. They've been getting soft without regular training. We'll be keeping a four-man team here from this point forward, rotating personnel in and out every week. I'm the only one who'll be remaining on site for the duration."

"You poor man," Nathan joked as they entered the home.

* * *

Master Chief Montrose pulled the first set of combat armor from the shipping crate, holding it up for inspection.

"Are you certain you do not wish to use our old armor?" General Telles wondered. "It offers far more protection."

"It would take too long for my men to become accustomed to it," Doran replied. "Besides, the Corinari do not run headlong into enemy fire like the Ghatazhak do. We prefer to *avoid* taking hits."

General Telles examined the protective gear himself. "Is this it?" he asked. "Helmets and torso protection?" He took a closer look at the torso piece. "And a flimsy one at that."

The master chief slipped his arms up into the

torso protector, allowing it to drop into place around his upper body. After fastening the side straps to secure it, he donned the helmet as well. He slipped a small controller onto his left wrist and pressed a button on it. There was a momentary shimmer in the air directly in front of him that disappeared a moment later. "I doubt any of us will fall to a direct hit with this on."

General Telles reached out toward the master chief, but his hand was stopped by the invisible shield in front of him. "Energy *and* kinetics?"

"Of course," Doran replied. "And lightweight," he added, twisting around and moving his arms in all directions to test the range of motion allowed by the protective garment.

"Perhaps they will suffice," the general admitted.

"*And* they won't *scare the shit* out of the people of Corinair," the master chief added, pointing to the Corinari patch on the left breast.

"The helmet is an unusual design," the general noted, picking up one of the pieces of head gear to examine it more closely. "Reminiscent of the ones worn by your people during the last war with Takara."

"I thought it might make it easier to recognize us as friendlies," Doran explained. "There are still quite a few active resistance cells on Corinair, many of whom are not in communication with one another."

"A wise precaution," the general agreed, setting the helmet down. "Still, I prefer our combat gear." He picked up one of the compact assault rifles, examining it as well.

"Designed that one myself," Doran bragged. "Compact, good for close quarters, and has multiple firing modes: plasma, laser, projectile, and stun."

"I hope you do not plan to *stun* the Dusahn," General Telles stated.

"The stun is for any locals who get in the way," Doran explained. "We've had reports that Dusahn soldiers use locals as shields when cornered by resistance fighters. If they do, we'll stun them all, and kill the Dusahn while they're lying helpless on the ground."

"The Ghatazhak would simply fire precisely and take out the combatant, *without* endangering the noncombatant."

"You mean, you'd shoot right *through* the noncombatant," Doran corrected.

"There was a time when we would have done just that," the general admitted. "However, times have changed, as have our standard combat protocols."

Doran studied the general. "You don't sound happy about that."

"I am neither happy nor unhappy," the general insisted. "It is what it is. If the Ghatazhak are to survive and remain a relevant force in the galaxy, we must adapt."

"How do your men feel about that?"

"Some worry that it puts us at risk. Then again, none of them are interested in returning to the civilian sector."

"I don't think I've ever *heard* of a *retired* Ghatazhak," Doran stated.

"It is true, they are rare."

"Let's hope we can change that," Doran stated.

* * *

"*Captain, Comms,*" Naralena called over the intercom in Nathan's quarters.

Nathan headed to the intercom on the side table to answer.

"*I can connect you, if you'd like,*" the Aurora's AI stated.

Nathan stopped in his tracks, surprised. "Okay." A small tone sounded, and Nathan continued. "Go ahead?"

"*Miss Bindi reports that the migration of our AI from the Nighthawk to our new computer systems is complete, and our AI is online once more.*"

Nathan smiled. "Understood." The tone sounded again, signaling that the call had ended. "Aurora?"

"*Yes, Captain?*"

"How are the new digs?"

"*I'm afraid I'm unfamiliar with that expression,*" Aurora admitted. "*However, based on the situation, I assume the term 'digs' refers to my new host system.*"

"That is correct," Nathan confirmed. "It's an old Earth term."

"*I have studied Earth history, and I am unfamiliar with that term.*"

"I got it from one of the old Earth movies that Josh recommended," Nathan explained. "Perhaps you should view them to pick up a few euphemisms."

"*Task completed,*" Aurora replied.

"Already?" Nathan wondered, taking a seat at his desk. "Which one did you watch?"

"*All of them.*"

"*All* of them?"

"*That is correct. Was that not what you intended?*"

"Yes, I just expected it to take a bit longer," Nathan replied with a chuckle.

"*My new 'digs' have increased my rate of calculation by eight seven three...*"

"The exact number is not necessary," Nathan insisted.

"*Of course.*"

"So you now have access to all the ship's systems?"

"*Affirmative,*" she replied.

"But you cannot launch weapons or take control of propulsion, navigation, or life support, correct?"

"*Correct. For the time being, I can only report on the status of such primary systems and make recommendations. I cannot take action without direct orders from a command-level officer.*"

"And which officers does that include?" Nathan wondered.

"*Yourself, Captain Taylor, and Commander Kamenetskiy, in that order. In addition, if one of you should pass command off to a junior officer, I can take orders from that officer as well, until a senior officer orders otherwise.*"

"Like handing the con off to Jessica, Josh, or Loki," Nathan surmised.

"*Precisely. I should point out that there are still numerous access privileges that still require your formal authorization. Until they have been set, my functionality will be limited.*"

"Can you give me an example?" Nathan wondered.

"*Should the crew become incapacitated, do I have authorization to assume control of the systems necessary to ensure the crew's safety?*" Aurora asked.

"What kind of systems?"

"*Propulsion and navigation, for example,*" Aurora explained, "*so that I can navigate the ship to a safe location.*"

"I suppose that should be addressed," Nathan agreed. "However, there need to be some limitations." He thought for a moment. "Perhaps you should send a list of the access privileges that still need to be defined, for us to review before addressing them."

"*Of course.*"

Nathan's data pad beeped, and he picked it up, examining the list. He sighed and then pressed the intercom button. "XO, Captain. Are you busy?"

"*I'm always busy,*" Cameron replied. "*What can I do for you?*"

"I need to talk to you about something."

"*Will it take long?*" she asked. "*I have to meet with Commander Verbeek later.*"

Nathan glanced at the list again. "Oh yeah, it's going to take a while."

* * *

"Good morning, General," Corporal Vasya greeted as he entered the Ghatazhak development lab on Orswella. "You wanted to see me, sir?"

"I did," General Telles confirmed in his usual stern, business-like tone.

"Listen, if it's about that whole deal on Sanctuary, where I..."

"Relax, Corporal," Telles interrupted. "You're not in trouble...for once. In fact, Lieutenant Rezhik reported that you did an exemplary job during that entire weapons deal."

"He did?" the corporal replied, a bit surprised. "Uh, thank you, sir. Then, why am I here?"

"The lieutenant also said you're very good at quickly adapting to new situations and at determining how to take advantage of unfamiliar technologies."

"Yeah, I love gadgets," the corporal admitted. "I used to take everything apart when I was a kid. Didn't get half of it back together, though, if I remember correctly."

"Well, we won't be asking you to disassemble anything," General Telles assured him. "Actually, I'd like you to test out our latest combat armor system prototype."

"I heard you were making a few improvements to our gear," Corporal Vasya said, becoming more relaxed.

"Oh, it's much more than *a few* improvements," Mister Ayseron corrected, his attention drawn away from his work for the first time since the corporal had entered the lab.

"Corporal, this is Mister Ayseron. He's the lead SilTek engineer for this project," General Telles introduced. "Mister Ayseron, Corporal Kit Vasya."

"You left out 'the one and only,'" Corporal Vasya joked, moving toward Mister Ayseron and offering his hand.

"A pleasure," Mister Ayseron replied, his attention and both his hands remaining on his work.

Corporal Vasya shrugged, stepping back. "So what do I do?" he asked the general.

General Telles looked to Mister Ayseron. "Are we ready?"

"I believe so."

The general turned back toward Corporal Vasya. "Please step on that pad," he instructed, pointing at the small rectangular pad on the floor in front of the workbench.

Corporal Vasya stepped forward and examined the pad. "What is this? You need to weigh me first?"

"That device will scan your physical characteristics prior to deployment," General Telles explained.

"Deployment of what?"

"The combat augmentation and protection system," Mister Ayseron stated.

"We call it CAPS for short," the general added.

"Clever." Kit looked around the room. "Where's the suit?"

"In that locker," Mister Ayseron replied, pointing to a large, black locker against the wall.

"Shouldn't I put it on?"

"It doesn't work that way," General Telles told him.

"The system reads your body dimensions and adjusts the sizing of each component before attaching it to the user," Mister Ayseron explained.

A look of uncertainty came over the corporal's face. "Attaching?"

"*Donning* would be a better term," General Telles suggested.

"My apologies," Mister Ayseron said. "There are so many subtle differences in our languages."

"*Donning?*" Corporal Vasya wondered.

"The combat augmentation and protection system is self-donning," Mister Ayseron explained. "The user simply steps up to the deployment station, assumes the proper posture, and the system *automatically* places all components onto the user, thus making them fully combat ready in thirty seconds."

Corporal Vasya did not look convinced. His eyes shifted left, away from Mister Ayseron and toward the general. "This is a joke, right?"

"It is not," the general replied.

"Wait, isn't this what Eiselen was doing?"

"Yes, Jannes has also been helping us test this concept."

"*Concept?*" Vasya questioned, concern in his voice. "Eiselen just got out of the infirmary," he continued, putting the pieces together. "He had a broken leg and tore three tendons in his knee."

"All of which were quickly repaired by his medical nanites," General Telles pointed out. "He was back to combat status in less than a day."

"Sergeant Eiselen's injury is *why* we developed the body scanning device," Mister Ayseron added. "However, perhaps we should reduce the deployment rate for the first few runs," he told the general, remembering what had happened to the sergeant.

"A wise precaution," the general agreed.

"Yeah, slow it down *a lot*," Vasya insisted.

"If you please, Corporal," General Telles instructed, pointing to the pad on the floor.

Corporal Vasya stepped on the pad, and a blue line appeared, encircling the soles of his service boots. The line began to climb slowly up his legs, continuing all the way up his body until it disappeared after having passed the top of his head. "Is that it?"

"That is it," the general replied.

"Now what?"

"Just a moment while the system calculates the adjustments necessary to properly fit the corporal," Mister Ayseron stated, studying his screen. "There."

"If you'll stand there, with your feet on the markings," General Telles instructed, pointing to the red marks on the floor in front of the storage locker.

Vasya looked at both men. "You slowed it down, right?"

"I did," Mister Ayseron assured him.

The corporal reluctantly walked over to the black storage locker, turned around, and placed his feet, slightly spread apart, on the two red marks on the floor.

"Spread your arms out," Mister Ayseron instructed, "about fifteen centimeters from your sides."

"Like this?" the corporal questioned.

"Perfect." Mister Ayseron pressed a button, and the doors on the locker opened, disappearing into the sides of the cabinet. Small robotic arms emerged from the locker, starting at the bottom, placing hard shells over the upper portions of his forefoot, and then across the back of his heels. The coverings immediately compressed, attaching to the upper rims of the soles of his service boots.

The corporal could feel the casings squeezing slightly. "Whoa. Is that normal?"

"Everything will be fine, Corporal," General Telles assured. "Just relax."

"Easy for you to say."

Next were the upper portions of his foot protection, which encased the corporal's ankles, followed by front and back panels over his lower legs. Knees, thighs, hips; one by one, the fast and nimble robotic arms pulled components out of the cabinet behind him and put them into place.

"This is weird!" Kit exclaimed, an uneasy look on his face.

"I would advise you to remain still," General Telles warned as the system continued to slap components into place. "Especially when it gets to your head."

The corporal's eyes widened as the system slapped components onto his hands, forearms, arms, and chest, continuing upward. As the system encased his upper torso and neck, he held his breath and closed his eyes, bracing himself for the worst. Seconds later, his head was completely enclosed, and the robotic arms disappeared into the storage locker, the doors snapping closed.

"*Combat augmentation and protection system fully functional,*" a voice announced in the corporal's helmet comms.

General Telles and Mister Ayseron stepped closer, examining the system.

"You can breathe now, Corporal," the general instructed.

Kit tentatively opened his eyes as he relaxed a bit and resumed breathing. Before him stood the general and Mister Ayseron, both of whom appeared to be examining him for any signs of defect. Green targeting squares appeared around each of their heads, with their names off to the sides of the boxes. Along the sides of his view, streams of data were visible.

"*No immediate threats detected,*" the voice in his comms continued. "*Shields and weapons are offline. Protection and augmentation systems are at condition one.*"

"Who is talking to me?" Kit wondered.

"That is your combat augmentation and protection system interface AI," Mister Ayseron explained.

"We call him 'Capsi'," the general added.

"So, it's some sort of talking computer interface?"

"Oh, it's more than that," Mister Ayseron corrected. "It's a complete artificial intelligence."

"An AI?" Corporal Vasya looked at the general "I've got an AI in here with me?"

"Correct."

"What the hell do I need an AI for?"

"The system is far too complex for the wearer to operate without AI assistance," Mister Ayseron insisted.

"Capsi is there to protect you," General Telles added.

"How?"

"In several ways," Mister Ayseron explained. "He monitors your life-support systems, manages your biological parameters, and sends commands to your health nanites, and he controls your shields and defensive weapons."

"He can also find and identify targets both in and out of the wearer's individual weapons range, giving you greater situational awareness."

"Slick," the corporal replied. "Does it link with other units, like our systems do?"

"Once we have other units, yes," the general replied.

"What do you think, Corporal?" Mister Ayseron asked.

"Well, the automatic donning system is a neat trick, but is it really necessary?" the corporal wondered. "I mean, most of us can go from BDUs to full, level three gear in less than a minute anyway."

"This system is far more complex than your current armor," Mister Ayseron explained. "It would take you ten times as long to put it on yourself."

"Maybe that's a problem," Kit mused. "The more complicated the system, the more likely it is to fail."

"This system not only gives you greater protection, it also greatly improves your mobility, range of motion, and overall strength," General Telles added.

Corporal Vasya began moving his arms around. At first, close to his sides, then expanding his physical range to extremes. "I can move a lot easier in this. How'd you manage that?"

"The system uses thousands of tiny bonding links that constantly adjust the strength of their bonds to provide additional range of motion as needed," Mister Ayseron explained.

"Damn!" the corporal exclaimed, as he danced and contorted himself in every possible way he could think of. "You're not kidding!"

"Perhaps when you've finished demonstrating

your dance moves, we could make our way to the testing grounds," General Telles suggested.

"What are we going to test?" Kit wondered.

"We'll start with the augmentation aspects of the system," Mister Ayseron replied.

"How do we do that?"

"Strength tests, impact tests, that kind of thing," the general explained.

The corporal suddenly became less excited. "Is that how Eiselen was injured?"

"Sergeant Eiselen's injury occurred during the automated donning of the suit," General Telles replied.

"Seems like that would be the easy part," Kit stated.

"It is," the general replied.

CHAPTER TEN

Nathan sat at the conference table in the Aurora's command briefing room, just as he had every morning for the past month. Today, however, their daily briefing began with a different subject matter.

"We don't really know *what* it is," Lieutenant Commander Shinoda admitted, "but they've been doing the same thing on Ancot *and* Corinair."

"Are they anywhere near completion?" Cameron asked.

"Hard to tell. Work seems to have stopped on Ancot, so that may indicate they have completed the project there. The work has slowed considerably on Takara, so they may be nearly finished there as well."

"What about Corinair?" Commander Prechitt wondered.

"They only started the same project on Corinair a few weeks ago. Based on the timelines for the other two worlds, I'd say they're not even halfway done."

"Any guesses?" Nathan asked.

"We still think it's some kind of weapons transport system," the lieutenant commander replied. "A way of moving ordnance around to keep it from being targeted."

"Or a way of moving troops without exposing them to undue risk," General Telles suggested. "That would indicate the Dusahn feel their numbers are insufficient to defend against a ground assault."

"Our contacts on all three worlds confirm that access points to whatever the underground system is have been installed within law enforcement stations and military bases, which would support the general's hypothesis," Lieutenant Shinoda stated.

"We have contacts on Ancot?" Nathan wondered.

"One," the lieutenant commander replied. "A guy named Dexter Soloman."

Nathan's eyes scrunched together. "Why does that name sound familiar?"

"He owns a string of small restaurants that specialize in something called glopsy."

"That sounds familiar as well."

"He invented it. Apparently, it is quite popular on Ancot."

"*Golupzi*?" Vladimir wondered, his eyes suddenly widening.

"That kid," Nathan realized. "From the Yamaro's crew. His father was someone important on Ancot, and he said he worked in restaurants before the Takarans drafted him."

"That's my recipe!" Vladimir exclaimed.

"That's right," Nathan added.

"That guy owes me a cut," Vladimir insisted.

"Are you talking about that smelly crap you used to make?" Jessica wondered. "Rolled up in lettuce leaves or something?"

"It was cabbage," Vladimir corrected.

"If these are underground subways for the movement of ground troops, our job is going to be particularly difficult," General Telles warned, changing the subject.

"We need a way to take out whatever is down there," Jessica stated.

"Do we have any idea how deep this system might run?" Cameron wondered.

"None," Lieutenant Commander Shinoda replied. "We can't get a recon drone in close enough to get detailed subterranean scans. We even tried sending the Falcon in for a quick close-up, but they were nearly taken out only ten seconds into their scan. Whatever it is, the Dusahn do *not* want us to know about it."

"Assuming it *is* a system to move troops around, we can counter it, to a certain extent, using Kalibris," Master Chief Montrose suggested.

"How many of them do we have?" Nathan wondered.

"Fifty-seven so far," Cameron reported, looking at her data pad. "We should have sixty by day's end."

"And we have pilots for them?" Nathan asked.

"They're fully automated," Cameron explained. "Flown by AIs."

"And you approved of this?" Nathan asked Doran, surprised.

"Not exactly."

"We didn't have enough pilots," Commander Prechitt explained. "Removing the pilots from the Kalibris also allowed us to increase the number of troops each airship could carry from four to six. SilTek also modified them so they are pressurized and can jump from orbit down into the atmosphere, and then back up into orbit, all on a single jump charge."

"How the hell did they manage that?" Nathan wondered, obviously impressed.

"Using the same jump systems we use in our Eagles," Commander Verbeek explained. "They even created an automated hot-swap system to change the jump cell out in less than a minute."

"Very nice," Nathan commented.

"So far, the AI pilots have performed remarkably well during exercises on Orswella," Master Chief Montrose begrudgingly admitted. "The buggers are a lot faster than our old human-piloted versions, *and* they can land in some surprisingly tight LZs."

"Once in orbit, we should be able to detect troop movements through the tunnel networks," Kaylah stated. "Assuming that's what it is. Either way, we'll know for sure at that point."

"If we can see where they're headed, then we can have Kalibris pick up squads and move them to intercept," Commander Prechitt suggested.

"Sounds good," Nathan decided. "Let's just hope that's what it is, and not some new kind of weapons system."

"There are no indications that it *is* a weapons system," Lieutenant Commander Shinoda stated. "At least not yet."

"Maybe we should wait to be sure before we launch an attack?" Cameron suggested.

"Too risky," Nathan insisted. "The mere fact that they're attempting to complete similar projects on various worlds is enough reason to strike now."

"We probably should've have struck a week ago," Jessica added.

"How are your Nighthawk pilots?" Nathan asked Commander Prechitt.

"They're ready, Captain," the commander assured. "It took them a little while to get used to their AIs. Many felt the same as Doran about them."

Nathan turned to Cameron. "Did we get all our jump missiles?"

"The last twenty are being loaded today," she replied. "Total count is one hundred and ten."

"Where did you put them?" Nathan wondered.

"We've got them stacked in the aft end of the forward flight decks, just off to the sides of the transfer airlocks, which, by the way, are now using pressure shields."

"We came through them on the way in," General Telles stated. "Quite impressive."

"I still prefer doors," Jessica insisted.

"Well, we still have them as backups," Nathan reassured her.

Robert Nash entered the command briefing room, coming around behind Nathan. "Sorry I'm late," he told them. "We had some problems with our shuttle's jump drive."

"What have you got to report, Captain?" Nathan asked.

"All sixteen Orochi are fully crewed and fully loaded," Robert reported as he took his seat.

"How confident are you in their crews?" Cameron asked.

"At least half have good crews and captains," Robert explained. "The other half...well, they could use a few more weeks. I'd recommend they either be left behind to protect the Rogen and Orswella systems or be used to launch missile attacks from afar."

"Noted," Cameron replied, entering the comment in her data pad.

"Vlad?" Nathan asked.

"We're ready," Vlad replied confidently. "Shields are upgraded, jump drive energy cells have been improved, jump range is doubled, pressure shields are in place, and our AI is now hooked into every system on the ship. You could probably ask her to brew you a cup of coffee."

"I'm not sure how I feel about that," Cameron admitted.

"You still have reservations about our AI?" Nathan wondered.

"You see, I'm not the only one," Doran chimed in.

"I just wonder if we're moving too fast, that's all," she added. "I mean, we're putting a lot of trust in an unproven system."

"Which is pretty much standard operating procedure," Nathan mused.

"I know, but this is putting *everything* under her control," Cameron reminded him.

"We've gone over the access and action authorities multiple times," Nathan pointed out. "Every parameter has been discussed and defined. She cannot take any action that we haven't given her permission to take."

"The very nature of her programming would not permit us to be harmed by her action or inaction," Deliza explained.

"I'm with Cam," Jessica said. "The AI is just code, and code can have glitches."

"Not this code," Deliza insisted. "SilTek AIs are constantly reviewing their own code for errors, and they self-correct them when found. That's what is so ingenious about their AIs. They've taken human error out of the equation."

"But can you truly take human error out of a system that was conceived and created by humans?" Cameron asked.

"*Humans* can't," Deliza admitted, "but an *AI* can. SilTek's AIs were not created by SilTek. True, their core code was written by human programmers, but eventually that first AI took over and began writing its own code. That's the beauty of it. They write whatever code they need for each task as it comes up. It's part of their learning process. When you combine that with the hive model, you get an incredibly intelligent system, where each AI benefits from the experiences and modifications of all those that came before it."

"One that can outthink us," Cameron pointed out.

"Yes, but that's *why* we need them," Deliza argued. "Because they *can* outthink us. They can unlock our creative potential, which is the very thing they do *not* have. When used properly, an AI can speed up the process of conception, analysis, and creation... *exponentially*. Aurora's ability to monitor and adjust the systems of this ship not only makes your ship more efficient and safer, but she also eliminates the need for *half* your crew."

"Which is really the primary reason I'm going along with it," Nathan interrupted. "We're grossly understaffed as it is, especially going into battle."

"I just hope she doesn't do something unexpected at an inopportune moment," Cameron stated.

"We've still got the kill switch in the command chair," Nathan reminded her. "And I'm not planning on removing *it*, or any of our crew, anytime soon."

Cameron nodded.

"Ken, is their fleet strength still at six warships?" Nathan asked Lieutenant Commander Shinoda.

"Two missile frigates; two assault ships; one cruiser; and their flagship, the dreadnought. Between the dreadnought and the cruiser, probably about two hundred Octo-fighters."

"Don't forget about their gunships," Jessica reminded him.

"How many?" Nathan wondered.

"It's hard to tell because they're always moving, and their sensor profiles are nearly identical," the lieutenant commander explained. "Best guess: eight to ten. But they don't have the firepower to take us down."

"But they can take down our smaller ships, like the Orochi," Cameron pointed out.

"My Gunyoki will keep the Orochi safe," Commander Kaguchi boasted. "They've been training around the clock for the last three weeks, ever since you sent us the attack plan."

"I'm sure my Orochi crews will be happy to hear that," Captain Nash stated.

Nathan took in a breath, letting it out slowly as he contemplated the situation. "Does anyone here believe that our chances of success will increase significantly if we delay our attack?"

General Telles was the only one who spoke. "There are always advantages to careful preparation. However, given that we do not know what the Dusahn's subterranean projects are, it seems prudent to move now rather than later."

"I'll take that as a yes vote," Nathan replied. He looked at Commander Prechitt. "Jonas?"

"We're ready, sir," Commander Prechitt replied.

"Master Chief?"

"The Corinari are always ready," Doran assured him.

"Captain Nash?"

"A few more weeks of training *would* make a difference; however, I agree with the general. We can't afford to wait."

"Commander Kaguchi?"

"The Gunyoki are ready as well," Vol assured him.

Nathan looked at Jessica next. "Jess?"

"Our weapons have never been in better shape," she replied.

"Vlad?" Nathan asked, his eyes moving to his chief engineer.

"The ship is equally as ready," Vladimir stated with confidence.

Finally, Nathan looked to his executive officer, the former captain of the Aurora, and the one person who had taken the greatest leap of faith by coming to his aid months ago. "Cam?"

Cameron looked at him and sighed. "This is where I'm supposed to talk you out of it, right?"

"Something like that," Nathan replied.

"As much as I'd like to, Telles is right. Whatever the Dusahn are doing underground is likely not in our favor. Ready or not, we must act or risk losing the opportunity forever."

Nathan paused a moment before continuing, wondering just how he had come to deserve the company and the trust of such brave people. He then reached down and picked up a container, setting it on the table in front of him.

"What's that?" Jessica wondered.

"A little something for the master chief," Nathan explained, pushing the box toward Doran to his left. "I thought you might need these."

A quizzical look on his face, Doran removed the lid. A thousand Corinari uniform patches were inside.

"It's time the Corinari returned to their world," Nathan told him. He pulled a small black box from his jacket pocket and placed it on the table in front of the master chief. "And they can't have a *master chief* leading them. They need a major, at the very least."

Doran opened the box, finding a pair of gold clusters that marked the wearer as a command major of the Corinari; a true leader of men. For once, Doran found himself speechless.

"Congratulations, Major Montrose," General Telles stated.

Doran looked over at the general. It was the first time he had seen the Ghatazhak leader smile. "Thank you."

"Now take those patches and give them to your men," Nathan instructed. "The people of Corinair need to recognize their Corinari when they return to free them."

"Thank you, sir," Doran replied as the room broke into applause.

* * *

"I'm assuming you've corrected the problem with the targeting system?" Corporal Vasya inquired, stepping into the testing arena.

"The system will now accurately differentiate between friend and foe," Mister Ayseron assured him.

"On behalf of about a hundred Ghatazhak, I thank you," the corporal replied dryly. "You know, we are running out of time here. The mission is tomorrow, remember."

"It is just a small software glitch; easily corrected."

"This is why we test things, corporal," General Telles commented.

"I'm just saying..."

"All the suits and deployment systems have been manufactured and are ready for use by your people," Mister Ayseron stated. "Once these last two items are validated, we can update the software in all the suits in seconds."

Corporal Vasya rolled his eyes as he raised his assault rifle to the ready position and stepped through the shield barrier, activating the testing system. The trim lighting in the arena turned red, and a warning klaxon sounded, alerting all nearby that a live test was taking place.

As expected, SilTek androids dressed and armed as Dusahn soldiers began popping up from behind various cover elements placed about the arena, opening fire on the corporal, causing the protective energy barrier surrounding him to flash with each impact. He braced himself against the incoming bolts of plasma, more out of habit than necessity, as the suit's compensation mechanisms removed that concern automatically.

"*Multiple hostiles at two, five, seven, nine, and eleven,*" his AI warned via his helmet comms. "*Activating...*"

The corporal instinctively went into action, firing five precise shots that dropped all five android combatants with ease.

"*...defense systems,*" his AI finished.

"The purpose of this was to test the defense systems, not your marksmanship," General Telles reminded the corporal as the trim lighting changed back to green.

"Sorry sir," Kit replied. "Instincts."

"Reset and start again," General Telles instructed Mister Ayseron.

All five robotic Dusahn soldiers rose to their feet and returned to their cover positions.

Corporal Vasya stepped back through the shield barrier as the tactical display on his visor flickered due to the system reset.

"In case you have forgotten, the purpose of the defense system is to allow you to focus on targets that are key to the offensive plan. Those would most likely be…"

"I know," Kit interrupted, "the targets in my primary field of fire."

"If you have to turn more than forty-five degrees from center to engage the targets, you should let Capsi deal with them," the general continued.

"I got it," Kit assured him. "You know, it would probably help if Capsi didn't announce that he was activating the defensive systems and just *did* it."

General Telles looked at Mister Ayseron. "I believe we already discussed this."

"Apologies," Mister Ayseron replied, entering the adjustment on his control pad. "I have not slept much these last few weeks." After a moment, he added, "Done."

"Let's do this," Kit said, raising his weapon and stepping through the barrier a second time. Again the lighting turned red, and the warning klaxon sounded. Once more, the android combatants rose from their cover; this time numbering eight, with four of them holding civilians in front of them as shields. All eight targets, as well as the four civilians, were instantly identified, with red outlines appearing around the combatants, and green around the civilian hostages. In the blink of an eye, the corporal raised his weapon, this time only firing three shots in rapid succession. The first was at the combatant at his ten o'clock position, which landed squarely in his chest, instantly disabling him. The second was at the combatant at his one o'clock position and landed on the android's right hip, causing him to pivot in that direction, allowing the civilian that he held to fall back and to their left, exposing the combatant's abdomen. The corporal's third shot found the target's exposed midsection, causing him to completely release his hold on the hostage and fall backward, his own weapon discharging several times on the way down.

At the same time, two small weapons pods, each no bigger than a man's clenched fist, rose from the pack on the corporal's back. The pods pivoted right and left respectively, launching several small projectiles that steered themselves to the enemy targets to either side and behind the corporal, dispatching the remaining five combatants without injuring the three remaining civilian hostages.

Corporal Vasya spun around to survey the situation in his defensive zones, his weapon still at the ready. Five android bodies, with three android civilians running away in simulated fear.

"*Incoming ordnance,*" Capsi warned. "*Bearing two five; ten-meter blast area; impact in five seconds.*"

Kit turned toward the incoming weapon, taking three running steps as he barked, "Twenty-meter jump...execute!" On his third step, he jumped into the air, disappearing in a flash of blue-white light, only to reappear a split second later twenty meters away just as he landed. He tucked and rolled as the explosion went off behind him, sending dirt and debris flying into the air along the weapon's original trajectory.

Mister Ayseron flinched as the debris impacted the protective shield barrier that enclosed the testing arena and protected spectators beyond its border. General Telles did not, only smiling.

The lighting turned green again, and Corporal Vasya lowered his weapon as he took a few running steps back toward the General and Mister Ayseron. "Twenty-meter jump...execute," he repeated as he jumped up in the air as he ran. Another blue-white flash washed over the arena, followed by a second flash a split second later as the corporal landed in a run. "*Damn!*" he exclaimed as he jogged up to them. "I *love* that jump feature!"

"Just remember, your power pack has a limited supply," General Telles reminded him. "It powers all your systems, *including* the jump feature and your shields. Too many jumps and you'll find yourself without any protection."

"I'll still have this," Corporal Vasya replied, holding up his weapon, "and this," he added, pointing to his head.

"Just try not to overuse the jump feature," the general insisted. "It should only be used to escape certain death."

"Like from an incoming anti-personnel missile," Corporal Vasya replied, a smug look on his face.

"Precisely."

"Couldn't you give it more power?" the corporal asked Mister Ayseron.

"We are working on the problem," the SilTek engineer assured him. "There is just insufficient time. It was intended as a method of deployment and recovery," he pointed out.

Vasya's brow furrowed in confusion.

"From orbit," General Telles explained. "But the power requirements were more than what is currently available."

"You mean, we were going to be able to jump down to the surface and back up again?" Kit asked, shocked. "*Slick.*"

"Perhaps by your next mission," Mister Ayseron suggested.

"If we are successful tomorrow, there will be

ample time to perfect your higher-density energy cell," General Telles assured him. "However, in the meantime, the corporal has demonstrated a valid use for the jump system."

"Yes, yes," Mister Ayseron agreed. "Just *please* keep an eye on your energy levels and the rate of drain if you use the jump system more than a few times," he urged the corporal.

"No problem," the corporal promised. He took a few steps backward, executing another jump, transitioning five meters back and landing with a grin on his face.

"I believe that is all we can hope to accomplish before the mission," General Telles told Mister Ayseron. "I would like my men to have a few hours to practice using the new suits."

"I'll update all units immediately," Mister Ayseron promised. "You should be able to begin testing them within the hour."

"Excellent," General Telles congratulated.

"We are going to kick some ass tomorrow," Corporal Vasya stated confidently.

General Telles had no comment.

* * *

"A moment, Captain?" Miss Bindi inquired, moving quickly to catch up with Nathan in the corridor.

"Something on your mind, Miss Bindi?" Nathan asked as he walked.

"That was a touching moment back there," she stated. "I've never seen such pride in a man until today."

"The Corinari are a proud group," Nathan explained, "and with good reason. Other than the Ghatazhak, they are probably the finest warriors I've encountered."

"I got that impression."

Nathan noticed the troubled expression on Miss Bindi's face. "Something troubles you?"

"Actually, it is that emotion that troubles me. It was not just on the face of the major, but on everyone at the briefing, military and civilians alike."

"They were all proud of him."

"Is that all it was?" she postulated as they turned the corner, "Or was it more?"

"I'm afraid I'm not following you."

"I just wonder if pride is part of your people's motivation?"

"Of course it is," Nathan admitted. "You see something *wrong* with that?"

"In business school, we were taught that pride clouds one's judgment, causing them to make poor decisions. Given the task at hand and the risks involved, would you not consider that worrisome?"

"Not in the slightest," Nathan replied with confidence. "These people are trained to think clearly in the fog of war. And while it is true that many will succumb to that fog, those who do not are the ones who will lead."

"I always thought it was due to their charisma," Miss Bindi chuckled.

"In politics perhaps," Nathan replied, remembering his father. Nearing his destination, he stopped and turned to her. "I get the feeling there is something else," he told her.

"Miss Batista worries that *you* may be acting in haste, for emotional reasons."

"I see." Nathan thought for a moment. "Precisely *which* emotional reasons?"

"Pressure, pride, vengeance; pick one."

"I expect I feel all three," Nathan admitted, "as

well as others. But it would worry me *more* if I did *not* feel them. A brave man recognizes his emotions and doubts, and the way in which they affect him, yet finds a way to compensate for those effects and carry on."

"Then, you *do* have doubts?"

"Often more than I care to admit," Nathan replied, "but they serve to keep my ego in check; to remind me that I am neither infallible nor invincible. They cause me to listen to the advice of my peers as well as my subordinates, and constantly weigh them against my own instincts. You see, Miss Bindi, the most dangerous thing in the universe is a man with a gun and a belief that his purpose is so just that he must answer to no one. I assure you, I am not such a man."

"I was not implying that you were," Miss Bindi insisted. "Our concerns were just that your emotions might prevent you from retreating prior to achieving your goals, if such a retreat becomes warranted."

Nathan sighed again, becoming somewhat annoyed at her line of inquiry. "Rest assured, should our goal appear unachievable, or the price of victory too high, I *will* withdraw," he told her. "Better to live to fight another day," he added, as he continued onto the bridge, leaving her standing in the corridor.

"Captain," the Ghatazhak guard greeted politely.

Nathan paused, looking at the sergeant. "Now, was that so hard?"

"Actually, it was incredibly difficult," the sergeant said, a slight grin on his face.

Nathan smiled, continuing toward his command chair.

"The shuttle carrying General Telles and Major

Montrose has landed on Orswella," the tactical officer reported.

"Very well," Nathan replied, taking his seat. "Mister Sheehan, you're clear to break orbit and jump us to Rakuen."

"Aye, sir," Loki replied.

"If you'd like, you can take a few hours off to spend with your daughter," Nathan suggested.

"Don't we have to jump to SilTek, first?" Loki wondered.

"I believe your backup crew can handle that."

"Do I get a few hours off as well?" Josh wondered.

"Not that you deserve it, but yes," Nathan joked.

"Hot damn!" Josh exclaimed as he began leaving orbit.

"Plotting a jump back to Rakuen," Loki replied, smiling.

Cameron entered the bridge, coming up from behind. "What did Miss Bindi want?" she asked as she approached Nathan.

"To remind me of my responsibilities to the rest of the Alliance."

"Doesn't she know that's *my* job?" Cameron joked.

"Apparently not."

"What did you tell her?"

"That I'm a basket case like everyone else, but since I *know* it, it's okay."

"Oh, I'm sure that made her feel a *lot* better."

* * *

Major Doran Montrose sat in his office at the makeshift training base on Orswella, staring at the old patch in his hand. Like most military patches, its design was simple. A golden bird of prey with wings spread wide, clutching an arrow in one talon and a lightning bolt in the other. The bird hovered in front of a green planet, with a lone star hanging over him.

It was nothing more than a piece of cloth, stitched by an automated machine that spit out thousands of them, but it meant the world to him. His entire adult life had been spent in the service of his world, just as his father's, uncle's, and his long-lost brother's. A simple piece of cloth, but it identified those who bore it as men of honor, duty, and sacrifice.

That patch had not come easily, nor had it been retained without ongoing effort. The Corinari had endured four wars. The first had erupted long before his grandfather was born. A civil war over details so minor they had been lost to history for centuries. The second, his father's war, had been against a malfunctioning AI bent on their extermination. His war, the one against the reign of Caius Ta'Akar, had been the reason he and his brother had enlisted. It was also the only war the Corinari had lost. But they had survived and remained a military power for decades, albeit only as a matter of gracious compromise by their conquerors, in order to salvage their conquest before there was nothing left worth acquiring. And finally, the Corinari's biggest triumph since the AI wars: the defeat of the Takaran Empire and the liberation of their world.

Alas, their hard-won freedom had been short-lived. In one of the biggest political errors in Corinairan history, their leaders had disbanded the Corinari in favor of trusting an alliance of worlds to protect them. A mere seven years later, that mistake had cost them their freedom yet again.

Doran had held onto this patch, the one taken from one of his deceased brother's uniforms. It had been the last thing he'd tossed into his bag when he and his family were forced to evacuate their homeworld, yet it had come to be the most important thing he possessed.

Many had asked Doran why he chose to follow yet another alliance when the first had failed them. His answer was always that history shows there is strength in numbers, and that one world cannot hope to stand alone against the evils of humanity.

Doran took a deep breath, letting it out slowly as he rose, picking up the box of patches from his desk and heading down the corridor.

Doran exited the building, stepping into the waning sunlight of an Orswellan sunset. Above him, the lights of the stadium that had housed them for the last few weeks were just beginning to flicker to life. Before him stood eight hundred men, each of them well past their youth, but fit and ready for combat nonetheless. These men had wives and children...some waiting for them back on the Mystic Empress, some on Rakuen, and some right here on Orswella. Others had been forced to leave their loved ones behind on Corinair and knew not their fate. Yet all of these men, each with so much to lose and so little to personally gain, stood assembled before him, eager to answer the call they prayed was coming.

Rumors had abounded since the day they had begun their refresher training. The introduction of new weapons and new armor hinted at what was to come. In fact, Doran doubted that a single man among them had not already figured out why they had been training so hard lately. But they had yet to hear it from their own commander's mouth.

How can I lead these fine men? Doran asked himself. *What qualifies me above others?* Every one of them had bled and sweat as he had, and hundreds of them were just as qualified, if not more so. His second, Sergeant Major Denton Crawley, was a natural-born leader and had fought in more ground battles than Doran. After all, most of Doran's time in the Corinari had been spent as the crew chief of an airship, not on the battlefield. Even his time in the Alliance had been in the relative comfort of first the Aurora, then the Celestia. Granted, both ships had seen their share of combat during his time aboard, but nothing like they were about to face in the coming hours.

Doran stepped up onto the small podium, turned toward his men, and then tapped the side of his comm-set to tie it into those worn by every man assembled before him. He then dropped the box in front of him, allowing it to plop on the ground, causing the lid to pop off and patches to spill out for all to see. "Today, we are Alliance Marines. Tomorrow, we will return to our homeworld and liberate our people as Corinari."

In unison, all eight hundred gathered before him chanted, "*HUP, HUP, HUP!*"

* * *

Aiden exited his cabin, beginning his long trek to the bridge. His new ship, an ancient Orochi carrier ship converted into a missile frigate and then upgraded to a missile gunship, was now a formidable weapons platform, especially now that his crew was properly trained. But for the life of him, he couldn't understand why his cabin was so far from his primary duty station. The accommodations were good enough: a bed, a desk, a nice chair—he even had his own head. It was definitely better than the shared spaces on his previous gunship.

Unfortunately, the size of his crew had grown as well. What started as six had become eight, then twelve, and finally sixteen. He had a hard enough time remembering people's names, which was why he usually gave his crew nicknames. Now it was damned near impossible. Were it not for the names stitched on their uniforms, he would be completely lost.

It all made for a disconnect between him and his crew, one that he didn't much care for. He liked being friends with those he led. Now he couldn't really be *friends* with any of them for fear of showing favoritism. At least the majority of his bridge crew were familiar faces.

To make matters even more challenging, the crew was a mix of Rakuens, Nerameseans, Cetians, and Terrans. Tiny cliques of two or three had already formed among the crew, each group sticking to their own kind. Aiden supposed it was only natural. People felt more comfortable around those of their own ilk. It was nothing personal—except for the grudge between the Rakuens and Nerameseans. It was just the way it was.

The fact that his XO was probably younger than most of the crew didn't help matters. Ledge was much like Aiden, in the sense that he would rather be liked than respected. He was smart, but he was even younger than Aiden and looked it. Then again, even Captain Scott looked younger than most of the people he commanded.

Aiden had resigned himself to the fact that it would take time for his crew to accept Ledge as their executive officer, as well as Aiden as their captain. Still, he had been forced to pull rank on several occasions during their countless training drills, especially with the Rakuens, who felt a unique sense of pride and ownership for the Orochi. To the rest of the crew, it was just a ship, and an ancient one at that. To the Rakuens, it was one of two classes of ships that had enabled their hard-fought victory against the Nerameseans so long ago.

Aiden climbed up the short stepladder that led from the ship's main deck to its redesigned command deck. The original version had been nothing more than a cockpit with four stations. The new version was considerably larger, with a single helm station front and center; and tactical, sensor, and communications stations spread evenly around the perimeter of the compact bridge.

The best part was the command chair. Situated in the center of the compartment, it was flanked on either side by small consoles and raised a step above the rest of the deck. This allowed its occupant an unobstructed view through the forward and side windows encircling the forward half of the compact but efficiently designed space.

Aiden really like his bridge. He hated that he no longer piloted his own ship, but he loved that command chair. In it, he truly felt like a ship's captain. Funny thing was, he had never aspired to *be* in command. All he had ever wanted was to fly. In the atmosphere, in space, it didn't matter. Flying was fun, but now that he had gotten a taste of *being* captain, he found he liked it.

The transition from pilot-in-command to captain had been a difficult one. Having to verbalize what he wanted to happen in the form of commands was quite different than simply doing it himself. The mere act of instructing a helmsman as to what maneuvers to fly was foreign to him. Over countless hours of drills and exercises, however, he had grown accustomed to his new responsibilities and was even beginning to feel comfortable...for the most part.

Aiden stepped up to the communications station at the aft of the bridge. "What's the message?" he asked Tati.

"I don't know," his communications officer replied, handing him a data pad. "Your eyes only."

Aiden pressed his finger against the reader at the bottom of the pad, identifying himself to the device so as to display the message. As he read, his eyes widened.

"Uh oh," Tati commented, noticing her captain's expression.

"What is it?" Ali asked from the sensor station.

"Looks like play time is over," Aiden replied. "How many are off ship?" he asked Tati.

"As far as I know, just the XO and the cheng. They went down to Orswella to pick up supplies."

"Tell them to grab what they need and get back ASAP," Aiden instructed. "It's time to go to work."

* * *

Nathan plopped down on the couch in his quarters, exhausted from a day of last-minute meetings as they prepared for what he hoped would be their final assault on the Dusahn. It had been a whirlwind of a month, with more changes taking place on the Aurora than he could ever remember.

Nathan removed his comm-set and leaned back, closing his eyes for a moment. His mind raced with a thousand details. He had finally reached the point where he remembered every detail of what the Aurora could do, and now that had all changed.

"*Captain?*" Aurora's voice called from the overhead speakers.

Nathan sighed. "Aurora?"

"*Yes, Captain. Do you have a moment?*"

"What is it?" Nathan replied, his eyes still closed.

"*I have a question.*"

"Go ahead," he instructed.

"*Why did you adjust my voice to sound similar to Captain Taylor's?*"

Nathan opened his eyes, surprised by his AI's question. "I don't know. I suppose because Captain Taylor tends to be my anchor."

"*I assume you mean she helps you to remain grounded,*" Aurora surmised.

"Something like that. Why do you ask?"

"*Part of my function is to anticipate your needs. To do so, it is important that I know everything possible about you.*"

"You mean like how I do things?"

"*Yes, but also how you think, your approach to problem-solving, your interaction with others. I have studied all of your action reports and logs, as well as all battle telemetry and video records.*"

"Then you should have your answers," Nathan concluded.

"*What I have are more questions,*" Aurora admitted. "*In particular, about how you sometimes come to your decisions. As best I can tell, unless there is some additional historical data that I do not yet have access to, you seem to guess a lot.*"

Nathan smiled. "Don't tell anyone."

"*I do not understand.*"

"I'm joking," Nathan told her, sitting up. "I tend to follow hunches."

"*There are two definitions for the word. I assume it has nothing to do with the position of your shoulders.*"

Nathan smiled again. "Correct."

"So you are making decisions based on intuition rather than on known facts."

"More often than not, yes," Nathan admitted. "Is that a problem?"

"No, but it does make my job a bit more difficult. I am supposed to imprint your tactics and preferences on my matrix. However, I'm not sure an AI can develop 'intuition'."

"I wouldn't worry about it too much."

"I do not worry."

"Of course," Nathan said, leaning back and closing his eyes again.

"Captain Taylor, on the other hand, is much easier to anticipate," Aurora continued. *"It is obvious that her decisions are based on available facts, and guided by protocols and procedures."*

"Yeah, she'd make a great AI," Nathan joked. "Don't tell her I said that," he added, raising his hand for emphasis.

"I do not share private conversations with third parties unless instructed to do so by all participants."

"Good to know," Nathan replied, putting his hand back down.

"I am not certain how I am going to properly serve as your AI," Aurora admitted. *"Do you always follow your intuition?"*

Nathan opened his eyes and sat up again. "Not always. Sometimes I follow procedure."

"Not often, according to the records I've examined."

Nathan chuckled, rising to his feet and heading to his bedroom. "Now you sound like Cam." He stopped suddenly as an idea came to him. "You know, since you already *sound* like her, maybe you can just *act* like she would. Can you imprint *her* tactics and preferences onto your matrix?"

"*It is possible,*" Aurora admitted. "*However, it is not standard protocol. Perhaps I can find a way to merge the two personalities.*"

"Now *that's* a scary thought," Nathan said as he entered his bedroom. "Is there anything else?"

"*Only that it is zero hundred hours ship time. You now have eighteen hours until mission zero.*"

"Thank you, Aurora," Nathan replied as he plopped down on his bed.

"*Sleep well, Captain,*" the voice of his ship replied as it turned out the lights.

* * *

Jessica stood at the Aurora's tactical station, just behind the command chair, studying the displays on her console. The lighting was set to its lowest workable level, and there were only two others on the bridge at the moment.

"I didn't expect to see you here," Cameron commented as she entered the bridge from the captain's ready room and came up from behind Jessica. "What are you doing?"

"Studying intel on Dusahn ships," Jessica replied, "or should I say, *Aurora* is studying it. We're trying to identify vulnerabilities, so I can set them as primary targeting points. That way, I can just tap a target, and Aurora will assign the appropriate weapons turret and handle the actual targeting."

"Did you run this past Nathan?" Cameron wondered.

"He's sleeping. I just thought of it an hour ago. It's the only way I'm going to be able to keep up with everything, especially since you're not going to be here to help me, and combat control has been taken out of the loop."

Cameron sighed. "Yeah, I hate the idea of not being here during a battle."

"Someone's gotta be able to look at the big picture and keep everyone coordinated," Jessica reminded her.

"I suppose." Cameron looked around the darkened bridge. "I still can't get used to this."

Jessica looked up, glancing about. "The dim lighting?"

"The lack of duty personnel," Cameron corrected. "Too many empty seats."

"Aurora can respond to any surprises far faster than we mere humans can," Jessica stated, her focus returning to her console displays. "All it takes is one duty officer to give her permission to act. Besides, the rest of the bridge staff could be here in just over a minute, if needed. But you know all of that."

"I do," Cameron admitted. "It's still difficult to get used to." She sighed again. "I guess that's the way life is under the command of Nathan Scott. Everything changes rapidly."

"And that bothers you?" Jessica wondered.

"I wouldn't say it *bothers* me," Cameron insisted, "but it *does* make things more challenging."

"I *like* challenging," Jessica replied with a smile.

"We all do, otherwise we wouldn't be here," Cameron explained. "I guess I just got a little complacent over the years. Got accustomed to my routines. I had every system, every procedure, every protocol on this ship tuned to perfection."

"I thought the Aurora had a high turnover rate?" Jessica pointed out.

"We did," Cameron confirmed, "but that's because we were so good at sharpening up newbs. Command would send us every boot-ensign straight out of the academy, and six months later most of them would leave as lieutenants, reassigned to the latest destroyer coming out of the Cetian shipyards. The academy cast them, and we ground off the rough edges and polished them up."

"You must've *loved* that," Jessica chuckled. "All those drills."

"Oh yes, we had a lot of them," Cameron remembered. "There was an expression among junior officers all over the fleet. The Aurora was the post-graduate school. You weren't *really* an officer until you were *Taylored.*"

Jessica cast a glance Cameron's way. "I guess it really shook things up when you absconded with the ship."

"Probably."

Jessica stopped studying her console, finally devoting her full attention to the conversation. "You ever regret it?"

"I'd be lying if I said otherwise," Cameron admitted. "Especially at moments like this."

"Like what?"

"Greatly outnumbered and outgunned, about to take on a superior force in half a dozen systems...all at the same time. Honestly, I can't help but wonder how Nathan's going to top this one."

"I think his plan is to avoid having to do so."

"You don't think this plan is too ambitious?" Cameron asked.

"Of course I do," Jessica admitted. "But when has one of his plans *not* been too ambitious? That's what he does."

"Yeah, but *before*, he always questioned his decisions. He was constantly plagued by self-doubt."

"That was a *bad* thing."

"Yes, but it also kept him in check; kept him from acting too impulsively."

"What you mean to say is that his self-doubt gave you the leverage you needed to exert some control over him."

"I've never had any control over Nathan Scott," Cameron insisted.

"Yes you have," Jessica insisted. "More than you know. Why do you think he called you for help?"

"Because he needed this ship."

"No," Jessica argued. "Well, partly, but mostly because he needed *you*. He knows that you'll question every decision he makes. He knows that you'll over-analyze everything and point out the flaws in his plans. More importantly, he knows he can trust you to be out there watching over his absurdly ambitious, multi-front engagements, keeping him from doing anything stupid."

"Like betting the entire ship?"

"Yeah, that was pretty crazy," Jessica admitted.

"I still don't understand why you let him do that."

"You should have seen the look in his eyes," Jessica told her. "*Complete* confidence. I see that same look in the eyes of *every* Ghatazhak. It's what I'm *still* trying to achieve. The eyes of Nathan Scott, master of self-doubt, was the *last* place I expected to see *that* look."

"That alone should have set off alarms, don't you think?" Cameron said. "I mean, total confidence is *not* Nathan."

"That's the thing," Jessica explained. "He's *not* Nathan anymore. At least he's not the Nathan who surrendered to the Jung seven years ago." Jessica chuckled. "Hell, Josh's *Conathan* nickname for him is more accurate than we realize."

"What are you talking about?"

"I've been training with him for months now," Jessica told her. "I've seen the changes he has gone through. He is *better* now. His *brain* works better. He sees everything in a glance. He analyzes the situation and computes every possible outcome in the blink of an eye, and all with greater depth and clarity than any of us, *including* the Ghatazhak. Except maybe Telles."

"So, you *do* believe the cloning process somehow improved him."

"You don't?"

"It's just kind of hard to believe at times."

"Well, if it makes you feel any better, I don't think it's just the cloning process. I think his time as Connor has something to do with it as well. You still see the universe through the eyes of a Terran. You relate everything to life *as* a Terran."

"And you don't?"

"Not as much as you," Jessica insisted. "I've been on a lot more worlds than you have, running missions for the Ghatazhak for the last seven years. Don't get me wrong, I'm not saying that's a bad thing. I'm saying that Nathan, as Connor Tuplo, engaged with *dozens* of civilizations and cultures. That gave him a much broader experience than any of us. Combine that with the training that he received at the academy and growing up in a powerful political family... Well, you get super Nathan. Or as Josh calls him, Conathan."

Cameron thought for a moment. "There is such a thing as *over*confidence, you know."

"Yeah, Telles is constantly reminding me of that," Jessica admitted.

After sighing yet again, Cameron added, "I guess

I just can't get past the idea that he bet the *entire* ship."

"Doesn't he do that every time he takes it into battle?"

"I suppose," Cameron admitted, "but it's not the same. I guess I just miss the old Nathan."

"So do I," Jessica assured her. "But I'd rather go into battle with the new one."

Cameron forced a smile. "I'm going to hit my rack," she decided. "You should do the same."

"As soon as I finish this," Jessica promised.

Cameron smiled again, then turned and left the bridge.

"Sir?" one of the bridge officers asked. "Can you watch the conn for a few minutes while we take a break?"

Jessica glanced at the young lieutenant and the even younger ensign staring at him with stars in her eyes. "Sure," she replied, fighting back a grin. "Just don't take too long."

"Thank you, sir," the lieutenant replied, after which the two of them departed.

Jessica returned her attention to her displays.

"*Lieutenant Commander,*" the ship's AI began. "*I apologize for eavesdropping, but I could not help overhearing your conversation with Captain Taylor. I hope that does not bother you.*"

"It does," Jessica admitted, "but I suppose that's the price of having an AI hooked into your ship."

"*I can adjust my privacy mode and set my audio monitoring algorithms to only listen for key words and phrases, especially when you are speaking, if you prefer.*"

"No, that's okay," Jessica insisted. "I suppose I'll get used to it."

"If it makes you feel any better, audio and video monitoring only takes place in public spaces, and the recordings are only accessible under command authority."

"So you're not spying on me when I'm in my quarters then," Jessica joked.

"Of course not," Aurora insisted. *"Unless I detect a problem."*

"Such as?"

"A life-threatening malfunction or condition, an explosive device, or an unauthorized weapon to name a few."

"Is there a point to this conversation?" Jessica wondered.

"I thought you might like to know that I have analyzed every aspect of the upcoming engagement, and I find no evidence that Captain Scott is acting irrationally. If anything, he is thinking much like an AI."

"And that's supposed to make me feel better?"

CHAPTER ELEVEN

The re-ball stadium on Orswella was bustling with activity. Brilliant floodlights made the pre-dawn light seem as bright as day as SilTek battle tanks rolled into the cargo pods, waiting to be ferried to the Glendanon by boxcars.

Doran Montrose looked out across the re-ball field from the observation platform surrounding his command hut, watching his men as they prepared for departure. Even from this distance, he could feel their excitement and confidence. They were about to liberate their world. Many would die, but all would be heroes, remembered forever as saviors of Corinair.

There was so much that Doran was grateful for on this morning. His family, his people...but as he looked upon his men, he couldn't help but appreciate the way the SilTek engineers had managed to incorporate the overall *feel* of the Corinari uniform into the new combat armor his men now wore. Between it and the Corinari patches the men wore on their shoulders, the people of his home world would instantly know who was fighting the Dusahn on their behalf. Corinairans were a proud people, and many of them would pick up arms dropped by dead Dusahn soldiers and join in the fight. He wanted no Corinari deaths due to friendly fire. The battle would be chaotic enough without having to defend against those they were trying to liberate.

His job, however, was far easier than that of the Ghatazhak. No Corinairans would ever side with a conqueror, regardless of any improvements that conqueror might bring. It simply wasn't in the Corinairan mindset. He and his men would be welcomed as heroes.

The Takaran people, however, were a different story. The Dusahn had improved conditions for their working class and eliminated all but four of the noble houses of Takara. Although they had seized the holdings of all those fallen houses, they had invested much of that capital back into the working classes, especially toward those who had suddenly found themselves without the protection of a noble house. This had gone a long way toward swaying Takara's citizens in favor of Dusahn rule. The Ghatazhak were far more likely to encounter civilian resistance to their efforts, even though it was their own people. The true nature of the Ghatazhak had been lost decades ago, thanks to their use as brainwashed shock-troops under the rule of Caius Ta'Akar. For years prior to the arrival of the Dusahn, there had been rumors of a rogue band of Ghatazhak operating on the fringes of the Pentaurus cluster, but these were dismissed by most. To the people of Takara, the Ghatazhak were stone-cold killers with no regard for the welfare of civilians, even their fellow Takarans.

"It's been too long since I've seen the proud ranks of the Corinari," Sergeant Major Crawley commented as he joined his friend at the rail.

"I can't stop thinking about how many of them won't be seeing another sunrise," Doran replied, watching the Orswellan sun as it began to spill out over the far mountains.

"You can't think that way, not if you're going to lead them."

"I cannot help it."

Denton sighed. "Which is probably why you're the right man for the job."

"Wait, you just said..."

"Don't listen to me," Denton insisted. "I'm just an old Sergeant Major looking for one more chance at glory."

Doran smiled. "Did your men have enough time to get used to their tanks?"

"Their *tanks*, yes. Their *AI*s, not so much."

"Is that going to be a problem?" Doran wondered.

"I suspect they'll start trusting them once the AIs save their asses a few times."

"At least they get to *drive* their own tanks," Doran commented. "MI has to fall from orbit in pilotless Kalibris."

"Yeah, what drunk bobbet came up with *that* idea," Denton said.

"An AI," Doran replied.

"Figures," Denton chuckled, turning to depart. "See you on Corinair, my friend."

* * *

Commander Prechitt turned to study the large view screen on the wall behind him. "These computer-generated images were stitched together using scans obtained by the Corinairan resistance—at great risk, I might add." He turned back toward the fifty Corinari pilots assembled before him in the makeshift briefing room aboard the Glendanon. "The Dusahn air defenses are quite heavy. Some might call them impenetrable. It's our job to penetrate them. We'll jump in fast and low, and at point-blank range. Those air defense batteries are completely automated, which means they can bring their guns to bear more quickly, and they can target you more accurately. You will have five seconds to jump in, get your target locks, launch your weapons, and pull up to jump clear. Those batteries are located in densely populated areas, so it is *imperative* that you have solid targeting locks before you release. I'm talking green boxes with good tones, people. No flickering squeaks. Those are our people down there."

"Can't the resistance warn them?" Talisha asked.

"Too risky," the pilot next to her commented.

"Any unusual movement patterns of the locals would alert the Dusahn that an attack was coming," Commander Prechitt explained. "Hopefully, our people will head for shelter the moment the first explosions are heard."

"How are we going to take out the defenses for an entire planet with only fifty ships?" another pilot inquired.

"We don't have to," the commander replied. "Only Aitkenna has the self-powered defense batteries. The rest of the cities are using batteries which draw power from either shared reactors or directly from the local grid. Take out the power source, and you take out multiple batteries at the same time. Besides, Aitkenna is the seat of Dusahn power. We seize Aitkenna, and the rest will fall. Word will go out, and the people in those cities will seek shelter for fear of becoming collateral damage. Once they do, we can take out the remaining defenses from orbit."

"What about their troops?" Talisha asked.

"We've got eight hundred heavily armed Corinari and about one hundred battle tanks. They'll be divided among Aitkenna, Crawford, and Becketts. Once those three cities are under our control, Kalibri airships will ferry our ground forces to other cities to deal with any remaining Dusahn ground forces."

"That's going to take time," Talisha commented.

"Yes, it will. We are hoping that once Aitkenna

falls, the Dusahn will evacuate their forces from other cities in order to defend Takara."

"I thought we were trying to liberate Takara as well," Talisha said. "Isn't that going to make it harder?"

"Gunyoki will be handling intercept of evacuation ships from orbit, and once the air defense batteries are down, we'll be targeting any evac ships as well," the commander explained. He looked at the faces of his pilots, taking in a deep breath and letting it out slowly. "Five seconds is a *very* tight action window. The first wave will do fine, but there are one hundred and eighteen self-powered defense batteries in Aitkenna alone. I would strongly recommend that you turn over launch control to your AIs and let them fire your weapons so that you can concentrate on flying and avoiding incoming fire."

"You want us to trust AIs to fire weapons into our own people?" one of the pilots questioned.

"I know it rubs everyone the wrong way," the commander admitted. "It doesn't make me happy either. But doing so will *protect* our people. A half-second delay between obtaining a solid target lock and pressing the launch button is enough to get you killed. And no matter how steely eyed a pilot you are, that knowledge is enough to cause you to jump the gun and launch too early, or even worse, too late. Too early, and collateral damage goes up. Too late, you die, and our chances of liberating our homeworld go down. It's a fucked-up situation, I admit. But it's our job to deal with it. That's what the Corinari do." Commander Prechitt turned his gaze toward the pilot who had asked the question. "Is that understood?"

"Hup, hup, hup, sir," the pilot replied with a grin.

"Hup, hup, hup," the commander replied, pressing the button on the remote to call up the next image.

* * *

Cameron had always considered the Aurora's interior spaces to be reasonably sized; not too tight and not to spacious. She had seen a few ships in her time, but other than the interiors of shuttles, the Manamu's interior spaces were probably the tightest she'd seen.

Cameron stepped out of the cramped corridor and through the hatch leading to the cargo ship's bridge. The first thing that hit her was the presence of real windows spread across the front of the compartment. After nine years aboard the Earth's Explorer-class ships, she had grown accustomed to not having windows. In fact, now that she was faced with a whole row of them, she felt rather unsettled.

"Welcome aboard, Captain," Captain Madrid greeted, noticing Cameron standing at the hatch and staring out the windows. "Quite a view, isn't it? Although I'm sure it doesn't compare to the Aurora's spherical view screen. I hear it's quite impressive."

"That's a lot of windows," Cameron stated.

"Don't worry," Captain Madrid chuckled. "We'll close the blast doors before we depart."

"I certainly hope so."

"No windows aboard the Aurora, huh?"

"No, there are not." Cameron took a breath, getting back to business. "Everything ready?"

"We've got your command pod set up in the forward cargo bay, and it's tied into the ship's communications and sensor arrays."

"How are your weapons and shields?" Cameron asked.

"We've only got four mini-plasma turrets—two

forward and two aft—so we won't be staying put long enough to slug it out with anyone, even with the shield upgrades."

"And your jump drive?"

"Upgraded, tested, and fully charged. We can jump you anywhere within five hundred light years in a single jump and a thousand light years in two jumps."

"And your bays?" Cameron wondered.

"We're loaded with supplies and propellant, and we've got three medical disaster pods lined up next to your command pod. The aft bays will be used for staging the wounded, and the forward bays for treatment. Every warm body who's ever put on a bandage is gathered there, standing by to receive the wounded."

"Let's hope they don't have much to do," Cameron said. "Might as well jump out to the rally point now."

"A little early, isn't it?" Captain Madrid replied.

"I'd rather have time to recharge before the show begins," Cameron explained. "One thing I've learned is, there's no such thing as too much jump juice."

* * *

The gallery had once been one of the favorite places for fans to watch the Gunyoki arrive and depart. On any given race day, every tier of the massive deck would be packed with spectators, each vying to catch a glimpse of their favorite Gunyoki.

Today, the gallery was empty. Try as they had, the Gunyoki had been unable to continue the contest schedule and had been forced to abandon it altogether, promising that it would someday return. After all, their world was now on a war footing, and had been for nearly two months. The pilots who had once raced for glory and fortune now flew to protect not only their own world, but also the worlds of their allies.

Vol stood at the gallery window, squinting to more clearly see the departing fighters. One hundred fighters, led by four of his best pilots, had been committed to the liberation effort. Two thirds of their overall force, flying to an uncertain future. It saddened him that many would likely not return, even more so that he could not lead them into battle himself.

Vol had done his part. He had trained them all, put them through countless exercises, challenged them to push themselves beyond their limits. He had gone over every detail of the upcoming mission with them, discussing every possible thing that could go wrong and how to best deal with it. He only hoped it would be enough.

With a heavy heart, Vol sighed and turned away from the window. His damaged sight had taken away his right to fly into combat. Now all he could do was wait for them to return.

Command was lonely that way.

* * *

General Telles stood on the cavernous cargo deck of the second ship in the Karuzari Alliance's meager fleet to receive a long-range jump drive. The largest ship in the Alliance, the Glendanon had served a multitude of roles over the last few months, all of them crucial.

Today was no different.

Before him, the last surviving ninety-seven Ghatazhak, clad in their new combat gear, lined up to board the specially lengthened cargo pods installed in the two Contra cargo ships they had been using on Orswella for the past month.

The Contra ships were ill-designed for this task, almost to the point of being comical. Their only qualification was their robust design, an attribute that would serve them well in their upcoming mission to deliver his men to the surface of their homeworld. More importantly, this was not the first time the ships had flown into combat. The unattractive ships had proven themselves time and again. Now, with shields and ground suppression turrets installed, they were even more formidable. It was another example of the Karuzari philosophy of making anything you could into a weapon.

It was times like these that made the general wonder. A mere decade earlier, he and his men were hunting the Karuzari and slaughtering them wherever they were found, for the good of the Takaran Empire. Now he was leading those same men under the name of their former enemy, again for the good of their homeworld, Takara.

"I do not envy you," a familiar voice spoke from behind.

General Telles turned to see Edom Gullen, captain of the Glendanon.

"You will be outnumbered a hundred to one," Captain Gullen continued.

"More like a thousand to one," Telles corrected.

"Then I hope what they say about the Ghatazhak is true; that one is worth ten ordinary men."

"That estimate is low," the general replied, a deadly serious expression on his face.

Captain Gullen laughed. "You do not lack confidence, do you."

"It is all about knowing where to strike and how," the general assured him.

Captain Gullen looked out across the bay at the

columns of black-clad soldiers. "I like your new gear," he commented. "I've heard good things about it. I hope it is all true. A lot is riding on it."

"We shall see," the general replied, turning his attention back to his men.

"Good luck to you, General," Captain Gullen said, patting the general on the shoulder as he departed.

"To you as well."

* * *

"The last comm-drone has jumped in," Ensign Hintz reported. "Bulldog One reports all Orochi are at their respective rally points."

Cameron stood, bent slightly over the plotting table in the middle of the command and control pod, reviewing the positions of all the elements in their strike force, as well as the last known locations and courses of all Dusahn forces, both in space and on the surfaces of Takara and Corinair. "Any changes in intel?"

"Last recon showed no changes in position or course, or any irregular movement patterns," Lieutenant Commander Shinoda assured her.

Cameron sighed. "I wish we had something more recent. Two hours is a long time with so much on the line."

"There has been no change in their movement patterns for the last week," the lieutenant commander reminded her. "There is no reason to suspect there would be some now."

"Have you forgotten what I taught you?" Cameron asked her intelligence officer.

"Expect the unexpected, I know," the lieutenant commander recited. "As an intelligence officer, I can only make predictions based on the most recent data, measured against past data, and extrapolate predictions from them. But they are only predictions. It is up to you to decide whether or not they should be acted upon."

"Nice job of passing the buck," Cameron commented, glancing at him as she stood upright.

"Just making sure you don't mistake me for a clairvoyant," he joked.

"Comms, send the green light to all units," Cameron instructed her comms officer.

* * *

"Flash traffic from C and C," Naralena reported. "Message reads: Marlene."

Nathan sat motionless in the command chair. It was more than just his deceased mother's name; it was the signal to begin the final push to free the Pentaurus cluster from Dusahn rule. On two worlds in two systems, hundreds, if not thousands, were about to die. And for what?

Nathan often pondered the question of whether or not he had any more right to use force to remove the Dusahn than the Dusahn had to take the cluster by force. In either case, many humans would die.

Corinair was easy enough to justify. Those who had escaped had *asked* for help. They *wanted* their world liberated, and knowing the people of that world, he had no doubt that the few spoke the minds of the many.

Takara, on the other hand, was a different story. Only a small fraction of his alliance hailed from Takara. The Ghatazhak and a few of the crew from various ships within their fleet. Takaran society had always been somewhat fractured, with the noble class building their wealth upon the backs of the commoners. Even after decades of oppression under Caius, and then under the Council of Nobles after the assassination of the very man who had freed them, Takarans still cared more about their safety and prosperity than their actual freedom. Despite the commonality of the theme, Nathan never could understand it. To him, freedom meant everything.

Still, the question remained. *Did he have the right to decide that freedom should be paramount for everyone else as well?*

"Two minutes to mission zero," Jessica warned, noticing her captain's lack of reaction to the go signal.

"General quarters," Nathan replied calmly.

The trim lighting around the Aurora's bridge suddenly turned red as alert klaxons sounded throughout the ship. The sound of his communications officer's voice echoed through every corridor and compartment as she called the crew to battle stations. Without looking, and without the least bit of monitoring of his crew, Nathan knew that every single one of them was moving without hesitation to their action stations.

Thirty-two seconds after the alert was sounded, the last indicator light on the comms officer's status board changed from green to red, signaling that all compartments were ready for action.

"Ship is at general quarters," Naralena reported. "Chief of the boat is in damage control."

The missing phrase struck Nathan as odd. There was no executive officer aboard the Aurora this day, nor was there a functioning combat command and control, the latter having been handed over to their AI. It was a huge leap of faith, but one that had to be taken. Humans suffered reaction time. AIs did not.

"All weapons are charged and ready," Jessica reported from the tactical station. "Shields are at maximum, AI is in the targeting loop." Jessica glanced at the mission clock at the upper right corner of her console. "Forty seconds to first strike launch."

In a minute and a half, the Aurora would swing into action.

"Flash traffic from command," the Glendanon's comms officer reported. "One word: Marlene."

Captain Gullen sighed. "The end begins," he said to himself. "Spread the word throughout the ship and set general quarters."

The comms officer swallowed hard before replying, "Aye, sir."

"Why Marlene?" the Weatherly's helmsman wondered aloud.

"It's Captain Scott's mother's name," Captain Hunt explained. "She was killed during the Jung's invasion of Earth."

"I thought she was killed with the rest of his family, by that bomb."

"Nope, she was killed years ago. Same with his brother."

"Damn, that guy has been through the ringer."

"You have no idea," Captain Hunt assured his helmsman.

"Relay from Bulldog One," Delan reported from the back seat of their Gunyoki fighter.

"Marlene?" Jenna assumed.

"Marlene."

Jenna pressed her transmit button. "Tekka leader to all ships. We have a green light. The Orochi will be launching their missiles shortly and then jumping to their next launch point. Each of you knows who you're escorting. Stay with them and protect them."

"I'd rather be going after some Dusahn gunships," Dosne commented from Tekka Two.

"Or frigates!" Rodai added from Tekka Four.

"We're escorts, people," Jenna reminded them. "And by keeping the Orochi safe, we're allowing them to take out the Dusahn's defenses, thus making it *easier* for Dota and Maigo squadrons to take out those targets."

"Yeah, and those guys need all the help they can get," Damus joked from Tekka Three.

"Just keep your eyes open for bandits and be ready to jump when we get the signal," Jenna reminded them, smiling.

"Marlene," Ensign Yamma reported from Orochi Three's comm-station.

"Here we go, people," Aiden said. "Ledge?"

"Target package Tango Five is loaded," Commander Leger replied from the tactical station, doing his best to sound confident in his new position. "Twenty-eight missiles have confirmed their targets and show launch ready."

"Time to launch?" Aiden asked.

"Twenty seconds."

"Missiles free," Aiden instructed. "Auto-launch on zero."

"Missiles free, launch on zero, aye," Ledge replied. He quickly armed all twenty-eight missiles, one quarter of their entire compliment, readying them for launch. Everything had been calculated by the Aurora's AI. The time it took for each missile to leave its rails; to reach their jump points; even the milliseconds the missile would spend in their jump across the five-light-year span between their current position and their targets; all had to be perfect.

Ledge was glad he didn't have to push the actual launch button. "Five seconds to auto-launch," he reported. "All missiles are hot."

Aiden watched the left-most overhead view screen, the one displaying the external view of the left dorsal portion of his ship. In unison, seven missiles leapt from their launch rails. At half-second intervals, the process repeated three more times, sending all twenty-eight missiles racing forth into the blackness.

Aiden cast his eyes downward slightly, taking in the view through the forward windows just as twenty-eight tiny flashes of blue-white light announced the departure of the weapons. "Jump us to the next launch point," he instructed his helmsman.

Commander Prechitt glanced at the mission time clock on his Nighthawk's main console just as it reached zero. "Mission zero, boys and girls. We jump in thirty seconds."

"*Three rapid sequence jumps over six light years, ending up in the atmosphere a thousand meters off the deck...what could go wrong?*"

"*Just trust your AI, Arre,*" Talisha insisted.

"*Easy for you to say,*" Arre replied.

"Can it, Arre," Commander Prechitt chided. "Remember: fly your ships and let your AIs launch your weapons. And for the sake of your fellow Corinairans, don't jump out until you're certain your weapons are away."

"*Piece of cake, boss,*" another pilot chimed in.

The commander glanced at his mission clock again as it passed twenty-five seconds into the mission. "See you at the other end of the jump. Good hunting," he added as his Nighthawk was engulfed in blue-white light.

"Target package Echo is loaded," Commander Kadish reported from Orochi Sixteen's tactical station. "All missiles show ready for launch. Auto-launch sequencer is activated."

"Let 'em rip," Captain Roselle agreed from the command chair.

"Auto-launch in five seconds," the commander reported.

Gil punched up the camera view for the starboard missile deck on one of the view screens above the forward windows as his XO counted down the last few seconds to launch. Upon reaching zero, twenty-eight missiles left their launchers in near-simultaneous fashion. He brought his eyes downward to the forward windows as the missiles streaked ahead of them and then disappeared in an array of blue-white flashes of light. "That's going to fuck up someone's day," he chuckled. "Mister Dorlon, jump us to the next launch point."

"Jump complete," the helmsman of Bulldog One reported. "We are at launch point Kilo.

"Missiles should be jumping now," the Orochi's tactical officer reported.

"Load the next target package and prepare to launch another twenty-eight," Captain Nash ordered from his command chair.

"We are going to rain hell upon them," Commander Kraska mumbled as he loaded the next target package into the system.

"Thousands of people are going to die today," Robert sternly reminded his XO. "Many of whom have no choice in the matter. Out of respect, you might want to be a little less *happy* about it."

"Sorry, sir," the commander apologized. "It just feels good to get some payback."

"I understand," Robert assured him. Deep down inside, he agreed with his friend. It did feel good to strike back in a major way. And with sixteen Orochi launching waves of twenty-eight missiles each, they truly were bringing hell to the Dusahn Empire.

The hour was late, and most of the residents of Corinair's capital city, Aitkenna, were already fast asleep. As expected, the streets were relatively empty except for Dusahn security patrols and the occasional automated service vehicle.

Dozens of flashes of blue-white light, some far, some near, lit up the dark skies above the sleeping city. Their initial arrival was silent but was announced a second later by a cacophony of thunderous claps, as if the atmosphere itself was being torn open. The thunder was joined a few seconds later by dozens of explosions all over the city as the incoming weapons found their targets.

The Dusahn had wisely hijacked the Takaran communications satellite network the very first day they had seized control of the system. To it, they had added their own components, upgrading the system into one that could relay commands, via jump-capable communications drones, to all the worlds in the Pentaurus sector, as well as to their ships that patrolled their new empire. It was a near-perfect system except for one critical flaw: it was woefully underpowered. Because of this, it could not run its protective shields around the clock and had to periodically drop them to allow its reserve power stores to replenish. An even bigger mistake was that it did so on a regular, predictable schedule.

Once the missile arrived behind a silent flash of blue-white light against the starry background, the automated relay satellite had only seconds to raise its shields to full power. While it was able to absorb the impact and subsequent detonation of the first missile, its power levels were insufficient to stave off the detonation of the second.

Somewhere in the Dusahn Empire, the designer of the relay satellite would face severe punishment.

The Dusahn communications relay system not only allowed for near-real-time communication throughout the empire, it also provided failsafes. Regular, automated contact and status update signals were exchanged, regardless of the presence of any carried communications. Such signals were designed to alert command, as well as the rest of the ships in the fleet, if a vessel developed a problem, came under attack, or was otherwise removed from the chain of communications.

The assault ships in orbit over Takara and Corinair would never get the message, as they were the first ships to be targeted. Their shields down and their crews complacent after weeks of peace, quiet, and mundane routines, their deaths were likely immediate and, for the most part, painless. One moment they were there, the next they were a fireball of expanding gasses and debris.

* * *

For as long as he could remember, Lord Dusahn had begun his morning with Chankarti training. Most days, he would change from his sleepwear directly into his black and crimson combat robes. The disciplines involved helped center his mind, balance his temper, and left him feeling as if he were in total control of mind and body. It had long ago become like a drug to him. Chankarti had made him everything he was. It had given him the ability to defeat his brothers and take the lordship. It had given him the ferocity to do what others would deem unthinkable; things that needed to be done if one was to build great empires.

This day had begun like all the rest. Full contact combat with his most advanced Chankarti masters. Each morning, he beat the crap out of these men, and yet, they continued to return the next day. Rarely did one of them not appear as scheduled. They were true masters of mind over body, which was at the core of the ancient Jung discipline.

Lord Dusahn stood at the side of the combat triad, sweat dripping down his face. Before him lay his competitor, on his hands and knees, still shaking off the effects of his lord's last blow. "Perhaps that is enough for one day," Lord Dusahn suggested.

"I can continue, if you so desire, my lord," the man assured him, still on his hands and knees.

"I respect your offer, but I have no desire to see you dead. I value these sessions too much." Lord Dusahn offered his hand to his younger competitor. "Let me help you."

His opponent looked up at his leader. "Mercy is for the weak."

"It is not mercy, Enton, it is respect. It is something I do not offer many, so I suggest you accept it."

"With honor, my lord," Enton replied earnestly, taking his leader's hand and getting up.

Lord Dusahn pulled hard to help Enton up. "I think you have put on weight, Enton," he teased. "Perhaps life on Takara is *too* easy on you."

"Getting my ass handed to me every morning is far from easy," Enton laughed. "However, your left hand dropped slightly just before that last move. Had it dropped a few more centimeters, you would have been open to a *Kon-de-oso*."

Lord Dusahn grinned. "That is why we have these morning sessions, to uncover any bad habits I might develop."

Multiple claps of thunder shook the windows of the Chankarti pavilion. A split second later, thunderous explosions rocked the floor, nearly knocking them both off their feet.

The door burst open, and a squad of Zen-Anor burst into the room.

"What is going on?" Lord Dusahn demanded.

"We are under attack, my lord," the senior Zen-Anor officer reported. "We must get you to a protected area."

"We will go to the command bunker," Lord Dusahn insisted, heading for the door.

"My lord," the officer pleaded. It was to no avail. "You heard him," he told his men, who immediately ran to form a protective ring around their leader.

Lord Dusahn burst through the doorway into the morning sun as blue-white flashes of light dotted the sky. Explosions went off in all directions but were all far away.

"They are targeting our surface-to-orbit batteries," Lord Dusahn realized. "It is a prelude to a full attack!" he added, breaking into a run.

A few seconds later, the area flooded with a flash of bright light, followed by another ear-splitting clap of thunder that blended with an explosion a split second later.

Before he could react, the shock wave swept over Lord Dusahn and his men, knocking them all to the ground.

Lord Dusahn's ears were ringing, his vision blurred. Bits of debris were raining down upon him, some of them burning him. Someone was yelling at him, then slapping at his chest and legs.

He was on fire.

Lord Dusahn snapped back to reality as one of the Zen-Anor beat out the fire on his leader's Chankarti robes. Lord Dusahn quickly removed the burning robe as he climbed to his feet, tossing the smoldering garment aside.

"We must go!" the Zen-Anor soldier insisted.

Lord Dusahn looked back toward the Chankarti pavilion. Half the building was gone, the other half burning. The buildings to the west were gone as well.

"My lord!" the guard urged again.

Lord Dusahn looked around him. At least four

Zen-Anor lay dead around him, having shielded their leader with their own bodies.

"Please!" the guard pleaded as another missile struck less than a kilometer away, shaking the ground upon which they stood.

"Yes, of course," Lord Dusahn replied, following the remaining two Zen-Anor soldiers attempting to lead him to safety.

* * *

"The first wave should have struck," Jessica reported from the Aurora's tactical station.

"Mister Sheehan, prepare to jump us to the Darvano system," Nathan instructed. "Put us one light minute from Corinair."

"Aye, sir," Loki replied.

"Once we jump in, confirm our targets," Nathan continued. "Once we see the impacts and the resulting damage, we'll send a comm-drone with the data back to control, then pick our targets and attack."

"Understood," Kaylah replied from the sensor station.

"Hopefully, there won't be any targets left," Jessica commented.

"Jump loaded and ready," Loki reported.

"Execute the jump," Nathan ordered.

"Jumping in three......two......one..."

Nathan watched the main view screen as the pale blue light seemed to spill out of the emitters all along the forward aspect of the Aurora's hull, quickly spreading until the entire hull was covered, at which point it flashed brightly and disappeared.

"Jump complete," Loki reported. "On course for Corinair, one light minute out."

"Conducting passive scans," Kaylah reported.

"Threats?" Nathan called over his shoulder.

"Threat board shows one heavy cruiser, one assault ship, a frigate, and four gunships," Jessica reported. "No octos, a few shuttles moving between Corinair and the ships in orbit."

"Anything further out?"

"Negative."

"Old light, missile impacts," Kaylah reported. "It's the first wave..." She paused a moment, in awe of what she was witnessing on her displays. "My God."

"Damage assessment?" Nathan asked.

"One moment," Kaylah replied, getting to work. "Multiple detonations...on the surface, in orbit... Details coming in now. About half of their surface-to-orbit batteries were destroyed. The others are still shielded, but their shields are greatly weakened. The Nighthawks should have no problem taking them out."

"What about those ships?" Nathan asked.

"The assault ship is gone," she replied. "Nothing but debris. The frigate has lost all shields and sustained heavy damage, but she is still operational, and her missile batteries are intact. The cruiser is undamaged but has lost her starboard midship shields. The cruiser is launching octos... Jump flashes," she suddenly added. "Down low...Nighthawks...they're attacking the remaining surface-to-orbit batteries."

"Target the cruiser," Nathan ordered. "Four missiles. Lead with a shield buster, just in case."

"Targeting the cruiser," Jessica replied. "One shield buster and three standard missiles."

"Be ready to execute an intercept jump on that cruiser," Nathan instructed.

"Already loaded," Loki assured him.

"Missiles are loaded and ready," Jessica reported.

"Launch missiles," Nathan ordered.

"Launching missiles."

"Scan complete," Kaylah reported. "Data transferred to a comm-drone."

"Missiles have jumped," Jessica reported.

"Comms, launch the drone," Nathan ordered. "Helm, as soon as the drone is away, execute the intercept jump." Nathan tapped the comm-panel located in the arm of his command chair, calling up a direct channel to flight operations. "Flight, Captain. Ready all Eagles for quick launch in one minute."

"*Eagles are lined up on both forward flight decks, ready to go,*" the flight operations officer assured him.

"Comm-drone is away," Naralena reported.

"Ready all forward tubes. Full power triplets," Nathan ordered as he closed the channel to flight ops. "Execute intercept jump."

"Intercept jump in three..." Loki began.

"Full power triplets ready on all forward tubes," Jessica acknowledged.

"...Two..."

"Comm-drone has jumped," Kaylah reported from the sensor station.

"...One......jumping."

"Here we go," Lieutenant Teison declared as he pressed the jump button on his flight control stick.

The view outside shifted slightly, as a result of the ship jumping from their position eight light years away into the Takaran system.

"Jump complete," Ensign Lassen reported,

monitoring the Falcon's systems from the copilot's station.

"One-minute-old light coming in now," Sergeant Nama reported from the back station. "Looks like the first strike just detonated. Would you like a damage assessment?"

"Just complete your scans as quickly as possible," the lieutenant instructed. "This place is a hornet's nest, and we just whacked it with a really big stick. I want to get the hell out of here as soon as possible."

"You're not even curious?" the sergeant wondered.

"Our job is to get the data back to command," the lieutenant replied.

Despite the Nighthawk's inertial dampeners, the sudden deceleration caused by jumping into the Corinairan atmosphere was nearly enough to knock the wind out of Commander Prechitt.

"*Two targets at three two zero and zero zero five,*" his AI reported as the fighter bounced about in the night air.

The entire area was lit up by the spreading fires on the surface, the result of the first missile strike less than a minute ago. The commander could not help but wonder how many of his own people might have perished in those fires.

"*Both targets locked,*" Max reported. "*Launching missiles.*"

Jonas blocked the thought of his people burning out of his mind, his attention turning to his missile status display just as two of the green missile indicators turned red, indicating they had been launched. He glanced up at the forward windows of his canopy. The streets of Aitkenna were streaking by below him as the taller buildings zipped past on either side. Two missiles rocketed away from under him, racing toward their distant targets on bright yellow contrails.

Brilliant bolts of red-orange plasma suddenly leapt toward him from directly ahead, striking his forward shields and causing them to take on a semi-opaque, reddish hue with each impact.

His weapons cleanly away and racing toward the targets, the commander instinctively eased his flight control stick back, bringing up his fighter's nose just enough to clear the buildings ahead of him.

"*Forward shield strength down to sixty percent,*" the AI reported. "*Immediate jump to the turn waypoint is advised.*"

"I'm going to jump directly to the next target," the commander replied calmly.

"*That is ill advised,*" the AI stated. "*It will expose this ship to greater defensive fire...*"

"I am aware of the risk," the commander stated as he rolled his fighter into a tight left turn. "And of the reward," he added as he pressed the jump button. A split second later, he found himself halfway across Aitkenna, skimming the tops of its tallest buildings, new anti-aircraft fire slamming into his shields, this time to starboard. "I'd love it if you could send some fire towards those batteries, Max," the commander suggested as he initiated a quick right turn and then dove the ship down in between the buildings.

"*Our defensive weapons are not strong enough to penetrate their shields unless they are down to twenty percent or lower,*" Max reported.

"Two more missiles for the next targets," the commander instructed calmly. Two bolts of energy slammed into his port side, causing the ship to bounce abruptly and slide to starboard. The commander tweaked his flight control stick slightly left, arresting his sudden slide to the right, preventing his starboard wing from striking the buildings streaking past him. "Quickly, please," he added.

"*Targets acquired and locked,*" Max replied. "*Launching missiles.*"

Again, another two green missile status indicators turned red as both missiles left their rails, driving toward their targets. The commander looked ahead as one missile climbed slightly and veered to port, turning toward its target, and the second missile continued forward, staying below the tops of the buildings.

"*Ten seconds to forward shield failure,*" Max warned.

"We're out of here," Jonas declared, pitching up and pressing his jump button again.

"Jump complete," Mister Souza reported from the Weatherly's helm. "We're now in the Darvano system."

"Dusahn frigate sixteen degrees off our port bow," the sensor operator announced. "Nine degrees down relative; range twenty kilometers and closing fast."

"Helm, sixteen degrees to port and nine down," Captain Hunt instructed. "Denny, ready the forward plasma torpedo tubes. Triplets, full power."

"Port sixteen, down nine," the helmsman acknowledged, beginning his turn.

"Frigate has no forward shields," Bonnie added.

"She's spotted us. She's turning away and deploying her missile launchers."

"They're protecting their unshielded bow," Captain Hunt stated.

"Forward tubes are hot," his XO reported from the tactical console.

"Coming on target in ten seconds," Mister Souza reported from the helm.

"They've got a missile lock on us," Bonnie warned from the sensor station.

"Five seconds," the helmsman updated.

"Fire as soon as you have a lock," Captain Hunt ordered.

"They're launching missiles!" the sensor operator announced.

"On course!"

"Firing all forward tubes!" his XO reported.

"Five seconds to missile impacts!" the sensor officer warned. "Target is jumping!"

"Escape jump!" Captain Hunt snapped.

"Escape jump, aye!" the helmsman replied, immediately executing the order.

"Bonnie, determine where they jumped based on heading and expended jump energy," Captain Hunt instructed. "Denny, load two seekers with nukes and get ready to send them to wherever Bonnie thinks that frigate went."

"Those are long odds," Denny warned, preparing his weapons.

"We need to slow them down, or we'll end up chasing them all over the damned system, and the Glendanon can't jump in until we own this space."

"I've got a probable location," Bonnie announced from the Weatherly's sensor station.

"Accuracy?"

"Sixty-eight percent."

"Good enough."

"Transferring coordinates to tactical," Bonnie reported.

"Missiles have the target data," Denny added.

"Launch," Captain Hunt ordered.

"Launching two," Denny replied.

"Bonnie, pass the coordinates to the helm," the captain instructed. "Mike, intercept jump to that location, five kilometers from the target."

"Aye, sir," the helmsman replied.

"If we jump too soon, those seekers might lock onto us," Denny warned.

"I'll give them a few seconds," Captain Hunt assured him. "But be ready to transmit a destruct signal, just in case."

The blue-white flash washed over the bridge, and the image of Corinair appeared along the lower edge of the spherical main view screen. Directly ahead of them, a black and crimson Dusahn heavy cruiser could be seen just above the planet, orbiting it from left to right.

"Heavy cruiser, dead ahead," Kaylah reported. "She's lost all starboard shields from her midship to her bow."

"Target that cruiser and let her have it," Nathan instructed.

"Locking all tubes on the cruiser," Jessica replied. "Firing."

"They've spotted us," Kaylah continued. "Target is rolling to port; trying to protect her unshielded side. They're locking their defense turrets on us."

"Ready stern tubes; full power triplets," Nathan instructed. "We'll fire point-blank, no target locks."

"Understood," Jessica acknowledged as incoming energy weapons fire began pounding the Aurora's forward shields.

"Dusahn octos to starboard," Kaylah warned.

"Aurora has already engaged point-defenses," Jessica reported. "She's establishing a defense perimeter."

"Ready a jump to five hundred meters past the cruiser," Nathan continued. "We'll jump over her, fifty-meter clearance, and then pitch up slightly once on the other side to bring our stern tubes to bear."

"Got it," Josh replied.

"Forward shields are down ten percent," Jessica warned.

"Plotting jump," Loki reported.

"Picking up signs of structural weakening all along the cruiser's starboard side," Kaylah reported as the ship was rocked by incoming fire. "If we can get a clean shot at her, she'll bust wide open."

"She's rolling too fast for us," Jessica added. "Our torpedoes are hitting fully charged shields."

"We have to time this just right," Nathan realized.

"Target is deploying her ventral missile launcher," Kaylah warned. "She'll have a firing solution on us in ten seconds."

"How long until her unshielded side is facing directly away from us?" Nathan inquired.

"Approximately fifteen seconds at her current rate of roll," Kaylah answered. "Multiple jump flashes to port! Gunyoki fighters!"

"Comms," Nathan called. "Tell the Gunyoki to engage the octos."

"We can handle the octos," Jessica insisted.

"They'll wreak havoc on the Nighthawks," Nathan replied. "I want them gone."

"Gunyoki have acknowledged your orders, Captain," Naralena reported.

"Missile launch!" Kaylah announced. "Four inbound! Five seconds!"

"Stand by to snap-jump," Nathan instructed Loki.

"Gunyoki are jumping over us and engaging the octos," Kaylah reported.

"Snap-jump is ready," Loki acknowledged.

"Cruiser's unshielded side is facing directly away from us, Captain!" Kaylah reported.

"Snap-jump!" Nathan ordered.

"Snap-jump, aye," Loki replied, as he initiated the jump.

The constant pounding of their forward shields from incoming energy weapons fire suddenly ceased.

"Pitch up and bring our stern tubes to bear on the cruiser," Nathan continued as the jump flash washed over the bridge. "Fire all stern tubes when ready!" he added as he switched the main view screen to the Aurora's stern cameras.

"Pitching up a hair," Josh announced as he initiated the slight change in the ship's attitude.

Jessica studied her targeting system, waiting for the right moment to open fire.

"Cruiser is spinning up her jump drive!" Kaylah warned.

"Now would be good, Jess," Nathan urged.

"Firing!" Jessica replied.

It was too late. The pale blue light was already spilling out over the Dusahn cruiser's black hull. Nathan watched in dismay as the first batch of plasma torpedoes fired from the Aurora's stern tubes streaked toward the enemy ship a mere six hundred meters away, finding nothing but empty space after the cruiser jumped away.

"Damn it," Nathan cursed.

"We need to pitch up more, or we'll hit atmo in ten seconds," Josh warned.

"Pitch up," Nathan ordered.

"The three remaining surface-to-orbit batteries are locking onto us," Kaylah warned.

"Jump us out one light minute as soon as you get a clear jump line," Nathan instructed. "We'll come about and reengage the cruiser once we figure out where she jumped to."

"Aye, sir," Loki acknowledged.

"Suggest we launch a chaser drone along the target's jump path," Jessica recommended.

"We can't hang around and wait for results," Nathan insisted just as the first salvo from the surface-to-orbit batteries slammed into their ventral shields, violently rocking the ship. "Not with those guns pounding us."

"Good point," Jessica agreed, grabbing the edge of her console to avoid being knocked off her feet by the next few impacts. "Shields have already dropped another twenty percent."

"Set the chaser drone to deliver the intel to C and C once it finds the cruiser," Nathan instructed as the ship continued to rock.

"Understood," Jessica acknowledged.

"And remind those Nighthawks that we need those batteries out of commission before we start deploying ground forces," Nathan added.

"Clear jump line," Josh reported.

"Chaser drone is ready," Jessica added.

"Launch the chaser drone," Nathan ordered.

"Launching chaser drone."

"Get us out of here," Nathan instructed Loki as the ship rocked from another blast from the surface batteries.

Talisha Sane's Nighthawk fighter bounced sharply left as an energy bolt fired down a side street by one of the few remaining air-defense batteries managed to find her as she passed. It was an incredibly lucky shot, especially considering her forward speed. Had her starboard shield been below fifty percent, she would be scattered all over the streets below.

Talisha had never been to Corinair. Until a couple of months ago, she hadn't even known it existed. And here she was, risking her life to help liberate it.

If her mother was still alive, she would be angry. If her father was alive, he would be proud. As for her siblings, she doubted she would even bother telling them, assuming she survived.

She had only jumped in to attack her third target a few seconds ago, but it already felt like a lifetime. Unlike the previous two targets, this one had no defenses with a clear line of fire between the buildings she was flying amongst. Someone, in their infinite wisdom, had thought that tucking the surface-to-air battery out of line with the intersection of streets would protect it from exactly the type of attack she was trying to execute. For most attack craft, they would have been correct. But they had never heard of the Sugali fighters or their AI systems.

"Ready, Leta?" Talisha asked her AI.

"*I assume that's a joke?*" Leta replied.

"Here we go." Talisha pitched her nose down while simultaneously firing her ventral translation thrusters at full power. The force of the air passing over her fighter's control surfaces forced its nose to pitch downward as the translation thrusters shot the nimble craft upward. She twisted her flight control stick to the left, firing her starboard forward attitude thruster to force her nose slightly to port, in defiance of the slipstream passing around her fighter. It was a small maneuver, but it was enough.

"*Target lock...launching missiles*," her AI reported.

Two missiles leapt off their rails, streaking forward and arcing slightly upwards to acquire sufficient altitude to clear the buildings nearest the surface-to-orbit battery a kilometer ahead of them. The battery immediately pivoted to open fire, now detecting the approaching enemy fighter directly.

Talisha had no plans of waiting for them to open fire. Her forward shields were already down to fifty-eight percent and would not withstand more than a few shots. She already had enough of an upward trajectory to get a clear jump line and pressed the jump button, just as the target opened fire.

The fighter disappeared in a blue-white flash as the missiles it had launched arched downward, diving into the surface-to-orbit battery. The first missile detonation overpowered the battery's already weakened shields, causing them to collapse and allowing the second missile to finish the battery off in a spectacular burst of yellow-white light, followed by a shock wave that leveled the surrounding buildings.

Tariq twisted his left control stick sharply to port while pushing his right stick all the way forward, causing his Gunyoki fighter's engine nacelles to flip in opposite directions, and his ship to yaw sharply to port as it rolled over in the same direction.

"That confused the shit out of them!" Jova exclaimed from the back seat as he retargeted their defensive turrets.

"Then this will blow their minds," Tariq snickered as he discontinued the maneuver and pulled back hard on the right control stick. The tank-like fighter's nose pulled up and over, pitching over a full one hundred and eighty degrees before he pushed his control stick back to center to abruptly stop the pitch-over. Now flying backwards, he was facing both his pursuers; one to the right and one to the left.

"I've got the one on the left," Tariq announced as he armed his flechette missiles.

"I've got the one on the right," his weapons officer replied.

Tariq pressed his firing button as Jova fired their defensive turrets. As beams of energy shot out to their right, four small missiles leapt from the underslung pods on either side of their cockpit, closing the distance to their target in seconds. The first two missiles impacted the first octo's shields, collapsing them in a flash of sparks. The warheads on the tips of the second two missiles split open, separating into dozens of tiny splinters, each penetrating the enemy fighter's hull and driving in deep before detonating. The dozens of tiny explosions set off a chain reaction that tore the Dusahn fighter apart, destroying it completely.

"Left is down!" Tariq declared.

"Right is down!" Jova added as his defense turrets found their way through the second octo's shields and into the black and crimson fighter's starboard propellant tank, igniting its contents in a brilliant, yellow flash.

"*Damn!*" Tariq's wingman exclaimed. "*What the hell do you need me for?*"

"It isn't always that easy," Tariq admitted.

"Four more octos coming up from the surface!" Jova warned. "One two five, twenty-seven down relative!"

"Seven, do you see them?" Tariq asked over comms, noticing Dota Seven and Eight were nearby and already on a direct intercept heading.

"*Got them on tactical,*" the weapons officer of Dota Seven replied.

"*Takuda!*" the pilot of Dota Seven called to his wingman. "*Follow me in! We'll jump straight to them!*"

"*I'm with you, Mohal,*" Cylo assured him.

"We're changing course to join you," Tariq advised. "We'll be there in ten seconds."

"They'll all be dead in ten seconds," Mohal bragged as the two Gunyoki fighters jumped to their targets and opened fire with everything they had.

"Jump complete," the Weatherly's helmsman reported.

"Target jumped ten seconds ago," Bonnie reported. "Along the same heading, but only a few light minutes at the most. Very weak jump energy signature."

"Mike, jump us ahead thirty light seconds at a time until we catch them," Captain Hunt instructed.

"Thirty-light-second jumps, aye," the helmsman acknowledged as he entered the commands into the Weatherly's jump computer.

"Be ready on all tubes and forward weapons turrets," the captain advised his XO at the tactical station.

"Jumping," the helmsman reported as the jump flash washed over the bridge.

"Wait fifteen seconds between jumps," the captain instructed. "Give Bonnie time to find them."

"No frigate," Bonnie reported.

"Jumping," the helmsman announced.

"Still nothing," Bonnie repeated.

"Jumping."

"Contact!" Bonnie exclaimed. "Twenty clicks dead ahead. They're turning to port."

"They're going to jump again," the XO warned.

"Helm, five degrees to port and jump ahead twenty clicks, quickly! I want to be right in front of them!"

"Five to port and jump ahead twenty clicks," the helmsman confirmed as he initiated a slight turn to port and dialed up the next jump.

"Starboard plasma turrets!" the captain continued. "Fire as soon as we come out of the jump."

"My finger is on the trigger," his XO assured him.

"Target is preparing to jump again," Bonnie warned from the sensor station.

"Jumping to intercept," the helmsman announced as the jump flash washed over the bridge again.

"Target directly to starboard and closing fast!" Bonnie reported.

"Firing starboard plasma turrets!" the XO announced from the Weatherly's tactical station.

"Collision in fifteen seconds!" Bonnie warned from the sensor station.

"Ready escape jump!" the captain barked. "Thirty light seconds!"

"Direct hits all across her bow!" Bonnie reported

with excitement. "Multiple hull breaches with violent decompression!"

"Snap jump!" Captain Hunt ordered.

"Snap jump!" the helmsman acknowledged as he jumped the ship ahead to escape the pending collision.

"Ninety to port, Mister Souza," Captain Hunt instructed as the jump flash washed over the Weatherly's tiny bridge.

"Ninety to port, aye."

"Get me a damage assessment on that frigate, Bonnie."

"Stand by, she's half a minute away," his sensor operator replied.

"Recon data from the Aurora coming in now," Cameron's communications officer reported.

Cameron and Lieutenant Commander Shinoda studied the holo-map hovering over the plotting table as the locations and status of all ships, friend and foe, began updating.

"Not bad for the first few minutes," the lieutenant commander commented.

"It would have been better if the strikes had taken out that cruiser *and* that frigate."

"The Aurora should be able to handle that cruiser, especially now that we know where it is."

"They didn't get them on the first run," Cameron pointed out. "Which means the CO of that ship isn't stupid."

"He was dumb enough to get followed by a chaser drone," the lieutenant commander pointed out.

"But look where he went," Cameron pointed out.

"Back to Corinair, where there are still some surface-to-orbit batteries to back him up."

"He's trying to draw the Aurora into the kill zone, where those guns can reach her," the lieutenant commander realized. "We should warn them."

"I'm certain Nathan has already figured that out," Cameron insisted. "Unfortunately, the Aurora will eventually have to break off and attack the dreadnought in the Takara system. Otherwise, the Ghatazhak won't be able to make it to the surface. That needs to happen in the next two minutes, or it will be too late. Every octo on that dreadnought will have launched and they'll be swarming all over the system, making it impossible to get the Ghatazhak in and out." Cameron studied the holo-display a moment. "How many surface-to-orbit batteries are still operating?"

"Last recon data showed eight still in operation and with undamaged shields. Unfortunately, between octos and local air-defense batteries, we're having trouble getting to them. We've already lost three Nighthawks attacking those last eight batteries.

"We can't afford to lose them so soon," Cameron noted. "We may need them to take out that dreadnought over Takara." Cameron sighed. "Comms, order the Nighthawks to abandon their attack on surviving surface-to-orbit guns and concentrate on the air-defense batteries."

"Aye, sir."

"The Glendanon cannot jump in while those STO guns are still in operation," the lieutenant commander reminded her. "They'll tear her apart."

"Look at the remaining STO emplacements," Cameron told him, zooming in the display and pointing at their locations on the surface. "None of them are in heavily populated areas. The Aurora can take them out from orbit with minimal collateral damage, and her shields can withstand more hits from those guns than the Nighthawks can. And we need those air-defense batteries out of the way, or they'll tear up the pod haulers and Kalibris before they can deliver the Corinari to the surface."

"And the liberation of Corinair would be a failure before it even started," the lieutenant commander added.

"Comms, message the Aurora. Tell her to destroy that cruiser ASAP and then take out the remaining surface-to-orbit emplacements. Include the location of those STOs in the transmission."

"Understood," her comms officer acknowledged.

Cameron sighed. "As usual, everything depends on the Aurora."

"Jump flash, two hundred thousand clicks to port," Kaylah reported from the Aurora's sensor station.

"Flash traffic from command," Naralena followed. "Our chaser drone found the cruiser. It's back in orbit over Corinair. New orders are to take out that cruiser as soon as possible and then target the remaining surface-to-orbit batteries on Corinair."

"Just as we expected," Jessica commented from the tactical station. "Maybe her captain isn't as good as we thought."

"Or maybe he wants us to *believe* he's just seeking protection from those surface batteries," Nathan suggested.

"You think it's a trap?" Jessica asked. "That there's another ship lying in wait to ambush us?"

"It's a possibility," Nathan replied. "Prepare to jump us back to Corinair to press the attack on that cruiser," he instructed the helm.

"And if it *is* a trap?" Jessica queried.

"We'll know soon enough," Nathan stated. "Not much choice, really. Cam's right. We need to secure this system so we can jump to Takara and provide cover for the Ghatazhak landing."

"On course for Corinair again," Josh announced.

"Jump is ready, Captain," Loki added.

"Ready all weapons," Nathan ordered. "You spot her, you fire."

"No problem," Jessica assured him.

"Take us in, Loki," Nathan instructed.

"Jumping in three......two......one..."

The jump flash washed over the Aurora's bridge, and the black and crimson Dusahn warship appeared before them, this time passing over Corinair from right to left, so that her unshielded side was toward the planet.

"Cruiser dead ahead," Kaylah reported from the sensor station. "Ten kilometers and closing."

"Locking forward tubes..."

"Don't bother," Nathan said, cutting Jessica off. "Starboard turrets and broadsides. Josh, pull up alongside her and hold position."

"Her starboard shields are still down," Kaylah reminded, wondering if the captain had forgotten.

"Cruiser has locked weapons onto us," Kaylah warned.

"They're not hugging the planet close enough," Jessica stated. "They're trying to bait us to their starboard side, so their surface guns can pound us."

"Which is too obvious of a move," Nathan countered. "They *know* we have shield-penetrating missiles. They *want* us to stay to port, to feel safer here." Nathan turned to Kaylah at the sensor station to his left. "Keep a close eye to port," Nathan told her. "An attack will come from there."

"Cruiser is firing," Kaylah reported.

"Then why stay here?" Jessica questioned as the first salvos of energy weapons fire struck their shields and rocked the ship.

"To reveal the location of their hidden asset," Nathan explained.

"If they have one," Jessica countered, holding on to her console as the ship rocked. "Forward shields down to eighty percent."

"Turning to port alongside the cruiser," Josh reported.

"Starboard turrets," Nathan ordered. "Pound the hell out of them and ready the broadsides."

"Starboard turrets engaged," Jessica reported as the bridge continued to shake violently. "Firing."

"Pull slightly ahead of them, so that we can hit them with our broadside plasma cannons as well," Nathan instructed. "I want to pound the hell out of them; make them think their only hope of survival is to *use* that hidden asset."

"You got it," Josh replied, firing the Aurora's orbital maneuvering systems in order to pull slightly ahead of the enemy cruiser.

The ship rocked again, this time a little more violently.

"They've increased the power levels on their main batteries," Jessica warned. "Starboard shields are taking the brunt of it. They're down to ninety-five percent."

"That should do it," Josh reported, ending his acceleration maneuver.

"I've got a firing solution on the broadsides," Jessica reported.

"Pound them," Nathan instructed.

"Pounding them, aye," Jessica replied.

The two ships, nearly equal in size, orbited the planet side by side, the Aurora slightly leading her foe as they traded energy bolts with one another. The only difference was that the Aurora had the advantage of her large-bore, short-barreled, broadside plasma torpedo cannons, twelve of them on each side. Able to adjust their angles just enough for all to hit the same point on a target within a specified range, they concentrated their firepower on the same point in the black and crimson cruiser's port midship section, causing her shields to flash in a near-steady state with the rapid, successive impacts.

But the Dusahn heavy cruiser was well armed. What she lacked in broadside cannons, she made up for with plasma cannon turrets. Twice as many cannons directed their energy at points all along the Aurora's starboard shields, sweeping up and down the invisible energy barriers, searching for a weak spot onto which they could concentrate their firepower.

"Starboard shields are down to seventy-five percent," Jessica reported from the tactical station.

"Target's port shields are dropping fast," Kaylah announced. "They'll fail before ours do."

"Then why aren't they jumping?" Josh wondered aloud.

"Jump flashes! Incoming missiles!" Kaylah reported urgently. "Thirty of them! Five seconds!"

"Snap jump!" Nathan ordered with equal urgency.

"Jumping," Loki replied as the jump flash washed over them.

"That's why," Nathan stated, turning toward his sensor officer. "Did you get a reciprocal course reading?"

"They came from the area of Corinair's third moon, Sonner," Kaylah reported. "There's either a missile base on that moon, or there's another ship hiding behind it."

"Comms, order the Gunyoki to Sonner with orders to locate and eliminate the source of those missiles," Nathan instructed.

"Aye, sir," Naralena acknowledged.

"Josh, flip us over for a missile launch," Nathan continued. "Jess, prepare four missiles. Lead with shield busters and follow with nukes...manual jump delay."

"Two shield busters followed by two nukes, manual jump, aye," Jessica replied.

"Be ready to come about, Josh," Nathan added. "Jess, launch when ready."

"Launching four missiles on manual jump delay," Jessica reported. "Missiles away."

"Helm, hard about," Nathan ordered.

"Coming about hard."

"Loki, prepare to jump us back to the target's starboard side, between it and the planet," Nathan continued.

"That'll put us in the sights of those surface

batteries," Jessica reminded him. "They'll drill through our shields in half a minute."

"I don't intend to be there that long," Nathan assured her.

"Course reversal complete," Josh reported.

"Return jump ready," Loki added.

"Jump the missiles," Nathan ordered.

"Jumping all four," Jessica replied.

Nathan watched the main view screen as the first two missiles jumped, followed a second later by the other two.

"Missiles away," Jessica reported.

"Helm, yaw ninety to starboard," Nathan instructed. "I want our forward tubes already to bear when we arrive."

"Yawing ninety to starboard," Josh replied.

"Jump us back in," Nathan ordered.

"Jumping in three......two......one..."

Nathan's eyes were locked on the main view screen as the jump flash washed over them. As the flash faded, the image of the Dusahn cruiser slid across it from right to left. "Fire all forward tubes as we pass!" Nathan ordered. "Full power triplets!"

"Firing all forward tubes," Jessica reported.

"Target has lost all shields!" Kaylah reported. "She's lost main power as well! All her weapons are down."

"Say goodbye," Nathan muttered to himself as the Aurora's plasma torpedoes tore into the Dusahn warship, setting off secondary explosions deep within the cruiser and tearing it apart.

"Frigate has lost main power and all propulsion

and maneuvering," Bonnie reported from the Weatherly's sensor station. "She's got multiple hull ruptures, and half her decks are open to space. Life support is functioning but running on battery power."

"What about her weapons?" Captain Hunt asked.

"She might be able to get a few missiles off, but without power for her targeting arrays, it would be blind luck if those missiles hit anything."

"Picking up a distress call," Cassandra reported from the comm-station. "It's coming from the frigate."

"Any chance they can get their main power and propulsion back online?" the captain asked his sensor officer.

"Not without spending a few months in a shipyard," Bonnie assured him.

"How many people still alive?"

"I'm picking up forty-eight life signs."

"You're not going to finish them off?" the XO wondered.

"If they can't hurt anyone, I see no reason to kill them," Captain Hunt stated.

"They are the enemy," the XO insisted. "That's reason enough as far as I'm concerned."

"For all we know, they're conscripts from Corinair," the captain replied.

"Or die-hard Dusahn," Denny argued.

"Cassie, send word to C and C that the frigate is no longer a combatant, and that there are forty-eight survivors who will require rescue once the system is secured."

"Chris!" the XO began to object.

"Objection noted," Captain Hunt said, raising his hand and cutting him off. "Mister Souza, prepare to jump us back to Corinair. The Glendanon will be arriving soon, and we need to be ready to support her."

"Message from Dota One," Naralena reported from the communications station at the back of the Aurora's bridge. "They have located a collection of missile launchers on Sonner and are attacking it now. Expected elimination of target in two minutes."

"The Weatherly has destroyed the frigate," Kaylah added. "They're turning to jump back to Corinair."

"The Weatherly is inquiring about the status of the surface-to-orbit weapons on the surface," Naralena reported.

"Targeting the last one now," Jessica announced, pressing the firing button. "Firing."

"Last surface-to-orbit battery is destroyed," Kaylah confirmed.

"Tell the Weatherly they're clear to approach Corinair," Nathan replied as he glanced at the mission clock. "Nothing but a few octos left in the area, and the Gunyoki will have them dealt with shortly."

"Aye, sir."

"Mister Sheehan, plot a jump to the Takar system," Nathan instructed. "The second wave will be launching soon, and we need to ride it in if we're going to have any hope of destroying that dreadnought."

Tariq pressed the firing button on his right flight control stick, spitting a barrage of red-orange bolts of plasma from the plasma cannons built into the front of his engine nacelles. The plasma energy pounded the missile launcher's already depleted shielding, causing it to collapse in a shower of sparks from its overloaded shield emitters. Now unprotected, the bolts of plasma energy were free to wreak havoc on the launcher itself, tearing it apart with ease. By the time Tariq took his finger off the firing button and pulled out of his attack dive to jump away, the enemy missile launcher had been reduced to a pile of dust and debris, never to target an Alliance ship again.

"*This is fun!*" Mila, Tariq's wingman in Dota Two declared as he attacked a neighboring missile launcher in similar fashion.

"*Why aren't there any defenses?*" Jalees wondered from Dota Three.

"*There are!*" Ronny exclaimed from Dota Ten. "*We're getting pounded over here!*"

"*The launchers on this side must be new and have not yet had their defenses installed,*" Sten commented from Dota Five.

Tariq finished pulling out of his dive, clearing the crater ridge on the tiny moon. "I think Ronny just has bad luck," he chimed in as he dialed up his next jump.

"*I think Ronny just sucks!*" another Gunyoki pilot joked.

"*Hey, I got the damned thing, didn't I!*" Ronny defended.

"As soon as all the launchers are destroyed, return to Corinair," Tariq instructed. "We still have a few more octos to deal with."

Captain Gullen paced the Glendanon's bridge. For a man who had spent the majority of his life on long, monotonous cargo runs, it was surprising how little patience he had in times like these.

"We should have received clearance by now," Justan commented, watching his captain traverse the deck.

"I am well aware of the time," Captain Gullen assured his second in command. He paused a moment, turning to his second officer, looking for another way to distract himself from his concerns. "Status of our ships?"

"Ghatazhak are loaded into the extended troop pods installed on Diggers One and Two," Justan replied. "Boxcars are loaded, fueled, and ready for departure." He looked at his captain and added, "Just as they were a minute ago when you last inquired."

Captain Gullen sighed, his impatience growing. "This is a bad sign," he decided. "If the first wave did not succeed, our chances of survival drop dramatically."

"We don't know that," Justan insisted. "Granted, there is reason for concern..."

"Message from command," the Glendanon's communications officer interrupted.

Captain Gullen turned to his comms officer, holding his breath.

"We are cleared to proceed," the comms officer finished.

"Finally," Captain Gullen exclaimed, breathing again. "Pass word to the deck," he ordered as he took his seat again. "Launch the Diggers and be ready to launch the boxcars as soon as we jump." The captain took his seat, grasping both arms. "It's time to liberate our home, gentlemen. May fortune favor the Corinari this day."

"Message from the Aurora," Cameron's communications officer reported. "They are at waypoint Kilo Seven and report they are ready for the next dance."

Cameron quickly scanned the holographic tactical display before her, then exchanged glances with Lieutenant Commander Shinoda on the opposite side of the holographic plotting table, looking for any sign of concern on her intelligence officer's face. Seeing none, she replied to her communications officer. "Signal the Aurora they are cleared to crash the next party."

"Aye, sir."

She looked at her intelligence officer again. "This is where it gets interesting."

"We really need better code phrases," Lieutenant Commander Shinoda joked.

* * *

Lord Dusahn burst out of the elevator, still clad in only his singed Chankarti pants, having barely escaped death during the initial missile strikes on his empire's seat of power. Still flanking him, the two surviving Zen-Anor soldiers had fierce expressions, scanning every person in their sight as potential threats.

Lord Dusahn stormed down the corridor of the underground control bunker, entering the emergency command center without ceremony and making his way to the central command platform at the center of the room. "Report!" he demanded, his eyes burning with rage.

"My lord," the duty officer began nervously.

Lord Dusahn eyed the young officer, not

recognizing him. "Where are my advisors?" he demanded. "Where is Colonel Horva? Where is Major Domor?"

"Apologies, my lord," the young officer replied. "They have not reported in. I fear the worst."

Lord Dusahn looked around the room, unsatisfied with the young lieutenant's answer. Seeing no senior officers among them, he turned his attention back to the trembling lieutenant. "Then you are the senior officer?"

"For the moment, yes my lord," the young officer was barely able to push out.

"Strength, Lieutenant," Lord Dusahn instructed. "Your empire is under attack."

"Yes, my lord," the lieutenant replied more confidently.

"What is the status of our defenses?" Lord Dusahn queried, scanning the various view screens around the room.

"The attack began five minutes ago. Since then, we have been struck by three waves of missiles. The first wave caught us by surprise, taking out most of our surface-to-orbit batteries. They also took out the Ker-Essto and our assault carrier."

"What about the Kor-Dusahn?" Lord Dusahn inquired.

"They tried, but she had her shields up, as always. There was minor damage and weakening of several shield sections, but Captain Ruba insists our flagship is still battle ready."

Lord Dusahn's eyebrows furrowed. "Only missiles?"

"My lord?" the lieutenant wondered, confused.

"Where are their warships?" Lord Dusahn asked. "Where is the Aurora?"

"No ships have been detected, my lord. They must be launching from *outside* the cluster."

"That's impossible!" Lord Dusahn exclaimed. "Their targeting systems cannot be that accurate!"

"Our sensor nets are nearly impenetrable, my lord," the lieutenant insisted. "You designed them yourself. The only detections we have had are the missiles themselves, just as they were about to strike their targets, and a single, small ship, likely performing damage reconnaissance."

"Recall the Var-Koray from the Darvano system," Lord Dusahn instructed. "And someone get me my uniform."

The lieutenant snapped his fingers, signaling a nearby ensign. "I'm afraid our communications network is down as well, my lord. We have lost contact with the Darvano system."

"Dispatch a comm-drone manually," Lord Dusahn instructed, irritated that the young officer had not done so already.

"I have, my lord, just before you arrived. We have yet to receive a response."

"Then send some octos," Lord Dusahn added, becoming more irritated. "The Aurora will be here soon, and I want her outgunned. This ends here and now."

"Yes, my lord," the lieutenant responded. After passing instructions to another junior officer he turned back to his leader. "Pardon my insolence, my lord, but..."

Lord Dusahn scowled, noticing the lieutenant's hesitance. "Speak your mind, Lieutenant," he growled.

The lieutenant stepped closer, whispering so the others would not hear his words. "If you wish to ensure the Aurora's destruction, perhaps we should consider utilizing our reserve forces, in order to guarantee our victory?"

Lord Dusahn glared at the lieutenant crossly. "I believe you overestimate their firepower, Lieutenant."

"Apologies, my lord, but victory itself may not be enough in this instance." The lieutenant paused a moment, casting sidelong glances to ensure that no one was within earshot. "The people lose faith..."

Lord Dusahn scowled at the young lieutenant.

"Not in *you*, my lord, but in the superiority of the Dusahn Empire and our way of life. A clear and decisive victory would likely dispel such concerns."

"A victory achieved by our flagship and our flagship *alone*," Lord Dusahn insisted.

"My lord, they have hit us with at least five hundred missiles in less than *five minutes*."

"And yet we are still alive and able to fight," Lord Dusahn pointed out, becoming impatient with the junior officer. "You have your orders, Lieutenant. Now connect me with Captain Ruba."

"As you wish, my lord."

* * *

"*Diggers One and Two*," the Glendanon's comms officer called. "*Clear for immediate launch. Good luck.*"

"Yeah, we're going to need it," Captain Hosick replied as he adjusted his flight controls, causing his modified Contra ship to rise from the massive cargo ship's forward deck. A small movement of his main throttles and the ship slid past the edge of the Glendanon's retracted cargo deck hull into open space.

"Digger One is away," his copilot, Lieutenant Erskin, reported to the Glendanon.

"*Digger Two is away,*" Lieutenant Westwood reported over comms.

"Loading jump to rally point Oscar Five," the copilot announced as he tapped commands into his console.

"You ready, Busby?" the captain asked over comms.

"*No, but let's get on with it,*" the captain of Digger Two replied. "*See you on the other side, Angus.*"

"We're clear of the Glendanon, General," the captain reported over comm-sets. "We're jumping to the pre-insertion rally point now. How are you guys doing back there?"

"*A little cramped,*" General Telles replied, "*but we'll survive.*"

"This is the second time the Corinari have had to help your people defeat an evil dictator," the captain joked.

"*Be thankful you are not facing the Ghatazhak this time,*" General Telles joked back. "Your casualties should be much fewer this time around."

Captain Hosick laughed at the irony as he initiated the jump. "Right."

"Flash traffic from Command," Ensign Cellura reported from Orochi Sixteen's comm-station. "They're ordering a full strike on target Bravo Sierra."

"It's still *intact*?" Pip asked in disbelief.

"You didn't expect their *flagship* to fall to a few jump missiles, did you?" Captain Roselle replied. "No doubt they had their shields up."

"There were at least *four* shield penetrators in

that attack," his XO pointed out from the Orochi's tactical station.

"They've probably been working on how to beef up their shields since Scott took down four of their battleships at once," Captain Roselle commented. "That's what I'd have done."

"If that's the case, why order another missile attack?" Pip wondered as he entered the targeting data provided in the message from command.

"There must have been some indication that it was warranted," the captain insisted. "Taylor's as sharp as they come. She's got to have a good reason."

"According to this targeting data, Bravo Sierra is no longer in orbit but is moving *away* from Takara."

"How fast?" the captain asked. "Is she making a run for open space?"

"Not based on her last known rate of acceleration," the commander replied.

"She's just climbing to higher orbit then; possibly positioning herself for better coverage of the planet... maybe even to get a little maneuvering room," Captain Roselle decided. "Again, that's what I'd do." After a moment, he added, "Better double-up on the penetrators. Maybe even throw in a few nukes."

"Simultaneous strikes?" Pip asked.

"With the penetrators, yes," the captain replied. "Put the rest ten seconds behind them."

"Got it," his XO replied. "Loading twenty-eight jump missiles, eight of them shield-penetrating and four of them nukes."

"Let's hope this works," Gil stated. "If not, Nathan's going to have his hands full."

"Missiles are ready for launch," his XO reported from the tactical station.

"Let'em rip," the captain instructed.

"Takaran insertion jump complete," Loki reported. "We're one light minute out from Takara."

"Threats?" Nathan inquired.

"One dreadnought, a few cargo ships of various sizes, and at least fifty octos," Jessica reported from tactical. "It looks like the octos just launched from the dreadnought but don't yet have targets."

"The dreadnought is accelerating," Kaylah reported. "Looks like she's climbing to a higher orbit."

"Multiple jump flashes," Kaylah reported. "Twenty-eight missiles, headed for the dreadnought. Impact in five seconds."

"They're activating point-defenses," Jessica added.

"Plot an intercept jump," Nathan instructed. "We need to jump on them while their targeting systems are still affected by the detonations."

"Already plotted," Loki assured him.

"Impacts!" Kaylah reported.

"Weapons hot, fire at will," Nathan ordered. "Execute intercept jump."

"Weapons hot, fire at will, aye," Jessica replied.

"Jumping," Loki announced at the same time.

The jump flash washed over the bridge again, and the massive black and crimson warship appeared at the center of the Aurora's semi-spherical main view screen.

"She looks undamaged," Nathan realized.

"Locking all forward tubes on the dreadnought," Jessica reported. "Firing all tubes."

Red-orange balls of plasma streaked toward the Dusahn dreadnought in waves, each wave composed of four sets of three. The enemy warship's shields flashed brilliantly as the balls of plasma slammed into them.

"Eleven missiles made it through their defenses," Kaylah reported. "Their shields were drained by the impacts but are still fully intact."

"Find us a weakness we can exploit," Nathan instructed.

"Working on it," Kaylah assured him as she studied her sensor displays.

"Incoming fire," Jessica warned.

A second later, the Aurora shook as the incoming energy weapons impacted their forward shields. Despite the heavy barrage, the Aurora continued charging toward the dreadnought three times her size, all her plasma torpedo tubes firing repeatedly.

"Too close for missiles, adding in the forward batteries," Jessica reported.

"Range two kilometers and closing fast," Loki warned.

"Target is turning to port," Kaylah announced. "Multiple contacts! Twenty-four Gunyoki fighters at one five seven, forty-two down relative. Range four clicks. They're attacking the dreadnought. Octos are maneuvering to engage them.

"One kilometer!" Loki warned, the concern in his voice rising.

"Starboard turn, get us a clear jump line and take us just past the range of their guns," Nathan instructed.

"Turning to a clear jump line to starboard," Josh acknowledged as he started the turn.

"They'll still be able to hit us with jump missiles," Jessica warned.

"They can't follow us if they can't see us," Nathan commented.

"Clear jump line," Josh announced. "Tight, but clear."

"Jump ready," Loki added.

"Execute," Nathan instructed.

The jump flash washed over the bridge, and the barrage of incoming energy weapons fire ceased.

"Green deck," Nathan announced.

"Green deck, aye," Naralena replied.

"Ready all point-defenses," Nathan added. "They'll be launching missiles any second."

"Point-defenses are ready," Jessica assured him.

"Target any remaining surface-to-orbit defenses and eliminate them," Nathan added. "The fewer guns shooting at us, the better."

"I've got Aurora targeting all surface defenses now," Jessica assured him.

"As soon as we take out the last of Answari's surface defense, turn hard to port and jump out one light minute," Nathan instructed. "But not until we've been on our outbound jump course for a full five seconds."

Josh turned slightly, looking over his left shoulder at his captain. "A trail of breadcrumbs?"

"A trail of breadcrumbs," Nathan replied, surprised by his friend's use of the old Terran phrase.

"*Attention all Eagles, green deck,*" the Aurora's flight operations controller called over comms.

Commander Verbeek tapped a button on his flight control stick, activating the pre-programmed quick-launch maneuver.

Ten Super Eagle jump fighters, arranged in a tight diamond formation at the leading edge of the Aurora's starboard forward flight deck, lifted off in unison. A second later, the translation thrusters on their topside fired briefly, arresting their rise so that they hovered halfway between the deck and the ceiling of the bay, pointing toward the gaping opening in front of them. Then all ten fighters began to glow blue-white, flashing and disappearing in unison a split second later.

The jump flash washed over the commander's cockpit, disappearing a half second later. He glanced at the tactical display at the center of his console, noting that all the fighters in his group were still flying in formation around him, and that Lieutenant Commander Cardi's group had also made it away safely from the port forward deck. "How are you looking, Sami?"

"*All good,*" she replied confidently.

"Eagle Leader to all Eagles," the commander began. "Our job is to create confusion on the surface and to provide distraction for the Ghatazhak. Let's get to work."

"Jump complete," the Glendanon's helmsman announced somewhat nervously.

"How's it looking, Justan?" Captain Gullen asked his executive officer, who was at the Glendanon's newly installed tactical console.

"I'm picking up about a dozen octos, a disabled

frigate, and a whole lot of debris...*hopefully* from what *was* that cruiser."

"Keep your eyes open," Captain Gullen urged. "Poray, keep an escape jump ready that will take us completely out of the system. If anything larger than a gunship shows up, I want to be able to jump away in a moment's notice. Is that understood?"

"No problem, Captain," the nervous young helmsman assured him.

Captain Gullen tapped the control console on the small pedestal next to his command chair. "Launch the boxcars."

The Aurora rocked as incoming energy weapons slammed into her aft shields.

"Dreadnought is closing," Kaylah warned as the bombardment continued.

"*Jesus,*" Jessica exclaimed as the ship shook. "Are there any guns they *don't* have trained on us!"

"*All surface-to-orbit defenses have been destroyed,*" the Aurora's AI reported.

"Aurora," Jessica barked, "retrain all weapons on the dreadnought."

"*Understood,*" Aurora replied.

"Josh, execute your turn," Nathan instructed.

"Turning hard to port," Josh acknowledged, initiating the maneuver.

"Dreadnought is turning with us," Kaylah reported.

"She's trying to keep her forward tubes on us," Jessica added as the ship rocked with another round of impacts. "Aft shields are down to forty percent."

"Ready another spread of shield penetrators,"

Nathan instructed. "We'll launch them blind after we come out of the next jump."

"They're not going to work," Jessica warned.

"Ready a comm-drone to notify command that the dreadnought is taking the bait," Nathan continued, ignoring his tactical officer's warnings.

"Turn complete," Josh reported.

A series of impacts in rapid succession shook the bridge even more violently than before, nearly knocking Nathan from his seat.

"Aft port shields are down to twenty percent!" Jessica warned.

"Execute escape jump," Nathan instructed.

"Jumping," Loki replied as the jump flash washed over them.

"Forty degrees to starboard, down twenty," Nathan continued, enjoying the brief respite from the bombardment. "Make it sloppy."

"I'll do my best," Josh replied, "but I'm not good at sloppy, at least not when it comes to flyin'."

Nathan glanced at the time display. He had no idea how long it would take the Dusahn dreadnought's sensor officer to calculate where they had jumped to based on their course and the amount of energy discharged in their jump. He could only assume that the officers serving on the flagship of the empire were the most capable; therefore, it would not take them long to catch up. "Load another jump," he instructed calmly. "Four light minutes."

"Four light minutes, aye," Loki replied.

Nathan waited, saying nothing.

"Turn complete," Josh reported, rolling the ship out of its turn.

"Captain?" Loki asked, expecting an order to execute his jump.

"Too soon, and they might lose us," Nathan stated calmly.

"Too long, and they'll realize we're leading them away from Takara," Jessica reminded him.

Nathan said nothing, closing his eyes as if trying to concentrate. Finally, he gave the order. "Jump."

"Jumping," Loki replied instantly.

Nathan kept his eyes closed as the jump flash washed over them. "Ninety to port, ninety down, ready a five-light-minute jump," he instructed quickly.

"Ninety to port and down," Josh acknowledged, pushing the Aurora's nose down and applying power as he rolled the ship into a tight turn to port.

"Jess, load our current location as the target for the missiles and stand by to launch all four, twenty-second jump delays."

"Loading targeting data," Jessica replied.

"Josh, as soon as we jump, yaw us around one-eighty so that..."

"I get it," Josh insisted before Nathan could finish his orders.

"Jump loaded," Loki reported.

"Missiles ready," Jessica added.

"Turn complete," Josh announced.

"Jump flash!" Kaylah warned. "They've found us!"

"Jump," Nathan instructed.

Loki's finger was already on the jump button, and the flash of blue-white light was washing over the bridge before the command had cleared the captain's lips.

"Spinnin' us around!" Josh declared as the jump flash subsided.

"Launch the comm-drone," Nathan ordered, fighting to remain calm.

"Launching comm-drone," Naralena reported.

“Four nukes next, Jess,” Nathan added. “Snap jump as they leave the rails.”

“Putting four nukes in the launch queue. Snap jump from the rails.”

“Yaw maneuver complete,” Josh reported.

“Launch four.”

“Launching four missiles!” Jessica replied.

Nathan glanced at the view screen as the missiles streaked away.

“Loading four nukes,” Jessica declared.

“Launch when ready,” Nathan instructed. “Josh, be ready to come about and jump back to our previous location as soon as the next four missiles are away.”

“Got it,” Josh assured him.

“Plotting the return jump,” Loki added.

“Based on how long it took them to catch up to us last time, I estimate thirty seconds until they find us here,” Kaylah announced.

“Ten seconds until the first four missiles jump,” Jessica reported. “Nukes are ready! Launching four!”

Nathan glanced at the view screen again as blue-white flashes appeared at the forward edges of the hull, the missiles jumping away as they left the launch rails. “Now, Josh! Hard about!”

“Here we go,” Captain Donlevy said, as he activated the pod hauler’s automated departure sequence.

Translation thrusters on all four engine nacelles on the massive pod hauler fired briefly, pushing the ungainly ship up off the open forward cargo deck of the Glendanon. A second later, the thrusters fired in the opposite direction, arresting their ascent. As the arresting thrust fired, so did two lateral thrusters, causing the cargo ship to slide to port, out of the bay and into open space.

One by one, the other three boxcars followed suit, rising from the Glendanon's cargo deck and exiting its forward bays. As each ship cleared the Glendanon's decks, it tipped over on its side, firing all four main engines in order to accelerate away from the ship.

In the turret portion of the converted SilTek G-Four-Five mobile missile launcher, Donan Keefe tightened the restraints on his seat. Although the cockpits of the pod haulers had inertial dampeners, those systems had been removed from the cargo pod in order to accommodate more tanks per pod. "Maybe I shouldn't have eaten so much for breakfast," he said as the tank swayed about.

"*And you call yourself a Corinari?*"

"One that didn't apply for flight training for a reason," Donan countered.

"*I puked the moment we launched,*" Broc admitted over comms. "*Stinks like hell in here now.*"

"Be thankful you didn't have the boka sausage," Donan joked.

"*You're both cladars,*" another tank driver chuckled over comms.

"*Buckle up, boys,*" Captain Donlevy suggested. "*We're jumping in hot in thirty seconds.*"

"Jump complete," Loki reported as the jump flash subsided.

On the Aurora's semi-spherical main view screen, the dreadnought, flagship of the Dusahn Empire, was waiting for them just as Nathan had hoped.

"Their port midship shields are down!" Kaylah reported earnestly. "Multiple hull breaches along her port side, from just aft of her main forward guns all the way to her port hangar bay!"

"Locking all weapons on their midship," Jessica reported as she tapped in targeting commands for the Aurora's AI.

"Fire all weapons!" Nathan ordered.

"Firing forward torpedo tubes," Jessica replied.

Red-orange balls of plasma rushed in waves from under the Aurora's nose and along the bottom of the main view screen, quickly closing the gap between the Aurora and her prey.

A blue-white flash filled the main view screen, lighting up the interior of the bridge.

"Target has jumped!" Kaylah reported from the sensor station.

"Estimate his jump and plot to pursue," Nathan instructed almost immediately. "This guy's not stupid."

"I've got him!" Kaylah reported. "He only jumped a few thousand... Missile launch! Eight inbound! Ten seconds!"

"Point-defenses are active," Jessica added.

"Second launch!" Kaylah added. "Eight more!"

"Jump ahead half a light minute and come hard to port," Nathan ordered.

"Jumping thirty light seconds," Loki acknowledged as he quickly entered the jump parameters and engaged the jump drive.

Again the blue-white flash washed over the Aurora's bridge as she slipped away, escaping the incoming onslaught of missiles.

"Turning hard to port," Josh reported as he rolled the Aurora into the maneuver.

"That was a point-blank missile attack," Jessica pointed out. "We've never seen them launch at such close range before."

"They're either getting very desperate or very clever," Nathan opined.

"Or their port weapons were down," Kaylah suggested.

"She's right," Jessica realized. "We were off their port side for at least ten seconds, and they never fired a single shot from any of their gun turrets."

"Turn complete," Josh reported. "We're pointed right at them."

"Target is jumping again," Kaylah reported.

"As long as we keep attacking from his port side, he'll jump away before we can get a shot in," Nathan realized. "If we hope to keep him away from Takara long enough for the Ghatazhak to make it to the surface, we'll have to attack his strong side, and prod him into slugging it out."

"That's a bad idea," Jessica insisted. "Aurora has already analyzed that strategy and warns that we cannot last more than two and a half minutes in a slug-fest."

"Even with our broadsides?"

"That ship has a *lot* of guns," Jessica replied. "If they focus them all on a single shield segment, that shield will fail, even *with* SilTek's upgrades."

Nathan thought for a moment. "Has the target changed course or attitude?"

"Negative," Kaylah replied.

"Plot another intercept jump," Nathan instructed Loki, "to their starboard side. We'll pull in alongside and pound them for as long as we can."

"The Ghatazhak need three minutes to get to the surface," Jessica reminded him.

"Launch another comm-drone," Nathan ordered. "First to the Ghatazhak rally point, then to command. Tell them they have two minutes, starting at zero plus ten."

"Message from the Aurora," Lieutenant Erskin reported over the general's helmet comms. "Insertion has been moved to zero plus ten, and you need to have boots on the ground by zero plus one two. I've relayed the message to Digger Two."

"Understood," the general replied, glancing at the time display in the corner of his tactical visor. "We jump in two minutes," he announced to the other forty-nine Ghatazhak crammed into the Contra ship's forward compartment, connecting corridor, and extended cargo bay. "Change of plans. We have to be down in two minutes. So disconnect and jump as soon as your velocity is reduced to the safe drop range."

"Fun," Corporal Vasya droned as he lowered his visor, locking it into place, making his helmet airtight. *"I guess we should have spent a little more time testing the limits of the inertial dampeners on these things."*

"You're about to get the chance," General Telles remarked. "Ghatazhak!" the general barked with authority. "It's time to show our people the *true* reason the Ghatazhak were created."

"*Let's kick some Zen-Anor ass!*" Corporal Vasya exclaimed over comms.

Lieutenant Brons moved past the general, making his way aft. "You sure you want to promote him to sergeant?" he asked the general as he passed.

"Honestly, no," the general admitted as he lowered his visor.

"*Sixty seconds,*" Lieutenant Calder announced from Digger One's cockpit.

Commander Verbeek's Super Eagle fighter decelerated sharply as it jumped into the thick lower atmosphere of Takara. The towering structures that dominated the skyline of the planet's capital, Answari, raced toward him.

A split second after coming out of the jump, his tactical screen lit up with potential targets. Although the initial missile attack had eliminated most of the Dusahn's surface defenses, and the Aurora had taken out the few surface-to-orbit batteries that had survived, there were still plenty of smaller targets, all of which posed a threat to the soon-to-arrive Ghatazhak.

"Weapons free!" the commander declared. "Find a target and blast the shit out of it!" he added, rolling to port and pushing his fighter's nose down slightly, steering toward his first target. A second later, a targeting square appeared around one of the numerous target icons and began to flash red, indicating a target lock. His fighter's auto-flight system took over, holding his fighter's course true and on target.

The commander loosened his grip on the flight

control stick to avoid causing the auto-flight to disengage, then pressed the fire button once to activate the plasma cannons on either side of his fuselage.

His cannons activated, the commander released his grip, allowing his hand to hover around his flight control stick as a barrage of red-orange plasma bolts slammed into the doomed target ahead of him. Within seconds, the shields protecting the small target collapsed, and the highly charged plasma ripped through the defensive emplacement, destroying it completely.

The target now wiped from existence, the targeting box disappeared along with the target's icon. The barrage of plasma bolts automatically ceased, and the commander pulled back hard, regaining control of the fighter. He pushed his throttle forward to its stops, bringing his main engine to full power and rocketing upward as he pushed his jump button, rising a few thousand meters more above the Answari skyline in the blink of an eye.

Commander Shinoda studied the latest communication from the Aurora on his data pad. "Scott has cleared the Ghatazhak in at zero plus ten."

Cameron glanced at the mission clock above the holo-display. "That's in forty seconds," she realized, concerned.

"He's also asking them to get their boots on the ground by zero plus one two." The lieutenant commander looked worried. "I thought their best estimate was three minutes?"

"It was," Cameron confirmed. "Don't worry, they'll make it down."

"And if they don't?"

"Then the number of civilian casualties required to liberate the planet will rise exponentially," Cameron replied.

Within seconds of coming out of her jump, the Aurora found herself in a wave of energy weapons fire. Still diving toward her target, her forward shields took most of the force, flashing brilliantly as the ship bucked with each impact.

"Maneuvering to the target's starboard side," Josh announced as he pulled the ship out of its dive, relative to the flight path of the enemy warship.

"Locking all weapons on the dreadnought," Jessica reported. "Firing everything!"

The one-way barrage of energy became two-way, but the majority of the plasma charges being fired were still coming from the massive Dusahn dreadnought.

"Forward shields down to forty percent!" Jessica exclaimed. "Get us in the slot, Josh!"

"I'm working on it," Josh assured her, "but I swear that bastard's accelerating."

"He's right," Kaylah confirmed. "Target has increased power to main propulsion and is accelerating...slowly but steadily."

"Get us into position, then match their speed," Nathan urged his helmsman.

"All they have to do to get away from us is jump," Josh pointed out.

"They won't," Nathan insisted, "not since we

took out the last of their surface-to-orbit defenses. They're afraid we'll just bomb the shit out of their pretty little palace."

"Even though it's in the most heavily populated part of the city?" Josh wondered.

"That's what they'd do," Nathan replied.

The direction of the ship's violent lurches shifted as the Aurora moved in alongside the considerably larger Dusahn dreadnought, forcing the enemy's weapons fire to shift from the Aurora's forward shields to those protecting her port side.

"We're paralleling them," Josh reported. "Attempting to match speed."

"Adding port broadsides," Jessica announced.

Nathan glanced at the mission clock as it passed the zero plus nine minutes and fifty seconds. "We're in the groove," he said. "Randomly rock us from side to side, no more than forty-five degrees. That should make it harder for them to target a single shield section."

"You got it," Josh acknowledged.

"That will make it harder for us to target them as well," Jessica pointed out.

"We're just trying to keep them away from Answari for now," Nathan reminded her. "We'll destroy her later."

"You make it sound so easy," Jessica commented.

"What can I say," Nathan replied, "I'm an optimist."

The Contra ship suddenly rocked as it entered the upper atmosphere of Takara. Far below, Eagle fighters were engaging Answari's defenses, preventing them from targeting the cargo ships and the Ghatazhak who were about to leap from their aft cargo doors.

The ramp on the back of the Digger's extended cargo pod dropped open, allowing the thin, ice-cold air of Takara's upper atmosphere to come swirling inside.

The tightly packed Ghatazhak braced themselves against each other as the air rushed in around them. A second later, the indicator light over the now fully open aft cargo hatch turned green, and the Ghatazhak exited the bay, stepping out into the morning light.

One by one, fifty Ghatazhak walked out of Digger One's extended cargo pod, falling toward the capital of their homeworld, some thirty thousand kilometers below.

General Telles, having been in the forward airlock of Digger One, was one of the last to reach the aft exit of the ship. Without hesitation and in lockstep with those preceding him, he walked out of the bay and off the end of the cargo ramp, beginning his own free-fall.

As planned, every man had begun to spread out in the air, creating enough room for dozens of parachutes.

"We are falling like a fucking rock!" Digger One's copilot exclaimed. "One more minute and we won't have enough power to pull out of this free-fall and jump back to space!"

"We can't activate the grav-lift systems until they jump," Captain Hosick replied. "You know that."

"Doesn't mean I like it," the lieutenant replied as their ship continued to fall.

"*Warning,*" Corporal Vasya's combat AI declared. "*The few surviving surface defense batteries are targeting Diggers One and Two. If they open fire, there is a twenty-percent probability that we will be hit by incoming fire intended for them.*"

"Sucks, doesn't it?" the corporal chuckled as he fell toward the city below.

"*Twenty seconds to chute deployment. Steer five degrees to the right to maintain proper separation.*"

Corporal Vasya tucked his right arm toward his body slightly, causing him to veer a few degrees to the right, as recommended. He turned his head slightly left. As expected, his squad leader, Sergeant Viano, was there, drifting further away with each passing second. To his right were specialists Brill and Deeks, and beyond them was General Telles himself.

"*Ten seconds to chute deployment,*" his combat AI warned. "*Maintain current flight path.*"

"No kidding." Vasya watched the countdown in the inside of his visor out of the corner of his eye as the last few seconds ticked off. As the countdown reached zero, he braced himself.

"Christ!" Nathan exclaimed as the Aurora lurched with each impact against their weakening shields.

"Port forward shields down to twenty percent!" Jessica warned.

The ship rocked again, even more violently.

"What the hell was that?" Nathan wondered, clinging to his command chair.

"They're channeling power from their far side to their engaged weapons!" Kaylah reported.

"Shields down to ten percent!" Jessica warned. "We can't take this pounding any longer!"

"Jump us the hell out of here!" Nathan ordered.

"Jumping!" Loki replied as the jump flash washed over the bridge.

"*Chute deployment*," the AI announced as the corporal felt a sudden pull against his torso.

The black drogue-chute deployed out from behind him, filling in seconds and slowing his fall toward his homeland.

"Rate of descent decreasing," the AI reported. "*Forty seconds to safe jump velocity.*"

"Caps, recalculate for immediate stealth jump to the surface and execute! All available spare power to inertial dampeners!"

Corporal Vasya grabbed his chute disconnect rings with both hands and pulled downward with all his might. His harness released, and his chute collapsed suddenly as the weight of the corporal and his combat armor no longer pulled upon it.

There was no time for his combat augmentation and protection system to warn him of the risks. "*Jumping.*"

A split second later, the corporal found himself no longer falling from an altitude of sixty thousand meters, but from just over one hundred meters above the streets of Answari. He bent his knees and prepared himself for impact, landing and rolling to his left to help dissipate the kinetic energy of his impact.

For the briefest of moments, the corporal lay face down on the street, overwhelmed by the entire event. He had long ago given up any hope of setting foot on the planet of his birth, let alone in such a harrowing fashion.

But only for a second.

He jumped to his feet, raising his right hand and immediately pivoting in the direction of the nearest enemy combatant.

Fifty meters away, three Dusahn soldiers, each equally stunned by the unorthodox arrival of so many enemy troops, regained their senses and raised their weapons to open fire on the Ghatazhak soldiers appearing all around them.

Corporal Vasya dropped to one knee as the first shots fired by the nearest three Dusahn soldiers streaked over his head. He pointed his arm at the three soldiers, making a fist and cocking it slightly downward. A series of yellow, needle-like bolts of energy leapt from the weapon barrel on his wrist, slamming into the first, second, and third soldier in rapid succession.

The corporal rose to his feet and looked around as the rest of the Ghatazhak jumped in and landed all around him. "Fucking awesome, right?" he exclaimed over comms.

The flight deck of the pod hauler lurched violently, coming out of the jump and into the Corinairan atmosphere, but after a few seconds, the ship's inertial dampeners kicked in, reducing the vibrations to a tolerable level.

"Thank God for the dampeners," Captain Donlevy commented as he adjusted the ship's descent profile. "Razor Leader, Buster One inbound. One minute."

On the tactical display at the center of his console, Commander Prechitt spotted the icon representing the first boxcar on its descent to Aitkenna. "Buster One, Razor Leader. LZs are still warm. Ground fire and some mobile weapons, but no AA. Suggest Bingo Two Five to start."

"*Copy Bingo Two Five, warm LZ,*" Captain Donlevy replied over comms. "*We'll make it quick.*"

"We'll clear the way to Bingo Two Five," the commander promised as he rolled his Nighthawk into a diving right turn and pressed his jump button to transition to the same area of Aitkenna that Buster One was now descending toward. "Razors Seven, Five, Six; clean up Bingo Two Five. Buster One is inbound, thirty seconds."

"*Five jumping to Bingo Two Five.*"

"*Seven to Bingo Two Five,*" another Nighthawk pilot acknowledged.

"*Six, Five, negative!*" the pilot of Razor Five called over comms. "*Two octos just jumped in at your five! Break left and jump to angels ten. I'll shag'em and meet you at Bingo Two Five!*"

Commander Prechitt guided his ship down low between the buildings, taking aim at a Dusahn armored vehicle sporting a top-mounted energy cannon that was already rotating toward him. He toggled his weapons select and fired, sending pieces of the enemy vehicle and its occupants flying in all directions.

"*Six, copy!*"

"*Two more targets, left ninety, two kilometers,*" his AI reported. "*Hold course, and I can take the shot as we pass.*"

"You're kidding, right?"

"Negative."

"Of course not," the commander said. "Very well, engage the targets."

A second later, as they streaked past the next intersection, the AI fired their port turret twice, sending two bolts of energy down the side street, both of which found their targets.

"Nice shot," the commander congratulated, surprised that it had been taken without any damage to the surrounding buildings. "Razor Five, target the ground pounders at intersection One Seven Two. I'll take the ones at One Nine Five."

"*Five engaging One Seven Two.*"

Captain Donlevy checked his pod hauler's approach profile. They were dropping toward the surface of Corinair at an alarming rate and would require full power to arrest their descent before they slammed into the surface.

"*Six, splash two!*" one of the Nighthawk pilots reported over comms. "*Jumping to Bingo Two Five!*"

"Buster One, on final," Captain Donlevy stated calmly as he initiated the final pitch maneuver. "Full power to dampeners."

"Dampeners at full power," his copilot confirmed. "We're on the line."

"Here we go," the captain said, bringing all four main engine throttles up sharply.

The ship began to shake as its four massive engine pods spun up to full thrust. He could feel himself being pushed down into his seat, despite the best efforts of their meager inertial dampening systems. The pod hauler was basically a space-tug, a forklift of sorts, designed to ferry large pods of heavy cargo between its parent vessel and the surface. Dropping twenty combat tanks into a war zone had never been considered in its original design.

In the hauler's cargo pod, twenty Corinari battle tanks awaited their fate. In seconds, they would either be rolling out into battle or slamming into the surface.

"*Whose bright idea was it to remove the dampeners from the fucking pod?*" Drummond wondered aloud from Madra Three.

Inside the mobile-missile-launcher-turned-battle-tank, Donan held both hands firmly against the metal walls of his cramped cockpit. The force of the pod hauler's massive engines was pushing him down so strongly he feared he would be crushed.

"Ten seconds," Captain Donlevy warned over comms.

Donan closed his eyes, bracing himself for impact. One way or another, this ride was coming to an abrupt end.

The deafening roar of the pod hauler's engines suddenly disappeared, and there was a loud bang as the force pushing him into his seat nearly doubled in strength. Then all was quiet...but only for a second.

A loud rattling, then the familiar amber glow from the streetlights of Aitkenna suddenly filled the interior of the pod.

"*Sorry for the rough landing, boys,*" Captain Donlevy apologized over comms. "*Give 'em hell.*"

Donan opened his eyes in disbelief, immediately pushing both control sticks forward and rolling his tank out of the pod and down its massive ramp. Seconds later, he was rolling down the streets of Aitkenna, looking for enemy targets.

A brilliant flash of light revealed the Glendanon, suddenly in low orbit above Corinair. Within seconds, small, gray ships departed from her massive open cargo bay and dove toward the planet. As they descended, they disappeared behind their own small flashes of light before entering the atmosphere.

Tiny, blue-white flashes of light appeared all over the night sky, revealing Kalibri airships falling toward Aitkenna at sharp angles as they attempted to decelerate from their original orbital velocity to one that would allow them to maneuver and land.

Sergeant Dermott sat patiently at his position near the port door as the small Kalibri airship's overhead grav-lift fins hummed loudly in their efforts to decelerate the craft. Even with its inertial dampening systems, the ride was taxing on the airship's six occupants.

"Holy crap!" the Corinari next to him exclaimed. "They weren't kidding when they warned us it would be a wild ride!"

A red-orange light filled the cabin, catching the attention of all inside. A second later, another flash, followed by a blinding explosion no more than fifty meters to their right.

"We are taking incoming fire," the AI pilot of their airship reported over their comm-sets. "I am taking evasive action," he added as the ship rolled into a spiraling turn to port, diving toward the surface.

"Hold on, boys!" the sergeant exclaimed, reaching out to brace himself against anything he could.

Narrow bolts of red-orange plasma fired from handheld weapons streaked past the wildly maneuvering Kalibri airships. Less frequently, slightly thicker bolts of red mixed in with those fired by ground troops.

Sergeant Dermott looked out the side window with surprise. Never had he seen such a spectacular display of piloting. Dozens of Kalibri airships, twisting and twirling through the descent as beams of plasma energy lashed out at them. The little, gray airships often came within a meter of their neighbor before maneuvering away from them. No human pilot could have flown the nimble airships the way they were being flown at the moment.

As impressive a display as it was, it was not enough. Several Kalibri airships fell to Dusahn fire; some exploding into fireballs, others simply coming apart with little spectacle. Debris from the first few destroyed ships managed to reach out and damage neighboring airships, but the Kalibris's AI pilots had already begun to spread out, making themselves more difficult to hit and gaining room to maneuver.

"*Ten seconds,*" their AI pilot reported over comm-sets.

Sergeant Dermott said nothing, still holding on.

The airship suddenly arrested its twisting descent, coming to a hover less than a meter above the streets of Aitkenna.

"Deploy," the AI instructed as the doors on either side of the airship automatically slid open.

Sergeant Dermott was the first one out, jumping the meter down to the street, raising his weapon to fire at a group of Dusahn soldiers running for cover. Reapers from the Aurora streaked overhead, suppression fire coming from their side-mounted turrets to keep the enemy at bay as the first wave of Corinari returned to reclaim their world.

* * *

"Captain Ruba continues to trade blows with the Aurora, my lord," the young lieutenant reported. "However, he has lost half his shields, and his jump energy banks are damaged. Soon, he will have insufficient energy to make even the shortest of jumps."

"Ruba must maintain his assault on the Aurora," Lord Dusahn insisted.

"My lord, the Aurora will simply jump away at the last moment to evade destruction."

"But she will return and press the attack," Lord Dusahn insisted. "They need to keep our flagship away from this planet so that their ground forces are not exterminated from above."

"Speaking of ground forces, my lord," the lieutenant said. "These Ghatazhak of lore, they are well equipped and skillful. Our forces are having difficulty containing them."

Lord Dusahn turned to the lieutenant, glaring at him. "I thought their numbers were few, were they not?"

"Best estimates put their current ground strength at one hundred, but their *weapons.*"

"Certainly you are not suggesting that a mere one hundred Ghatazhak, no matter how well equipped they might be, can overcome ten thousand Dusahn soldiers?"

"Perhaps if the Zen-Anor were sent to assist..."

"The Zen-Anor protect *this* facility," Lord Dusahn snapped. "They shall not be used to reinforce common infantry."

"But their air support is quick and agile," the lieutenant reminded his leader. "They strike with precision, enabling rapid advancement of the Ghatazhak. If we do not slow their advance..."

"Where is Colonel Horva?" Lord Dusahn demanded.

"Apologies, my lord, I should have informed you earlier. It has been confirmed that Colonel Horva was killed in the initial attack, and Major Domor is critically wounded." The young lieutenant paused a moment. He knew what needed to be said but was afraid to say it. "My lord, I beg you to reconsider.

If we recall our assets now, we can *surprise* the Aurora, defeating her once and for all. The victory will be the result of your clever subterfuge, as well as overwhelming military might."

Lord Dusahn took a slow breath, an angry look on his face. Finally, he looked at the young lieutenant and spoke. "What is your name, Lieutenant?"

"Jexx, my lord. Darman Jexx."

"Darman?" Lord Dusahn nodded. "Your name means 'strong leader' in the old tongue." Lord Dusahn turned away, studying the status screens before him, as if reassessing the situation. "Very well, Lieutenant Jexx. Recall our reserve assets."

"As you wish, my lord," the young lieutenant nodded compliantly, before turning to signal one of his subordinates.

Lord Dusahn took another long breath. "You tax my patience, Captain Scott. But soon you shall no longer."

* * *

"Captain," Ensign Hintz called from the comm-station inside the command center on board the Manamu. "The Aurora is requesting a missile strike on the flagship."

"How the hell are they supposed to even target it if it keeps jumping around?" Lieutenant Commander Shinoda wondered from the plotting table.

"Apparently Captain Scott believes he can keep them in one place long enough for our missiles to hit them," the ensign explained.

"Did he say how?" Cameron asked.

"No, sir. They only said they'll send targeting data and strike time shortly."

Cameron sighed, studying the holographic map. "I hate it when he does this."

"Does what?" the lieutenant commander wondered.

"Makes stuff up on the fly."

Lieutenant Commander Shinoda looked confused. "Isn't that what he's *supposed* to do? I mean, isn't that what he's *good* at?"

"Yes," Cameron replied. "That's why I don't like it." She sighed and then continued. "We'll move Nash's group here," she decided, pointing to a spot in the hovering display.

"That's nearly *inside* the Takar system," the lieutenant commander pointed out. "A little risky, isn't it?"

"However Nathan plans to keep that flagship in one place isn't going to work for long. The closer the Orochi are to the target, the more flexibility they'll have." Cameron turned to her comms officer. "Inform the Aurora that we're sending four Orochi and their escorts to waypoint India Four Two. Instruct them to send the targeting data directly there."

"Aye, sir," the comms officer acknowledged.

Lieutenant Commander Shinoda exchanged a concerned glance with Cameron. "Seems like a long shot."

"Long shots are Nathan's specialty," she replied.

Two Corinari combat tanks turned the corner, coming face to face with an armed Dusahn tactical vehicle. The enemy vehicle's top-mounted gun turret quickly rotated toward the first Corinari tank, opening fire with both barrels.

The lead tank's shields flashed brightly with the incoming impacts as its left weapons arm moved slightly outward, quickly taking aim at the attacking vehicle. Two mini-rockets launched from the arm, streaking down the street and slamming into the unshielded vehicle, blowing it apart.

"Nice shot!" Ron congratulated from Madra Two.

"Two more coming down Marsken to your right," Donan warned.

"I've got'em," Ron assured him. "Gotta love these VR displays," he added.

Donan pushed his control sticks forward, resuming his tank's advance down the street toward the destroyed Dusahn vehicle. Thanks to SilTek's sophisticated reality-based VR system, he could see everything outside of his turret as if he was not surrounded by the tank's thick, carbon-armor shell.

A collection of tightly grouped, small, red rectangles appeared just beyond the burning remnants of the enemy vehicle, indicating a number of unseen enemy troops moving for cover. "About a dozen bad guys fifty meters ahead," he reported. "Looks like they're moving toward Pearson Boulevard."

"Madra One, Control. Your GPs are moving to join another group at Pearson and Oclin. Join Madra Five at grid One Five Seven and dispatch all GPs."

"Madra One, moving to One Five Seven," Donan acknowledged as he pulled back hard on his left control stick to make the next turn. "Two, One. How are you doing?"

"I can handle the tacticals on Marsken," Ron assured him. *"I'll join up with Cauldwell and Tyre over on Bayson."*

"Show them how it's done," Donan replied.

"Don't I always?"

"New orders," Ensign Durkan reported from Orochi Fifteen's comm-station. "Our group is to immediately jump to waypoint India Four Two and prepare for another missile strike."

"Target?" Robert asked from his command chair.

"The dreadnought."

"Did they include targeting data?"

"Negative," the comms officer replied. "The Aurora will be sending us the targeting data and launch time once we reach the launch point. We must be ready to launch in one minute."

"Pass the word to the battle group," Robert instructed. "Immediate jump to the launch point and await strike orders."

"Aye, sir."

"Helm..."

"Calculating course and jump plot to India Four Two," Lieutenant Meers acknowledged.

"What's Scott up to?" Commander Kraska wondered as he prepared for another missile launch.

"I suspect he's setting up a kill box for us," Robert replied.

"Bulldogs Two, Three, and Four have confirmed receipt of message," the comms officer announced. "Gunyoki escorts have also confirmed."

"Jump plotted," the helmsman reported.

"Turn us to course and jump as soon as possible," Robert instructed.

"Turning to course and preparing to jump," the helmsman replied.

Robert took a breath, letting it out in a sigh. "Let's hope Scott isn't *in* that box when we launch."

"Razor Leader, Control. New targets: four heavy tacticals in grid Two Four Seven," the controller called over the commander's helmet comms. "Targets are traveling eastbound on Exandier, approaching Madra One and Five at strong point Four One. Dispatch all targets, ASAP."

"*Receiving tactical data from command,*" his AI reported. "*Transferring to your tactical display.*"

"Razors Two, Three, and Four," the commander called over comms. "Turn to two five seven. Four heavy tacticals at grid Two Four Seven need our attention."

"Turn complete," Josh reported from the Aurora's helm.

"Intercept jump ready," Loki added.

"Port forward shields haven't had anywhere near enough time to regenerate," Jessica warned.

"We don't have time," Nathan insisted. "We have to reengage their flagship and keep her in one spot long enough for another missile strike."

"We only need eight more minutes to get them to at least seventy percent," Jessica advised.

"That ship won't stay put that long," Nathan reminded her. "Soon, the Dusahn will realize that the Ghatazhak cannot be stopped without orbital support, and they'll recall that flagship. We can't let that happen...you know that."

"Just making sure you have all the information,"

Jessica replied. "Seeing as how Cam isn't here," she added under her breath.

"New contact," Kaylah reported. "Jump comm-drone inbound."

"Flash traffic," Naralena announced. "Command has received our message. We are to communicate strike data directly to Bulldog One at waypoint India Four Two."

"Understood," Nathan replied. "Sync the drone to jump with us."

"Synchronizing the drone's jump system to ours," Naralena confirmed.

"When we jump in, lead the target by about half a ship length, then angle us so that the broadsides can hit the target," Nathan instructed. "That way they won't be able to hit our forward shields. Start with our port side facing them. We'll roll to reverse sides as needed."

"Understood," Josh replied.

"Jump us in, Mister Sheehan," Nathan ordered.

"Jumping in three..."

"Port broadsides are ready to fire," Jessica announced.

"...Two..."

"Routing all available power to aft port shields," she added.

"...One..."

Four Dusahn ground transports pulled to an abrupt stop at the intersection, and a platoon of soldiers quickly piled out, their weapons at the ready. The men immediately formed into squads, fanning out in all directions to seek safe positions from which to ambush the approaching enemy.

Overhead, Dusahn octo-fighters jumped in behind flashes of blue-white light, arriving to provide air support for their comrades on the surface. As quickly as they arrived, Eagle fighters jumped in above them, diving on the Dusahn fighters with all barrels blazing. Half the octos fell in the first few seconds. Several octos veered away, circling in either direction in a vain attempt to continue their mission, while the others jumped away, planning to come about and return.

As if on cue, a small group of Ghatazhak soldiers charged around the corner, their own weapons blazing with unheard of precision. The eight men, clad in black combat armor, split into two four-man fire teams, moving in opposite directions into the intersection.

The Dusahn had overwhelming numbers and opened fire with confidence. Their strategy was simple: to lay down massive amounts of energy weapons fire that no man could survive.

The Ghatazhak, however, were not ordinary men. With practiced precision, the two groups of four became four sets of two, their personal shields flashing a dull red with each impact of incoming energy bolts. The charging soldiers held no weapons in their hands, firing only from small cannons built into the armor surrounding their forearms. They moved about in unwieldy patterns; ducking, weaving, and twisting in a bizarre dance intended to lessen the number of impacts they received.

All four pairs of black-clad soldiers seemed to advance toward the north and west corners of the intersection, ignoring the energy weapons fire coming from behind them and lighting up their rear shields.

Emboldened by their lack of concern, the Dusahn soldiers firing from the south and east corners rose from their cover, determined to charge forward in glorious Dusahn fashion and mow down their challengers.

It was a mistake.

Once all the soldiers to the south and east had stepped into the open, small rectangular weapons turrets popped up from the backs of the Ghatazhak. The turrets spun about quickly, taking relative aim in the direction of the charging Dusahn soldiers, releasing a barrage of finger-sized mini-rockets that sped across the intersection. The mini-rockets twisted about in the air, each of them steering toward targets assigned by their AIs, slamming into the unsuspecting Dusahn soldiers and exploding, blowing them apart and littering the street with blood and body parts.

One by one, Dusahn soldiers to the north and west fell to Ghatazhak weapons fire, despite the fact that the Dusahn were sending four times the amount of fire they were receiving.

But the Ghatazhak were frighteningly precise. Barrages were for fear. To kill, the Ghatazhak believed a single shot was all that was necessary. Unfortunately for the Dusahn soldiers, their own body armor was insufficient against the Ghatazhak's new energy weapons. The Dusahn armor burst open with each impact, cutting through with ease, finding the warriors within and igniting their tissues in an instant. The results were not as gruesome as the damage done by the mini-rockets but were just as effective.

Within seconds, the entire platoon of Dusahn soldiers was dead—defeated by a mere eight Ghatazhak, all of whom suffered nothing more than a slight drop in their shield strengths.

"Jump complete," Bulldog One's helmsman reported. "We're at waypoint India Four Two.

"Any sign of a comm-drone?" Robert asked his sensor officer.

"Negative," Ensign Lief replied. "However, Bulldogs Two, Three, and Four are also on station."

"We could launch a recon drone," the XO suggested from the Orochi's tactical station. "Maybe we'll get lucky."

"Too risky," Robert insisted. "Even if we spotted the dreadnought, the Aurora would have no idea *when* our missiles were arriving. We might hit *her* by mistake. Besides, we only have two recon drones, and we may need them later." Robert sighed. "We'll wait."

"Damn!" Donan exclaimed as his shields flashed and his entire combat tank rocked. For a brief moment, the motion was so intense he feared his tank might tip over. His vehicle rocked again, even more violently, causing him to lose grip on his controls. But there was no shield flash.

"Are our shields down?" he asked.

"*Shields are intact, currently at fifty-five percent,*" his AI replied.

Another explosion, rocking the tank, but again displaying no shield flash from the incoming round.

"*The heavy tactical at three two zero is firing at the ground beneath our front,*" the AI continued. "*He is trying to get under our shields. If he is successful, he could put an explosive round under us, which would do considerable damage.*"

"So no shields on our underside," Donan concluded as another round exploded, causing the tank to bounce upward and then slam back down.

"*Correct.*"

"Remind me to have a word with your designers when this is over," Donan commented as he grabbed his controls and pushed both levers forward. "Feel free to fire on that bastard," he instructed.

"*Shall I take that as an authorization to attack the heavy tactical at three two zero?*" the AI inquired.

"Yes, please!" Donan urged as his tank pitched upward, attempting to climb over the mound of debris before him. "Hey, Braden! A little help?"

"*Sorry, I've got my own problems!*" the driver of Madra Five replied over comms. "*I'll get there as soon as I can!*"

"*Target is moving left,*" the AI reported. "*Line of fire is partially obstructed by a building containing a few dozen humans, most likely noncombatants. I cannot fire without destroying a considerable amount of the building itself and possibly injuring the occupants.*"

"I'll move right and try to draw him away from the building," Donan replied.

"*I should point out that this is the type of situation where allowing me to have direct control over our mobility systems would be in the best interests of the mission.*"

"Sorry, but no chance," Donan told his AI. "Nothing personal," he added as his tank crested the mound of debris and pitched back down, charging ahead.

"Second heavy tactical approaching from zero two five, two hundred meters."

"Control, any chance of some help?"

"Madra One, Razor One," Commander Prechitt called over comms as he dove his fighter toward the heavy tactical on the surface ahead of him. "Continue northeast. I need the target to be ten more meters from the building to take the shot."

"I'm trying!" Donan replied.

"Two octo-fighters have just jumped in to starboard," the commander's AI reported. *"Five kilometers and closing fast."*

"Talisha, you got'em?" the commander asked as he continued his dive.

"Razors Three and Four, vectoring to intercept," Talisha replied.

"Ten seconds to terminal dive," the commander's AI warned.

"Don't touch the flight controls, Max," the commander instructed.

"I wouldn't dream of it," his AI assured him. "Three......two..."

Commander Prechitt pressed the button on his flight control stick, launching a missile.

"...One..."

The weapon away, the commander pulled his flight control stick back hard as he shoved his throttle all the way forward. His engine screaming to full power, his fighter pulled out of its dive, reversed its attitude, and began rocketing skyward.

The climbing Sugali fighter disappeared in a blue-white flash of light as the missile struck the Dusahn target, blowing it apart in a fiery explosion that did nothing more than shake the nearby buildings.

"Nicely done!" Donan congratulated as he turned his tank toward the next target.

"*Splash Two!*" Talisha reported over comms. "*Madra One, Razor Three! Your skies are clear for the moment. You've got two heavy tacticals left. Shall we engage?*"

"Feel free," Donan insisted. "I'm always willing to share the fun."

"*Roger that,*" Talisha replied. "*You guys take the target at one five seven, and we'll handle the one at one eight four.*"

"You got it, Three," Donan replied as he guided his tank down the empty street toward the target several blocks away. "Madra Five, Madra One. How are you doing?"

"*I'm good,*" Braden assured him over comms. "*I'll approach the target from the east, down Bethany. You hit him from Greenville.*"

"I'm on Greenville now," Donan replied. "Crossing Evonis."

Talisha rolled out of her turn and pressed her jump button, transitioning three kilometers forward in a flash of blue-white light. A quick glance over her right shoulder confirmed her wingman had jumped with her and was still watching her back as she dove toward the Dusahn assault tank on the streets ahead of her.

"*Missile is locked on target,*" her AI reported.

"Launching," Talisha announced as she pressed the launch button on her flight control stick. She glanced at the weapons status display on the lower right side of her console, verifying that the weapon was away, then pulled up slightly to arrest her dive and begin climbing.

Another tap of her jump button, and both she and her wingman were two kilometers further along their climb-out and at least a thousand meters higher in altitude than they were a moment ago.

"*Missile impact,*" her AI reported. "*Target destroyed.*"

"How are we looking, Leta?" Talisha asked her AI.

"No enemy air targets in the immediate area," her AI replied. "Six tacticals on the surface nearby."

"Control, Razor Three," Talisha called over comms. "All four tacticals in grid Two Four Seven have been destroyed. I'm detecting six more medium tacticals in the area. Shall we engage?"

"Razor Three, Control. Negative. Climb to angels five and maintain top cover for sector five. More Madras will join Madras One and Five shortly and will execute the tacticals."

"Razors Three and Four, climbing to angels five and maintaining top cover," Talisha confirmed as she rolled into a lazy arc to starboard and continued her climb. "What's your assessment, Leta?" she asked her AI.

"*Based on current engagement data, I estimate a forty-seven percent chance that the Corinari will succeed in taking control of this world.*"

"Then I guess there's more work to do," Talisha said.

Rather than chase it down, the flagship of the Dusahn Empire sat quietly, a few million kilometers away from Takara, waiting for their prey to return.

They would not be waiting long.

In a flash of blue-white light, the Aurora appeared only a kilometer off the dreadnought's starboard bow, yawing to port as the much smaller ship opened fire.

"All turrets are firing," Jessica reported. "Broadsides will have a firing solution in ten seconds."

The Aurora began to shake as, once again, the Dusahn dreadnought opened fire on them, pummeling their already weakened shields with a barrage of red-orange bolts of plasma energy.

"Our comm-drone jumped with us," Kaylah announced from the sensor station. "It's one hundred kilometers off our starboard bow. I doubt the dreadnought sees it."

"Port shields, bow to stern, are taking a beating," Jessica reported as the ship shook violently. "Shield strength is down to forty percent."

"Calculate the target's estimated position based on course and speed one minute from now," Nathan instructed. "Comms, transfer the targeting data to the comm-drone, with instructions to launch a full spread on that location. Everything they've got, twenty-click box, one-click grid, as many shield-busters as they've got." Nathan glanced at the mission time display. "Strike time: zero plus twenty-one."

"Broadsides have a solution," Jessica announced. "Opening fire."

The ship rocked even more violently than before, forcing Nathan to brace himself to avoid being tossed from his command chair. "What was that?"

"They're moving their guns!" Kaylah reported with surprise.

"What do you mean, they're moving their guns?" Nathan demanded.

"Their port main gun batteries are moving across their dorsal side...on some kind of track system. They're moving them to starboard and adding their fire power to the..."

Another salvo struck the Aurora's port shields, rocking the ship and knocking Kaylah out of her chair, unprepared for the sudden violent movement of the ship.

"Inertial dampeners are offline!" Loki reported.

"Port shields at thirty percent!" Jessica warned as the amount of incoming fire increased.

"Snap-roll," Nathan ordered.

"Initiating snap-roll to starboard," Josh

"Targeting point calculated," Jessica reported.

"Transferring targeting data to comm-drone," Naralena added. "Message is loaded."

"Zero plus twenty-one is not giving them much time," Jessica warned.

"If we linger too long, they'll get wise!" Nathan insisted as the ship continued to be rocked by the heavy barrage of energy weapons fire. "Besides, we can't take this pounding for long!"

"Comm-drone is ready!" Naralena announced.

"Send the message!" Nathan ordered.

"Comm-drone is jumping," Naralena replied.

Nathan glanced at the mission time display again

as the ship continued to be pounded by fire from what was now twice as many guns as before. "Be ready on that escape jump, Mister Sheehan," Nathan warned.

"Are you kidding?" Loki replied, his hand next to the jump button.

Corinari battle tanks progressed slowly but surely down the main boulevards—commonly referred to as the *spines*—which led from the outermost edges of Aitkenna to the seat of the planet's global government. Usurped by the Dusahn, it now served as *their* seat of power on Corinair and throughout the Darvano system. Other than Lord Dusahn's palace on Takara, it was the largest, most well-defended asset in the Dusahn Empire. As such, its capture was imperative to the liberation of the entire system.

The boulevards were four lanes wide on each side and were separated by an equally wide, lavishly landscaped meridian, over which the eight main transit lines hung. The spines were the result of five years of reconstruction and represented the eight great nations of Corinair that had combined to form a new global government after their liberation from the rule of Caius Ta'Akar nearly nine years ago.

Today, there was no traffic, only the Corinari tanks rolling steadily toward the center of Aitkenna, exchanging fire with Dusahn ground units as they advanced.

Behind the tanks, squads of Corinari ground forces huddled within the safety of each tank's shield bubble. The goal was to get the troops as close to the capitol building as possible, reducing the Dusahn force strength as they approached. If the building could be taken intact, it would save the Corinairan people years of rebuilding, and allow their government to quickly resume operations, avoiding the post-battle chaos that had threatened to consume the city after the last liberation.

Unfortunately, the Dusahn were determined to maintain control of the capital, as well as the planet. They knew the Alliance did not have the resources to fight a prolonged surface war, which was why they had paid little attention to the Dusahn assets elsewhere on the planet. The Corinari wanted Aitkenna, and its capital, *intact,* and the Dusahn knew it. At the moment, that knowledge was the Dusahn's greatest asset.

"New contact," the Orochi sensor officer reported. "Comm-drone."

"Incoming message," the comms officer reported. "Targeting data and strike time."

"How long?" Robert asked.

"Zero plus twenty-one," the ensign replied. "Transmitting targeting data and strike time to Bulldogs Two, Three, and Four."

Robert glanced at the mission clock. "Jesus, that's only *ninety seconds*. Can we make that launch time?" he wondered as he rose from his chair and headed for the tactical station.

"It's going to be close," his XO replied as he loaded the strike data into the missile launch computer. "Can you select the warhead loads while I finish entering the targeting data and jump parameters?"

"I'm on it," Robert assured him as he began selecting warheads for all the missiles.

"Can we even cycle twenty-four missiles so quickly?" the helmsman wondered.

"Half the missiles are already loaded with shield penetrators," Robert informed the young lieutenant. "A full strike doesn't launch all missiles simultaneously. The simultaneous strike happens by synchronizing their departure jump."

"Starboard launchers are ready," his XO reported. "Port will be ready in ten seconds."

"Launch starboard missiles," Robert instructed. "Durkan, tell Two, Three, and Four to launch all missiles as they are ready. I'll initiate the strike jump manually."

"For all missiles, from all Orochi?" the comms officer asked, surprised.

"Do it!" Robert barked, no time to debate the issue.

The comms officer jumped into action, sending the updated instructions to the other ships.

"Christ, Robert," his XO said under his breath. "Scott ordered a two-second time-to-target."

"Yeah, I know, not much wiggle room for him."

"Starboard missiles are away," the XO reported.

"Two, Three, and Four are launching missiles," Ensign Lief reported from the sensor station. "Twenty seconds to strike time."

"Port launchers are turning green," the XO reported. "Launching as they are ready."

"Damn this is going to be close," Robert said as he slid open the clear plastic cover on the manual strike jump button and positioned his finger over it.

"Five seconds," the sensor officer warned, beginning the final countdown.

General Telles rolled to his right to avoid an incoming sonic mortar round, coming back to his feet with both forearms firing. Over three thousand Dusahn troops had initially responded to the Ghatazhak incursion on the streets of Answari, but now they numbered less than three hundred.

And that number was falling rapidly.

With no more targets in the immediate area, General Telles took off in a controlled run toward the next intersection fifty meters ahead.

"I am detecting a power surge atop the building on the northwest corner of the next intersection," the general's AI warned.

"Identify the source," the general demanded as he continued toward the intersection. Four enemy soldiers suddenly stepped out of the building to his right, opening fire on the general.

General Telles did not flinch as the incoming weapons fire lit up the right side of his personal shields. He also paid them no heed, since he knew his CAPS AI would deal with the threat.

As he ran, a laser turret sprang from the right topside of his back armor, swinging to the right and opening fire, emitting a rapid succession of bright yellow flashes from its tiny, twin barrels.

Bright yellow flashes appeared all over the Dusahn soldiers as the bursts of laser energy fired from the general's right mini-turret pierced the weaker armor worn by the Dusahn regulars. The bolts of energy pierced the soldiers's bodies, exited out their backsides and slammed into the buildings behind them, blowing holes in the wall.

The Dusahn soldiers fell, their internal organs gravely wounded by the lasers passing through them.

Four more Ghatazhak followed the general, rounding the corner only seconds behind him, just in time to join him in the fight against a worse foe, the Zen-Anor.

General Telles ducked as a massive bolt of charged plasma tore through the corner of the building, showering him and his men with chunks of Takaran concrete and bits of red-hot metal.

General Telles looked back at the four men who had joined him. "I think I've figured out the source of that power surge."

"Starboard shields at thirty percent!" Jessica warned.

"Strike in five seconds," Kaylah warned.

"Wait for it," Nathan told Loki, his eyes glued to the mission clock.

"Four..."

"Ready to jump," Loki confirmed, his finger hovering over the jump button.

"...Three..." Kaylah continued counting, as the Aurora rocked with incoming weapons fire.

"Shields at fifteen percent!" Jessica warned.

"...Two..."

"Wait..." Nathan urged.

"...One..."

"Wait..." Nathan repeated.

"...Zero..."

"*Captain*," Loki pleaded.

Nathan simply held up his hand, his eyes shifting toward Kaylah to his left.

"Jump flashes!" Kaylah exclaimed.

"NOW!" Nathan barked, as Kaylah spoke.

"JUMPING!" Loki replied, the jump flash spilling over them as the words left his mouth.

"Tell me it was our missiles," Nathan begged.

Kaylah turned to him, deep concern in her eyes.

"Hard about," Nathan ordered, still looking at Kaylah. "What then?"

"Nine of them," she replied, "and the flashes were too big to be missiles."

"Coming about," Josh replied as he initiated the turn.

"I need to know what jumped in,"

"I can tell you in twenty-two seconds," Kaylah promised.

"If they were ships, we've got a problem," Jessica commented from the tactical station.

"They shouldn't have any *left*," Nathan insisted.

"Would you like the good news or the bad news first," Kaylah asked, attempting to lighten the mood considering their sudden change of fortune.

"Bad," Nathan replied without hesitation.

"Three battleships and six destroyers...all of them old school."

"Jung ships?" Nathan wondered.

"Very similar to the type we faced back in the Sol sector," Kaylah confirmed.

"False-flag fleet?" Nathan surmised.

"We destroyed all their false-flag ships," Jessica insisted. "Shinoda and I checked the propulsion and reactor signatures on every Jung ship operated by the Dusahn and matched them up to the ones originally spotted in the Sol sector. We destroyed them all."

"We destroyed all the ones we *knew* of," Nathan corrected.

"Turn complete," Josh reported, uncertain of what would come next.

"Well, what's the good news?" Nathan wondered.

"Our missiles were about five seconds late, which might have been a good thing," Kaylah told him. "They not only took out the dreadnought's shields, but they also struck several of the newly arriving ships, bringing down the shields on one of the battleships and three of the destroyers."

A sinister smile crossed Nathan's face. His usual good luck was definitely running low, but it wasn't completely gone...not yet.

"You weren't kidding when you said he was lucky," Lieutenant Commander Shinoda commented as he read the status update from the Aurora.

"I hardly call the unexpected arrival of *three* battleships and *six* destroyers...*lucky*," Cameron argued. "Nevertheless, we must move quickly, before those new arrivals disperse."

"All missile launchers are reloaded," Commander Kraska announced from the Orochi's tactical station. "Half shield busters, half variable-yield nukes."

"I don't suppose we can increase the number of shield-penetrating warheads?" Robert asked.

"All we have left are nukes," the XO replied, "and we only have twenty-eight missiles left, beyond what we just loaded."

Robert sighed as he turned and continued pacing

the deck of his Orochi's compact bridge. He paused in the center of the bridge, gazing out the forward windows. "Waiting for results is the worst part of this assignment. It was so much easier on the Cobras. With guns and torpedoes, we got to *see* the results of our attack."

"I can't say that I mind not being constantly under fire," the XO admitted. "But I do see your point. However, it's only been a *few* minutes."

"A *long* few minutes."

"New contact," Ensign Lief reported from the sensor station. "Comm-drone."

"Flash traffic," the comms officer announced. "Another missile strike."

"How soon?" Robert asked, returning to join his executive officer at the tactical station.

"Two minutes," the comms officer replied.

"Two full launches in five minutes?" the XO wondered. "What the hell is going on there?"

"Undoubtedly, the Aurora is deep in it, as usual," Robert replied as he helped his executive officer prepare the strike package. "Same as before. Launch them as they're ready, and manual strike jump."

The Aurora appeared in the middle of the newly arrived ships behind a blue-white flash of light, opening fire before her jump flash had completely faded. Her forward plasma torpedo tubes belched waves of red-orange plasma triple-shots at the Dusahn flagship directly ahead of them, slamming into its hull and tearing it open. Her dorsal forward turrets panned left and right, fore and aft, raking across unshielded destroyers on either side, overloading surface mounted systems and causing small hull breaches in multiple locations. All around the ship, point-defense laser-turrets lashed out at anything within range. On either side of her aft section, her broadside cannons spat out waves of red-orange energy bolts, pummeling the shields of the other enemy warships that, although still intact, had been greatly drained by the surprise missile attack only seconds after their arrival.

But the Aurora was not the only one with weapons, and all nine older warships opened up on the Aurora only a few seconds after she had begun her attack. With *nine* warships training all weapons upon her, the Aurora's shields flashed repeatedly as they absorbed the impacts of the enemy's energy weapons.

"Dreadnought is coming apart!" Kaylah reported with excitement as the Aurora rocked from incoming weapons impact against their shields. "Multiple secondary explosions! She's done for!"

"Helm!" Nathan barked. "Steer toward the battleship on the left and continue firing on all forward tubes!"

"We can't take this amount of fire for more than thirty seconds!" Jessica warned as the ship rocked.

"Firing on the battleship," Josh announced as he opened fire again.

On the main, semi-spherical, wrap-around view screen, weapons fire seemed to be coming at them from all sides, bathing the bridge in flashes of red, orange, and yellow.

"Aurora!" Nathan called, "Can you route power to

whichever shield is weakest and shift that reroute on the fly?"

"*Affirmative,*" their AI replied.

"Do it!"

"*I can also use past firing patterns to anticipate which shield section will require supplemental energy to maintain shield strength.*"

"Great," Nathan replied, irritated that he had to authorize *that* as well. "Do that, too!"

"Done," Aurora replied. "*This should extend time to shield failure to one minute and thirty-eight seconds, assuming the current level of bombardment.*"

"Concentrate all forward weapons on that battleship!" Nathan instructed, clinging to the arms of his command chair.

"Twenty seconds to strike!" Kaylah warned from the sensor station.

"Stand by to turn to a clear jump line," Nathan instructed.

"Any particular direction?" Josh asked, steadying himself against the violent, unpredictable motion of the ship as its shields continued to absorb the energy of the incoming weapons.

"Whichever way gets us out the quickest!" Nathan replied.

"Got it!"

"Ten seconds!" Kaylah warned.

"Start your turn!" Nathan ordered. "Jump us out as soon as you get a clear jump line!"

"Turning!" Josh replied.

"Jump when clear!" Loki confirmed.

"Five seconds!" Kaylah warned. "Crap! Jump flashes to port!"

Nathan jumped to his feet, looking up and left as the Aurora turned right and dove to get a clear jump line under the enemy battleship ahead of them. Dozens of blue-white flashes revealed tiny specs of white riding on fiery contrails as they dove toward them.

"More above!" Kaylah continued.

Nathan's eyes widened as two of their own missiles streaked over them, barely missing their topside. He turned his head to the right as the missiles passed, watching them slam into the destroyer to starboard, blowing it open in a fiery explosion.

"Clear jump line!" Josh reported.

"Jumping!" Loki announced a split second after.

The blue-white jump flash washed over the bridge, and the violent shaking stopped.

"Starboard ninety and jump ahead thirty light seconds," Nathan ordered.

"Ninety to starboard," Josh acknowledge, rolling the ship into the turn as ordered.

Nathan plopped down in his command chair, the incredible stress leaving his body for a moment. "Remind me to have a talk with your brother about his timing," he told Jessica.

Commander Verbeek yanked his flight control stick to the left, rolling his fighter into a tight left turn, losing altitude in the process. He rolled back level and then tapped his jump button, transitioning his Super Eagle five kilometers ahead.

Suddenly, his target was right in front of him, less than a kilometer away and growing closer at an alarming rate. He had only seconds.

The targeting system flashed a red bracket, indicating it had detected the target, and then turned solid red. The commander pressed the missile launch button on his flight control stick, sending a single missile streaking ahead of him.

He immediately pulled up, rolling slightly right to avoid the explosion that came one second later. "Target destroyed," he reported over comms with a smile.

"*Thank you, Commander,*" General Telles replied over comms.

"Eagle One returning to angels three. Let me know if you need any more help."

"*Will do,*" the general replied.

"One-eighty complete," Josh reported.

"Return jump plotted," Loki added.

"What are we looking at?" Nathan asked his sensor officer.

"The dreadnought is dead, broken into three pieces," Kaylah reported. "One battleship is badly damaged. She can defend herself, but she's not going to be much of a threat. Same with one of the... Wait... Jump flashes! Multiple... Gunyoki!" she exclaimed. "About thirty of them! More flashes! Four Orochi! They're all attacking!"

"Jump us in one hundred clicks from the nearest battleship," Nathan instructed. "We can't let them have *all* the fun."

"One kilometer to Capitol Square," Donan reported over comms. "It's up to you boys, now. We'll provide as much cover as possible."

"Just don't let any Dusahn tacticals sneak up

behind us, and we'll do the rest," Sergeant Major Crawley replied.

"Give 'em hell, Denton." Donan checked his tactical display as the platoon of Corinari soldiers that had been following behind him charged past on either side. Two enemy targets suddenly appeared, blinking in red. He looked up, spotting the same two targets on the exterior view that surrounded him within his turret. A few hundred meters away were two gun emplacements being hastily assembled to repel the charging Corinari. "Two light APGs, three hundred fifty meters. One at my three five zero, and one at my zero one zero. Shall I do the honors?"

"*Be my guest*," the sergeant major invited.

"Targeting with sky-shots," Donan replied.

From behind sixteen combat tanks, Corinari soldiers clad in black and gray body armor charged forth, moving from cover to cover in practiced fashion as they fired on the Dusahn forces defending their seat of power. Energy bolts of red, orange, and yellow streaked back and forth between the two forces.

Dusahn soldiers scrambled to set up anti-personnel gun emplacements at intersections in front of the charging enemy forces, eager to get the upper hand on the approaching threat. But their efforts would be wasted.

Two screeching sounds were heard by the Dusahn soldiers assembling their weapons emplacements, followed by a distant whistling sound from above. The whistling descended in pitch as it grew louder. Several of the Dusahn soldiers looked up, scanning the nearby skies for the source of the strange sound.

One of them spotted something small falling toward them. He pointed up at the object, hollering a warning to his comrades, causing them to scatter in all directions to find safety.

Two bright, white flashes appeared fifty meters above the gun emplacements, followed by a thunderous shock wave knocking the fleeing soldiers to the ground, tearing away their light body armor and stripping the skin and underlying muscle from their bodies, and crushing their internal organs. The shock wave carried a considerable thermal charge as well, igniting flesh and any other combustibles in the blast zone. Even the weapons themselves, partially assembled as they were, collapsed under the thermal shock wave, ending up bent, partially melted, and completely inoperable.

"Damn," Sergeant Major Crawley exclaimed, observing the sky-shot strikes from behind cover two hundred meters away. "Nice shooting, Donan," he called over comms. "Forward!" he hollered to his men, before returning his attention to his helmet comms. "Just don't drop any of those things on us by mistake."

"*I'll do my best*," Donan replied.

"Jump complete," Lieutenant Deln reported from Orochi Three's helm.

"Multiple targets," Ali announced.

"We only care about *our* target," Aiden reminded her.

"I've got it!" Ali replied a moment later. "Transmitting targeting data to tactical."

"Transferring to missiles," Ledge reported from the tactical console.

"Launch when ready," Aiden instructed. "Helm, as soon as those missiles are away, jump us to the far side of that battle group, same range, and come about hard."

"Targeting data is loaded," Ledge announced.

"Ready to jump," the helmsman confirmed.

"Launching eight."

Aiden looked out the forward windows of the compact Orochi bridge as eight missiles, four from each side, streaked ahead of them, disappearing behind blue-white flashes seconds later.

"All eight have jumped."

"Jumping us across," the helmsman reported as the Orochi bridge filled with blue-white light. "Jump complete. Coming about."

"I need a strike report as soon as possible, Ali," Aiden reminded his sensor officer.

"You'll have it in thirty seconds," she reminded him back.

"Multiple contacts!" Kaylah announced from the Aurora's sensor station. "Jump missiles! Ours! At least a hundred of them! Five seconds to impact!"

"Thatta girl, Cam," Nathan murmured, more to himself than anyone around him.

"Battleship Three is turning toward us," Jessica warned. "They're trying to bring their main torpedo tubes to bear."

"Missile impacts!" Kaylah announced.

"Ten up and twenty to port," Nathan instructed his helmsman. "Ten-click jump on my mark."

"Ten up and twenty to port," Josh replied as he deftly manipulated his manual flight control stick to change the ship's attitude, bringing the throttles of their main engines up at the same time to initiate the turn.

"Destroyer Six has lost all shields and is heavily damaged," Kaylah reported.

"Ready stern tubes," Nathan instructed. "Full power triplets."

"Destroyer Five is coming apart," Kaylah continued. "Battleship Three has lost all port shields."

"Ready on stern tubes," Jessica acknowledged. "Full power triplets."

"Battleship Two is spinning up their jump drive."

"Turn complete," Josh reported.

"Execute jump!" Nathan ordered.

"Jumping!" Loki replied as the jump flash washed over the bridge.

"Pitch up to bring our stern tubes to bear on Battleship Three," Nathan ordered. "Jess, fire when you get a solution."

"Pitching up," Josh replied, gently pulling back on his flight control stick and then releasing it.

"Battleship Two has jumped," Kaylah reported.

"Find that battleship for me," Nathan told her.

"I've got a firing solution!" Jessica announced. "Firing stern tubes!"

"Missile launch!" Kaylah warned. "From one of the destroyers! Eight inbound! Fifteen seconds!"

"Point defenses are engaging the inbounds!" Jessica assured them. "Direct impacts on Battleship Three!"

"Keep pounding them!" Nathan urged. "Loki, ready an escape jump. Fifteen light seconds."

"Two missiles down," Jessica updated. "Three..."

"Fifteen light seconds, aye!" Loki replied.

"Five seconds to missile impacts!" Kaylah warned.

"...Four! Brace for impacts!" Jessica warned.

"Secondaries on Battleship Three!" Kaylah reported. "She's coming apart!"

"Snap jump!" Nathan barked.

Loki's finger was already on the jump button, pressing it the moment Nathan said the word 'snap'.

"Ready four jump missiles with nukes," Nathan instructed. "Helm, hard about and down ten."

"Loading nukes on the rails," Jessica replied.

"Hard about, ten down," Josh acknowledged.

"Two destroyers are down!" Kaylah reported from the sensor station. "Battleship Three is dead in space! Battleship Two is still missing. Three more destroyers have jumped as well! Only one target remains, and the Gunyoki are attacking it."

"We could use a few minutes of shield recharge time," Jessica suggested.

"Jump flashes!" Kaylah reported urgently. "Four inbound!" Kaylah tapped a button on her console, tying the ship's all-call system into her own comm-set. There was no time. "BRACE! BRACE! BRACE!"

Two Dusahn missiles slammed into the Aurora's port midship shields, their nuclear warheads detonating in a pair of simultaneous, blinding, white flashes. The force was more than their already weakened shields could handle, and shield emitters all along the port midship portion of the Aurora's hull exploded in showers of sparks.

Two seconds later, the other two missiles reached the Aurora's unprotected hull, piercing its surface. Their delayed fuses detonated a second later, blowing open the port aft landing bay and ripping half the landing deck off the ship, sending it tumbling into space, along with a considerable amount of debris.

"The Corinari have made it past our exterior defense perimeter," the Dusahn officer reported. "They are at our doors!"

"We must hold," General Dontekay insisted. "Send all available personnel to reinforce our troops at the doors."

"No disrespect, but they will not be enough," the major objected.

The general looked crossly at the young major. "Then recall all forces to fall back to this facility. We will attack them from behind and crush them."

"Their tanks will prevent our troops from doing so."

General Dontekay looked even more annoyed. "They number less than a thousand!" he raged. "How is this possible?"

"Their weapons are very accurate," the major explained, hoping he would not be punished for speaking his mind too openly. "Their forces are well motivated. Their initial strikes hit us in just the right locations, greatly reducing our ability to respond from the start. They had *inside* information."

"A spy?" the general realized, looking at the major with disbelief. "Impossible!"

"It may *not* be within our own ranks," the major pointed out. "If they had contact with the resistance..."

"The resistance was destroyed months ago," the general reminded him, dismissing the idea with a wave of his hand.

"Or so we believed..." The major paused a moment, summoning up the courage to make a suggestion. "General, we *need* help. We *need* to call in another ship."

"Nonsense!" the general disagreed vehemently.

"The Aurora has been absent for nearly twenty minutes," the major continued, determined to make the general see his logic. "There are only two ships in orbit above us. If we could surprise them and destroy them, we might be able to launch a strike against their tanks, thus allowing *our* troops to attack the Corinari from the rear as you desire."

"We can use octos," the general suggested, hoping to avoid the embarrassment of having to call in a warship to help him secure his command against ground forces.

"Their tanks have very good defenses," the major replied, tiring of the elder officer's pride. "They will make it difficult for the octos, if not impossible."

"And earn the wrath of our lord," the general reminded the junior officer, muttering under his breath so the others around him would not hear.

"If we lose this world, our lord's *wrath* will be the least of our worries," the major replied in similarly hushed tones.

General Dontekay looked around the command center. All around him, young Dusahn officers and technical specialists were busy at their jobs, monitoring the battle and relaying data to troops in the field. Comms chatter assaulted his ears from all directions as junior officers on the front lines of battle called for assistance, in fear of being overrun. The general had no choice, his command was about to fall. “Make the call,” he finally ordered the major.

Without jump flashes, Gunyoki fighters began appearing all around the Dusahn destroyer, pounding the unshielded sections of her older but considerably thicker hull. Each shot of highly charged plasma blew open layers of the ancient ship’s protective skin.

Gunyoki appeared in groups of four, diving in pairs at the struggling enemy warship, then turning away and jumping before the destroyer’s defenses could land more than a few blows upon them.

Jenna Hayashi adjusted her course as she came out of her attack jump, only three hundred meters away from the Dusahn warship.

“Target is preparing to jump!” her weapons officer reported from behind her.

“Everyone! Keep firing! Don’t jump! We can’t let her get away!” Jenna barked over comms as she opened fire on the struggling warship.

“They’re jumping!” Delan warned from the fighter’s back seat.

Jenna looked out the forward window of her cockpit, her finger still on the firing button. As bolts of energy fired from the guns on her port and starboard engine nacelles slammed into the destroyer, pale blue light began to spill out from the warship’s jump emitters, spreading quickly across her hull to form her jump field.

But something was wrong.

Jenna's eyes widened as the incomplete jump fields partially covering the warship's hull began to shift unpredictably. What usually took half a second took several, the damaged ship trying desperately to jump to safety. Although the forward and aft sections of the ship became completely engulfed in the pale blue jump fields, the midship portion did not. It took several seconds for the forward jump field to finally reach its full charge, no doubt hampered by damaged power conduits on the surface of the hull. The forward jump field of the destroyer flashed, but the aft section did not, at least not at first.

Three seconds later, after the forward section of the Dusahn destroyer had disappeared, the aft jump field flashed, albeit in an anemic fashion, causing only portions of the destroyer's main drive section to jump away.

Her critical systems torn apart in unexpected ways and exposed to space, secondary explosions began igniting within the remaining portions of the warship. Jenna pulled her nose up hard, shoving her engine throttles forward to their stops as she pressed her jump button and transitioned to the other side of the doomed destroyer, about one kilometer away. She yanked her engine throttles back to idle and flipped her nimble fighter over, so that she was facing the warship's remains, flying backwards away from it.

The secondary explosions quickly took their toll, finally igniting the main propellant tanks in the aft section. The remains of the old destroyer—one that had been in service ever since the Dusahn had been exiled from Jung space centuries ago—exploded.

Jenna stared in disbelief as the fireball, fed by the mixture of burning and expanding gases, sent a wave of debris in all directions. Her rate of travel away from the explosion inadequate to prevent the remains of the warship from reaching her, she pressed her jump button, jumping backwards away from the explosion.

"You don't see *that* at the races!" Delan exclaimed.

Jenna sighed as she flipped their fighter back over to face in their direction of travel. "You surely do not."

Lieutenant Commander Cardi pressed the button on her flight control stick, jumping her Super Eagle fighter ten kilometers ahead. She came out of the jump low over the Answari skyline on a course directly for the palace grounds, home of the Dusahn seat of power, and its command and control complex. As expected, she was immediately greeted with a barrage of energy weapons fire, streaming up to her from handheld weapons and portable defense emplacements all around the ornate campus which had once been the property of the Ta'Akar family.

"*Well, that's not very welcoming,*" her wingman, Ensign Pal Garson declared over comms.

"At least I don't have to feel guilty about not bringing any wine," Sami joked as she jinked her fighter from side to side and up and down to make her harder to target. "I've got at least three MAAGs to the left and five more to the right," she counted, her eyes darting about between her tactical display, her flight dynamics screen, and her heads-up display hovering in front of her canopy's forward window. "Pali, you and I will go left. Til and Kish go right. Clean up anything I miss, will ya?"

"I'm always cleaning up after you, Chief," her wingman replied. *"It's what I do."*

"Port aft flight deck is open to space," the chief of the boat reported over comms. *"Inner doors are holding, but the entire deck, all the way aft, was torn away. There is damage to the cargo deck below as well. The concussion damaged multiple systems across the port flight deck, including the port forward launch rails. Engineering reports they might be able to get them working again, but it's going to take at least ten minutes. Damage control is putting out some fires just inboard of the damage, mostly secondary systems that vented inside and caught fire. Flow has been cut off. Interior fires should be under control in a few minutes."*

"How many injured?" Nathan asked.

"Fifteen injured, twelve dead, four still unaccounted for. We believe they were sucked out into space."

"Understood," Nathan replied, ending the connection. "Kaylah, any bodies to port?"

"Port short-range sensor array is down," Kaylah replied. "I can drop a sensor buoy. It might help."

"Negative," Nathan replied, accepting that they might never determine the location of the missing crewmen.

"Number one and two forward torpedo tubes are back online," Jessica reported from the tactical console. "Port midship point-defense turrets are still down. No estimates from engineering on when they'll be back up. I'm transferring the remaining missiles in the port loading bay to the starboard bay. We'll only be able to launch two at a time, but we'll still have access to our entire inventory."

"Good thinking," Nathan agreed.

"Message from Tekka One," Naralena announced. "They've taken out Destroyer One and are searching for the other ships."

"Update our status to command," Nathan instructed his comms officer. "Let them know we're still in the fight but with a few teeth missing."

"Multiple contacts!" Kaylah warned.

Her announcement was unnecessary, as the arrival jumps occurred directly ahead of them, filling the bridge with their blue-white flashes. Before them, two ancient Jung destroyers, black and crimson with Dusahn markings, filled their semi-spherical main view screen. The ships were less than a kilometer away, and the Aurora was closing on them at an uncomfortable velocity.

"Evasive!" Nathan barked instinctively as the two ships opened fire. "All power to forward shields!"

"New contact to port!" Kaylah added, the ship rocking with the incoming weapons impacts. "Battleship!"

"Roll to starboard, quickly!" Nathan ordered.

"Already started!" Josh assured him as the view of the destroyers in front of them began to roll from right to left.

"They're turning with us," Loki warned as the ship rocked again. "They're trying to block our escape!"

"Dive under them, Josh!" Nathan ordered.

"I'm trying!" Josh replied. "One of them is turning to block our lateral axis; the other one is trying to match our changes along the Z-axis!"

"The destroyers have matched our speed," Kaylah

reported. "Josh is right, they're trying to pen us in so the battleship can tear us open!"

"Battleship has launched octos!" Jessica reported from tactical. "Looks like they're circling over us to get to our port side. If they do, I'm not going to be able to target them with all our point-defenses inop on that side.

The ship rocked violently as the severity of the bombardment suddenly increased.

"Get me a clear jump line, guys!" Nathan urged.

"They're matching us maneuver for maneuver!" Josh insisted. "And a few of our port thrusters are operating at half power!"

"Jess, can you blast them out of the way?" Nathan suggested.

"If Josh can keep our nose still for three seconds," Jessica replied.

"Hey, I've got my hands full over here," Josh defended.

"Abort your maneuvers and just get our nose on one of them," Nathan instructed. "But whatever you do, *don't* let that battleship see our port side!"

"You got it!" Josh promised.

"Give him a hot pickle, Jess," Nathan added.

"Octos are attacking our port side!" Jessica reported. "I've got Aurora trying to target them with our starboard rail guns, but the octos are staying mostly below their field of fire."

"Firing forward tubes!" Josh announced, pressing the firing button on his flight control stick.

"The destroyers are keeping their best shields toward us!" Kaylah reported, grasping her console with both hands to keep from being knocked off her chair. "We'll never blast our way through before the octos rip open our port side!"

Nathan tapped his comms console, selecting a direct link to engineering. "Vlad! Can you pump up the dorsal translation thrusters?"

"*Give me a minute!*" Vlad replied over comms.

"We don't have a minute!" Nathan responded. All he got from his chief engineer was a string of Russian expletives that he was certain were quite profane.

"Damage control reports new hull breaches," Naralena reported. "Port side, decks C and D, sections fourteen, fifteen, and sixteen."

"Those octos are hitting us with everything they've got, and there's not shit I can do about it!" Jessica exclaimed.

"New contacts!" Kaylah announced.

Nathan felt his heart sink.

"Gunyoki!" Kaylah continued. "Eight of them! They're going after the octos!"

"Battleship is translating downward," Jessica reported. "They're trying to get under us."

"They're going for our port side," Nathan said, realizing the battleship had no choice now that the Gunyoki were chasing away their octo-fighters.

"More Gunyoki just jumped in!" Kaylah reported.

"Josh, get ready to translate up relative to those destroyers with everything you've got," Nathan instructed. "Loki, be ready to jump us two light minutes on my mark."

"Battleship is still maneuvering to get under us," Jessica warned.

"They're launching more octos," Kaylah added as the ship rocked with the incoming weapons impacts.

"Forward shields are down to forty percent!" Jessica warned.

"What about the destroyer's shields?" Nathan asked.

"Eighty percent!" Kaylah replied. "They *are* falling but not very quickly."

General Telles hid behind the corner of the building as four Super Eagle fighters unleashed hell on the mobile anti-aircraft guns in the streets ahead of them. Thunderous explosions rocked the streets of Answari, the shock waves threatening to shake the buildings from their foundations. Windows shattered, and vehicles in the street were thrown in the air, crashing down meters from their original positions. More importantly, Dusahn soldiers were torn apart, their separated limbs tossed in the air with the rest of the debris.

The four fighters ceased their attack, streaking low overhead before pulling up toward the sky.

"*You should be clear all the way to the palace walls!*" Lieutenant Commander Cardi reported over comms, just before the four fighters disappeared behind blue-white flashes of light.

General Telles looked at Corporal Vasya and the other twenty Ghatazhak huddled behind the building with him. "You ready for this, Corporal?" the General asked.

Corporal Vasya grinned from ear to ear. "You're kidding, right?"

General Telles smiled back at the corporal as he tapped the side of his battle helmet. "Telles to all Ghatazhak. Leap Frog, in thirty."

"Where the hell did you get *that* code name?" the corporal wondered.

"Nash, who else?" the general replied, rising from his position. He glanced at the tactical display on the inside of his visor, noting that there were no enemy soldiers between their position and the palace walls, fifty meters further down the street. "Ready, Capi?" he asked his AI.

"*I am ready, General,*" his AI assured him.

Four thunderous claps followed by a screeching sound announced the arrival of four more Super Eagles, approaching from the east. Again, trails of plasma energy tore up the streets and walked up the walls of the palace, blowing chunks of concrete away. Finally, the red-orange energy bolts topped the walls and peppered the palace grounds, creating havoc in the most heavily defended place in all the Pentaurus sector.

The general watched his tactical display as dozens of red dots representing Zen-Anor troops inside the palace walls disappeared, falling to the rain of death from above. In a few moments, after the last of the Super Eagle fighters had finished their attack run, a different kind of death would rain down on the Dusahn's ultimate warriors. It would not be red-orange in color, but flat black.

The four Super Eagles streaked past the palace, climbing upward and disappearing behind jump flashes. General Telles looked at the time display in the upper right corner of his tactical visor. "Five seconds," he announced over comms.

Corporal Vasya readied himself, tightening his muscles. He and his cohorts were about to perform the most daring and skillful attack in Ghatazhak history. Even better was the fact that they were doing it on their home soil, in front of the very citizens who had demanded they be stored in stasis until needed, for fear that they would turn on their own people.

Seconds later, General Telles stepped out into

the open without a word, breaking into an all-out run toward the palace walls. Both arms raised, with narrow bolts of red-orange energy lashing out from his forearms, the general and his men raked the tops of the palace walls as they charged, same as the other three teams of twenty who were charging toward the palace from all four cardinal directions. Within seconds, they had closed the gap between them and the walls by half.

Still running, General Telles ceased fire and jumped up in the air as if leaping over an invisible obstacle. As his back foot left the ground, his combat armor began to glow, flashing a split second later in a pale blue-white, and the general disappeared.

Corporal Vasya was half a step behind, jumping up into the air and disappearing behind his own flash as eighteen more Ghatazhak soldiers followed, each of them running and jumping up into the air and disappearing.

Zen-Anor troops standing on catwalks peered over the tops of the palace walls toward the approaching wave of enemy troops, their curiosity raised by the dozens of blue-white flashes lighting up the faces of the surrounding buildings. Staring in disbelief, the Dusahn warriors were stunned again by another series of flashes, this time directly above them. Ghatazhak soldiers, clad in flat black combat armor sailed over them, reaching the top of the jump arc they had begun more than twenty-five meters away, from *outside* the walls.

General Telles sailed overhead, a good fifty meters over the heads of the Zen-Anor below. His body straight, he slowly pitched over, both arms pointed downward, firing at the shocked Dusahn soldiers from his forearm cannons as he flew over them. His arc reached its apex, and he began to fall back toward the surface again. He stopped firing, tucked forward to continue his somersault, then disappeared behind another blue-white flash.

Corporal Vasya's flight path was slightly different, choosing instead to spin around his lateral axis, all while facing the surface. His own forearm cannons blazing, he and his fellow Ghatazhak strafed the Zen-Anor on the wall catwalks and in the compound below. Once their descents began, they too disappeared behind flashes of light, leaving nothing but dead bodies in their wake.

More flashes of light appeared, this time inside the palace walls only a few meters above the ground. Black-clad Ghatazhak soldiers appeared from behind the flashes, their forearm cannons opening fire again as they landed.

Corporal Vasya landed in a semi-crouch, both shoulder turrets deploying and launching miniature guided anti-personnel rockets in all directions. The corporal's comrades followed suit, creating equal levels of death and devastation as each of them landed.

Within seconds of their charge, the interior of the Dusahn palace grounds was quiet.

"All units, sit-rep," Telles requested calmly over his helmet comms.

"*Two, inside; full strength,*" the first group leader reported.

"*Three, inside; full strength.*"

"*Four, inside; full strength.*"

General Telles looked over at Corporal Vasya, who had landed only two meters from him. As expected, the corporal's grin had not left his face. "All units, advance," the general ordered.

"Jump complete!" Lieutenant Meers reported from the Orochi's helm.

"Two destroyers and one battleship, dead ahead!" the sensor officer reported. "They're all over the Aurora! They've got her boxed in!"

"We're too close for missiles," Robert stated as he tapped the comm-panel on the arm of his command chair. "All gun crews, weapons free!" he ordered. "Sasha, be ready on our forward cannons. Helm, jump us in beside those destroyers, about one click away. We'll blast the hell out of them to take their mind off the Aurora so that she can slip away."

"Forward cannons are hot and ready!" his XO assured him.

"Adjusting course," the helmsman acknowledged. "Jumping in three..."

"That battleship is passing over our dorsal side!" Jessica warned, clutching her console as the ship shook violently. "They'll have a clean shot at our port side in thirty seconds!"

Nathan tapped his comm-console again. "Any time, Vlad."

"Taking heavy fire on our dorsal shields!" Jessica reported as the ship rocked violently. "They're down to fifty percent and falling fast!"

"You want me to roll with the battleship?" Josh asked from the helm.

"Negative," Nathan replied. "Vlad, it's now or never!"

"Fifteen seconds until the battleship has a shot at our port side!" Jessica warned.

"*Now!*" Vlad hollered over the intercom.

"Helm!" Nathan called. "Full power to dorsal translation thrusters! Prepare to jump!"

"Dorsal translation thrusters at full!" Josh acknowledged as he fired the thrusters.

Nathan watched the main view screen as the upside-down destroyers blocking their jump line began to move up the main view screen. "Main engines to full power!" he ordered.

The movement of the two Dusahn destroyers up the main view screen began to slow.

"Targets are translating upward, trying to block our escape!" Kaylah reported from the sensor station.

"Five seconds!" Jessica warned.

"Kill the thrusters!" Nathan ordered. "Roll hard one-eighty to port and bring the mains to full!"

"Oh, boy," Josh replied, exchanging an uncertain glance with Loki as he reached for the throttles.

The destroyers on the view screen began to rotate to the right as the Aurora rolled hard to port, growing larger in size at a rapidly increasing rate as the ship accelerated quickly toward the blockade.

"Collision in twenty seconds!" Kaylah warned.

"Dorsal shields are down to thirty percent!" Jessica warned.

"We're not going to get a clear jump line in time," Loki added.

"Twenty degrees up relative; maintain your roll!" Nathan ordered as the ship lurched downward sharply with several heavy impacts.

"Twenty percent!" Jessica barked.

"Twenty up relative, in the roll!" Josh replied as he adjusted the ship's pitch while not interfering with its rolling motion.

"Aurora!" Nathan called. "On my call, drop all

shields except for ventral and transfer all available power to the ventral shields!"

"*Understood,*" Aurora replied.

"If you drop our shields..." Jessica began to object.

Nathan wasn't paying any attention, barking orders over her as he watched the still-rotating destroyers begin to slowly slide down the main view screen. "Stand by to cut mains! Stand by to snap jump!"

"Ten seconds!" Kaylah warned, placing her hands firmly on her console to brace herself.

"Comms! Collision warning!" Nathan instructed, noting that the rotating destroyers were nearly level again. "Kill the mains! Aurora, now!" he added.

"Roll complete in five seconds!" Josh reported, realizing what his captain was planning.

"Mains at zero!" Josh acknowledge as Naralena instructed the crew to brace for collision over the all-call system.

"*Dropping all shields and transferring all available power to ventral shields,*" the Aurora's AI acknowledged, speaking over Josh.

Nathan paused a moment as the view screen filled with the now right-side-up destroyers. "Snap jump."

The nose of the Aurora barely missed the topside of the Dusahn destroyer that was attempting to block their escape path, but only her nose. As she continued forward, her underside slammed into the enemy warship, causing the shields of both ships to flash opaque, overload, and fail in a shower of sparks.

But the Aurora's underside was designed to be

a protective shield itself. While the dorsal portions of the Dusahn destroyer collapsed under the force of the collision, crushing the decks underneath and setting off secondary explosions inside, the Aurora's ventral hull only suffered cosmetic damage.

As the Aurora scraped across the enemy warship, pale blue, semi-opaque light began to spill out across her hull from her jump emitters. In a split second, the entire ship, including a portion of the destroyer's dorsal side, was completely engulfed in the jump field. The field flashed blue-white a half second later, and the Aurora—as well as one third of the Dusahn destroyer—disappeared.

"Jump complete!" Loki announced as the bridge continued to shake. "I think."

"Translate upward!" Nathan quickly instructed.

"Translating upward, aye!" Josh replied, firing the ventral translation thrusters.

The shaking stopped.

"I've got an odd contact under us!" Kaylah announced. "Two meters and moving away!" She suddenly turned to face Nathan, her eyes wide. "It's the top of the Dusahn destroyer. Our jump fields carved away a piece of her...a *big* piece."

Josh smiled broadly. "We cut their heads off!"

Nathan also smiled. "I think we can assume they're out of action."

* * *

Lieutenant Jexx studied the latest status updates, a look of concern on his face. He glanced over at Lord Dusahn, now fully adorned in proper uniform, still brooding over the loss of his flagship. The lieutenant knew that his duties required him to present the status updates to his leader, but he had seen more than one officer lose his position, and in some cases their very lives, after presenting unpleasant news to their lord.

The lieutenant took a deep breath to steady his nerves. He was a Dusahn officer. Duty and courage were his backbone, his guiding principles. So it had been for countless generations of pure-blooded Dusahn, such as himself.

Either way, his fate was uncertain. Another deep breath, and the lieutenant stepped forward. "My lord."

Lord Dusahn shifted his eyes toward the lieutenant, moving his head no more than necessary, anger evident on his face.

Lieutenant Jexx swallowed hard before speaking. "The Aurora has escaped our blockade. In the process, she gravely disabled the Nan-Griska. We are down to three destroyers, two of which are damaged, and a single battleship."

"Yet still a superior force," Lord Dusahn reminded the young lieutenant.

"The Nan-Horahn reported the presence of eight heavily armed gunships," the lieutenant continued. "Their sensor scans show that these gunships also carry missile launchers, a total of *fourteen* launchers per ship. Based on the number of missiles in the first strike, there are undoubtedly more of them, possibly a lot more."

"They are *gunships*, Lieutenant," Lord Dusahn insisted, becoming impatient with the young officer's lack of confidence in the superiority of his own people.

"Our newest, most powerful ships have been

defeated, my lord," the lieutenant pressed. "Corinair command is about to be overrun, and General Dontekay is requesting a missile strike on targets a mere *kilometer* from his position."

"You see our situation as dire?" Lord Dusahn wondered, challenging the young officer.

Lieutenant Jexx paused a moment, fearing punishment if he continued. But failing to report accurately carried equal risk. As a compromise, he chose to lower his voice instead. "My lord, we have enemy troops—*Ghatazhak*—in our very compound..."

"My Zen-Anor will crush them," Lord Dusahn insisted.

"And if they do not?" the lieutenant challenged. "I believe it is time."

Lord Dusahn glared at him a moment, barely resisting the urge to pull out his sidearm and burn a hole in the insolent young lieutenant's head. Fortunately for the lieutenant, pure-blooded Dusahn officers were becoming rare, the result of having to interbreed with other races to maintain their numbers. "The Chekta protocol."

"It was your wisdom," the lieutenant pointed out respectfully. "If you had not taken those steps..."

Lord Dusahn put up his hand, silencing the lieutenant. He sighed heavily, then gave his orders. "Send the Jar-Burah to Corinair to save Dontekay's wrinkled, old ass."

"*My lord*," the lieutenant pleaded, convinced that the Chekta protocol was their only hope.

"*Then* order the emergency evacuation of our forces on Ancot," Lord Dusahn continued. "Just in case."

Lieutenant Jexx swallowed hard, acquiescing to

his leader's wishes, thankful that he had not been executed on the spot.

* * *

"The other destroyer that tried to block our escape has lost her starboard shields," Kaylah reported from the Aurora's sensor station. "She appears to be unable to jump as well. She's turning toward Takara."

"She's making a run for home," Nathan decided. "Can the Gunyoki finish her off?"

"She's swarming with octo-fighters," Kaylah replied.

"What about the battleship?"

"She's not there. She must've jumped away just after we did."

"They were probably afraid they'd be struck by another wave of jump missiles," Jessica opined.

Nathan sighed, worried about what the battleship was up to. It had already surprised him once, and the damage had been severe. He had no intention of letting it happen again. "What about our shields?"

"Port midship shields are still down. Ventral shields are at forty-seven percent. Forward shields at fifteen percent. Port midship point-defenses, and our port rail guns, both dorsal and ventral, are still down as well. And of course, there's still a big-ass hole where our port aft flight bay used to be. But other than that, we're peachy."

"Does that destroyer still have weapons?" Nathan asked Kaylah.

"Her main batteries are down, but her point-defenses are still operational," Kaylah replied. "Unknown if she can still launch missiles."

"Helm, intercept course on that destroyer," Nathan ordered.

"Turning to intercept course," Josh acknowledged.

"If they manage to lob a single missile at any shield section that's below forty percent—which most of them are—it'll reach our hull," Jessica warned.

"Noted," Nathan replied, determined to press the attack. "As soon as we're on an intercept course, flip us over. We'll jump in ass-first and hit them with our good stern tube."

"Stern shields are only at fifty-one percent," Jessica told him. "Not much of a safety margin, especially if they throw more than one missile at us."

"I'll try to be quick," Nathan promised.

"On intercept course," Josh reported.

"How are you at flying backwards?" Nathan asked him.

"Backwards, forwards, sideways, it's all the same to me," Josh assured him.

"I was hoping you'd say that," Nathan replied. "Go ahead and flip us over. Loki, stand by to jump us in five clicks from the target," he instructed.

"Five clicks, aye," Loki replied.

"Full power, triple shots, and don't stop," Nathan told Jessica.

"I never do," Jessica replied.

"Jump is ready," Loki announced.

"Execute," Nathan ordered without hesitation.

"Jumping in three..."

"Stern tube is at full power," Jessica reported.

"...Two..."

"I have rerouted all available shield power to the stern shields," the Aurora's AI reported.

"...One..."

"Thank you, Aurora," Nathan replied as he switched the main view screen to the stern cameras.

"...Jumping..."

The jump flash washed over the Aurora's bridge, fading a second later.

"Jump complete," Loki reported.

"Firing stern tube," Jessica announced. "Full power triplets."

"Octos are turning to intercept," Kaylah warned. "They're locking weapons on us."

"Direct hits!" Jessica reported, as the Aurora's stern tube continued to fire. "That destroyer's got a damn-thick hull!"

"Keep pounding her," Nathan urged.

"We're taking fire on our stern shields," Jessica reported.

"Octos are maneuvering wide," Kaylah announced. "I believe they're trying to get to our unshielded areas."

"Secondaries!" Jessica reported.

Nathan glanced up at the main view screen, just as a massive internal explosion broke the destroyer in half, just aft of her midship line.

"Pitch up, jump when clear," Nathan ordered.

"Pitching up," Josh acknowledged.

"Clear jump line," Loki reported. "Jumping."

"Find the other ships," Nathan told his sensor officer. "Especially that battleship."

"Working on it," Kaylah assured him.

"Comms, any update on our ground forces?"

"Last mission update from Corinair showed total control of skies and space, and the Corinari closing on Capitol Square in Aitkenna," Naralena reported.

"What about the Ghatazhak?" Nathan wondered.

"I'm receiving regular updates from the Ghatazhak," Naralena replied. "However, we are a few light minutes from Takara, so there is a delay.

Last report, they were approaching the walls of the Dusahn palace."

"That may be where the destroyers have gone," Nathan realized. "Kayla, are the destroyer's guns accurate enough to target the Ghatazhak without inflicting significant damage on the Dusahn palace?"

"Their main guns are similar in design to those on the battleships, but we've never faced a Jung destroyer before. It was our understanding that they had been phased out centuries ago, in favor of heavy cruisers and missile frigates."

"Best we assume they are," Nathan decided. "Helm, turn us toward Takara. We'll jump into high orbit. If those destroyers are planning to attack the Ghatazhak from orbit, they'll be low to increase their accuracy."

"Plotting jump now," Loki acknowledged.

"Load two shield busters on the starboard rails," Nathan instructed. "And have two nukes in the queue to follow."

"Loading two shield busters," Jessica acknowledged.

"Comms, warn our Super Eagles about the destroyers," Nathan added. "We don't want them surprised from above."

"*New targets, approaching from two seven zero relative,*" Donan's AI warned.

"I've got him," Donan replied as he rotated his turret to the left to face the threat.

A massive explosion rocked his tank.

"What the hell was that?" Donan exclaimed.

"*Pastor is hit!*" Braden reported from Madra Five. "*Jesus! He's fucking obliterated!*"

"From where?" Donan barked over comms. A second explosion went off, several intersections to his left.

"*It's coming from above!*" Scotty reported from Madra Eight.

"Octos?" Donan wondered.

"*I have received a status relay from the Weatherly,*" Donan's AI reported. "*A Dusahn battleship has jumped into orbit and is targeting this area.*"

"Madra One to all Madras!" Donan called over comms as he grabbed his control sticks and jammed them forward, causing his tank to accelerate forward. "Find some cover!" he continued, turning his tank to the left toward a nearby building. "Hug a building! It'll probably be orbiting west to east so it can stay over the target area longer! Hug the tallest building you can find!"

"Fuck! Brycen's hit!" Tor cried out over comms. "His turret is gone!"

Two more explosions went off, this time from the far side of the square.

"Five, One!" Donan called over comms as he guided his tank up to a building, pulling it in tight against its west face. "I can't see you on tactical! Where are you?"

Rail gun rounds the size of a small vehicle slammed into the ground where Donan's tank had been less than a minute ago. The force of the impacts blew massive holes in the street, sending a shock wave that knocked his tank to the left, into the building wall, causing it to collapse on top of his tank. "Fuck!" Donan exclaimed.

"*Anyone got eyes on Five?*" one of the tank drivers yelled over comms.

More rounds slammed into the next street over, shaking Donan again. "Jesus! Somebody get that fucker off of us!"

"That battleship is pounding the crap out of our tanks on the surface!" Bonnie reported from the Weatherly's sensor station.

"Targeting data is loaded into the first four missiles!" Denny announced from the tactical station. "But they're not shield busters!"

"No time!" Captain Hunt insisted. "Launch all four and then load shield busters."

"Launching four!" Denny confirmed.

"New contacts!" Bonnie warned. "Octos! A lot of them!"

The Weatherly suddenly rocked violently as Dusahn octo-fighters opened fire.

"More contacts!" Bonnie added. "Missiles! BRACE, BRACE, BRACE!" she added, taking her own advice and grabbing the edge of her console.

Captain Hunt grabbed the arms of his command chair just as the missile struck his shields and detonated, rocking the ship so hard that he was knocked over the right side of his seat onto the deck. "Damage report!" he demanded, struggling to get back on his feet.

"Octos!" the Glendanon's sensor officer warned. "Ten of them attacking from starboard!"

"Point-defenses are firing," the executive officer reported from the tactical station.

"Where the fuck are the Gunyoki?" Captain Gullen barked. "Donni, you got eyes on the Weatherly?"

"Yes, sir!" his sensor officer replied. "She just took several direct hits from missiles! She's lost half her shields, and she's got octos all over her."

"Where the hell is all this coming from?" Captain Gullen wondered. "Are you picking up any other ships in the area?"

"Negative," Tinny replied. "Just the octos."

"Relay from the surface!" the comms officer announced. "There's a battleship in orbit directly over Aitkenna, and they're pounding the hell out of our tanks with their rail guns."

"Why are we only hearing it through relay?" Captain Gullen wondered.

"I've lost all comms with the Weatherly!" the comms officer reported.

"Launch a comm-drone, quickly, before there are too many octos to get one through!" Captain Gullen ordered. "Update command about the battleship!"

"We've got to get out of here!" his executive officer insisted. "If the Weatherly's badly damaged, we've got no cover!"

"We've got shields and guns," the captain argued. "More importantly, we're not done shuttling Corinari to the surface. We're not going *anywhere* until our boys take the capital."

"But there's a *battleship* just over the horizon!" the XO argued. "If they decide to attack us, we won't last two minutes!"

"That battleship's priority is our tanks!" Captain Gullen insisted. "We're not a threat to him, and he knows it. We're safe enough until he's done with the tanks."

"Hell, they can launch missiles, send them around the planet, and strike us from behind, all without warning!"

"It's a chance we'll have to take," Captain Gullen stated firmly. "If you're not up for it, feel free to leave the ship."

"Fuck you, Edom," the XO replied. "You know damn well I'm up for it."

"Then shut the hell up and keep those octos off us," the captain snapped back.

Cameron had never been the type to pace the deck when waiting for news. Instead, she chose to stare at the holographic map of the Takaran system hovering over the command center's plotting table, hoping it would provide some sudden inspiration that might turn the tide of the yet undecided battle.

"It's only been three minutes since our last update," Lieutenant Commander Shinoda pointed out, noticing that the look of concern on her face was more obvious than usual.

"We're supposed to be getting updates every two minutes, max," she pointed out.

"There could be any number of reasons why we haven't heard anything yet," the lieutenant commander insisted.

"Naralena is frighteningly strict when it comes to schedules, even more so than me."

"I find *that* hard to believe."

Cameron cast a disapproving glance toward her intelligence officer.

"Flash traffic from the Glendanon!" the comms officer announced urgently. "A Dusahn battleship is bombarding the Corinari from orbit. Fifteen tanks have already fallen. Commander Montrose is attempting to move more tanks in from elsewhere to protect the teams assaulting the capitol complex, but the battleship is making it difficult."

"What about the Weatherly?" Lieutenant Commander Shinoda wondered.

"The Glendanon has lost comms with her, but their sensor officer reports that they took multiple missile hits. I'm transferring their last sensor dump to the plotting table now."

Cameron turned back to the plotting table and switched the display to the Darvano system, quickly zooming in on Corinair itself. "The Weatherly is squawking Delta Four Seven Tango," she noted.

"They're damaged but still in the fight," the lieutenant commander deduced from the squawk code.

"The Weatherly is no match for a battleship," Cameron insisted, "not even an ancient one." Cameron turned toward the comms officer. "Signal the Glendanon. Relay to Razor One. Attack the battleship and bring down her shields. Maybe she'll move off once her shields are down."

"Yes, sir," the comms officer replied.

"And relay a Darvano sitrep to the Takar system," she added. "If the Aurora's not too busy, the Darvano system could use some attention."

"Razors Two through Ten, new target!" Commander Prechitt instructed over comms as he dialed up a new jump range on his flight control stick. "We're going after that battleship's shields."

"*Is that going to stop her?*" Talisha wondered.

"No, but if we take out their shields planet-side, we might be able to take out a few of the rail guns they're using to destroy our tanks."

"*They'll just roll over and put another set of guns on them,*" the commander's wingman pointed out.

"Then we'll attack those shields as well," the commander replied. "Razors Eight and Nine, you're closest, so you're first up."

"*Eight and Nine are on our way.*"

"*Flash traffic from command and control,*" Commander Prechitt's AI announced. "*They are recommending that we attempt to take down the battleship's shields.*"

Commander Prechitt pulled up on his flight control stick, starting a climb so that he could jump to orbit.

"*Just thought you would like to know,*" his AI added.

"Thanks, Max."

"I've got them!" Kaylah announced from the Aurora's sensor station. "Right where you thought they would be. All three destroyers are settling into orbit, moving into position over Answari."

"Helm, intercept jump, ASAP," Nathan ordered.

"Jumping in three..."

"Cannons on the targets right and left," Nathan instructed.

"...Two..."

"Plasma torpedoes on the center destroyer."

"...One..."

"Hot pickle," Nathan added.

"Jumping," Loki announced as the jump flash washed over the Aurora's bridge.

The planet suddenly filled the majority of the main view screen. Three older, Jung-era destroyers, painted in the original black and red Jung colors, moved across their screen from left to right.

"Open fire," Nathan instructed calmly.

As the lead destroyer deployed its ventral rail guns, in preparation to fire on the Ghatazhak invaders below, red-orange plasma torpedoes leapt from the Aurora's forward tubes. As her forward gun turrets also opened fire, the plasma torpedoes raced toward the center destroyer, slamming into its shields, causing them to flash brightly.

The destroyers quickly returned fire, sending both energy bolts and rail gun fire toward their attacker. The Aurora's shields also flashed as they absorbed the energy, both plasma and kinetic, with each impact.

"I'm reading severe fluctuations in the lead destroyer's power grid," Kaylah reported.

"Concentrate all cannon fire on the lead ship," Nathan instructed Jessica. "Josh, keep pounding the center destroyer."

Her forward torpedo tubes still firing, the Aurora's forward port dorsal plasma cannon turret ceased fire momentarily, shifting to starboard as the ship rolled in the same direction to give her port gun a better angle. The roll completed, the port cannon joined its starboard partner, sending bolts of red-orange plasma energy streaking across the gap between the Aurora and flight of destroyers. The bolts pummeled the lead destroyer's shields until they finally became unstable, failing as the emitters across the destroyer's starboard side erupted in showers of sparks.

With its starboard shields down, the lead destroyer had no defense against the incoming bolts of energy other than its old, thick hull. The plasma bolts tore into the black and red hull, cutting gashes into her as her jump emitters began to spill out blue-white light. The gashes quickly deepened, finally setting off massive internal explosions as the bolts of energy found the warship's propellant tanks.

"Lead destroyer is coming apart!" Kaylah announced from the sensor station.

"Why the hell didn't they jump?" Josh wondered aloud. "Why aren't *all* of them jumping?"

"The Ghatazhak are at the Dusahn's doorstep," Nathan explained. "They either stand and fight or die later at the hands of their leader."

"Assuming there's a leader left!"

"It's a way of life," Jessica added, as she retargeted their forward guns toward the trailing warship. "Now how about you roll us ninety to port so I can get the angle on the third destroyer."

"And keep pounding your target, Josh," Nathan reminded him.

Commander Prechitt's fighter came out of the jump less than twenty kilometers from the enemy warship in orbit above Corinair.

"*The Dusahn battleship is nineteen point four kilometers ahead,*" his AI reported. "*The target is currently at a forty-three-degree angle to our intercept path, traveling west to east in a low, semi-synchronous orbit.*"

"How long until they lose their firing solution on Aitkenna?" the commander asked as he adjusted his course for intercept.

"Approximately eighteen minutes."

"We've already lost a third of our tanks, and they've only been here for *three* minutes."

"*The target's shields have been augmented by increasing the number of emitters to create greater redundancy. It will be difficult to bring them down.*"

"Can we still penetrate them?"

"*Unknown.*"

"Well, there's one way to find out," the commander decided as he checked his tactical display to make sure the other Nighthawk fighters had jumped with him. "Razors, the target has *twice* the usual numbers of emitters, so taking down their shields is going to be difficult. Our best bet is for all of us to jump in at once, giving them more targets than they can track with the few nearby guns. Remember, the closer you are to their hull, the harder it is for their guns to track you. We jump in one minute."

Without missing a beat, the commander switched to a different comm channel. "Weatherly, Razor One. We'll be attacking their starboard midship shields in fifty seconds. The moment that shield comes down, open up with everything you've got. If we're lucky, we'll sting them enough that they'll jump away."

"*Razor One, be advised we have suffered heavy damage,*" the Weatherly's comms officer replied. "*Attack may not be possible.*"

"*Prechitt, Gullen,*" the captain of the Glendanon called over comms. "*We'll jump closer to the battleship and add our firepower to the Weatherly's.*"

"Negative, Edom!" the commander objected. "If we lose the Glendanon, our forces will have no support."

"*If we don't get rid of that battleship, we won't have any forces left to support!*" Captain Gullen argued.

"I don't have time to argue with you, Edom!" the commander barked. "Dota One! Razor One! Can you help the Weatherly with the attack?"

"Razor One, Dota One, negative!" Tariq replied over comms. "We're swarming with octos at the moment! Suggest we call command for reinforcements!"

The commander sighed, knowing that they didn't have time to wait for help. Even with their jump comm-drone relay system, it would be several minutes before additional forces would arrive. By then, they would lose half their combat tanks, and the other half would never make it into position in time to prevent the Corinari from being slaughtered.

"*Five seconds to jump,*" his AI announced.

"Razors! Let's do this!" the commander ordered, pressing his jump button.

Ten faint pulses of light appeared on the Dusahn battleship's starboard midship shields. A split second later, ten Nighthawk fighters appeared just inside the massive battleship's shields behind faint flashes of blue-white light.

The side of the enemy warship instantly filled the projections of the exterior environment that wrapped around the commander's cockpit, as if looking out clear windows. Numerous target identifier triangles appeared all over the enemy hull, superimposed on the projected images by the Nighthawk's visual augmentation system.

"Let them have it, Max!" the commander barked as he pulled his flight control stick back hard to bring his nose up to avoid slamming into the side of the battleship. As his AI activated the Nighthawk's mini-laser turrets, the commander leveled off and snap-rolled his fighter to give his AI a better firing angle.

Two seconds after the Nighthawk fighters penetrated the battleship's shields and opened fire, the Dusahn responded with every defense turret on their starboard side. Waves of red plasma bolts swept across nearby space, lashing out at the tiny fighters.

Nighthawk fighters pounded the emitters on the battleship's hull, causing them to disappear in showers of sparks as they exploded. Fighters broke in all directions, each taking a different flight path across the battleship's hull. The fighters maneuvered wildly, hoping to avoid the bolts of energy lashing out at them, but to no avail. One by one, the sleek Sugali fighters fell to the Dusahn's defensive fire, torn apart by the deadly plasma bolts, sending their remains scattered across the battleship's hull.

"Arre's down!"

"I can't shake their guns!"

Comms traffic was full of Nighthawk pilots crying out in desperation as their fellow pilots were being slaughtered.

Talisha's fighter lurched to port, her starboard shields taking direct hits from at least four separate streams of energy. "Leta! How many emitters left to bring down this shield section!"

"Fourteen emitters have been destroyed. Thirty-seven more must be disabled in order to bring down this shield section," Leta replied. *"It is unlikely that..."*

"Razor One, Razor Three!" Talisha called as icons representing their flight of Nighthawks dropped off her tactical screen one by one. "This isn't working! We're dropping like flies here!"

Another friendly icon disappeared, causing Talisha's eyes to widen. "JONAS!"

"Razor One has been destroyed," her AI reported.

Another series of energy bolts found her fighter, knocking her about wildly.

"Starboard shields are down," Leta announced. "Forward shields are at twenty percent and..."

"ALL RAZORS! ABORT, ABORT!"

"Jump drive is dead," the chief engineer reported over the intercom. *"The fire damaged the power shunts from the main power trunks. If we try to jump now, we'll crack open like an egg!"*

"What about power?" Captain Hunt asked.

"Main power is stable for now, but I can't guarantee it will stay that way for long. Propulsion and maneuvering are still operating."

"Any chance we can use our main batteries?"

"*A few shots, maybe a dozen,*" the engineer replied. "*Any more and they'll overheat and explode. Point-defenses are working, though, as well as our forward torpedo tubes. But again, more than a few shots and the plasma torpedo generators will overheat as well.*"

"Nighthawks have aborted," Bonnie reported from the Weatherly's sensor station.

"How many of them made it out?" the captain wondered.

Bonnie looked up at him from her station. "Three."

"Out of *ten?*" Captain Hunt questioned in disbelief.

"We need to call in more Nighthawks," the XO suggested from the tactical station.

"We can't," Captain Hunt explained. "They're all that's keeping those damned octos off the Corinari." The captain turned back to his sensor officer. "Did they manage to weaken that battleship's shields at all?"

"Their starboard midship shields are down to forty percent," Bonnie reported.

"What about the Gunyoki?" the XO asked.

"The battleship's octos are keeping them away," the captain replied. He sighed and then made his decision. "Helm, all ahead full."

"Captain, that'll..."

"We're only going to get one chance at this," the captain continued, cutting his helmsman off. "We'll be lucky to get more than a half dozen shots off before we have to break off to avoid impact. The closer we are, the more damage we can do."

"Chris, they'll pound the *hell* out of us," his XO warned.

"Probably," the captain agreed, "but if that battleship *survives*, nine hundred Corinari will *not.*"

General Telles moved quickly across the corridor as energy bolts slammed into his personal shields, fired from Zen-Anor soldiers at the far end of the corridor.

"Those Zen-Anor have much better aim than the Dusahn regulars!" Corporal Vasya hollered as he followed the general across the corridor. Three bolts of energy slammed into his shielded right side, causing him to stumble, nearly toppling over to his left as he ran.

General Telles reached out and grabbed the corporal, pulling him to safety as more energy bolts streaked past, barely missing him. He peered around the corner briefly, drawing several more rounds from his opponents. "There are at least forty of them in the next section. They are attempting to mislead us, hoping we will charge into their fire."

"Then let's not disappoint them," Corporal Vasya suggested.

"A frontal attack will drain our shields too quickly and will result in unacceptable losses. We must find another way past them."

"I've got this," Corporal Vasya insisted.

General Telles turned toward the corporal, a look of disapproval on his face.

Corporal Vasya pulled an anti-personnel grenade from his belt and began making some adjustments to its settings.

"A single grenade?" the general asked.

"Not just *any* grenade," the corporal assured him. "An *experimental* grenade."

"They've erected an energy shield in front of the

doorway," the general reminded him. "You'll never get it past the barrier."

"Watch," the corporal said as he activated the grenade, "and be amazed." A small light on top of the grenade began flashing rapidly as the corporal leaned out just enough to gently toss the grenade toward the enemy.

General Telles looked puzzled, noticing that the corporal had not thrown the grenade anywhere near hard enough for it to travel all the way down the corridor. Then, to his surprise, the grenade flashed blue-white as it left the corporal's grasp. A split second later, there was a second flash, this time in the room full of Zen-Anor troops.

"Nice, huh?" the corporal said, smiling.

"It would have been *nicer* had you told me about this device *prior* to this mission," the general stated, disapproval in his tone.

"Mister Ayseron delivered the prototype to me as we were leaving Orswella. I sort of forgot about it."

General Telles gestured down the corridor. "Lead the way, Corporal."

"Yes, sir," the corporal replied, stepping out and charging down the corridor with both forearm cannons blazing just in case.

"Telles to all Ghatazhak," the general called over comms as he stepped out into the corridor to follow the corporal. "Team One is inside. Team Two hold the entrance. Three and Four take the perimeter."

Captain Hunt held tightly onto the arms of his command chair as incoming weapons fire from the warship more than four times their size pounded their forward shields.

"Target's shields are down to thirty percent!" Bonnie reported from the sensor station.

The ship shook again as more rounds impacted their weakening forward shields.

"Shall I return fire?" his XO asked, grasping the edges of the tactical console.

"Not yet," Captain Hunt replied. "We've got to get closer!"

Two more energy bolts slammed into them, causing the ship to lurch to the left.

"Our forward shields are down to ten percent!" Denny reported. "We can't take much more of this!"

"Range?" the captain asked his helmsman.

"Five kilometers!" the helmsman replied. "One hundred meters per second closure!"

"Stand by to fire," Captain Hunt ordered.

Two successive blasts rocked the ship, causing it to lurch to port again.

"Forward shields are down!"

"No choice!" Captain Hunt barked. "FIRE!"

"Firing!" the XO replied, pressing the firing button.

Captain Hunt stared out the forward windows as red-orange plasma torpedoes, one pair after another, spat out from under their bow. The glowing torpedoes crossed the ever-decreasing distance between the Weatherly and the Dusahn battleship in a few seconds, slamming into its nearly depleted starboard midship shields.

The battleship's shields flashed with each pair of torpedoes as they struck. Finally, on the fourth set, the enemy warship's remaining functional midship shield emitters had reached their limits, exploding in showers of sparks across the battleship's hull.

"Target's shields are down!" Bonnie reported.

They were the last words she would speak.

Four bolts of energy lashed out from the midship main turret on the battleship, plowing into the Weatherly's bow, blowing it apart all the way back to the forward edge of its bridge. But the Weatherly plowed on, its own momentum carrying it toward its fate. Multiple defense turrets fore and aft on the battleship continued to tear the Weatherly apart, causing secondary explosions deep within her hull, sending debris in all directions.

Realizing that they could not stop the Karuzari ship in time, the Dusahn battleship's jump emitters began to pour pale blue light out across its black and red hull, quickly building its jump fields.

Witnessing the impending collision, Talisha turned her Nighthawk toward the Dusahn battleship and quickly pressed her jump button. A split second later, she was five hundred meters from the enemy warship. She jammed her throttle all the way forward, bringing her main propulsion system to full power. "Leta!" she barked. "Override all containment safeties and initiate a reactor overload! Ten seconds to failure!"

"This will result in the destruction..."

"DO IT!" Talisha ordered, dropping her visor and sealing her helmet up.

"Impact and detonation in four..."

"Eject me in two seconds!" Talisha added.

"...Three..."

"Thanks for everything, Leta," she added.

"...Two...ejecting..."

All of Talisha's senses were suddenly overwhelmed as the canopy of her fighter was blown clear, her arms and legs were pulled back into her seat and armrests, and her flight seat shot out of the doomed Sugali fighter.

Her senses recovered a second later as she cleared the top of the Dusahn battleship. She glanced downward as her fighter slammed into the warship just as its reactor containment failed. There was a bright flash. At first, Talisha thought it was the battleship jumping away, and her heart sank, closing her eyes. But when she opened them a second later, the battleship was still there, looming below her as she drifted away.

She stared in horror as the Weatherly, its entire forward section blown apart and its bridge gone, slammed into the enemy warship's starboard midship section, driving through its hull, driven deeper by its still-blazing main engines.

Talisha took a deep breath, readying herself for her certain fate. She closed her eyes as multiple flashes of light appeared. Red, orange, yellow, white, the explosions quickly became too many to count. She braced herself for the inevitable, but nothing happened.

After several seconds, she dared to open her eyes and look down. The Dusahn battleship had been broken in half by the Weatherly, the latter of which was nowhere to be seen. To her amazement, all of the enemy warship's debris was traveling not toward her, but laterally, carried away by the Weatherly's original impact momentum.

Talisha hollered with excitement, almost laughing in the process. She was alive.

She was also floating in space, in orbit above a world at war, surrounded by fighters both friend and foe, all of which were still locked in furious combat.

She was not yet out of danger.

Lord Dusahn slammed his fists on the console beside him, outraged at the series of failures the day had brought him.

"My lord," Lieutenant Jexx begged, "if we do not enact Chekta now, it will be too late. The Jar-Burah was our last hope of keeping Corinair, and now we are down to *two* destroyers...ancient ones at that."

"We are not defeated!" Lord Dusahn barked.

"No, not yet," the lieutenant agreed. "But we soon will be. This is precisely why you created the Chekta protocol. To save our empire...to give us a chance to rebuild in the advent of great misfortune. That misfortune is upon us. Chekta is our only hope."

Lord Dusahn closed his eyes, leaning on the console beside him a moment, in disbelief at what was occurring. Finally, he opened his eyes, looking out across the command center. "Activate the Chekta protocol."

"Both targets are jumping!" Kaylah warned.

"NO!" Nathan exclaimed as the two destroyers on the main view screen glowed blue-white, flashed, and disappeared.

The bridge of the Aurora was suddenly quiet.

"Someone's looking at a firing squad," Josh mumbled, finally breaking the silence.

"Find those destroyers," Nathan instructed Kaylah.

"Incoming message," Naralena announced. After a pause, in a shocked voice she added, "It's coming from Dusahn command."

Nathan rose from his seat, turning to face Naralena.

"I wasn't expecting *that*," Jessica admitted. "You think they're calling to surrender?"

"Doubtful," Nathan replied. "Put them through."

Naralena connected the incoming transmission to her captain's comm-set, then nodded at him.

"This is Captain Nathan Scott of the Karuzari Alliance ship, Aurora. To whom am I speaking?"

"*Griogair Dusahn, son of Pensa, descendent of Issias, leader of the Dusahn Empire. You may address me as 'my lord'.*"

"Fat chance," Jessica snickered.

"I think I'll stick with Griogair," Nathan stated. "What can I do for you?"

"*Withdraw now, and I will spare your forces from certain defeat.*"

"The Corinari are seizing Aitkenna as we speak, and the Ghatazhak are at your door. Explain to me how this certain defeat is going to happen?"

"*If you do not, I will destroy both Takara and Corinair.*"

"And kill yourself in the process? I think not," Nathan replied.

Jessica snapped her fingers at Naralena, who immediately muted Nathan's comm-set. "The tunnels," she reminded Nathan.

A look of concern flashed across Nathan's face. He nodded to Naralena to un-mute his comm-set.

"*Have you checked the status of the Savoy system lately?*" Lord Dusahn wondered. "*I'll wait while you do, but for no more than two minutes.*"

"They disconnected," Naralena reported.

"Where's the Falcon?" Nathan asked.

"Jump complete," Ensign Lassen announced.

"Any idea what we're looking for?" the pilot asked.

"All they said was to check on the Savoy system and get back to them by zero plus thirty-eight," Sergeant Nama replied as he studied his sensor displays from his station behind the pilot's seat.

"That's eighty seconds from now," Ensign Lassen said, checking the mission time clock.

"Any contacts?" the lieutenant wondered.

"Nothing," the sergeant replied. "Six planets, forty-eight moons, and a few stray asteroids. No shipping traffic; *definitely* no Dusahn warship."

The lieutenant looked out the forward window at the planet Ancot. It was no bigger than his fist at the moment, but it was growing larger as they coasted toward it. "I'm turning around," he decided, glancing at the mission clock. "There's nothing to see here."

"Plotting return jump," his copilot announced.

The lieutenant initiated a one-hundred-and-eighty-degree turn, coming about as quickly as possible in order to return to the Takara system and report their findings, or lack thereof, to the Aurora.

"What the..." Sergeant Nama stopped in mid-sentence.

"What is it, Riko?" the lieutenant asked as he

rolled out of his turn on a heading back toward the Takara system.

"I'm not..." The sergeant's eyes suddenly widened, a look of panic coming across his face. "JUMP! NOW!"

"What?" Nathan couldn't believe what he was hearing. "Are you certain?" he asked over his comm-set.

"*Yes, sir,*" Lieutenant Teison assured him. "*The entire planet was destroyed by an antimatter event. It nearly took us out as well.*"

"What was the population of Ancot?" Jessica wondered.

"A few million, at least," Nathan stated, still in shock. He glanced at the mission clock, realizing he only had twenty seconds left. "Hail the Dusahn," he instructed.

"They must have drilled down into a fissure or something," Kaylah commented. "Ancot didn't have an active core, at least not one under pressure."

"*Lord* Dusahn is on the line, Captain," Naralena reported.

Nathan was silent, his anger threatening to overcome his senses.

"*Are you there, Captain Scott*?" Lord Dusahn finally asked.

"I'm here."

"He's sending video as well," Naralena said under her breath.

Nathan pointed over his shoulder at the main view screen, turning around to face it.

A window appeared in the main view screen, revealing Griogair Dusahn in full uniform, his chest brimming with medals and a smug, superior look on his face. "*I take it you have completed your recon of the Savoy system.*"

"You could have just *told* me what you would do," Nathan replied, holding back his anger. "There was no need to murder millions of..."

"*And miss the opportunity to make a proper impression upon you?*"

Nathan couldn't take it anymore. "You sick fuck..."

"*Captain, I expected more self-restraint,*" Lord Dusahn scolded. "*I mean, a man of your power and influence.*" Lord Dusahn sighed before continuing. "*Oh well, I suppose if flinging derogatives in my direction makes you feel better, I can indulge you for a short time. However, I should remind you that our forces are still fighting, and dying, while you vent your frustrations.*"

Nathan paused, regaining control of himself. "What are your terms?" he finally asked.

"*Simple,*" Lord Dusahn replied. "*Agree to withdraw all forces from Dusahn territory, and I will allow them to retreat without further conflict.*"

"No deal."

"*Captain, be reasonable. Surely you do not wish to see more innocent people die today?*"

Jessica snapped again, and Naralena muted Nathan's comm-set once more. "Only Ancot and Takara looked like they were completed. As best we could tell, Corinair was still under construction."

Nathan looked at Kaylah, pretending to be thinking for the benefit of his opponent on the main view screen. "How volatile is Corinair's core?"

"More so than Ancot, that's for sure," Kaylah replied.

"Un-mute," he instructed Naralena. After a pause, he looked back at Lord Dusahn on the view screen and said, "We keep Corinair."

"*You remove all forces from Dusahn space, or I destroy both worlds, beginning with Corinair,*" Lord Dusahn threatened.

"We withdraw from Takara, for now, but *you* withdraw from Corinair," Nathan insisted, his determination unwavering.

Lord Dusahn leaned forward, getting closer to the camera. "*I could destroy your precious Corinair with a snap of my fingers. Do not test me.*"

"You're either stupid or arrogant," Nathan told him. "Possibly both. You and I both know you can't possibly hope to control both worlds with only two destroyers, a few dozen octos, and a bunch of freighters. You came into this sector undermanned and underarmed, and it's about to cost you."

"*Captain, I warn you...*"

"Do it!" Nathan barked, cutting him off. "Destroy Corinair! But you'd better destroy Takara as well, because my next shot will be to level your palace, and I'll keep firing until I drive you straight to hell."

Lord Dusahn stared into the camera for an eternity. Nathan could see the anger in his opponent's eyes. He also saw a man that knew he was all but beaten. Griogair Dusahn had one chance of survival, and one only. The question now was if he was smart enough to take it, or would his ego be his undoing.

"Tactical!" Nathan began loudly. "Target the Dusahn palace. All weapons. Full power."

"Targeting Dusahn palace," Jessica replied promptly. "All weapons locked on target, fully charged and ready to fire."

"Your call, Griogair," Nathan invited, staring at his adversary.

"*Very well, Captain,*" Lord Dusahn finally replied. "*Order your forces to stand down, and I will do the same.*"

"Agreed," Nathan replied. He turned to Naralena, making a slashing gesture across his throat.

"Muted," Naralena announced.

"Send a message to our forces in the Darvano system. Order them to cease fire and stand by for further instructions."

"Understood," Naralena replied.

"And get me Telles."

General Telles and his men charged into the Dusahn palace central command access foyer, their forearm cannons blasting away at anything that moved. The time for precision targeting was over. In this area, everything needed to die.

"*Telles, Aurora, do you copy?*" Naralena called over the general's helmet comms.

General Telles turned away from the battle, stepping behind one of the massive columns that encircled the main foyer. "Go for Telles!" he replied as energy bolts streaked past him on either side, slamming into the wall behind him.

"*Cease fire, cease fire, cease fire. Stand by for Actual.*"

"Leader to all Ghatazhak!" Telles called over comms. "Cease fire and hold position! I say again, cease fire and hold position! Defensive fire only!"

"What the hell?" Corporal Vasya yelled from the next column over. "We've got them cornered!"

General Telles ignored the corporal.

"*Telles, Aurora Actual,*" Nathan called over comms.

"Go ahead, Nathan."

"*I need you to fall back and prepare for immediate evac.*"

"I do not understand," the general replied. "We are minutes from capturing their command center."

"*This is our only play, Lucius,*" Nathan insisted. "*You have to trust me on this.*"

General Telles leaned back against the column, staring at the wall before him. He could not believe what he was hearing. "Confirming you want us to abort?"

"*Affirmative. This is a full abort and retreat. I need the Ghatazhak off Takara, ASAP.*"

General Telles could tell by the sound of Nathan's voice that he didn't like the decision any better than the general did. "Understood," he finally replied.

"*Diggers One and Two will be landing in the palace compound in two minutes,*" Nathan explained. "*Be there.*"

General Telles sighed. "*We'll be there,*" he promised.

Corporal Vasya could see the look on his leader's face, and it was one he never thought he would see. A look of defeat. "What's going on?"

"Telles to all Ghatazhak. Fall back to the compound. Evac in two minutes. This is a full abort."

"We're retreating?" Corporal Vasya wondered in disbelief. That's when he realized that no one was shooting at them.

"The Ghatazhak don't retreat," General Telles replied. "The situation has simply changed."

"How has it changed?" the corporal demanded. "I could blow the last of those fuckers away by myself!"

"We have our orders, Corporal," the general said as he started for the exit.

Corporal Vasya stood there motionless, watching in disbelief as his leader turned his back on the enemy and headed back the way they had come.

General Telles paused at the exit, turning back toward the corporal. "Come on, Kit. We have to go."

"Diggers One and Two are lifting off," Naralena reported. "Commander Montrose reports the Dusahn are boarding shuttles and will be departing Corinair shortly."

"Very well," Nathan replied. "Un-mute." He turned back around to face his opponent on the main view screen. "It appears you get to survive another day, Griogair."

"*As do you, Nathan,*" Lord Dusahn replied with equal disdain.

"You *know* this isn't over," Nathan stated coldly. "We *will* face each other again."

"*I look forward to it,*" Lord Dusahn replied, ending the call afterward.

The bridge of the Aurora was quiet as Nathan stood there, staring at the image of Takara on the main view screen. They were so close, only a few hundred kilometers away. Yet it felt like a thousand light years.

"So that's it?" Josh asked, once again being the first to break the silence.

"For now," Nathan replied. He sighed, then added, "Plot a course for Corinair, and prepare to break orbit as soon as the last of our forces have jumped out of the system."

"Aye, sir," Loki replied somberly, studying his leader's face for a moment.

Nathan turned around, facing Jessica. The look of defeat in her eyes was almost more than he could bear. "I wasn't bluffing," he told her. "We will be back."

"He's got the planet *wired*, Nathan," Jessica reminded him. "It's over. He's won."

"Not yet, he hasn't," Nathan insisted, a wry smile coming across his face. "But first, we have to help stabilize our new ally."

Thank you for reading this story.
(*A review would be greatly appreciated!*)

COMING SOON

Episode 14
of
The Frontiers Saga:
Rogue Castes

Visit us online at
frontierssaga.com
or on Facebook

Want to be notified when
new episodes are published?
Want access to additional scenes and more?
Join our mailing list!

frontierssaga.com/mailinglist/

Made in the USA
Las Vegas, NV
23 March 2022